PRAISE FOR ALAN F. TROOP'S "BRILLIANT"* DEBUT,
Named by *Booklist* as One of the
Top Ten Horror Novels of Recent Years . . .

The Dragon DelaSangre

"What a brilliant idea! Troop takes the loneliness, angst, and eroticism so often found in the works of Anne Rice and weaves them into a new kind of misunderstood monster. Push aside the vampires and werewolves . . . and enter the dragon."   —*Christopher Golden, author of *The Ferryman*

"Comparisons with *Interview with the Vampire* are almost inevitable. . . . However, *DelaSangre* ultimately carves out its own territory . . . unabashed fun, with just enough moral ambiguity to raise it above the level of a pure popcorn book. A promising debut."   —*Locus*

"Any book that has us cheering for a human-eating dragon is definitely well-written."   —*Chicago Sun-Times*

"*The Dragon DelaSangre* is only as equally fascinating as the man who wrote it."   —*The Miami Herald*

"Alan F. Troop has done for dragons what Anne Rice has done for vampires and Laurell K. Hamilton has done for werewolves. . . . An exciting fantasy. . . . Horror lovers will have a feast."   —*Midwest Book Review*

"*The Dragon DelaSangre* is the most original fantasy I've read in years, its strength coming in no small part from Alan Troop's remarkable ability to deliver a sympathetic but distinctly non-human protagonist. Just when I thought there was nothing new in contemporary fantasy, along comes Alan Troop's terrific *The Dragon DelaSangre* to prove me wrong! I loved this book!"   —Tanya Huff

continued . . .

"An exciting, inventive, unique novel with, in Peter, a surprisingly sympathetic protagonist."
—*Booklist* (starred review)

"A very thoughtful and rewarding read."
—*New Mobility Magazine*

"The new book by Alan F. Troop you won't be able to put down."　　　　　　　　—*Aventura News*

"Troop proves to be quite skillful at characterization. . . . Light and fast-paced . . . engrossing."　　　—*The Davis Enterprise*

"Troop paints his monsters in sympathetic colors, making us sympathize with Peter. . . . His dragons are wonderfully realized. . . . A fascinating read."　　　—ZENtertainment.com

"Alan F. Troop tells an intense tale of more-than-human characters who can be quite human in their souls. Very intense."　　　　　　—*The Weekly Press* (Philadelphia)

"Troop never lets up, he never loses focus, and he never loses the reader's attention . . . could lead to a great series. . . . [He] might really be on to something big."
—Trashotron.com

"A powerful, passionate, gripping tale that brings dragons into the modern era. . . . Just when you think dragons are overdone and nothing new can be said about them, this book comes along to challenge that notion and put it in its place. Don't ignore this one."　　　—The Green Man Review

Dragon Moon

Alan F. Troop

A ROC BOOK

ROC
Published by New American Library, a division of
Penguin Putnam Inc., 375 Hudson Street,
New York, New York 10014, U.S.A.
Penguin Books Ltd, 80 Strand,
London WC2R 0RL, England
Penguin Books Australia Ltd, 250 Camberwell Road,
Camberwell, Victoria 3124, Australia
Penguin Books Canada Ltd, 10 Alcorn Avenue,
Toronto, Ontario, Canada M4V 3B2
Penguin Books (N.Z.) Ltd, Cnr Rosedale and Airborne Roads,
Albany, Auckland 1310, New Zealand

Penguin Books Ltd, Registered Offices:
Harmondsworth, Middlesex, England

First published by Roc, an imprint of New American Library,
a division of Penguin Putnam Inc.

First Printing, April 2003
10 9 8 7 6 5 4 3 2 1

Copyright © Alan F. Troop, 2003
All rights reserved

Cover art by Kovec
Cover design by Ray Lundgren

 REGISTERED TRADEMARK—MARCA REGISTRADA

Printed in the United States of America

For Susan, my mate, my love

Acknowledgments

To Rocky Marcus for your insightful reading, ongoing advice and enthusiastic cheerleading. To Steve Marcus for your occasional patience. To Pat Rosenbaum for your enthusiastic support. To all of the BMC— Jimmy Stinson, Bob Hollander, Rick Rosenbaum, Mike Fisher, Geoff Weisbaum and Dan Palmer—for your relentless teasing. To my mother, who's probably purchased more copies of my first book than anyone else. And to Delaney, Zoe and Aaron, who won't be allowed to read this book until they're much, much older.

1

It's been almost four years since my wife, Elizabeth, died. No headstone marks her grave. No bouquet of cut flowers lies on the grass that grows above her. I see little value in such things. I know perfectly well whose dead body I lowered into the ground. I need no letters carved in stone to remind me to mourn my poor bride's passage. I need no dead vegetation to honor her memory.

Because Elizabeth loved the garden just below our veranda, overlooking our island's small harbor, I buried her next to it. Because she often sat and relaxed under the shade of the ancient gumbo limbo trees that dot my island, I took a cutting from the largest of the trees and planted it at the head of her grave.

That skinny twig's rapid growth has made me shake my head. Now over twenty feet tall, the tree stands guard over Elizabeth's resting place, breaking the force of the fierce winds that sometimes blow in from the sea, shielding the grave from the driving rain, shading it from the burning sun.

Like all of its kind, the gumbo limbo possesses a thick glossy green-brown trunk that weeps strands of red bark, as if it's in permanent mourning. Its gnarled branches spread out and up in asymmetrical disarray, hugging the air, connecting Elizabeth's resting place to the sky above.

I like to believe that Elizabeth would smile if she could know such a mighty tree grows above her. It would please her too, I think, to see how much her son has grown.

*   *   *

"Papa?" Henri says, just after breakfast, as soon as we arrive at the grave, "Did Mama ever see me?"

"No. She died just after you were born," I say, stifling a sigh. I dislike telling my son partial truths but I know better than to discuss something so complex with a young child. One day, I promise myself, when Henri's older, I'll tell him the full story of his mother's death.

For now I look at my son and ruffle his hair with my hand. Almost four, the boy's as large as most five-year-olds, far more precocious, already beginning to show the tendency toward muscularity, the wide shoulders that are typical of our people.

Not surprisingly, he's chosen to look like me, sporting the same middle-American appearance, the same blond hair, even the same cleft chin as I do. Had Elizabeth lived, I've no doubt he'd look much like her and — with the contrast of her dark skin and the emerald-green eyes all of our kind have — much more exotic.

Part of me wishes he resembled his mother more. But all he's ever known of her are the stories I've told him, the pictures he's seen on her passport and driver's license and the small grassy grave we visit each morning after breakfast, on every day the weather permits.

On each visit Henri asks me dozens of questions about his mother — all asked and answered more times than I care to remember.

"Yes," I answer today, "she was pretty. . . . Of course, she loved you very much. . . . No, she didn't expect to die. . . . Sure, one day I plan to find another wife. . . . No, I won't forget your mommy when I do. . . ."

Something slaps the water in the harbor — just loud enough to catch our attention. Henri turns, as do I, both of us staring at the fresh concentric rings of ripples expanding across the small harbor's surface. A few moments later, a gray fluke rises from the water and slaps down again. The manatee it belongs to pokes its snout above the water and blows out air in a single huff.

Henri looks at me. "Can I, Papa?"

Just as glad not to explain any more this morning, I nod, smiling as my son runs toward the dock.

The manatee has visited us before but this is the first time I've allowed Henri to greet the beast by himself. I sit down next to the gumbo limbo tree, lean against its trunk, let the sun-dappled shade beneath its branches cool me as I watch my son begin to unravel the hose I keep coiled on the dock near where my boat is tied.

I have to will myself not to interfere as Henri grabs the top coil with both hands and yanks, barely budging more than a few coils. The hose curls into a spiral as he pulls, resisting his attempts to straighten it, but the boy jerks and yanks until enough is free to make it manageable.

Henri gives it a final tug, looks up at me and smiles, then turns his attention to the spigot. Holding the hose nozzle with one hand, he attempts to turn the valve with the other. It refuses to give. To my son's credit, he just bites on his lower lip and tries again, struggling with the stubborn valve until it too succumbs to his attentions and begins to rotate.

Water flows, then shoots from the nozzle, the hose becoming alive, twisting and flexing. Henri holds on to it with both hands, tries to point it—first splattering water on the dock—then wetting the bow, the cockpit, the outboard motors of the boat.

For a moment I wonder whether the hose or Henri is in control. I start to get up but, before I can, the boy manages to direct the stream toward the manatee, the water shooting up, forming a shallow arc, splashing into the surface of the calm harbor.

The beast swims toward the dock, putting its head directly into the flow. Henri smiles. Crouching by the edge of the dock, leaning over the water, he offers the hose end to the ugly thing. It nuzzles and slurps at the nozzle like it's nursing. Almost taking it into its mouth as it drinks the fresh water, the manatee accidentally nuzzles my son's hand too and he giggles loud enough for the sound to reach me.

I grin. Too bad, I think, that Elizabeth never had the opportunity to hear him laugh. I shake my head as I lament the short time she and I had together—the emptiness I feel without her.

Henri's a beautiful boy, a worthy subject for my devotion. Still, it's been almost four years since I've felt any female's touch, almost four years since I've ventured to the mainland.

Arturo nags me constantly to leave the island. I've never explained that Henri lacks the necessary self-control to be around ordinary people or to have anyone but me watch him—nor would I. The man's paid to run my business and to do my bidding, not to offer personal advice.

Still, just the other day, he said again, "I admire your dedication to the boy. But you need to get out some. You need to have some sort of life. . . . At least let's arrange to bring you a woman. . . ."

I sighed into the phone. "Let's not. When Henri's four, he should be old enough for me to take from the island. I can wait till then."

Not that the waiting has been easy. I long to fill the void that Elizabeth's death has left in my life. But, as Arturo so obviously can't understand, no ordinary woman will do. I want, I need, one of my own kind.

I know whom I plan to pursue. I know where to find her. And as time passes, I think about her more and more.

At first, I felt twinges of guilt when I allowed such thoughts to intrude on my mourning—so soon after my bride's death. Time has eased that burden. After all, Elizabeth would have understood my need for a new mate. She certainly would have approved of my quest for one. Whether she would have been pleased with my choice of her sister, Chloe, is another matter entirely.

Chloe was hardly past thirteen when I last saw her, in Jamaica, when I first met Elizabeth. I still carry an image of her in my mind—a young thin dark girl with sparkling emerald-green eyes and a mischievous smile. I know she'll look older now, but she can't be more than seventeen. That gives me plenty of time yet, I tell myself, to leave my island and to travel to hers. She won't reach her maturity until after her eighteenth birthday.

True, if I could, I would have traveled to Jamaica long ago. But I've had to wait for Henri to be able to travel, for him to grow old enough to control his natural impulses.

For almost four years I've bided my time, taken care of my son and made my plans. For almost four years, I've thought of no women but Elizabeth and Chloe. The boy should be ready soon. As soon as I see he can behave, I plan to take him with me to Jamaica.

I'm sure there will be more waiting then. The moment must be right before I dare approach Chloe. If it is, I know she can't refuse me. Still, late at night, when I picture the girl in my mind, I worry that maybe, just maybe, I have waited too long.

Henri tires of the manatee—or the beast tires of him—and my son rejoins me just as I begin to weed the garden Elizabeth so lovingly restored. He studies me as I kneel and search the ground between the green stalks of the exotic herbs Elizabeth had planted, follows me as I look under the yellow-green flowers of the Dragon's Tear plants and the deep purple petals of the Death's Rose bush—seeking invading parasites, yanking them out, roots and all.

Finally, the boy pulls on a few green stalks of his own, slaughtering some innocent herbs and one deserving weed in the process. Henri holds them out for me to inspect.

"Good job," I say, and take them from him.

Henri beams. But rather than return to weeding, he looks away, toward the island's ocean side. "Papa?" he says. "Can I go to the beach?"

I yank another weed, and mutter, "Damn!" when its stalk snaps, leaving its roots buried in the dirt.

"Papa!" Henri giggles. "You used a bad word."

"You're right. I'm sorry," I say, digging in the dirt for the roots, wondering if letting him watch movies off our satellite dish has been a good idea. The few PG-13 ones I've let him see have certainly led to endless discussions about which words are good or bad.

"Can I go, Papa?" Henri says.

There's no reason I can think of why the boy has to stay with me. If I could, I'd avoid weeding too. I pull out the last of the weed's roots and frown at the rank, thick aroma of the broken vegetation around me. Standing, I turn my back on the garden, study the clear, light blue sky above us, the powder-puff clouds, the bright sun, its heat surprisingly strong for May. I can understand why my son would rather play on a day like this than do chores.

"Go ahead." I add, "Just be careful," even though I doubt that anything on the island can inflict any injury he can't quickly heal.

"Yes, Papa." He rushes off.

Brushing my hands on my jeans, I wait a few minutes, then follow the stone path from the garden to the wide, deep stone steps that lead to the oak-decked veranda encircling our three-story-tall coral house. Taking the steps two at a time, I get to the bay side of the deck just in time to check on Henri as he begins to scamper up one of the dunes across the island on the ocean side.

Barks and yelps break the morning quiet. As soon as Henri reaches the light brown slender stalks of the sea oats crowding the dune's top, better than a dozen of our dogs, all furry and thick framed, with overlarge heads and mouths, appear from the other side of the dune.

The younger ones and the puppies surround my young son, gambol about him and vie for his attention. I grin. As much as he's grown, the beasts still tower above him.

Only the few older dogs and the pack's leader, Scar, keep their distance. They know better than to trust our kind. The younger ones have no memories of the many times I've had to cull the pack. They have no understanding that I've been trying to let their numbers grow back to full strength from the few that were left after the attack that devastated their ranks four years ago.

Henri laughs as the dogs push against him. He pets some and allows others to lick him. When one of the larger pups jumps up and almost knocks him over, the boy just steps back and regains his balance. Ignoring the rambunctious beast, he resumes playing with the smaller pups.

The dog jumps on him again. This time my son glares at it and shoves it away—hard. The dog yelps, then slinks back. Ears flattened, hackles raised, it circles him.

To get closer, in case I'm needed, I walk to the ocean side of the veranda, stand by one of the open cannon ports placed every five yards along the waist-high coral parapet that rings the deck. But I've little doubt Henri can handle this challenge. The boy's been taught to cope with worse.

Henri knows to always keep his eyes on an attacker. He faces the beast, slowly revolves as it attempts to get behind him, allowing the dog no opportunity for surprise. Finally, it charges, knocking some of the smaller pups out of its way, snapping its jaws when it nears my son, then jumping back, lunging forward again.

"Back!" Henri yells. The dog freezes for an instant, then shoots forward, mouth open, fangs exposed. The boy steps back, puts up his left arm to guard his face just as the animal bites.

Its teeth sink into his forearm and Henri yowls once. Then the boy hisses—loud enough for me to hear from the veranda. The foolish beast ignores the warning, and refuses to let go.

Henri holds his right hand up and stares at it, his fingers narrowing and extending, his nails turning into sharp, curved claws in only a few moments. I nod, proud the boy could ignore the pain and the attack long enough to focus on what he must do to save himself. Like me, like his mother, like all of our kind, the boy is a shapechanger, a far more dangerous foe than the animal realizes.

Henri slashes out and this time the dog yelps. It howls as my son strikes again and again. The creature backs off, tail tucked in, blood flowing on the ground as it scurries into the underbrush.

"Good," I mutter. It's best that all these beasts understand that we are masters of this island. And it's time my son learned they've been bred to be our watchdogs, not our cuddly pets.

Henri shoves the other dogs away from him, then turns and holds up his left arm so I can see the red teeth marks of the dog's bite, the blood running down his arm. From the expression on his face, I'm not sure whether he's showing me because he's proud or because he needs my sympathy. *"Poor you,"* I mindspeak to him. *"Do you want me to guide you, help you heal?"*

My son shakes his head. *"No, Papa,"* he mindspeaks. *"I'm too big for that now. I'm almost four. Look, Papa!"*

He keeps his arm up so I can watch. Henri stares at the red puncture wounds on his forearm, frowns, knits his eyebrows and I grin at the concentration evident on his face. One day he'll be able to heal an injury as minor as this with a moment's thought.

The bleeding stops. The wounds turn from red, to pink, to normal flesh color, and Henri smiles again. *"See?"* he mindspeaks. *"I told you I could."*

"You're growing up, son," I say, frowning at the concept. A year ago he would have taken refuge in my lap and moaned while I nudged his mind toward the thoughts that could ease his pain and heal his wound.

Ready to move on, Henri waves at me with a clenching and unclenching of his chubby right hand. I smile, wave and watch him go over the top of the dune to the beach on the other side. Then I turn and go back to my chores.

It makes me chuckle when I think how many people assume it's easy to live on an island. How idyllic they imagine such a life to be. But on an island such as ours, life is anything but simple.

Sandwiched between the Atlantic Ocean and Miami's Biscayne Bay, surrounded by salt water on all sides, our small island—Caya DelaSangre, as my family calls it, or Blood Key as it's named on the charts—is in a constant state of erosion and decay. Wind and tide attack the shores relentlessly. Salt air penetrates everything.

As I weed, I mentally catalog all my chores. Besides working in the garden, maintaining Elizabeth's grave and straightening out the cavernous interior of our coral house every day, I have to spend my time going from machine to machine. I lubricate and repair generators and motors, fight rust where it appears and recharge batteries. Other regular chores include painting, replacing rotted planks of wood, making sure the well pumps remain primed, keeping the reserve water in the cistern fresh and servicing the twin Yamaha outboards on the boat so they function as they should.

Keeping supplied presents its own difficulties. All materials have to be brought by boat from Miami, just over the horizon, to our west. Since I trust no one to visit but Arturo, I've taught only him the twists and turns of the narrow channel that leads to our harbor. He alone is responsible for bringing all of our supplies, including frozen meat, from the mainland.

Since Henri's far too young to help, fresh food is entirely my responsibility. Our kind prefers fresh meat and whenever we feel the need for it, I have to go off on a hunt. Not that hunting is ever a hardship. It's what my people do.

Just the thought of hunting fresh prey makes my stomach growl. I look up at the sun, frown when I see it hasn't quite yet reached its apex. I sigh, swallowing saliva. If I could, I would go right now. But I'll wait. I know the only safe time to hunt is at night, in the dark, after the world has turned quiet.

I decide to wait until evening before I tell Henri of my plans. Otherwise, the day will go too slowly for my son.

At dinner, I serve Henri only half his regular portion of rare steak, as I do every time before a hunt. I don't want the boy to be too full to eat what I bring him. He looks at his plate, then at me. "Papa? Are you hunting tonight?" he says.

I nod, put my own much larger serving of warm, bloody meat on the table.

"Can I go too?"

"You know better," I say. "Not until you're older."

"But I'm going to be four. . . ."

"Older than that."

"Not fair!" he says, folds his arms and pouts.

I smile at him. "When you're bigger, we'll hunt together. For now, eat your food. There will be more later, when I come back after you're asleep."

Henri, still pouting, looks away from his plate.

I ignore his momentary food strike and make a show of cutting and eating my meat. In only a few minutes the heavy aroma of the blood on his plate and my feeding in front of him makes him too hungry to resist eating any longer.

After Henri falls asleep, I go out on the veranda and walk over to its ocean side. In the darkness, a dog barks. Otherwise, only the waves rushing at the shore, the wind rustling through the trees break the silence of the night.

A southeast breeze, I think, normal for this time of year. My mind turns to Chloe, living on that island so far south of mine. There's little chance the girl has come of age so soon. Still, I turn my face toward the southeast, sniff in the salt smell the wind carries. If Chloe has reached her maturity, her scent will surely be on the air. Thankfully, the breeze carries no hint of cinnamon and musk, the telltale aroma of a female of my kind in heat.

Grinning, I put my arms out, luxuriate in the caress of the wind. "It's time," I say out loud. I take off my shirt, my pants, my underwear, my socks and shoes, and stand naked on the oak deck of the veranda.

Flaring my nostrils, I breathe in the night air again, puffing my chest as it fills my lungs—the oxygen energizing my blood cells—my heart speeding its contractions, hammering in my chest as it pumps great bursts of blood throughout my body. I look up to the dark sky, the gray clouds scudding overhead, the pinpoint sparkles of the stars, the dull glow of a half-moon. I belong up there, I think.

I will myself to change, groaning at the pleasure/pain of stretching skin, the sweet agony of growing bones. Once I was ashamed of what I was. Once I wished to live only as a human. But now I welcome my metamorphosis to my natural form. I draw in a deep breath of the salt-tinged night air and let out a slow growl.

"I am Peter DelaSangre, son of Don Henri Dela-Sangre," I say into the night. My skin ripples, hardening, turning to dark green armored scales everywhere but my underbelly. Beige scales form there, double thick to protect me from any attacks from below. I grimace as my back swells, then splits, my wings emerging, growing, unfolding, my tail stretching out behind me.

My lips compress as my face narrows and elongates and my teeth lengthen and turn to fangs. My body stretches and thickens until I'm more than twice the size of my human form. My hands and feet reshape themselves into taloned claws and I groan at the pain and pleasure of it all.

Clasping and unclasping my claws, I stretch my wings to their full span—almost twice as wide as my height. I beat them once and then again, fanning air before me, switching my thick tail from side to side, stretching muscles that have rested too long—until every fiber of my being longs to fly.

With one bound I take to the air. The sky belongs to me. The night is my domain. I roar into the dark.

I pity those who have never experienced such a moment.

Each stroke of my wings takes me higher. As always before a hunt, I bank and circle Caya DelaSangre, looking down at the thin white lines of waves moving in the gloom, approaching my island's shore—the white froth as they break against the pale shadow of the beach.

The rest of the island shows itself only as a black mass floating in a slightly less dark sea. Only the warm, yellow glow of the lights I left on in the great room on the third floor of the house gives evidence of the island's habitation.

I spiral over my home, soaring higher, the air growing cold around me, the bright grid of the city lights of Coral Gables and Miami appearing, stretching inland to my west. Boats lights pierce the darkness of the ocean to my east. My stomach, emptied by the energy spent changing, growls and aches. Saliva floods my mouth.

Hungry as I am, I still have no desire to hunt near where I live. There's no challenge in capturing any nearby prey. Humans mob the mainland just a few minutes' flight away. Their boats crowd the water around my island. To take one of them would gain me only quick gratification and would risk that Henri and I might be discovered for what we are. Before any such easy prey tempts me, I turn toward the sea, flying over the fishing boats near shore, continuing past the craft plying the Gulf Stream.

Some nights I search over Bimini or Freeport, occasionally ranging as far as islands like Abaco, Eleuthera or Exuma. Other times I hunt over the farming regions of Cuba. I find there's little fuss raised on those islands when poor fishermen or impoverished rural people disappear. Likewise, no one takes notice when I attack the dilapidated wooden boats that illegally bring Haitian aliens to our shores or the rafts bearing those poor Cubans risking their lives to escape the thug of Havana.

Tonight I fly south, following the path of the Florida Straits as it wends between Key West and Cuba. I angle west, and begin to search the waters beneath me after I pass Key West. I prefer this hunting area to any other. Any rafters who float south of the Florida Keys without being discovered have little chance of survival. Their rickety contraptions are soon captured by a current which whisks them into the Gulf of Mexico, away from the shipping channels, without any hope of reaching land before they starve or die of thirst.

I take no pleasure that my hunger dictates the death of other beings. It strikes me that, when I find such rafters floating to their inevitable demise, I'm at least bringing them the blessing of a quick death.

No more than thirty miles past the Dry Tortugas, I spot a flash of orange bobbing in the water. It disappears and I circle back, staring at the dark waters beneath me. The orange shows again and I spiral down toward it. Had the night been moonless, I doubt I would have noticed. As proud as I am of my night vision, I must admit, not even creatures like me can see in the darkest gloom.

But this evening provides no such challenge. The clouds have cleared in this area and the half-moon provides more than enough light to enable even those with normal vision to see some things.

Below me, a second flash of orange paint appears no more than six feet from the first. I continue my descent until I make out two half-submerged, orange, fifty-five-gallon drums lashed to a few wooden beams, the wood attached to a plywood deck which slants into the water. A sole man lies on the plywood, facedown, his head toward the drums, his hands grasping the rope which holds everything together, his feet trailing in the water.

Poor soul, I think, imagining the storm which swept away the other drums and drowned his companions. I drop to within a few feet of the water, skim over the waves as I approach the rafter. As close as he still is to the Keys, I doubt he'll be too emaciated to take. If he is, I decide, I'll perform a quick mercy killing and continue my hunt.

There were times in the past, I admit, that Father and I would pick up such a wasted creature and bring him home to heal and fatten in one of the six cells built beneath our house for that very purpose. But Father is long gone now and, ever since Elizabeth's death, the thought of keeping any human prisoner makes me shudder.

I fly over the man, close enough that the wind from my passage ruffles his shirt, ripples the water around him. To my delight, he appears still healthy, even thick, a little running to fat.

"QUÉ?" he shouts as he turns over, rubs his eyes. The Cuban draws his knees up, scoots closer to the drums. Searches the water around him.

Circling above, I wonder what injustice caused him to risk his journey. Or was it just the desire for a better life? My stomach growls and I sigh. Whatever brought this man this far will never be known to me. All I can be sure of is that his voyage has been for nothing.

I fold my wings and dive, gathering speed as I hurtle toward the water, spreading my wings at the last moment so that I shoot forward toward the raft.

The Cuban sees me as I rush toward him. His eyes widen. He shouts, *"ENDRIAGO!"* an instant before I strike.

I grab him with my back claws, jerk him from the raft and cut through the back of his neck with one bite. His body goes limp in my grasp, his warm blood fills my mouth. Beating my wings, gaining altitude, I swallow, then roar into the night.

Tearing flesh from the carcass as I fly, mindful of leaving enough meat to share with my son, I mull over what the man had yelled. *Endriago,* a Spanish word for dragon.

That the man identified me for what I was in the few seconds before his death, in the half-lit gloom of the night, earns my admiration. Most of his kind merely scream.

Still, "dragon" is only a term that humans chose for us long ago. We call ourselves the People of the Blood. Part of me wishes the man could have known what kind of creature took his life. Not that it would have comforted him or changed anything about his demise. But at least he would have known his life wasn't taken by some fairy-tale monster, that he didn't die from the attack of some mindless beast.

I take another bite from my prey, savor the sweetness of the fresh meat. Henri will like this, I think, picturing how my son will rush to join me once I arrive home and place my kill on the veranda. We'll feed together then, father and son, both in our natural forms, side by side.

Chloe comes to mind too. I wonder whether she's flying this night over the rugged terrain near her home. I wish she were here, flying beside me. Soon, I promise myself. Henri's birthday is only days away. We should be free to leave for Jamaica within weeks after that. Then, there's only the final wait.

I sigh, wishing that was over too.

2

"Papa! Wake up!"

Two small hands push against my back—once, twice. "Papa," Henri says, "it's today isn't it? My birthday? I'm four now, right?" He pushes on my back again.

I groan, let Henri's voice and his insistent prodding rouse me from sleep, take me away from the seductive comfort of unconsciousness. Opening my eyes just a little, as if my eyelids alone can keep me from fully awakening, I turn toward my son. "Yes," I mutter, "you're four."

Henri leans his elbows on the bed, cradles his face in his hands and stares at me. "Then we're going to shore today? You promised!"

Certainly I did, many times. Something I regret at this moment. I nod. Wondering what time it is, I open my eyes farther, and blink at the sunlight streaming through the cracks between the wooden slats of the bedroom's window shutters. The narrow lines of brightness cut through whatever gloom remains from the night, leaving pockets of darkness only in the corners farthest from the windows.

Henri's fourth birthday, I think. I shake my head, marveling at the rush of time. Then, as always on each of my son's birthdays, I remember Elizabeth's death, feel it all over again. How unjust that my son's first day must always be linked to my wife's last, that my joy must always be diluted with my sorrow. I close my eyes again.

"Papa!" Henri says.

"Okay . . . okay." I stretch, sit up, reach for my watch.

Ten after six. I sigh. Ordinarily, Henri sleeps until I wake him. At worst, if he does wake by himself, it's never before eight. But I can't blame the boy for being excited today. He's never set foot on the mainland. I've been promising him the adventure of it for months.

Henri comes to the dock a few minutes after the twin, two-hundred-horsepower Yamaha outboards on the twenty-seven-foot, Grady White cough to life. I grin when I sense his presence. No matter where he is on the island, no matter what adventure he's in the midst of, the sound of the boat's motors invariably draws him near.

"Papa?" he says when I look up from working on the motors.

I stare at him, cock an eyebrow.

"Are we going now?"

"Would you like to be?" I ask.

Henri nods.

"Do you think you can behave?"

The boy furrows his brows, compresses his lips, as if he's taking on a serious mission. He nods again, twice.

Erasing my grin, I match my young son's solemn expression. I understand his concern. All he knows of the outside world is what I've taught him and what he's seen on TV. The only other being he's ever met has been Arturo Gomez, my business associate. "What are the things I've taught you?" I ask.

"That people on shore aren't the same as us. They can't understand someone thinking to them, mindspeaking at them, and they can't do the things we do and that makes them scared sometimes . . . and sometimes they try to hurt us, so we can't do everything like we do at home. . . ."

"Especially?"

"No changing." He shakes his head back and forth. "And no feeding."

I can't help but smile. I leave the motors, pick up Henri from the dock and hug him.

He squirms in my grasp. "Can we?" he asks.

"Isn't it your birthday?" I ask.

The boy nods.

"And how old are you?"

Henri holds up four fingers.

One of the Yamahas misses a beat, then returns to its normally smooth drone and I turn toward the motors, tempted for a moment to shut them down, check their fuel ignition systems. But I know it's unnecessary, just another delay. I've already made the boy wait until after breakfast, until after we visited Elizabeth's grave, until after all my morning chores were done and until after he cleaned and straightened his room.

While Henri was too young to be in control of himself, I could tell myself I was living sequestered on our island just for his sake. But now that the child has grown old enough for us to go, I'm surprised at my willingness to put off leaving the island, my reluctance to venture forth once again into the company of man.

"Papa?"

I look at my son, nod. "I guess it's time for us to go to shore," I say. "But remember, Henri, you have to be careful."

"I know, Papa," he says. "You told me."

Henri laughs and squeals every time we hit a wave. "Faster, Papa! Faster!" he shouts.

I laugh along with him, revel in the freedom I feel leaving our island behind. The boat strikes another wave, sending a fine light spray of salt water over us. Henri giggles, shouts, "More!" I lick my lips, taste the salt residue upon them and nod, pushing the throttle forward. The Grady White leaps ahead, skitters from wave crest to wave crest, pitches and bumps in a steady rhythm.

"Look back," I say. Henri turns his head as I do and stares at the white-foamed ever-expanding *V* of our wake and the small tree-topped island receding behind us. "That's our home, Henri."

"It looks little," he says.

I nod.

The boy points to the other small, green-covered islands within sight—Wayward Key so close to our north that from a distance it almost seems part of Caya DelaSangre, Soldier Key to the north of that and, to the south the Raggeds, Boca Chita and Sand. "Do other people like us live on those?" he asks.

"No," I say. "We're the only ones who live anywhere around here." Turning back to face the bow, I think about Elizabeth's family. "You have relatives though, on a much bigger island, far to the south."

Henri nods. He's heard this before.

I point forward to the smudges on the horizon that I know will soon grow into the condo towers and high-rise office buildings and hotels that crowd near the waterfront in Coconut Grove. "Watch, Henri, that's Miami."

We rush forward, Henri's eyes growing wider the closer to shore we come. Apartment buildings and hotels stretch into sight, then homes and marinas crowded with hundreds of boats.

"Papa," he says. "There are so many of them."

"Yes, there are," I say. "That's why you have to remember what I told you."

I guide the Grady White past the main channel into Dinner Key Marina, turn into the channel to the north of it, point at the cream-and-green-colored office building towering over the land just beyond the docks. "That's where we're going," I say.

Henri says nothing, only nods.

"As long as you do what I taught you, you have nothing to fear, son. Just remember to behave."

He nods again, his eyes wide.

Pulling my son close to me, hugging him, I say, "They're just humans, Henri. I won't let anyone hurt you."

Henri stares at everything around us, swivels his head from side to side, his mouth open as we approach Monty's docks, the boat gliding forward, its twin Yamahas purring.

He says nothing while I maneuver the Grady White, back it into our slip, tie off our lines and kill the ignition.

Silence washes over us, the boat rocking slightly, the heat of the late morning sun suddenly too intense now that we're no longer speeding along. "We're here," I say, looking around, surprised to see how little has changed—the boats docked near us mostly the same as four years ago— the cheekees, brown palm-frond thatched, open-sided huts, still providing shade at Monty's restaurant's outdoor patio just a few yards from the dock. The air still tinged with the aromas of stale cigarette smoke, greasy food, gas fumes and stagnant salt water.

Henri wrinkles his nose. "It smells funny."

I laugh. "It's early. It'll smell worse later."

Lifting my son, I place him on the dock, then step off the boat myself. I take his hand and lead him down the dock, toward the shore. Two couples pass us—the women, both blondes in bikinis, carrying towels and bags of food; the men, dark and Latin, wearing cutoffs, sharing the burden of a large red cooler.

"Great day for boating, isn't it?" says the larger of the men.

"Sure is," I say.

Henri gapes at them. His right cheek twitches, the skin tightening.

"Henri, stop! No changing!" I mindspeak before my son goes any further.

"But they make me hungry!" he blurts out.

One of the blondes hears him, stops. "What did he mean by that?" she barks.

I frown at her tone and resist the temptation to shock her with the truth. Instead, I shrug and say, "He's a child. Who knows?"

She stands still, stares at the boy's face as the skin on his right cheek twitches and smooths back to its regular chubby state. Then, shaking her head, she rushes off to catch up to her party.

"You have to be careful of what you say and what you do, Henri," I say.

The boy looks away from me. Watches the people make their way down the dock. "Why, Papa? They <u>did</u> make me hungry."

I sigh, shake my head. I knew it was unrealistic to hope that Henri's first venture into the outside world would go without incident. No matter how much I've taught him, the child's too young and his instincts are too strong. Still, if I hope to travel in the near future, he has to learn how to behave around humans.

"They don't know what we are, Henri," I say, my voice harsh enough to make Henri study his feet.

"Yes, Papa," he mumbles.

"If they did, it would scare them. Sometimes when people are scared of us, they try to hurt us. You have to remember that, Henri. You must never, ever change in front of them."

"Yes, Papa," he says, still looking down. Then he murmurs, "But I'm <u>still</u> hungry."

Sitting in the shade of a cheekee, I watch my son from across one of Monty's wood-topped tables. Henri's feet dangle from the wooden bench seat and he swings them while he sucks on the straw the waitress was good enough to put in his glass of water. I grin, watching him drain half the glass in a few sips. The boy's never used a straw before and, if given the opportunity, I'm sure he'd empty this glass and two or three more.

"That's enough for now, son," I say, taking out my cellphone, dialing LaMar Associates, my family's company.

It takes only a minute for Rita, the receptionist, to get Arturo on the line.

"Jesus, Peter!" Arturo says. "You told me you'd be over this morning. It's almost noon now. You should hear Ian. He's been complaining so much about you making us wait for you that for a minute I thought he was his father come back from the grave."

I laugh, say, "God forbid."

"So where are you? When are you going to be here?"

"We're at Monty's. Henri was hungry, so we stopped and ordered some burgers. We should be up in a little bit. . . . Sorry for the delay, Arturo, but this is Henri's first time around others. He's overwhelmed enough by all of it. I think it will go better if he isn't hungry too."

"You won't catch me arguing with you," Arturo says.

I wonder if the man is rubbing the scar on his right forearm as we speak. When he visits on the island, he tends to stroke it whenever Henri's near or I mention the boy to him. Not that I blame him. The bite took over thirty stitches to close. Of course, had Arturo listened to me when I first let him meet Henri, he wouldn't have reached out to my infant son. Henri never would have bit him without such temptation.

Any other human would have been shocked by such a thing, but the Gomez family has been serving mine since we first arrived on our island—long before the United States was even a dream in anyone's mind. Arturo was taught, I'm sure, to expect peculiar things from us and to look the other way when they occurred, as was his father and his father's father. For this, and their services, they've been well rewarded.

The waitress comes to the table carrying a tray with our meals and I get off the phone. She places a red plastic basket containing a burger and fries in front of Henri, another in front of me. I cut into my burger with a plastic knife and fork, nod when I see the meat virtually raw inside it. I say, "Perfect."

She lingers while I cut up Henri's burger for him. Watches him as he stares at the meat and waits for me to finish. "He's adorable," she says.

"Thank you," I say.

Resting her hand lightly on my left shoulder, she lingers a few more moments, then walks off to wait on another table.

She's the first female to touch me in four years. I know

some waitresses use physical contact to raise their tips, but still my heart speeds up. I draw in a breath, amazed I could be so affected by such slight feminine contact. I watch her walk away, study her tight shorts, her long legs and firm buttocks and wonder if my celibacy can be maintained for much longer.

Henri grabs a piece of burger, pops it in his mouth.

"Use your fork," I say.

"Why?" he says, picking up another piece with his fingers.

"Because if you don't do what I tell you, I won't bring you to land again."

Henri picks up his fork, spears his next piece of meat. I eat in tandem with him, watching him chew, smiling at his total concentration on his food.

"If you can behave all of today," I say. "I think we'll go shopping before we go home."

Henri looks up from his food, smiles.

"So you think you can behave?"

The boy spears another chunk of hamburger, says, "Sure," with his mouth full.

The Monroe building sits just across the street from Monty's parking lot. Henri holds my hand while we wait for the light on South Bayshore Drive to turn red. Every time a car drives by us, he squeezes hard. He cranes his neck as he stares at the top floor of the office building. "We're going all the way up there?"

I nod.

"It's all ours?"

The light changes and I lead Henri across the street. "All ours," I say, neglecting to tell him that our family's company, LaMar Associates, owns at least a portion of every one of the large buildings that tower over Bayshore's western side. There will be plenty of time, I think, when my son grows older, for him to learn what a wealthy and powerful company his grandfather built.

Henri's mouth drops open when we enter the building's

lobby. He half slides his sneakers across the slick marble floor as we cross the room toward the private elevator that accesses LaMar Associates' penthouse offices. Men in suits, women in business attire rush past us, coming and going from the bank of elevators servicing the other floors.

Where once there was one man standing guard, two armed men—one gray haired, the other balding, heavy set and younger—flank LaMar's private elevator, watch our approach. I shake my head at the show of force. I'd almost forgotten that Arturo had beefed up security after the incidents four years ago.

The balding guard steps forward when we approach. "Sir?" he says, frowning at my shorts and T-shirt, and the small, similarly dressed child I have in tow.

I grin, nod toward the older guard, try to remember his name but can't quite dredge it up. He nods back. The younger man, oblivious to our nonverbal exchange, adjusts his belt and growls, "Sir?"

Cocking one eyebrow at the man, I make a show of fishing in my pockets. I wait until a flush rises on the beefy man's cheeks before I finally produce my key to the private elevator, hold it out for him to see. "I'm Peter DelaSangre," I say. When the man doesn't react to my name, I add, "Mr. Gomez and Mr. Tindall are expecting me."

The guard frowns even more. "I'll have to check." He turns, reaches for a wall phone.

"Harry, for Christ's sake," the older man says. "Don't you know who Mr. DelaSangre is? Let the man go up. Now!"

Henri's eyes widen when the elevator door opens. Inside I pick him up, let him push the PH button. The door closes and he giggles when we accelerate upward.

Another guard greets us on the penthouse floor when the door opens. He points me to the new receptionist's station. I pause for a moment, examine the rich mahogany paneling, the matching wood furniture that's replaced the wallpaper and mica of four years ago and feel a pang of regret that Emily's no longer here to greet me.

Rita Santiago, the receptionist hired after Emily's unfortunate death, stands up, comes out from behind her desk as soon as she sees me. She smiles, stares directly in my eyes, holds out her hand. "Mr. DelaSangre. We finally get to meet."

Her gaze, delivered at equal height to mine, surprises me. I'm used to being taller than most men, towering over most women. Not even Elizabeth, who'd chosen a fairly tall human shape, could look directly into my eyes—even on her tiptoes. But, with only the aid of short-heeled shoes, this woman not only can, but does so with disturbing intensity.

I return Rita's smile, take her proffered hand. For the second time today, the mere contact with a woman's fingers affects me out of all proportion to the touch. It doesn't help at all that her eyes remind me of the deep blue water just beyond the shore of my island, or that her thick, red hair cascades down to her shoulders or that her body curves in symmetry with her height. Pockmarks—acne scars, I assume—mostly covered over by makeup, mar what otherwise could be a model's face. But I find that that slight imperfection makes her all the more attractive.

We stand frozen for a few moments—her hand growing warm in my grasp, her eyes holding mine captive, her mouth slightly parted. I don't doubt, should I lean forward, she'd accept my kiss.

Father told me once that after I'd been with one of my own kind, I'd have no interest in ordinary women. Oh, how he'd be disappointed in me today. I breathe in deeply, think of Chloe and attempt to slip my hand away.

Rita holds on, pulls me a little closer.

I know many women find me attractive. I'm no stranger to their attentions. It's my fault really. Father always teased me for being so vain as to model my features on those possessed by some of Hollywood's most popular matinee idols.

Those features served me well when I was interested in human women—when they could tempt me. But I want no such temptations now. "Rita," I say, before she can make any advance, my tone businesslike, "Arturo and Ian are waiting for me."

"I know Mr. DelaSangre," she whispers, her voice anything but seductive. "But I think you might want to hear about something I recently found out." She glances around, looks into my eyes again. "When I was hired, Mr. Tindall told me to never volunteer any information to you. He said you had no interest in anything that went on at the office, but . . ."

A man wearing a shirt and tie, someone from accounting I think, Benny something or other, walks past us and Rita lets go of my hand, backs up a little.

Arching an eyebrow, I wonder what devious scheme Ian Tindall has cooked up now. Not that anything a Tindall does could ever surprise me.

The woman turns her eyes from me to my son. Her dress hugs her, rides up to her mid-thigh as she crouches next to Henri. I look away from her long legs, her slightly too thick thighs.

"Aren't you a handsome young man," she says to Henri, then looks up at me and smiles. "Of course, anyone could tell this apple didn't fall very far from its tree."

"Papa," Henri says. He backs up, hugs my left leg with one arm, studies his feet. "When can we go?"

I grin. "We just got here, Henri. I still have to meet with Arturo and Ian. . . ."

Then looking at Rita, I say, "Don't mind the boy. This is his first time around people. He's just shy."

Rita stands, stares into my eyes and smiles. "I certainly hope his father isn't," she says. She walks to her desk, scribbles on a small piece of paper, folds it and offers it to me. "I'd like to talk more with you sometime . . . away from the office."

"I'm sure something can be worked out," I say taking the note, pocketing it, then adopting a more businesslike tone. "Please tell Gomez and Tindall to meet me in my office as soon as they can."

3

Ian Tindall appears at the doorway to my office just moments after I sit down in the big leather chair behind my mahogany desk. He knocks on the door frame, waits for me to acknowledge his presence. His Brooks Brothers suit hangs loose on his bony frame, the black wool material accentuating the pallor of his too white skin. Except for his obvious youth, his full head of black hair, I think it could be his father come back from his watery grave. I motion him in.

Behind me, Henri, intent on staring out the window, concentrates his attention on the ground far beneath us, the marina and the bay beyond it. He pays no attention to the man whatsoever. "Papa!" the child says. "I can see our boat. . . . It looks so small. Like when we're up in the air."

Before I can answer him, Tindall plops into one of the chairs in front of my desk, slouches and says, "About time you got here." He puts his hands together, interlaces his long skeletal fingers, studies the empty surface of my desk. "I hope I'm not keeping you from any important work."

I scowl at his sarcasm, spit out my words. "Work is what I pay you to do."

A pink flush blossoms on Ian's sunken cheeks, but he's wise enough to change the subject. "Arturo will be around in a few minutes," he says.

Nodding, I wonder, not for the first time, whether the Tindall family's services are worth having to endure their company. Father always insisted they were. "There are only two types of humans you should employ," he told me years ago. "Honorable men and scoundrels. The honorable ones, like the Gomez family, believe in loyalty. They'll never betray you unless you forsake them. You can trust them with your life. The scoundrels, like the Tindalls, believe in nothing—but you can count that, as long as their self-interest is served, they will do anything you want."

"But," I'd argued, "there's never been a generation of Tindalls that hasn't tried to cheat us in some way."

Father had chuckled. "We need lawyers who are willing to bend the law to our purposes. Do you expect that type of attorney to be anything but a scoundrel? Only greed and fear motivate the Tindalls. Just remember to reward them well for their services and punish them severely for their transgressions."

As my lawyer, and as chief legal counsel for LaMar Associates, Ian is rewarded very well indeed. Still, it amazes me that he could overlook the fatal punishment both his father and brother have received at my hands. I go over Rita's words in my mind, wonder if Tindall is plotting some sort of revenge or betrayal. I shake my head. Surely, I think, the deaths of two other Tindalls have taught him the foolhardiness of such acts. The man couldn't be that greedy or that stupid.

"Peter! Henri!" Arturo Gomez's voice breaks the silence in the room.

Henri turns from the window as Arturo enters the room, smiles at him, holds up one hand showing four fingers. "I'm four," he says.

"And a big boy you certainly are," Arturo says. I look from one man to the other and grin at the contrast between them. Where Tindall is skin and bones, Gomez is thick and muscular. As usual, the Latin's gray-streaked, black hair is slicked back perfectly in place, his sun-darkened skin sports the telltale reddish tinge of a fresh tan and his open-mouthed smile shows off a set of expertly capped, bright white teeth. He sits in the chair next to Tindall, nods toward him, says, "Ian."

I wince at the overpowering scent of Aramis cologne that follows Arturo into the room and immediately permeates the office's air. Sometimes I find I wish there were a way I could dull my sense of smell.

Arturo shifts in his chair, the gray silk of his Armani suit so perfectly tailored to his body's bulk that it barely wrinkles as he moves. He opens a black leather portfolio, takes out a manila folder, hands it to Tindall. He then produces another manila envelope, slides it across the desk to me.

I cock an eyebrow.

"Jamaica," he says.

Tindall opens his folder. "Jamaica?" he says, examining the brochure inside, the papers that accompany it.

"Peter had me buy some property for him in Jamaica . . . a while ago," Arturo says. He takes another folder from the portfolio, opens it, hands me three large photographs. He looks in the folder. "The Bartlet Great House, built in 1735, constructed of cut stone, on ten acres near Windsor, thirty miles inland of Montego Bay—"

"Seven hundred fifty thousand dollars?" Tindall looks up from his papers. "What the hell for?"

"I want to stay at my own place when I visit," I say.

"Last time you went to Jamaica, you just borrowed my father's boat."

"The last time I didn't plan to stay there very long."

"So how long are you planning for this time?"

"I don't know if that's any of your business, Ian," Arturo says, then turns to me. "Get this, two stories, six thousand square feet under air conditioning, four bedrooms, six baths, a great room and four other common rooms, plus a wraparound veranda and pool . . . cottages too. You could use them for servants' quarters."

I shake my head. "No. I only want day help. I want Henri and me to be left alone in the evenings."

Arturo shrugs.

Turning my attention to the pictures Arturo handed me, I admire the lines of the house, the high-pitched, stone-shingle roof. Henri crowds next to me, examines the photos too.

"Where's the water?" he says.

Grinning, I tousle Henri's hair. The child's lived his life within feet of both the ocean and the bay. To him it's only natural to expect the same everywhere. "There isn't any water near it."

"Actually," Arturo says, "the Martha Brae River runs right through the property."

"That's not the type of water Henri meant." I pick up one photo that shows a hint of mountains in the background of the picture. "And Cockpit Country?" I say.

Arturo nods. "According to the real estate agent, not very far at all."

Ian frowns. "What the hell's going on? If you wanted to go to Jamaica for a few months you could have rented a condo—or a house. You certainly don't need an estate like that. I'm your attorney for Christ's sake! I should have been consulted before you committed to something as big as this. . . ."

I sigh. "Damn it, Ian. You should be consulted when I want you to be. Anyway, this was done after your father died—before you were up to speed here. I told Arturo to find me someplace private, away from tourists, where Henri and I can live for a while . . . maybe for a year or more, maybe not."

"That's a long time to be away," Ian says.

"I just spent four years without coming to the office once. I think LaMar will do fine without me."

From the look of concentration on the thin man's face, I'm sure he's trying to calculate what opportunities might arise from my absence. "Sure," he says. "But I still don't get why you want to go there."

"And I care about that?" I say. "You don't have to understand. I want the house furnished and ready in two months. I want you to buy me a Land Rover too. Make sure someone will bring it to the airport whenever Henri and I decide to go."

*   *   *

After Tindall leaves the office, Arturo says, "You really going to leave in two months?"

I shrug, lift Henri, put him on my lap, hug him. "That depends on this one. If he shows he can behave on the mainland, then I think we'll be able to chance an airplane flight. . . . I was thinking I'd see how he does in crowds today, maybe take him toy shopping. Would you like that, Henri?" I say.

Intent on stuffing the brochure and pictures back into the manila envelope on my desk, Henri bites on his tongue, absentmindedly nodding his head, yes.

Arturo eyes the boy, rubs his right forearm.

I look at the Latin, think of my conversation with Rita. "Anything going on with Ian? You seeing anything suspicious?"

Arturo shakes his head, says, "He's a Tindall. I never trust him. But you know I always have some of my people watching him. They haven't reported anything irregular— no dramatic changes in his checking or savings, no new cars or houses, no meetings with people we don't know about. . . ."

"Something might be going on," I say. "I want you to watch out."

Arturo grins. "Sure. It'll be my pleasure. But you know, if I find something, you're going to have to think about what you want done this time."

"Because?" I ask.

The Latin's grin grows larger. "Because there are no more brothers, no cousins you can hire. Ian has no children yet. If something happens to him, there won't be any more Tindalls working for your family anymore."

I don't say it out loud, but honestly, I think, worse things could happen.

It's late afternoon before Henri and I return to the boat. The child falls asleep only moments after we get under-way, slumping to his side, his head resting on my left thigh, one ear of a large, pink, toy rabbit clutched in his right hand. I set the throttle just a few notches above idle and steer the boat toward the main channel with one hand while I rest my other hand on my son's shoulder.

I smile, marvel at the warmth he throws off when he sleeps, and envy his ability to fall asleep in an instant. I certainly can't fault the boy for running out of steam. This has been a big day for him, visiting the mainland for the first time, meeting so many new people, riding in a car, shopping for the first time.

A yellow-and-black Seatow boat crosses our bow and I hold on to Henri as I guide the Grady White over its wake, trying to minimize any pitching and bobbing of our craft. Henri shifts his position only slightly, releases the pink rabbit, lets it drop to the deck.

I lean over, pick it up and wonder why, with all the thousands of more exciting toys at the store to choose from, my son chose this one. I wedge it on the seat next to him, breathe in the salt smell freshening the air the farther we travel from the marina.

If I could, I would lie down beside my son and sleep too. There's something so restful about being on the water near the end of the day. I look out across the bay, check for other boats, see only a sailboat far to our south and the Seatow boat speeding toward Key Biscayne, most probably to rescue some stranded boater floating on the ocean just beyond it.

The water is so calm, the sea breeze so lazy, that it seems to me a shame to move so slowly. I push the throttle forward just enough to bring the motors up to half-speed. The Grady White rushes forward, leaves the channel behind in minutes. And Henri sleeps on.

I toy with the thought of detouring north, running up to the Port of Miami so Henri can see whatever big cruise ships are in port. But instead I head for the horizon, miles south of Key Biscayne where only the sky and the water are visible. Soon enough, I know, our island will begin to make its presence known.

Resisting the impulse to go faster, I stroke my sleeping son and concentrate on the movement of the boat and the water around it. Behind me the sun rides low enough in the sky for its rays to reach under the boat's canopy and burn against my back. To our right, a cormorant spooked by the nearness of our passage erupts from the water, fluttering and splashing as it takes flight.

Henri would have loved that, I think, but I let the child rest.

The far-off thunder of powerful motors breaks the quiet of the day. I turn, scan the water until I spot the boat exiting the Dinner Key channel far behind me. Over forty feet long, bullet shaped, the red-and-white Cigarette speedboat must be traveling at least sixty miles per hour. I glare at it, wish there were a way to stop it from disturbing a day like this.

The drone of the boat's motors continues to grow and after a few minutes, I look back again. The speedboat seems to be traveling in the same direction as we are and has already halved the distance between us. I watch it race toward me, remember Rita's words again, and wonder if she was warning me about Tindall, wonder if he would have the courage to arrange an attack. Shaking my head at the paranoia a few words can cause, I still alter my course to see if the boat's pursuing me or just accidentally traveling the same way.

At first, the speedboat continues on its original path. But just as I begin to feel silly about changing course, it curves toward me.

I toy with the thought of running to shore, but I know the approaching craft can reach almost twice my speed. Steering with one hand, I reach inside the compartment in the boat's console and feel around for the flare gun kit I put on board years ago. I pull the plastic case out, lay it on the dash in front of me, open it, remove the gun and a flare.

The engine sounds behind me continue to grow. I load the flare gun, cock it, hold it by my side and turn to find the boat closer than I expected, its bow pointed straight at the center of my stern as the speedboat rushes up the middle of my wake, where the water's the smoothest. A rooster tail of white water shoots up behind it, the speedboat's wake swelling up and spreading.

I get ready to aim the flare gun, then see the faces of the boat's driver and the blond woman beside him. Middle-aged, face bloated and flushed, the man looks like no assassin I've ever imagined.

The boat races closer until it's only a few lengths behind my stern. Too near for me. I begin to raise the flare gun, decide to fire at the driver's head if the boat comes much closer. But it approaches only a few feet more before it cuts to the right, jumping my wake, almost flying a few yards before it splashes down.

Jerk, I think, shaking my head. Most probably drunk, showing off for the woman. The speedboat turns back toward me, races up on the right side of my Grady White. I yell, "Henri! Hold on!" just before the roar of the Cigarette's massive motors makes any further shouting pointless. Dropping the flare gun, I gun the throttle with one hand, yank the wheel to the left with the other, trying to turn away from the boat before it overtakes me. But the Cigarette turns with me, finally passing with only a few feet between us.

Just as they come alongside my boat, I read the license numbers on the bow, FL332428, commit them to memory.

The Cigarette roars past, the blonde glancing back, pointing to her boat's wake as it smashes into us, both of them laughing.

The right side of our hull rises almost perpendicular to the water. Henri slides into me, cries out, "Papa!"

I turn us hard left, to stabilize the boat, then right, curving into the other boat's wake, the Grady White slicing through the waves, going airborne for an instant, slamming back into the water—white foam everywhere.

Henri falls forward, strikes his forehead on the edge of the console, gashing it open, blood immediately flowing down his face, into his eyes. "Papa!" he screams again and I cut back on the throttle, let the boat wallow in the remainder of the Cigarette's wake as I pick up my injured child, hug him to me.

"Shh," I say. "You're going to be okay. It just scared you. You know how to heal yourself. Do you want my help?"

My son shakes his head, the bleeding already stopping, the wound beginning to close.

I look away, wrinkle my nose at the stink of the gas fumes the other boat leaves behind. Reading the lettering on the boat's stern, DOCTOR'S RX, I memorize that too. I will permit no one to injure my son and go unpunished— not ever. Shaking my head, clenching and unclenching my fists, it takes all my self-control not to pursue them now.

It would take only a moment for me to change and take to the air, just a few minutes more for me to catch them and rip them from their boat. I wish the world were such that I could pursue my revenge in such a direct and expeditious manner. But I know I never could risk a daylight attack with the almost certainty of being seen.

"It's okay, son. . . . We're okay," I say. "That was just some idiot showing off. He'll learn his lesson soon enough."

As soon as we arrive home and get off the boat, Henri scampers off to play. I rush inside, take the spiral staircase to the great room on the third floor and go to the window overlooking Biscayne Bay. Sunlight streams through the glass, the sun already low enough in the sky to punish anyone facing west with its heat and its glare. Squinting, ignoring the warmth by the window, I study the water for any sign of a red-and-white speedboat. But I see nothing, not the Cigarette, not any other craft—just miles of empty, blue-green water.

Of course, I think, I should know better than to expect to find the boat within sight. When I last saw it, it was heading south and I was heading east. I turn from the window, pace the room, look for something to occupy my mind, divert my thoughts. But I keep picturing the smile on that fool's face when he blew by me in his Cigarette. He hurt my son. I want his name. I want to know where he lives.

I check my watch and curse. LaMar Associates closes at five. Already it's more than half an hour past that. Too late to call the office and demand that Arturo get me the name and address of the speedboat's owner.

Still, I toy with the thought of taking quick revenge. I pick up my cellphone. I know, if I called Arturo at home, if I insisted, he'd find a way to make someone research the boat's number for me, find out who owned DOCTOR'S RX and deliver the information to me before the night passed.

And then what? A quick attack, no matter what the time? I can picture—if he were here—how my father would shake his head. *"Rash actions often bring unexpected consequences,"* he warned long ago. *"Better to wait a short while than to rush into a disaster."*

If I could, I'd tell Father how tired I am of being careful. Elizabeth, who was always more reckless than me, used to argue, "What's the point of being powerful if you can't act powerfully?"

I yearn to lash out, but still I put down the cellphone. For now, I'm not willing to go against my father's teachings. I breathe deep, try to displace my anger with other thoughts.

Soon, I tell myself, we'll be on our way to Jamaica, to our new home at Bartlet House. A little while longer than that and I'll finally be able to see Chloe again. But rather than the thought reassuring me, it makes me sigh.

I've been daydreaming about the girl for years. Ordinarily, just picturing her in my mind calms me. But now that the time is coming closer, I wonder how she'll greet me, whether I'll be able to win her as my mate. And, if Chloe does eventually come into our lives, how will my son react to her?

I stare out the window, study the blue water and mutter,

"If only life could be simple." Then I remember my conversation with Rita and sigh again. Yet another problem.
Reaching into my pocket, I take out the folded paper she
gave me and smooth it out.

Studying the number, I shake my head. The last thing I
want to hear right now is any bad news from the office.
Not that Rita ever said there was a problem. She only said
she wanted to discuss something with me. But chances are,
I'm sure, I won't like what she says.

Somewhere below, Henri giggles. I smile at the sound
and decide Rita's problem can wait until after the boy's
asleep. For now, I'd far rather go see what new mischief
my son's invented.

4

"Mr. DelaSangre!" Rita breathes into her phone. "I'm so glad you called."

"I hope it isn't too late. I was sort of busy with Henri. He put up a major resistance to going to bed tonight and this is my first chance to call."

"No. It's not too late at all. I only got in a few minutes ago. Anyway, I never go to sleep before twelve. I was hoping to hear from you."

The woman confuses me. At the office her tone had alternated between warm and business brisk. Now she couldn't be warmer than if I were a new beau calling to make a date.

"You said there was something you heard that I should know?" I say, keeping my own voice businesslike.

"I didn't hear it; I read it. Please don't think I'm a snoop. I'm not. It's just that one of my jobs is to do the mail and when any legal papers pass by my desk I like to look at them," she says. "I'm going to Nova Law at night and I think it's good to see how they do it in the real world. I have to tell you, Mr. Tindall may not be the nicest man to work for, but his legal work is great to learn from. . . ."

"And you read what?" I say.

"This isn't going to hurt my job is it? I won't be through with Nova for a while yet and I like working at LaMar."

Rita speaks with just the right amount of earnest innocence. I smile at her ability to do so. Ian better watch out for this one, I think. Me too. "Somehow I don't think you'd be telling me anything you thought would put your job in jeopardy," I say.

She pauses for a moment, laughs. "No, I guess not."

"Would you also be expecting me to do something for you?"

Rita laughs again. "That would be up to you, Mr. DelaSangre. But I don't think ambition is a bad thing. Do you?"

Not as long as it serves my interests, I think, then say, "Why don't you tell me what you saw?"

"Well I didn't know that they could, because of it being in Biscayne National Park, like your island is, but did you know Wayward Key was privately held?"

"Yes," I say, thinking of the island just a hundred yards or so to my north. "The original owner bought it to keep it as a bird sanctuary."

"Which was the intent of his children and their children. But the current owner, Paul Deering, died a few months ago and, with no children of his own and no living siblings, the island goes to his only niece. She doesn't seem to care much about our feathered friends."

"And?"

"Somehow Mr. Tindall got wind of this. He and some friends have put a bid on the island."

"A lot of good that will do them. The park service doesn't want any development on any of the islands. They've been pestering me to sell to them for years. . . ."

"I thought so too. But Mr. Tindall received a letter from the director of the park service. He thanked him for being so innovative as to propose building Florida's first ecologically sensitive resort—all natural flora, vacation huts that blend in with the landscape, complete with solar and wind power, even eco-tours of the surrounding waters. He said that a project like that could possibly presage a new era of business and government working together to improve the environment. A few days later, I happened to be in Mr. Tindall's office when he had stepped out and there were some plans on his desk showing a resort—a sort of Ralph Nader meets Walt Disney vacation experience.

"Anyway," Rita continues, "the talk around the office is that you're pretty insistent on maintaining your privacy. I thought you might not like this at all."

"You thought right," I say. "So do you know how much Tindall paid for the park service director's support?"

"No, but I bet it was a lot."

The thought of vacationers staying at a resort on an island only a hundred yards from my island makes me shudder. "Has the deal gone through yet?" I say.

"I'm not sure. . . . I did see a letter from the Deering girl's attorney objecting to some of the terms of the first offer."

"Is Gomez involved?"

Rita laughs again. "You can't even get Mr. Gomez to order lunch with Mr. Tindall. No, he isn't involved."

"You didn't by any chance make any copies of all this paperwork you saw?"

"Mr. DelaSangre, that would be wrong!" she banters. "Of course, there might be some papers somewhere around here that I can get my hands on."

I smile. "You know, Rita, we just might have a place for you after you finish law school."

"You sure know how to talk to a girl, Mr. DelaSangre."

"Call me Peter," I say. "Listen, Rita, it would be great if a folder holding all those copies was placed on Arturo's desk first thing tomorrow morning. Leave him a note telling him I'll be calling to discuss it."

"Mr. Tindall will be furious."

"He may be." I grin at the thought of Tindall red faced and sputtering. I've long wanted someone else in office to use to help counter Tindall's machinations. The girl surely has her own agenda, but she could be the one. "But if things work out the way I hope they can," I say, "I don't think he'll be able to be sure who, if anyone, screwed his deal up."

"I hope so," Rita says.

"And Rita . . . thanks for the heads up. I'd like to be able to count on you to watch things in the future for me. Let me know about anything else out of the ordinary that you come across."

"Sure, Mr. DelaSangre. . . . I mean, Peter. Sure."

I try to sleep, tossing and turning for hours, thinking about Rita, Ian Tindall, DOCTOR'S RX and Chloe. When I finally drowse off, I dream over and over of finding my future bride flying above the irregular terrain of Jamaica's Cockpit Country and chasing her from valley to valley, skimming the ground, zooming high into the air, never quite catching her, never being able to make her slow, the girl ignoring all my pleas.

The frustrations the dreams bring build to such a level that I wake shaking with anger an hour before dawn. Glad to be done with my sleep and the disturbance it has brought, I get out of bed.

No matter how Chloe first receives me, I doubt she'll ever ignore me like that. Still, I have to do something to take my mind off the dreams and their troubling images and the other problems that now plague me—Tindall and his Wayward Key deal and the dolt who almost rammed me with his speedboat.

Since I won't be able to call Gomez for hours, I decide to at least do something about Chloe. If I really plan to be in Jamaica in two months, there's much that I need to get done. I throw on some clothes and descend the wooden staircase that spirals up the center of the house from the storage rooms and holding cells on the bottom floor to the great room on the top.

As I learned from my first wedding, my people's tradition requires both a proper present for my future bride, as well as a substantial gift for her parents. The choice of the correct gift for Chloe's parents, Charles and Samantha Blood, and where to find it causes me little concern. The answers to both questions reside beneath my house. But Chloe's present is another matter.

I wonder if she still wears Elizabeth's emerald-and-gold, four-leaf-clover necklace that I sent to her after my bride's death. If I know Chloe at all, I think, the girl not only wears it, but values it all the more as a reminder of her dead sibling.

Switching on the lights as soon as I reach the bottom step, I rush past the first few cells. Even with their iron-barred doors open, they remind me too much of their former occupants, the woman and the man who betrayed my trust. I still can't think of Jorge Santos without damning his memory.

I enter the last cell, the smallest, and pull up on the foot end of the cot. It resists only a moment before it begins to lift, the counterweights below taking hold, making my task simple, the cot and the floor beneath it rising, exposing a dark passageway into the bowels of the house.

Stepping down into the dark, I reach up, grab the line under the cot and bring it crashing down over me, leaving me in total blackness. When I was a child, I loved it when Father brought me here. He would insist that I lead him down the narrow stone stairs into the equally dark, small chamber below. *"Our kind relies too much at night on the stars and the moon. There will be times in your life when that light's not available,"* he said. *"It's best you learn now how to make your way in total darkness now."*

He would follow me as I found my way through the stone-walled chamber to the corridor beyond it. Offering no guidance, he'd wait until I made my way to the massive wood door that opened to the outside, behind the bushes near the dock. Only after I made my way out and stood blinking in the sudden glare of the day, would he join me and nod his approval. But he'd also always say, *"Remember, Peter, this passageway is our secret. Never tell anyone about it except your wife and children."*

Then, as a reward, he would take me inside, light a torch and lead me back to the chamber. There he would open an ancient iron door and lead me into his treasure room.

Having installed lights years ago, I've no need for any torches. I find the wall switch in the chamber, flick on the overhead lights and wince at the sudden brightness. The ancient steel-plated door to the family's treasure room is only a few feet in front of me. I turn around and look across the chamber at the other steel-plated door, no more than six paces from me.

Rusted, centuries' old padlocks secure equally aged and rusted chains crisscrossing the door. Before he died, Father made sure I knew where the ancient key to those locks was kept, showing me a secret panel behind the third stone to the right of the top of the door. But he never opened the door for me, never suggested I see what he kept inside the room.

"Open this door only if you have no other hope," he said. *"There is a chest inside that room that my father gave me, as his father gave it to him—from father to son as far back as anyone can remember. I'm told it holds a relic from a great war that was waged between our people ages before mankind gained its supremacy. I've never had any cause to open the chest, nor did my father, nor his. I've no idea what device it holds. I only know what my father told me—there is great power inside the chest and greater risk."*

As always I'm tempted to ignore Father's warnings and see for myself just what has been lurking beneath my house for my entire life. But I know I won't. Just as my father followed his father's wishes, I will follow mine. Besides, seeing the rust coating the padlocks, I doubt if Father's ancient key could even open the locks now.

I turn my attention to the treasure room. I long ago discarded the antique locks Father used to secure the chains on this door, preferring the convenience of modern, stainless-steel combination padlocks. Undoing the combination locks, I pull the chains clear and swing the door open.

Stacks of gold and silver bars, piles of twenty-dollar

bills, watches and jewelry, chests full of gold and silver coin clutter the room. I can't help but smile at the huge accumulation of wealth sitting in this one small room.

Of course my family's true wealth is invested on the mainland and worth hundreds of times more than the baubles before me. But like my father, I like the smell and feel of money, the cold weight of gold and silver, the glint of diamonds and rubies. Like Father did, I bring home the possessions of my prey and add them to the treasures in the room.

I frown as I count out enough gold coins to equal what I estimate would be three times Chloe's weight. Charles and Samantha Blood had been furious when I came to wed Elizabeth without bringing the requisite gift for her parents. I'd made amends by promising and sending them twice Elizabeth's weight in gold. This time I don't want to risk any chance of their displeasure. Still, it pains me to give them so much.

Certainly I'm not the first being to wish for more pleasant in-laws. But when I think of how unpleasant they'd been, I wish there were a way to pursue Chloe without dealing with them or rewarding them with any of my possessions.

For Chloe, however, I'd part with all the contents of this chamber. I search the room, sift through the jewelry, hoping to find something that would thrill my future bride. I look for anything in the treasure room that might be equal to or compliment the simple emerald-and-gold, four-leaf-clover necklace that I first gave Elizabeth. But each piece I look at is too massive or too gaudy or too plain or too ugly. Finally, I stop searching and sigh. Chloe's gift will have to be found on the mainland.

I call the office later in the morning. Rita, of course, answers.

"Mr. DelaSangre," she says. "How are you this morning?"

"Tired and cranky," I say, not mentioning that I'm also

irritated that I have to waste time over some human's machinations this morning. "Listen, Rita, does Arturo have the copies we discussed last night?"

"Of course, Mr. DelaSangre," she says, her voice turning coy. "I always do as I'm instructed."

I have to grin. If I were in the mood to be seduced by a human, she certainly would be one of my choices, but I've other concerns right now. "Sure you do," I say. "Please put me in to Arturo now—and Rita?"

"Yes, sir?"

"I told you, you can call me Peter."

"I don't know if I should here," she says.

"You should."

"But you do own everything around me. . . . You're Mr. Tindall's and Mr. Gomez's boss."

"So?"

"Well, they might not like it. They certainly don't want me to call them by their first names."

"Then don't call them by their first names. Anyway, I need to ask a favor of you after I finish with Arturo."

"Whatever you say, Peter."

"Goddamned Tindalls!" Arturo says as soon as he picks up the phone. "Can't they ever just go along for a year or two without trying something?"

"Guess not," I say. "Tell me what you think."

"You don't want to know what I think."

I know what he's going to say. I've heard it before. "Sure," I say. "Go ahead, tell me."

"The guy's not worth it. Let's cut our losses. I can arrange for him to go away, permanently. We could hire another attorney."

"Arturo, the man's useful to me. So far he hasn't done anything that would make me terminate him. If you want to be fair about it, the Wayward Key deal isn't any violation of his responsibilities to LaMar or of my trust."

"He has to know how you'd feel," the Latin says. "Technically he may not have betrayed you but any way I look at it, what he's trying to do is a massive disservice to you."

Nodding, even though the man can't see me, just as I'm sure Arturo is gesturing with his free hand, I say, "I agree with you. I'm sure Ian is taking pleasure in thumbing his nose at me. But I think we found out in time. We should be able to stop them."

Arturo says nothing.

"What?" I say.

"I made some calls before you phoned in. The sale may be a done deal."

"Are you sure?"

"Not completely. You know I couldn't approach anyone on Tindall's side of the deal. So I arranged for a broker to call the Deering side, feeling them out, if they would amenable to an offer. They didn't show much interest in hearing one."

"Damn!" I say. Even though I know, in the worst case, I can force Ian to stop, I prefer thwarting his plans without his knowing of my involvement. Ian is more helpful when he isn't sulking. Besides, there's no assurance that the other principals in the deal won't go on without him.

"Give me until next week. I'll see what I can work out," Arturo says.

I grunt assent, then say, "We wouldn't have known about this without Rita's help. I want you to review her salary, give her a good raise."

"It might raise eyebrows. Tindall will certainly find out."

"Let him. The girl's ambitious. She's going to law school. We might want to put her to work with him after she graduates."

Arturo chuckles. "Oh, he'd love that."

"He'd adjust."

"Hey, it's fine with me. We can move her there sooner if you want."

I mull it over. Do I want Rita working as one of Tindall's legal assistants just yet? "No," I say, thinking of her ability to screen all calls, review all of the office's mail. "I like her just where she is right now."

"Sure," Arturo says.

"I need you to do something else for me, Arturo," I say, telling him about DOCTOR'S RX, letting him know what I want.

5

The red Corvette and the silver Mercedes coupe remain parked near the valet stand at Monty's just where they were left four years ago. I study their glistening paint jobs and nod. It's a measure of Arturo's attention to detail that, after all the years of my neglect, my two cars still look like new.

"I want to ride in this one," Henri says, pointing to the Corvette.

Sometimes Henri's similarities to his mother amaze me. I grin at his instinctive choice of Elizabeth's car. Like she did, he gravitates to things that look fast. I put my hand on his shoulder, say, "Of course . . . but when it's just the two of us. Rita's coming with us today. She's meeting us here."

The boy looks toward the Monroe building. "But isn't she up there?"

"Not today." I say, checking my watch. "I told her to meet us here at ten-thirty." Lifting Henri, I put him on the Corvette's hood, so he can sit with his legs dangling. "We still have at least fifteen minutes before she's due to arrive." I lean back on the hood next to him.

Behind us, in the marina, a big Hatteras fires up its engines, battering the morning's calm, the noise drowning out all possibility for conversation. I wait a few minutes, until the boat's motors warm up and the captain throttles them down to a low growl, and then say, "It's Saturday. Didn't you notice how many boats were already on the bay this morning? Look around." I point toward the constant flow of joggers and bicyclists traveling up and down the sidewalks on both sides of Bayshore Drive. "Do you see anyone in a suit?"

Henri looks, shakes his head. "No."

"Right." I ruffle his hair with my right hand. "Most people don't have to work today."

"You don't have to work ever, do you, Papa?"

I think of all the chores I do back on my island—all the time and effort I expend taking care of my son—and smile. "No," I say. "I don't have to work."

Henri and I wait in silence. Overhead, a white cloud, already swollen and puffed out with moisture, shades us for a few moments as it passes on its journey west toward the Everglades. I watch it go by, knowing it will spend the day feeding on the humid air, growing until it turns dark and angry and then rushes east to menace us in the late afternoon.

Cars pull into Monty's parking lot, disgorging either groups of boaters laden with supplies or workers for the restaurant. Other cars pass us on Bayshore, some pulling boats on trailers, heading for the public ramps at Dinner Key a few blocks to our south. Finally a blue compact turns at the light and Rita waves from the driver's window. Henri waves back, as do I. "She was nice to me when we went to the office, Papa. I like her. Do you?"

I shrug, say, "She's okay—"

"For a human." Henri interrupts with my standard qualification, then giggles.

I tickle the boy, keep him giggling. "Yes, for a human."

But, I have to admit to myself, as she gets out of her car and walks toward us, even for a human, Rita Santiago in tight jeans and a simple yellow cotton T-shirt makes for quite an impressive sight.

"Mr. DelaSangre . . . Peter," she says, offering her hand. "I hope I haven't made you and Henri wait too long."

I take her hand and once again find myself enjoying her touch more than I want to. "No problem," I say, letting go, regretting the loss of contact. "Henri and I have been enjoying the morning air."

Rita draws in a breath. "It's beautiful today, isn't it? What a shame we're not going somewhere outside."

"I wanted to ride in that car." Henri points to the Corvette. "But Papa says we can't because of you."

"Really?" Rita looks at me while she says, "I don't see why not. If you don't mind riding on my lap. I think we can all squeeze in."

"Can we, Papa?" Henri asks. "Can we?"

At Rita's and Henri's prompting I take down the Corvette's top. "We're going to a jewelry shop near the Dadeland Mall," Rita says as she gets in the car, helps Henri onto her lap. "But it's too nice to drive down U.S. 1 today. Can we drive through the Grove, down Old Cutler?"

I nod. "I haven't been that way in years," I say. I take us through the middle of Coconut Grove's business district, then south on Ingraham Highway—the street shaded and cooled by a living canopy provided by the large oaks and ficus trees that line the roadway.

Henri sits on Rita's lap, swivels his head from side to side as he attempts to gaze at each home we pass, each jogger or bicyclist, each car.

"I called around like you asked," Rita says. "Mayer's Jewelers no longer carries the necklace you bought there. But a clerk there remembered the four-leaf-clover design. He told me one of his clients had matching earrings made by this jeweler, Sam Moscowitz. I called Mr. Moscowitz yesterday and arranged an appointment for us this morning."

"Thanks," I say. I glance at Rita and my son—the boy sitting on her lap with her arms around him. Both of them seem perfectly content with their seating arrangement. I smile. "I knew I could count on you to find what I need."

"We haven't found it yet." Rita returns my grin. "We'll see soon enough if this Moscowitz can do what you want."

"But it's probably unfair of me to make you come along with us. No doubt you have better things to do on your day off."

The woman leans her head back, stares at the branches and leaves shading the roadway, the flashes of blue sky that show through periodically. "Sure, I could be doing my laundry . . . or going grocery shopping . . . or I could be washing my car or studying," she says. "Or, let's see, I could spend the day being chauffeured around in a Corvette"—she hugs Henri enough to make him squirm in her grasp—"in the company of two good-looking men."

Ingraham gives way to Old Cutler Road and the road widens, its overhead canopy intermittently sparse, the houses larger and more palatial. "I can't believe so many people can afford homes like this," Rita says, then puts her hand to her mouth. "Of course, you could probably buy any one you wanted to."

I study the estates that we pass, their fake columns and overlarge doorways, their self-important gates and carefully manicured lawns and grimace. "I wouldn't want any of them. They're way too self-conscious. You should see my house. It's designed to be part of the landscape it inhabits—not to stand out from it."

Rita looks at me. "I'd like to see it."

Once again I've little doubt of Rita's availability. But, as tempting as she is, she isn't the one I want. "Maybe one day, if we have time."

Sam Moscowitz, short and round, with small thin fingered hands that seem to be perpetually in motion, either gesturing or rubbing together or picking up and straightening whatever objects might be nearby, says, "Sure. I remember," when I ask about the emerald, four-leaf-clover necklace and the earrings he made to match it. To my delight, he brings out pictures of the earrings and sketches of their design.

"Two weeks," he says. "They'll be ready. They'll be perfect. Your sweet lady here will love them."

Rita blushes. "They're not for me," she says.

"Oh. Some other lucky lady." Sam cocks an eyebrow at me. "Or should I say a very lucky man?"

Back in the car, Henri says, "I'm hungry, Papa."

"We can go get some burgers now, if it's okay with Rita."

"But I'm tired of burgers!" the boy whines. "I want a steak or something else big. . . ."

I sigh. "Not until tonight, when we get home."

"No, I want it now!"

Rita grins at the struggle of wills going on around her. "I've got an idea," she says.

Henri looks up at her. I say, "What?"

"Henri, have you ever been to Metrozoo?"

My son shakes his head.

"It's a place full of all different types of animals. We could go there and eat and see them all. Though the food isn't very good there."

"Animals?" Henri asks.

"Lions and monkeys and snakes and bears—all types. Would you like that, Henri?"

He looks at me. "Can we, Papa?"

We don't arrive at Monty's until well past five in the afternoon. Henri, tired from an afternoon of rushing from viewing one exotic creature after the next—and stuffed with two, far too well-cooked hamburgers, as well as an ice cream sandwich and almost a bag of buttered popcorn—sleeps so soundly that he barely moves in Rita's arms as she takes him from the car.

She cradles the boy so his cheek is pressed against hers, watches as I put up the Corvette's top. "He's so sweet," she says.

I nod, motion for her to hand him over to me.

"Can't I carry him to the boat for you?" she says.

Her cheeks and nose show the red tinge of a day spent in the sun. I look at her and smile. "Sure."

Neither she nor I say a word as we cross the parking lot and walk down the dock to my boat slip. Everywhere people coming in from a day on the water are pulling their boats into slips, washing down their windows and decks, piling leftover supplies on the docks, preparatory to bring-ing them back to their cars.

Gas exhaust and diesel fumes mix in the air with the smells of fried fish and beer that emanate from Monty's. The house band at the restaurant begins their first set by playing Marley loud enough to be heard from the farthest docks and I glance at my sleeping son and smile when he notices none of it.

At the boat, Rita says, "He was right, you know."

"Who was?" I take the boy, lay him down on the bench behind the driver's seat.

"The jeweler. Whoever you're buying those earrings for is one lucky girl."

I shrug, say, "That remains to be seen."

Rita wrinkles her forehead, stares at me. "Aren't you going with her already? What remains to be seen?"

"It's complicated," I say, thinking of Chloe, wondering how she'd react to seeing me with this woman, whether she'd care at all. "I don't know that I can explain."

I get off the boat, approach Rita and extend my hand. "Thanks for your help today . . . and for Metrozoo. It was a great idea."

"Oh," she says, "wait a minute. Mr. Gomez gave me something for you." She rushes off, goes to her car and re-turns with an envelope. "He said you'd know what to do with this."

Taking it, I nod, double it over, put it in my pocket. "Thank you again," I say turning toward the boat.

Rita doesn't move. "Peter, couldn't I possibly join you to see this house you were talking about? I mean I had fun with you today. I think you had a good time too." She says no more, waits for my reply.

I turn back. "I did have a good time," I say, looking at her, thinking how long it's been since I felt the warmth of another body pressed against mine. But I wonder about Rita's motives. She's human, ambitious, obviously well aware of the wealth that I control and an employee of my business—all good reasons to avoid entanglement with her. And then, of course, there's Chloe. I just don't want to hurt Rita's feelings. If things work out, the woman could be very useful for me.

"You went shopping with me today for a gift for another woman," I say. "I'll be leaving the country in a few months. If everything goes okay, I'll be marrying that woman in a year or two. I'm just trying to be fair to you. . . ."

"Why don't you let me decide what's fair for me?" Rita steps closer to me. "No one's looking to get married here." She moves even closer, so our bodies almost touch.

The scent of her perfume reminds me of jasmine. That, mixed with her natural scent, spiked with the slight hint of her sexual excitement and my four-year self-imposed abstinence, makes her almost irresistible. Hating my weakness, I put my hands on her hips, pull her the last few centimeters toward me and lean forward so my lips meet hers.

Overhead the late afternoon sun burns down upon us. We ignore its heat, pay no notice to the caress of the sea breeze as it plays with our clothes and our hair.

A couple, leaving their boat, walks by us, averting their eyes, giggling, whispering about our kisses and hugs loud enough to be heard. Rita tightens her embrace. "Screw them," she murmurs.

"Papa," Henri mindspeaks. *"Why is she still here? We're not going to eat her, are we, Papa?"*

"No, we're not," I mindspeak, pulling back from Rita.

"Good," Henri says. *"I like her."*

"Me too." Cocking my head toward the boat, I say out loud, "Look who's up."

Rita smiles toward Henri, smooths her blouse, straightens her hair. "I guess no boat ride for me today, huh?"

I shake my head. "Not today," I say. "It's probably for the best."

She shrugs, says, "Well, you know where to find me," and walks away before I can say anything else.

6

I'm ready to be gone. I wake each morning anxious to rush through the day so the next day can come and go. I call Tindall so often, to ask whether all the arrangements have been made in Jamaica, that he finally growls, "For Christ's sake, Peter, how hard do you think it is to hire a few house servants and an interior decorator? The house will be ready before you leave. Your Land Rover's sitting in Kingston at the dealer. As soon as I hire your groundskeeper, I'll have him pick it up."

Almost a week has passed since we went with Rita to the zoo and Henri continues to delight me with his progress around humans. I regret now that I set our departure date so far in the future. My boy already thinks nothing of being in any human crowd.

The other day, I let him play with at least two dozen other kids at the Dadeland Mall, in one of those brightly painted inside playgrounds malls built to encourage parents to come waste their money. All went well until a little girl, a head taller than him, shoved Henri out of her way so she could use the slide first. I took a deep breath. A few weeks ago, her life might have been at risk. But, rather than bite or slash her, Henri just waited for her to come down the slide and stand before he shoved her and knocked her down. He flashed me a grin when she ran crying to her mommy and then, rather triumphantly, took his own turn at the slide.

*   *   *

Henri follows me around the house today as I inspect each floor, try out each massive, wooden storm shutter, perform maintenance on the generators, wind turbines and solar panels that provide power for the island.

"Papa?" he says, after I start to inventory the foodstuffs and materials kept in the storerooms and the walk-in freezer on the bottom floor. "When can we go to the mainland again?"

"Not for a few days," I say and go into the freezer—to count the remaining cow carcasses hanging on hooks—while Henri wanders from cell to cell on the floor. He swings the unlocked barred doors open and closed until I begin to grit my teeth at the screech of their hinges and the clang and rattle of metal slamming into metal.

I resist scolding the boy. He has no knowledge of the poor souls who have been imprisoned in the dark bowels of our house or their sad endings. Certainly he knows nothing of the humans who betrayed me here or how close I came to my own death not so long ago.

Henri joins me in the freezer, blowing puffs of air, smiling at the little clouds of cold they create as he watches me recheck the temperature setting and make notes on a pad. "Why are you doing this?" he says.

"Because," I say, prepared to leave that as the final answer.

But my son frowns at me. "Papa, it's not fair. You always say that. I'm a little kid. How can I learn anything if you don't tell me?"

I sigh and smile at the same time. Henri's right. This question isn't like the endless patter of questions he usually barrages me with like, "Why do clouds float? What's inside dogs?" and, my favorite, "Why do I have to do what you say?"

"We're going to be in Jamaica a long time," I say. "I'm making sure everything will be okay when we get back."

"Why do we have to go? I like it here."

"You'll like it there too. Anyway, I want to see someone who lives there. She and I will like each other, I think."

"Are you going to marry her?"

"I might."

"Is she going to be my new mommy?"

I sigh again. That's how it is with Henri. One question leads to another and the answer to that leads to another. "I don't know, son. It depends on how she feels and how I feel and on how you feel about her."

Before he can ask another question, I say, "Come on, let me show you something special." Taking his hand, I guide him out of the freezer.

Henri giggles, says, "Your hand's cold."

I lead the boy outside onto the veranda, to the massive oak door between the doors to his and my bedrooms. "Watch," I say. Thinning my hand, I work it into a crevice on the side of the doorway, feel for the catch that will release the iron-sheaved crossbar that keeps the door closed. As soon as I find it, I push upward and am rewarded with a loud click.

Withdrawing my hand, letting it regain its shape, I shift the crossbar sideways until it engages an internal counterweight and pivots out of the way. I swing the door open. Warm air, smelling of mildew, oil, sulfur and must, flows out from the dark interior. Henri wrinkles his nose and backs up.

Stifling a laugh, I say, "It's okay, son. This is one of your grandfather's arms rooms. Some of the things in there are very old." I don't tell the boy that I haven't opened any of the four arms rooms that Father built into each corner of the house since the day of Elizabeth's death.

Mindful of the canisters of gunpowder stored in the room I wish now my laziness hadn't prevented me from installing electric lights in each of the arms rooms. Motioning for the boy to stay outside, I go in, find a torch and take it outside, where I can light it in the open air. Once it's burning, I carry it in, slip it into a metal sconce on the bare stone wall, far from any gunpowder. Then I say, "It's okay, Henri, come here."

His eyes grow large as he examines the one ancient cannon in the center of the room, the flintlock pistols, muskets and blunderbuss rail guns stacked on every shelf, the lead canisters full of powder and the bags of shot and stacks of cannonballs. "Wow," he says.

Nodding, I pat the barrel of the lone cannon. Once there were two in this room, as there are two in each of the others. But the mate to this one lies in the harbor now, encrusted and overgrown with barnacles and coral, decaying, I hope, until one day there will be no trace of what it once was capable of doing.

I look at my son, see the curiosity in his eyes. Before he can ask yet another, "Why?" I say, "Your grandfather brought all this to the island a long time ago. You know our kind can live a long time, don't you, Henri?"

The boy nods.

I think of the ancient, wheezing creature my father became at the end of his life. Life can be so unjust. "Some of us, like your grandfather, live for centuries."

"How old are you, Papa?"

It takes a moment for me to calculate. After all, for someone capable of maintaining any shape, able to manipulate his internal processes as well, age matters not a wit. The face I present to the outside world is that of a man in his late twenties. What does it matter that I'm far older? Among my own kind I'd still be considered young. "Sixty-two," I say. "But, Henri, I don't want you to ever repeat that to any human. It would just confuse them. Promise me."

He nods solemnly, then holds up four fingers. "I'm four now."

"Yes, you are." I smile. "Your grandfather was almost five hundred by the time he passed. He lived a long time — longer than he wanted, for my sake."

"Why, Papa?"

"Because he didn't want to leave me alone. He waited until he knew I could find a wife."

"Was that Mama?"

I nod, think about the old creature, how much he must

have loved me to hold on so long. "Anyway, a long time ago, Don Henri commanded a pirate fleet."

"And I'm named after him."

"Yes, you are," I say. "Do you know what a pirate is?"

"I saw it on TV. They have big sailboats and they shoot cannons."

I laugh, go about the business of lubricating the guns, fighting the rust that threatens to overtake them. "Yes, they do, Henri. Yes, they do."

Arturo comes out to visit us the next day. With my permission he brings along his oldest child, a daughter by the name of Claudia. "It's about time my daughter comes to work for the firm," Arturo said when he asked if he could bring her.

"The tradition is that your eldest son is supposed to come to work for us, not your eldest daughter," I said.

The Latin sighed. "You try telling Claudia that. The girl has been set on going into the business since the first time she heard about old Evilio Gomez sailing with your father in his pirate fleet. She's heard all the other stories too. She understands our family has always served your family's interests. She knows we have a special relationship that's never to be betrayed.

"Believe me, my wife and I tried to talk her out of it. We'd both prefer for her to marry some nice guy and give us some grandkids. I'd certainly rather my daughter wouldn't have to do some of the things I've done. But she has her own plans.

"Anyway, my eldest son is eight. I don't think he would be much help." he laughed. "We have to get with the times, Peter. Claudia's twenty-five now. She's been preparing for this since she was a child. She knows everything about what we do. She understands when to look the other way."

"But do you think she can handle the job?" I asked.

"She'll be fine, Peter," Arturo said. "She understands what a commitment this is. She knows she's continuing a relationship between our families that's gone on since the first Gomez came to work for your family in the New World. She's perfectly able and willing to do anything you need done.

"Besides, with you planning to be gone for God knows how long, I'll be damned if I'm going to stay out here on my boat, baby-sitting your island, feeding your damned dogs. Let me bring Claudia out to the island. After you meet her, I'm sure you'll be fine with it."

The dogs rush to the dock, baying and growling, before either Henri or I take notice of the approach of Gomez's boat. We follow the pack to the dock—shoo them away, back from the dock and the house—just before the thirty-five-foot SeaRay cabin cruiser motors into our harbor with Claudia at the helm. The dogs take turns darting out from behind the bushes, howling and barking. Arturo's daughter smiles toward us, and ignores the loud challenges of the dog pack as she expertly pulls the boat alongside the dock.

She approaches me as soon as she steps off the boat. "Mr. DelaSangre," she says, holding out her hand. "Thanks for letting me come."

I take her hand, admire her firm grip, the obvious ease she seems to have in my presence. Claudia turns from me, greets Henri with all the same courtesy as she greeted me.

Stepping back, I examine her while she talks with my son. The girl only comes up to her father's shoulders; otherwise, she could be a female clone of him. She possesses the same wide grin, the same square jaw, the same thick black hair, only longer. Fortunately for her, she seems not to have inherited her father's tendency toward beefiness, though her wide shoulders and defined muscles give testimony to her dedication to working out.

She looks up, catches my study of her. "Do I pass?"

I nod, turn to Arturo. "Well, she looks like you. If she works like you, we'll have no problem at all."

"You don't have to worry about me, Mr. DelaSangre," Claudia says. "I'll be glad to watch after things here. Pop promised to come relieve me every once in a while so I don't go too island crazy, but I think I'll enjoy it out here. As long as the fishing's good and I have some good books to read, I should be okay."

"Papa, can I show Claudy my room?"

"Claudia," I correct him. "If she wants to," I say.

"Sure," the girl says, allowing Henri to take her by the hand and lead her up the wide steps to the veranda.

Arturo watches them a few moments, then says, "Bad news."

"You can't break up Tindall's Wayward Key deal?"

"I'm not sure yet. But an offer was made that the Deering woman accepted and a fairly substantial deposit was given."

"Offer her twice as much," I say.

"We have, but she's worried about getting sued."

"Indemnify her."

"We offered to, but she's still dragging her feet."

"Threaten her."

"Peter, that's for later—if we have to. I have other ideas. Trust me."

I cock an eyebrow at the man. "If I come back from Jamaica and find a resort being built at my doorstep, I won't be very happy, Arturo."

He laughs. "It won't ever come to that, believe me. By the way," he says, "was the info I gave you on that speedboat useful? I don't think the owner's any threat to you. He's just some retired pathologist."

"I've gone over your notes a few times. It's exactly what I wanted," I say. "Matter of fact, I plan to review all of it again before we leave for Jamaica. Maybe I'll visit the good doctor, explain proper marine etiquette to him."

7

The ensuing weeks seem to crawl by for me. I continue to take Henri to the mainland. He and I go to malls, movies, restaurants and museums. To get him ready for flying on an airplane, we even take a few rides on city buses and one on the Metrorail, the elevated train that runs alongside U.S. 1 from South Miami to downtown.

At Henri's request, Rita Santiago joins us for that trip as she does for some of our other outings. "I'm glad you still invite me to come out with you and Henri," she says. "I like your son and enjoy your company. But don't worry. I understand my position. The raise you gave me was more than generous. I intend to earn it and hopefully more."

To my relief, there have been no repeats of the kiss and embrace we had after our first outing. She no longer flirts with me. She never asks to visit my island. Even more important, she begins to give me a weekly report on all she observes happening at the office.

Fortunately, nothing of much importance occurs. Tindall flies to Jamaica for a week to hire my help and make sure all will be in place for my trip. A lot of gossip goes around when Arturo brings Claudia into the company and assigns her to an office near his. But otherwise all proceeds as normal.

My thoughts focus more and more on Jamaica and the bride I hope to win. I dream over and over of flying above the conical hills and deep valleys of Cockpit Country. Some nights I find myself chasing Elizabeth; other nights,

Chloe. But where I sometimes catch Elizabeth, Chloe always eludes me. No matter how fast I fly, how well I maneuver, she almost always remains just beyond my grasp. In those dreams where I do come closer to her, when I reach out and grab her, I wake up before I can see her reaction.

Finally, the last week of waiting arrives. Tindall calls to assure me all is arranged. "Claudia's going to meet you at the island, ferry you to shore so we don't have to worry what to do with your boat. Arturo will take you to the airport. He has passports for you and your boy. You'll be met at the airport in Montego Bay by the man I hired for you, Granville Morrison. He goes by the nickname 'Granny.' He'll have your car and the keys to your house.

"You'll find Granny useful. He's in charge of maintaining the grounds, the house and the car, but he knows everything about the area too. If you and Henri want him to stock your stable, he also can handle horses. His wife, Velda, will be managing the house staff."

"Staff?" I say.

"Just two cleaning girls. Don't worry, Peter, they all know you like your privacy. I told them they have to be off the premises by five at the latest."

I begin to think about packing and realize I have only Elizabeth's one leather suitcase and Father's ancient portmanteau. Arturo laughs when I tell him. "But I never had any need to own any," I say. "The last time I went to Jamaica, I just threw my clothes on Jeremy Tindall's trawler."

"Don't worry," Arturo says. "I'll have Claudia take care of it."

The girl, by now able to negotiate our channel by herself, brings out the new suitcases the next day. "I got them at Dadeland this morning," Claudia says as she takes them off the boat and places them on the dock. "Can I help you pack?"

I shake my head. "I think I can handle it myself."

She shrugs. "Oh, I have something Pop wanted you to see." Claudia jumps on the boat, returns in a few minutes with the local section of the *Herald*. She points to a picture in the center of the page.

Taking the paper from her, I examine the photo. A man in shirtsleeves is addressing a crowd of protesters. I recognize him: David Muntz, a congressman from South Broward. My lip begins to curl just looking at his picture. I know all too well what a dunce he is, how incapable he is of any true reasoning. If it weren't for his innocent face, his Jewish background and my money, the elderly Jewish residents of the region's numerous condominiums would never have put him in office. But, I smile, at least he is *my* dunce.

The protesters' placards say, SAVE WAYWARD KEY, SAY NO TO DEVELOPMENT OF BISCAYNE NATIONAL PARK and SAVE THE BIRDS. The headline below the picture declares, CONGRESS-MAN MUNTZ VOWS TO SAVE WAYWARD KEY FROM DEVELOP-MENT.

"Pop thought you'd like that. He said to tell you, 'See there's more than one way to stop Tindall.'" Claudia laughs. "I can't wait to get to the office. I bet Ian is livid."

"I think he might be," I say, laughing too.

After Claudia leaves, I wander the island, go from floor to floor in the house, trying to make sure I haven't forgotten anything. I recheck all the items that need to be maintained, especially the wells and the cisterns. Henri follows me. "Papa, can't we do anything else?" he says.

"You can go play."

"I'm bored. I want to go to the mainland."

Shaking my head, I say, "Not until it's time to leave."

"Why?"

"Because there are things I need to do."

"Can't we do stuff with Rita?"

I sigh. "No, but I'll tell you what. How about if tonight, after it gets dark, we practice flying and then I'll go on a hunt for us."

"Fresh prey?" The boy salivates at the mention of it.

I nod, saliva flooding my mouth too. Just the thought of taking to the air and seeking prey awakens my hunger, speeds my heartbeat, makes me yearn for the dark to come more swiftly.

"Tonight," I say, thinking of Arturo's note sitting on my dresser and the information it details—Dr. Sean Mittleman's address, who lives with him, what their routine is.

Well after dark, I enter Henri's room. The boy is still wearing his daytime clothes, sleeping, his pink stuffed rabbit lying beside him. I turn on a dim lamp on his dresser, stare at him, shake my head. He looks so small, his bed seems so tiny and frail, dwarfed as they are by the dimensions of the room: the twelve-foot-high ceilings, the wide, double oak doors—one set leading to the veranda outside, and the other to the landing in the interior of the house.

Father didn't have children in mind when he designed this house. Every room of the house, every feature was fashioned to accommodate the most massive of our kind, in our natural forms. Toward that purpose all the sleeping chambers on this floor measure as large as an ordinary living room.

"Plenty of room, Peter," he chided me when I first took to sleeping in human form in an ordinary bed. *"That's all we need. A dry room and a good clean pile of hay."*

Henri's only recently taken to mimicking me—using his bed, sleeping in his human form. "I'm too big for straw now," he told me. Still, I maintain a fresh bed of straw in the far corner of the room, for whenever he chooses to change his habits.

I sit on the bed, rub Henri's back to wake him. He remains lost in sleep until I whisper in his small, perfectly formed ear, "It's dark out, Henri. Time for a hunt. Don't you want to fly with me before I leave?"

The boy burrows his head into his pillow, facedown. But I can see from his cheeks that he's smiling.

"So. Do you want to go flying, Henri?"

He nods his head into the pillow.

"Then let's go!" I stand up, walk toward the doorway.

Henri moves his legs over the side of the bed, lets their weight carry him down to the floor. He drags the rabbit after him.

"Stop playing," I say. "Leave the bunny on the bed."

He nods, carefully props the pink rabbit so it sits up against the pillow and then he runs for the doorway, giggling as he rushes past me onto the landing.

I allow him a lead, chase after him as he scampers up the open, thick wood slats of the staircase that spirals through the center of the house.

Henri shrieks when I catch up to him on the third-floor landing, laughs as I sweep him up in my arms and kiss him on the cheeks, his arms, the top of his head. "No, Papa," he says between giggles. "Please let me down. Please, Papa. I want to do it myself. I want to show you."

Putting the boy down, I follow him into the great room, throw the lights on and watch as he sits down on the planked floor and pulls off one sneaker, then the other.

"Do you want anything to eat?" I ask.

Henri pauses midway from pulling off one sock and looks up at me. "Can I . . . after I change?"

"Sure. I'll just get our meat ready now, while you undress." I leave the boy, walk to the kitchen in the far corner of the room and open the freezer. I smile at the thick, frozen steaks packed within it. Father had never been impressed with most of the improvements I'd installed over the years. *"Generators,"* he'd snorted. *"Airconditioning, electric lights—who needs them?"* But he'd never complained about my ability to keep fresh meat ready to be thawed in the microwave at a moment's notice.

I remove a huge steak and a smaller one, place both in the microwave and set it to run for a few minutes, just long enough to bring the meat to room temperature and eliminate the chill from its core.

"Papa! Look at me!"

Pressing the microwave's switch, I turn toward my son, who is standing above the pile of his cast-off clothes. "Me first," he says.

I grin at his naked form, put my hands on my hips and nod.

Henri's eyebrows furrow, his lips purse and tighten as he concentrates on his body. Nothing happens. The boy frowns, his eyebrows furrow even more. Still nothing. The microwave dings and I step forward, reach to touch my son, ready to change with him, to make it easier for the boy.

I don't remember it being that difficult when I was little, wonder if I should make him practice more, every day, like my father made me. *"Each of us has a size, both in our natural and human shapes, where our bodies are most comfortable,"* he taught me. *"That's the simplest form of shapechanging. Once you know your human form, it will grow just as your natural form does—without your thinking about it. But there will be times you'll want to force your form into other shapes and sizes. When you're older and more practiced, I'll teach you how."*

Henri steps back from me, shakes his head. "No, Papa. I'm a big boy now." His shoulders start to swell and a smile momentarily breaks out on his face. "See?" he says, his skin convulsing, tightening, forming scales—his jaws enlarging, his face stretching to accommodate them, as his teeth lengthen and his hands and feet turn into claws.

"Look, Papa!" He spreads his wings, fans me with a few quick strokes.

I study the pale green creature in front of me. Twice as large as his human form, the only resemblance he has to the naked boy who just stood in his place is the emerald-green color of his eyes. Still, there's no doubt he's a child.

I know eventually the pudginess around his jaws will go away, his light green scales will darken, the paunch of his cream-colored underbody will slim, his muscles will turn hard and bulge beneath his hide, his wings will lengthen and thin — and I have little desire to see any of it happen anytime soon.

"You certainly are growing up," I say. I go to the microwave, remove the lukewarm, raw steaks, put them on platters and place them on the massive oak table in the center of the room.

Henri eyes the meat, sniffs the blood pooling on the platter. *"May I, Papa?"*

I nod and the boy grabs the smaller steak, wolfs it down in only a few bites. I understand the boy's hunger. To be able to change shape is a wonderful gift nature has given us. But I've long ago learned, nature rarely gives anything without extracting some sort of a price in return. For People of the Blood, the cost extracted is our energy. Feeding is necessary to avoid growing weak.

Throwing off my clothes, I will my body to change, grunt with pleasure at the almost pain of my splitting skin, the itch of scales erupting to the surface of my body, the stiffness of my wings as they unfold and flex.

I spread my wings out to their full span and sigh at the relief of stretching them. This is the only room of the house where I can fully extend them. Measuring eighteen feet from nose to tail, with a wingspan twice that, I dwarf my son.

"Papa, you're so big!" Henri mindspeaks.

The aroma of fresh cow's blood catches my attention. With a half-growl, half-chuckle, I turn from the boy, seize the remaining steak in my claws and devour it.

"You'll be this big or bigger when you're grown," I mindspeak once the meat's gone.

"Soon?" Henri asks.

I nuzzle the boy, sniff his scent, take in the slightly sweet, slightly fresh leather smell that is uniquely him. I know I could recognize Henri from this aroma alone —

even from miles away, surrounded by dozens of his own kind.

"Shall we?" I mindspeak and turn to go down the staircase.

Henri rushes toward the room's southernmost window, the one facing the wide channel between us and the Ragged Keys. *"I want to go out here!"*

I shake my head. It's the only window in the room which can open large enough for the two of us to pass through, something Henri only knows because I'd demonstrated it recently. I wish now I'd never shown off for the boy, never dived through the window.

"It's better for us to go downstairs to the veranda. We can make sure it's safe . . . before we take to the air."

The boy shakes his head. *"I don't want to go downstairs. I want to fly like you did. Please?"*

"Come," I mindspeak.

"No!" The window catch clicks as Henri releases it. Warm, salt-tinged air rushes into the room as the child throws the window open and crouches on the sill and prepares to jump into the outside air.

I growl and rush toward him. *"Don't you dare!"* I mindspeak, twirling as I near him, slapping him from the sill with a quick stroke of my tail.

He falls to the floor and wails.

Approaching him, I lay one of my wings over his sobbing form. *"It's dangerous out there, Henri. We have to make sure we're not seen. You can't just fly out of a window anytime you want."*

"You did!"

In his natural form and in his rebellious behavior the boy reminds me of his mother. I find it hard to remain stern with him, and cuddle him some more. *"Sometimes you just have to do what I say,"* I mindspeak.

"Why?"

I sigh, find myself once again giving the answer that all parents give at one time or another. *"Because I'm your father."*

* * *

Henri pouts all the way downstairs, but his sulkiness gives way to delight as soon as we reach the veranda. *"Me first!"* he mindspeaks, running forward, extending his wings, flapping them just a few beats before going airborne.

"Stay low!" I warn him. Following behind, flying slightly above him, I study the sky. Dark thick clouds obscure what little moon there is this night. I welcome the darkness they ensure. Scanning the waters around the island for boaters, I make sure we're safe from human eyes, then fly higher, surrender to the pleasure of gliding through the evening's air.

Below me, Henri skims over the beach, waking the dog pack, leaving behind a pandemonium of growling, barking dogs as he flies out over the ocean, just barely over the tips of the waves. *"Watch Papa!"* he mindspeaks, wheeling around, gliding back to the beach, inches over the sand, in a collision course with the dogs.

He laughs as their barks and growls turn into yelps. They scatter before him and, with a few beats of his wings, Henri rises far above them.

I match his altitude and speed. Together we fly south over the Raggeds, then east over the ocean, then north, then west, making wide circles around our island—the lights in the windows of our house, warm and bright against the gloom of the evening sky. Henri follows me as I gain altitude and dive. He giggles when I chase him. Yelps with delight when I allow him to tag me.

My father taught me this way and I can think of no way better. *"You don't have to flap your wings so much,"* I remind Henri. *"Let the air do the work. Watch how I do it."*

I grunt, say, *"Good,"* when Henri mimics my motions exactly. Soon, I know, the boy will master the technique enough and build sufficient stamina to follow me on a hunt.

The thought of hunting, the hunger that's building within me prompts me to call an end to the play. I guide

Henri back to the island, circle the house and fly through the open window, into the great room. Henri follows laughing, half lands, half tumbles into me. *"You said we couldn't go through it,"* he mindspeaks.

I nuzzle him. *"And sometimes we can."*

Despite Henri's protests, I insist he go to bed before I leave to hunt. In return, he insists on remaining in his natural form and sleeping on his bed of hay. I wait for him to surrender to sleep and leave only after his breathing slows and his head slumps—leaving me with the improbable image of my dragon-child curled up in the hay, cuddling his cute, pink, stuffed bunny.

It's after midnight before I take to the air again and I've little patience to venture far to hunt and feed. I circle the island twice, discard the notion of flying to Cuba or the Bahamas, likewise decide against cruising the Straits of Florida in search of Cuban rafters. Safety be damned: I want both fresh prey and revenge.

Father would never have approved of my plan. *"Rich people are too visible. Leave them alone,"* he often said. *"The poor are easier to take. No one cares about them."*

I know he was right, realize he would have scolded me for such recklessness, but I can't let an injury to my child occur without retribution. Father would have given the task to Gomez. I want the pleasure of it myself.

Besides, thanks to Arturo's research, I know the risk is minimal. Dr. Sean Mittleman and his blond girlfriend live alone in a large house on a canal in Gables Estates. They rarely entertain and are usually in their bedroom by ten, as are most of their rich and elderly neighbors. Best of all, while guarded security gates restrict admission to the area, no guards patrol the waterways.

Flying low, I skim the water as I cross the bay and glide down the channel leading into Gable Estates. I've little fear of discovery. This is a rich man's enclave, with each mansion an exercise in excess. Security alarms protect each house from unwanted entry. I doubt such rich and protected people feel the need to scour the dark for potential attackers.

Except for an occasional dog's bark, no one, nothing reacts as I fly along the canals searching for Dr. Sean Mittleman's Cigarette speedboat. I find it docked on the northernmost canal, farthest from the bay where the homes, while still huge, are the smallest in the community.

Landing on the bow of the Cigarette, I study my surroundings. Except for the rustling of the leaves, the lapping of the water against the seawall, the night is still. No one is outside. Nothing makes noise. Without the few scattered windows glowing in the darkness, the area could be taken for deserted.

A large picture window on the second foor of the Mittleman house shows such a light. I mull my choices, consider if there's some way to lure Mittleman and his woman outside where they can be taken without fuss, without leaving traces of violence and blood for the police and the media to sensationalize.

Finally, I shrug, spring forward and take to the air. We are after all, I think, what we are.

The window explodes inward as I smash through it. A Klaxon horn sounds. In the king-sized bed the blonde, naked except for sheer white panties, screams. Mittleman, balding, the fat around his middle overlapping his muscleman briefs, shouts, "Christ!" and dives for his nightstand drawer, pulls out a small black automatic.

With little time before the alarm brings the security guards, I strike the blonde first, stunning her with one blow from my tail.

Mittleman backs up to the wall, shooting as I approach, gunshots cracking round after round, the man unaware that the gun is too small of a caliber for the bullets to do more than slap at my armored scales. I growl at his insolence, seize his throat in one taloned claw and drag him to the window. "What?" he gurgles. "Why?"

If time permitted I would change to human form and explain the peril and pain he inflicted on my son. But that is not an option now. I continue to choke him. When he collapses in my grasp, I throw him out the window.

I do the same with the blonde, leaping out after them, spreading my wings, scooping up their crumpled forms, one in each claw, from the backyard lawn as I zoom over them, the door chimes of the house ringing moments later as the security guards arrive and press the front doorbell button.

"Henri?" I mindspeak as I cross the bay. In my grasp Mittleman squirms and curses. The blonde remains limp. *"Henri?"*

"Papa?"

I sense that the boy is still sleepy, fighting to rouse himself from his slumber. I imagine him stretching in his bed of hay, rubbing his eyes with the backs of his claws. *"I'll be home in a few minutes,"* I mindspeak.

"I'm hungry, Papa."

"Me too. I have food for us."

"Fresh prey?" he mindspeaks.

My stomach growls and I realize how hungry I've become. *"Very fresh . . . meet me on the veranda."*

As I near the island, Mittleman increases his struggles, yells, "Let me go!" and tries to unpry my talons from their grasp. Beating my wings I fly higher until the air grows cold, then I release both humans, thinking Henri is still too young to participate in the slaughter of a human—even one as vile as Dr. Sean Mittleman.

Mittleman lets out a high-pitched scream. The blonde falls in silence. I dive after them, slash out as I pass them, killing each with a massive rip of my claws. I catch their bodies before they strike the water and carry them home.

Henri joins me a few minutes after I lay the bodies out on the veranda's deck. He approaches both, sniffs the thick aroma of fresh blood in the air, waits for me to take the first bite before he begins to feed beside me, his snout so close that it rubs against mine.

Beyond the walls the smell has drawn the dogs and they yelp and bark and growl while they wait for the remains they know we will feed to them.

"Papa?" Henri mindspeaks as he feeds. *"When can I go on a hunt?"*

"When you're bigger."

"But I am bigger."

I pause eating for a moment, smile, nudge the child feeding beside me. *"Not big enough,"* I mindspeak.

"When?" he asks.

"Don't be in such a rush," I say. I find a piece of meat that I know Henri will like and push it in front of him, watch him as he sniffs it.

He closes his eyes when he begins to chew, makes a mewing sound as he eats.

Mighty hunter, I think, and feed beside him.

8

I hardly sleep the night before we leave. Memories of Elizabeth flood my mind each time I close my eyes. I remember her touch, her wildness when we made love. No matter how I turn, no matter what thoughts I try to have, I can't pull my mind away from replaying scenes of our lovemaking. It brings me no pleasure to remember it now. It only sharpens a need I've tried to ignore for over four years.

Finally, before dawn, when I find myself wondering for the third time that night what sex with Chloe will be like, I give up any further attempt to rest and leave my bed. I dress and busy myself—wandering the house, making sure all is secure, going to the treasure room and bringing up the small wood chest filled with gold coins I plan to give to Chloe's parents. After carrying it to the dock, I make two more trips to bring out all our luggage too. I load all of it in the rear of the Grady White's cockpit, returning to the house, checking everything once more before I wake Henri.

He and I are done with breakfast, ready to travel before Claudia arrives to ferry us to shore. She finds us waiting for her on the dock.

I watch her maneuver the SeaRay alongside the dock, help her tie off the lines, noting the tight khaki shorts she's wearing, the white tank top with no bra. She steps off the boat and I struggle to keep my eyes off her. Shaking my head, I turn away. I should have no interest in this woman. I worry once again if I've gone too damn long without another's touch. Or is it the knowledge that I'll be in Jamaica before nightfall that's been flooding my mind with memories, weakening my self-control?

"Ready to go?" she says.

"Absolutely." Riding as a passenger this time, I let Claudia take the helm of the Grady White, the girl guiding us out of the channel, speeding us toward shore, Henri wedged between us, clutching his pink bunny.

It's a perfect summer morning—the blue sky just a few shades lighter than the flat bay waters, the puffy white clouds just numerous enough to offer intermittent relief from a bright July sun, the wind just strong enough to take the edge off the day's heat. From the water, our island looks like a small green paradise and as anxious as I am to go, as tired as I am of waiting, I still feel an emptiness as I watch it recede behind us.

The last time I left my home, I left at night, alone, cruising for weeks on a trawler before I finally reached my destination. By then I had already found and won my bride. This time I'm leaving in daylight, with a small child to look after. After only a short boat ride, an equally brief journey by car and an hour and a half flight, I'll be in Jamaica with no certainty how much longer I'll have to wait or whether my trip will have been in vain.

Henri picks up on my mood. "I've never been on a plane," he mumbles, hugging his bunny.

"It'll be fine," I say.

Still, the boy barely whispers, "Hello," when Arturo meets us at the dock, doesn't say "Good-bye," to Claudia. He follows us in silence as we carry the luggage to the car, doesn't even smile when Arturo tries to lift the wood chest and grimaces in surprise when he finds it's too heavy for him.

"There's gold in this," I say to Arturo as I pick up the chest, put it to the rear of the trunk. "I want you to arrange to have your agents deliver it to me in Jamaica." The Latin nods. He knows better than to ask why.

Neither Henri nor I feel much like talking and our monosyllabic answers quell any attempts Arturo makes at polite chatter. He only talks to me again at Miami International, after the skycap has taken our bags. "Here," he says, handing me a large envelope.

I open it, go through our tickets and passports, glance at the papers regarding Bartlet House, our new home in Jamaica. "Looks like it's everything we need."

"If you need anything else, just call," Arturo says. "Ian says someone called Granny will meet you at the airport?"

"Yes."

"He'll have all your keys and stuff too."

"I know," I say. "Ian told me."

Arturo grins. "Too bad you haven't be able to see him the past couple of days. He is pissed and taking it out on everyone. Wherever he goes in the office, people fall over each other trying to avoid him."

I smile. "He'll get over it."

"Or not," Arturo says, shrugging.

Henri wastes no time claiming the window position as soon as the Air Jamaica flight attendant points out our seat locations in first class.

"That boy sure is anxious, isn't he?" she says, her island accent subdued, just hinting at her background. She flashes me a grin, fussing over Henri, fastening his seat belt.

"I'm anxious too," I say, returning her smile. Her light brown, nearly mocha skin and her close-cropped hair remind me of Elizabeth—almost too much. I fight an impulse to touch her forearm, stroke her brown skin.

The flight attendant has no such compunction about touching me. She rests her hand on my shoulder and says, "First time?"

I shake my head. "Second time to Jamaica for me, first for him."

"Vacation?" she says.

Pausing before answering, I think of Chloe and my quest. "Visiting family," I say.

"Oh, is your wife already there?"

"She passed away years ago."

"So young," she says.

I shrug and her hand squeezes my shoulder. "If there's anything I can do for you, please let me know. My name's Althea," she says.

Once in the air, Henri can't keep his eyes off the window. "Papa this is higher than we've ever flown!" he says.

{*Mindspeak to me,*} I say. {*Practice being private.*}

{*I don't like to. It feels funny.*}

{*I told you this is how we have to mindspeak once we get to Jamaica. You might as well get used to it,*} I say.

It's a disagreement we've had since I first started teaching Henri how to mask his thoughts. I understand how he feels. I felt the same way when my parents taught me—it was as if I were squeezing my thoughts through a strainer.

Father said to think of my mind as a radio that had to be tuned to different frequencies. *"It's sometimes painful learning new habits, Peter,"* he said. *"But there may come a time, if you're with others of the blood, that you won't want your mindspeaking to be heard by all."*

"I don't like it!" Henri says out loud.

{*Mindspeak to me—masked!*}

Henri looks at his feet. {*Yes, Papa.*}

{*In Jamaica there will be others like us. There's a chance they might hear us if we mindspeak too strongly. I don't want them to realize we're there until I'm ready for them to know. When you mask your thoughts the way I taught you, only I can hear you and only you can hear me.*}

{*It makes my head feel fuzzy. I don't like it.*}

{*I didn't either when my father taught me. You'll get used to it.*}

{*Won't,*} Henri mindspeaks.

Althea visits us just before landing. I stifle a sigh when she crouches next to me, hands me a folded piece of paper. I've already found her tempting. I'd hoped she wouldn't make resisting her any harder.

"I live in Kingston," she says. "But I'll be visiting my

parents for a few days, in Wakefield, about thirty miles
from Montego Bay." She lets out a small laugh. "It's dead
around there at night, so if you'd like company, someone
to show you around in the evening, you'd be doing me a
favor. I'll be glad to drive to town and meet you, Mr. Dela-
Sangre."

"Peter," I say, taking the note, tucking it in my pants
pocket, wondering if I'll have the strength to throw it away
later. "But I'm staying inland, near the Good Hope Estate. . . ."

"That's great!" she says. "You're not far from me at all.
We can meet at their hotel for drinks."

"It depends. We'll just be settling in. I'm not sure if I
can leave the boy."

She leans closer, looks in my eyes, her perfume light
but musky, her breath sweet and warm on my face as she
says, "Try."

The smell of her stays with me after we leave the plane,
after we go through customs. As soon as Henri and I walk
outside Sangster International Airport's arrival doors, I
sniff the air, both to cleanse myself of Althea's scent and to
smell Jamaica once again. The breeze carries the usual mix
of aromas—sea salt, tropical plants and car exhaust, nothing out of the ordinary.

I hadn't expected otherwise. I know it will be months if
not more than a year before I will encounter any trace of
cinnamon and musk in the air. I feel for Althea's note in my
pocket, consider balling it up and discarding it. Instead, I
shrug, pat it and leave it in place. I can always throw it
away later.

The two red-capped porters whom I've hired to carry
our bags, stop behind us as I look around for the man and
the Land Rover Ian Tindall promised would meet us at the
airport. I shake my head when I see the bright yellow car
parked a few dozen yards away at the curb, stifle a laugh.
Tindall must have searched this whole island and maybe

more to find a Land Rover with this garish a color. How he must have gloated when he bought it.

My fault really, I think. I should have told the man exactly what I wanted.

Any hope the car might be waiting for someone else dies when I look at the large black man leaning against the car's hood and see the small homemade sign he holds with his right hand, dangling it by his side. Even from that angle I can make out the name printed in bold hand lettering— DELASANGRE.

The Jamaican is too busy gawking and grinning at three female flight attendants getting into a cab to hold it up— or to notice our approach. Bald-headed, mahogany dark and thick-framed, with a belly that hangs over a pair of too tight jeans, he looks like a heavyweight boxer five years past his last fight.

His wide grin makes me feel like smiling along with him, even though he should know he has better things to do than leer at women. But the way I've found myself looking at women today, I wonder if I have any right to judge his obvious lechery.

I just wish the man had bothered to meet us inside the terminal or at least to have been watching out for us. Walking up to the Jamaican, I try to keep any irritation out of my voice when I say, "Mr. Morrison?"

He swivels his head toward me. "Yah, mon?" Then he sees Henri beside me and stands straight. "You Mr. Dela-Sangre?"

I nod.

Belatedly raising the sign to his chest, he flashes his grin at me. "Sorry about that." Where the flight attendant had Americanized her speech, giving only a hint of her background, the man's accent is thick, his words lilting. He looks back toward the cab, the doors now closed, the women out of sight. "Three hotties in one car." (Tree hotties inna one cyah.) The man shakes his head and laughs. "Too many I think for this one mon. My friends call me Granny," he says. "So do everyone else."

Henri can't stop staring at the man. {*He talks funny, Papa,*} he mindspeaks.

{*It's just a Jamaican accent,*} I say. {*I'm glad you remembered to mask your thoughts.*}

My son smiles, says out loud, "What's a 'hottie'?"

The man laughs, drops the sign through the driver's window, then leans over and picks up Henri, swooping him up so quickly the boy has little chance to react. He holds him high over his head, looking up at him, grinning. "You should ask your da that question." He turns toward me. "Fine-looking boy you got."

"I think so."

Granny throws Henri into the air, catches him, then laughing, does it again. To my surprise, Henri laughs along with him. "Velda and me never had none," he says, putting the boy down, facing him. "You'll like it at Bartlet House. We got a pool for you to swim in and a river for fishing and, if your dad's willing, there are caves nearby to go exploring in. . . ."

"Not all in the same day, I hope," I say.

"And horses too?" Henri says.

The Jamaican looks at me.

I nod.

"Not yet," he says to Henri, "but soon come."

Granny drives. To my surprise, rather than travel down A1, the coastal road, to Falmouth and then turn inland from there, he takes us through Montego Bay, toward the interior of the island.

Once we're out of town, I tell him to turn off the air-conditioning and lower the windows. Breathing in the lush smell of the Jamaican countryside, I point out the trees and birds Henri's never seen, the sheep and goats kept on the side of many of the small rural homes. But by the time we take the right fork in the road at Adelphi, the warm air and the movement of the Land Rover are too much for the boy. His eyes close and his head drops as he falls off to sleep.

I've never driven in this section of the country and I pay

close attention to the road as it narrows and rises, the turns we take at the small towns of Lima and Somerton, so I can find the way by myself. Just before Hampden, we come into a large valley, the sides of the road walled by sugar-cane fields.

"Queen of Spain Valley," Granny says.

I nod, but it's not the valley that has my attention, it's the green-covered, conical hills far away, at the other side. My heart speeds up. If I could, I would go there now. "Cockpit Country," I say, wondering where Chloe is, what she's doing at this moment.

The Jamaican frowns, shakes his head. "Never go there, mon. Bad things happen there."

"It's just another place."

"No, mon. I had friends of mine, they used to hunt and camp in them hills. One day, they never came back."

"But people hike from Windsor to Troy all the time, don't they?" I say.

"Fool tourists do," Granny says. "Some of them, that don't pay for guides, come up missing too. It's no place I ever want to go."

I'm just as happy to hear him say that. The more most Jamaicans avoid the inhospitable terrain of Cockpit Country, the longer Chloe's family and their home in Morgan's Hole can remain undisturbed. I can imagine how dis-pleased the Bloods would be if the area ever became pop-ular with tourists, how furious Charles Blood would be if helicopters started touring over his valley.

We pass by stone buildings and churches, sugarcane fields and towering stands of bamboos, the road narrowing even more, turning rough. I continue to pay attention to the road and the sights, but I can't keep my eyes from drifting to the hilltops of Cockpit Country. I wonder how long I can stand to wait.

Henri's head lolls, his body sways with the bumps and jolts of the Land Rover. Not even the roughest motion dis-turbs his sleep. The Jamaican points ahead. "Past Bunker's Hill, the road gets even bumpier, mon."

"I've been out here before," I say, smiling, remembering my first jarring ride into Cockpit Country. "I've seen worse."

True to the Jamaican's promise, the road turns to mostly dirt. Granny slows the car, works the wheel, avoiding the worst potholes and puddles when he can. We pass a stone ruin on top of a small hill overlooking a river. "That's the Martha Brae," Granny says. "The Good Hope Estate's across that. They're your neighbor."

We go through a crossing with a ramshackle shop and yet another stone church and turn left shortly after that, passing through a cut-stone gateway onto a single-lane road—more tire ruts actually than roadway. Trees crowd the side of the road, obscure any view of what lies ahead; bushes scratch against the car's side.

"Home, mon," Granny says.

As bad as the road is, as much as it twists and turns, it's only minutes before we come to the clearing where the main house, the guest cottages and the stables are located. Granny pulls up to the front door, honks the horn.

Even that noise and the cessation of movement do nothing to wake my son. I get out of the car, lean in and pick him up, holding him against my chest, his legs dangling, his head resting on my shoulder. When he's like this, sleep warm, breathing against my neck, I'm always conflicted between waking him and holding him longer. I know the day will come, far sooner than I wish, that he'll be too grown to accept such attention.

"Henri," I whisper in his ear as I gently joggle him. "We're here."

The boy burrows his head into my shoulder, wraps his arms around me and squeezes. "We're here," I say, joggling him again.

He sighs, raises his head. Rubs one eye with one hand as he stares at the house. "It's big, Papa."

I look at the two-story, cut-stone building. Noting that it, the stables and the cottages seem freshly coated in white paint, I nod, both at what Henri had said and the obvious care given in preparing the house for our arrival.

It takes two more horn blasts before the Jamaican's wife and her two helpers appear at the front door. While she's no taller than the others and dressed no differently, there's no doubt which one is Velda as soon as she opens her mouth. "What are you doing, you claat fool? Think we couldn't hear you the first time? We been busy getting the house ready for this mon and his boy while all you been doing is driving and yapping your mouth."

Granny smiles at her. "Don't be rude with me, woman. Come greet our boss."

She's thinner than I expected, lighter skinned and far more formal than her husband. "Pleased to meet you, Mr. DelaSangre," she says, shaking my hand, her intonation still Jamaican but without any trace of the patois Granny and she had been using. "And you, Henri." She shakes the hand he offers her. "Welcome to Bartlet House."

Henri squirms and I let him down.

She introduces the other two women, her cousins, she explains, Charlotte and Margaret. While both look younger, neither has the fine cheekbones or graceful lips that accentuate Velda's face.

Granny hands me the keys to the car and the house. "There's a spare car key in a plastic box inside the wheel well." He pats the outside of the car's front driver's side fender. "It's held there by a magnet—in case you ever lose your keys."

Velda escorts us into the house as her husband and the others unload the car. To my relief, the rattan furniture in the great room is well placed, the colors subdued and matching. Tindall's petty rebellion seems limited to the car itself.

While I inspect the rest of the downstairs with Velda, Henri rushes to the staircase, scampers up to the second floor. "Which is my bedroom?" he shouts.

"Don't yell!" I shout back.

Velda grins. "It's the one closest to yours," she says to me. "The door just across from the staircase."

{*We'll be up in a minute,*} I mindspeak. {*We'll show you then.*}

Henri doesn't answer, but from below we hear the sounds of every door being opened and closed. By the time Velda and I get to the top of the stairs, Henri is sitting on the bed in the room across from us. "I want this one," he says.

"It's yours."

The boy beams. I walk across his room, look out the window. Across the lawn, beyond the trees I can see a glimpse of Cockpit Country. "Come here, son," I say. "Look." I point to the green egg-shaped hilltops. "That's where your mother's family lives."

He stares through the window, his mouth open, his eyes wide and I realize, except for TV, he's never known anything but the endlessly flat terrain of South Florida.

Henri nods. "We're going there?"

"Just not anytime soon," I say, wishing it were otherwise.

9

As per my instructions, Granny and Velda and the rest leave shortly before five. With them gone, the house turns silent. Henri stays close to me, watching as I put the last of his things away in his dresser and closet. He follows me into my room and stares as I do the same with my clothes.

I'm tempted to send him off to play, but I understand his unease. As well-laid out as the house is, as comfortable our rooms, we're used to living in our home. On our ten acres of land here, we're as cut off from the rest of the world as we were on our island, but nothing looks or feels the same. Here no ocean sounds can be heard, no seabirds, no dogs, no drone of motors from closely passing boats.

Only the distant blat of a lone goat, the raucous squawks of a flock of green parakeets passing overhead, the occasional rustling of unseen animals making their way through the brush on the perimeter of our lawn, break the quiet of the late afternoon. The strange sounds and the otherwise calmness of our surroundings weigh on me as I'm sure they do on Henri. I find myself wishing the wind would pick up so we could hear the constant rush and moan of it playing through the trees. I decide to tell Granny to purchase some watchdogs for us. I miss the barks and yelps that always filled the air on my island. I miss the ocean smells too.

Later, Henri follows me downstairs. Together we inspect the cavernous dining room, the enormous glossy slab of finished wood that serves as the table, the ten chairs lined on each side, the two others at each end. "Are we going to eat here, Papa?" my son says.

Shaking my head, I go through the kitchen door. A plain white table sits off to the side, six metal chairs around it. "There," I say, pointing to the table.

Visibly relieved, Henri sits down, swings his feet while I take two steaks out of the freezer and defrost them in the microwave. We eat together in silence.

After dinner, I remember the satellite dish on the side of the house, the TV in the upstairs family room. "Do you want to watch?" I ask Henri. He shakes his head and instead comes upstairs with me to the screened veranda overlooking the swimming pool. I sit in a rattan rocking chair. He sits in another beside me and together we rock and stare as the day darkens.

"Can we fly tonight, Papa?" Henri says.

I shake my head. "I need to learn more about the area before you can fly," I say. "It will be best if I go by myself first. Make sure you'll be safe."

"I'll be safe."

"No, son, I want to make sure. I'll go tonight after you're asleep."

"Will you hunt?"

"I doubt it," I say, looking past the trees to the hills behind. "First I have to see where we can go."

The air turns chilly as it darkens. Soon fireflies begin to wink in the dusk, stars appear, lizards and frogs croak in the gloom. The wind picks up and rustles the leaves, moans as it rushes through the branches. A sliver of moon shows itself. Henri puts his hand on my forearm. "I liked it better at home, Papa," he says.

Henri falls asleep in the rocking chair. I carry him to his room, place him in bed, undress him, put him in one of the overlarge T-shirts he likes to sleep in and tuck him under the covers. Then I go out to the veranda, turn on the pool lights and descend the stairs to the deck.

An owl hoots somewhere in the dark and I smile at it

and the other night sounds that seem to greet me—the whistling of the wind through the trees, the chirping of the crickets and the low croaks of a lone bullfrog. I undress and change, glad to be shed of my human form, anxious to assume my natural shape, eager to explore my new domain.

Taking to the air, I ascend in a tight spiral over Bartlet House, studying the lit pool beneath me, the lights glowing through the upstairs windows. How embarrassing it would be to lose my way back to my own home. Once I'm sure I can recognize the Bartlet House, I spiral higher, widening my circles, recognizing the Martha Brae river by the small glints of moonlight it reflects.

The smell of a barbecue reaches me and I soar over the Good Hope Estate, look down on an open fire, at least a dozen guests gathered around it. As secluded as my ten acres are, these beings stay too close for my comfort. I know I can't fault Arturo or Ian. They chose as well as they could. How could they know that some fool tourists would prefer to vacation so far from the beaches?

I turn inland, glide over a dark terrain intermittently lit by a single home's lights. The town of Windsor shows itself by the illumination coming from dozens of scattered homesites and then I reach the darkness of the edge of Cockpit Country.

My heartbeat accelerates as I fly over the first hilltop. I want to roar but don't dare risk being overheard. I want to hunt. I want to find a woman of my own kind to make love to—not an imitation like Althea. I dive into the small valley that follows the hill and soar over the next hilltop, keeping close to the dark ground in case any members of Chloe's family are about.

Flying this way, so from above my form is masked by the darkness below, I'm sure, if I wanted, I could make my way to Morgan's Hole, their home, without their detecting. Part of me wishes Chloe would discover me now. But I know no good can come of it.

Father explained it to me before I went off to find my

first mate. *"Among our kind,"* he said. *"To try to take a female as a mate before she reaches her first oestrus is for-
bidden. The female would resist and her family would be
duty bound to stop and kill whoever tried to take her. Our
females can only be approached after they've reached maturity and then, only when they're in heat.*

"Don't worry, son." he chuckled. *"Once our women
mature, before they mate, they come into heat every four
months. During oestrus, they have no choice but to accept
the first suitor who reaches them and that one becomes
their mate for life."*

I sigh and turn away from the direction that would lead
me to Morgan Hole. Until Chloe comes to term, she must
remain unapproachable for me.

Banking left, halfway to Troy, I stay low, brushing treetops as I see if I can find the homes at Barbecue Bottom
near where Elizabeth's brother Derek first took me off the
road into the true wilds of Cockpit Country. But either the
homes with lights still burning are too few, or it's been too
long since I flew over there for me to be sure of what I see.

I pass over a man leading a goat down a path, a thin
cord tied around the animal's neck. Circling, I wonder if I
should take him. Henri would be pleased if I returned with
such a treat. The man's oblivious to my surveillance and I
land a few hundred yards past him, hiding in the bushes by
the path while I weigh my hunger against the caution my
parents taught me to always take in new surroundings.

A dark shape hurtles over me—too fast, I think—flat-
tens its trajectory just moments before it crashes to earth,
striking the Jamaican from behind, yanking him into the
air, the rope falling behind him, the goat bleating into the
night. The man lets out one anguished cry before he goes
silent, slumped in the creature's grasp.

Knowing what it is, but not who, I back farther into the
shadows, under the trees, my heart racing.

"Got one!" someone mindspeaks.

"You bloody well got mine," another replies. *"At least
get the goat too."*

"You want it? Get it yourself."

I move closer to an opening in the tree covering so I can get an unobscured view of the sky. Even with the moonlight so dim, I can make out the forms of two of my kind circling overhead, one of them large—the other, smaller, burdened with the weight of the now dead man.

If I didn't recognize the larger one from his form, I'd still have no doubt from hearing his mindthoughts—Derek, Chloe and Elizabeth's older brother. The dead Jamaican carried under the smaller one blocks me from seeing who it is.

"Damn it, boy. Can't you learn to pay me any respect? If Pa were here, he'd give you a good thrashing. You know how he hates anything to go to waste."

It must be Philip, Chloe's younger brother, I think, smiling. The boy has to be twelve or thirteen now, certainly old enough for hunting. He's large for his age. Another five or six years and Derek better watch out for how he talks to his younger brother.

"I'm the one who has prey to bring home, Derek. You sure you don't want to hunt some more by yourself?"

"It's bad enough Pa makes me take you with me, you whelp." The larger form descends, passes directly over me, close enough that I can feel the wind from its passage. *"I told him you should have gone with Chloe instead, or Ma. You're too bloody young to tag along with me."*

"I'm the one who saw him first," Philip says. *"Not the one who's too old to see anything that's not standing still and waving for attention."*

"Damn your hide. I saw it the same time you did. I just thought we'd discuss which of us would attack. That's the polite way of doing it, you know."

Derek circles to pass over the goat one more time. As he does so the smaller creature starts to fly away. *"Let me know if you catch the goat!"* Philip laughs, increases his speed.

The larger male changes direction, follows the smaller.

*"Damn you, slow down! You better remember to leave me
my share this time. Not like before."*

Philip laughs again. *"See if you can catch me, old
man!"*

I stay in the shadows, grinning, until they race out of
sight. I really hadn't spent much time with Philip the last
time I was in Jamaica. The boy seems to have grown up
well. I'll be glad for Henri to meet this uncle. I think he
may learn some things from him.

The goat bleats again and I turn my attention to it. I may
have to return home without human prey tonight, but that
doesn't mean I have to go back empty-handed.

The animal watches me as I emerge from the shadows
and walk down the path toward it. Too frightened to run, it
shivers in place, bleating every few seconds. I check overhead, see nothing but the dark sky, the clouds and stars and
moon. Part of me wishes Chloe were near. I scan the sky
for any sight of her, strain for any sound of her thoughts,
hear snatches only of Philip and Derek's banter.

If I persist in coming here, I know it's just a matter of
time until I encounter her. Henri and I will have to take our
flying elsewhere. I'll have to hunt over other parts of the
island, maybe off the coast, like at home. Still, I know I'm
not going to be able to resist flying over Cockpit Country
some nights, risk or no risk.

I take a breath, will my heart to slow. I know part of my
excitement was over the possibility of being discovered,
but the rest was overhearing others of my kind again.

Picking the trembling goat up, I hold it with one claw,
careful not to injure it as I take to the air. When I get home,
I'll wake Henri, let him join me behind the house, let him
be the one who handles the killing before we feed. It's time
for him to begin to learn. I think of his uncle Philip. With
proper instruction, when Henri's that age I expect he'll be
every bit as good a hunter, if not better.

10

Being in Jamaica does nothing to ease my nights. In fact, I'm more plagued by nightmares and desire than I was at home. After two more evenings of restless sleep, I surrender to my impulses, open Althea's note and dial her parents' number.

"Lucky you called. Another day and I'd be gone," she says.

"Then I'd just have to ask your mother to fix me up with someone else," I say.

We make plans to meet in the evening, shortly after Henri's bedtime, at Good Hope Estate's main house. I find her sitting on the building's steps, waiting. She stands when I pull up in the Land Rover, gives a small wave with one hand as I get out.

Dressed in a light yellow silk dress that hugs her trim athletic body, she could almost pass for Elizabeth. Only her brown eyes, a larger mouth, thicker nose and slightly bowed legs differentiate her from my memories of my bride. I can't resist hugging her as we meet, lightly kissing her on the cheek.

She pulls back a little, touches her cheek, straightens her dress. "I don't usually do this, you know," she says.

I nod, say, "Me neither. If you'd rather, we can go someplace else. Or—if you want—we can both go back to our homes."

"That's not what I meant." She takes me by the hand. Leads me to the door. "I just didn't want you to think I asked men out all the time."

"I wouldn't think you'd have to."

The bar's mostly empty, just an elderly white-haired Jamaican serving drinks to the few white couples still up after ten. Althea orders a Gibson, frowns when I order only water.

"Alcohol's a problem for me," I say, knowing she'll take that as an indication that I have a substance-abuse problem rather than realizing that alcohol plays havoc with the systems of creatures like me.

"I understand," she says. "My last boyfriend—the son of a bitch—couldn't ever turn down a drink, or another woman." She tells me about her family, about growing up in rural Jamaica, asks about my family, what I do, why I'm not attached, finishing her Gibson, ordering another, moving her chair closer to me, touching me as she speaks.

I answer her questions, tell her about my life, some of the answers true; others, like my occupation, stockbroker, entirely fabricated. I can't help but keep staring at her, thinking about Elizabeth, wondering how much Chloe might look like the two women.

Althea smiles at my gaze. "You like the way I look, don't you?" she says.

I nod.

She sips at her drink, takes a deep breath, breathes out her words. "Too bad we don't have a room here. Who knows what you might get to see."

For a hundred-dollar bill the desk clerk finds an available room in the rear of a guest cottage a few dozen yards from the main building. Althea drains the last of her drink, kicks off her shoes as soon as we enter the cottage. Outside the door of our room, she puts her arms around my neck, kisses me on the mouth.

I hold her close to me, feel her warmth, smell her perfume, her scent. I can sense the excitement that's building within her. I know, if I let myself, it will build within me too. But the alcohol taste in her mouth reminds me all too well of her humanity. I pause before opening the door.

"Anything wrong?" she murmurs, pressing herself against me, kissing my neck.

How can I tell her I don't want her? I think. That no matter how good she is in bed, she can never equal any of our women? That sex with her will serve only as a poor release for my frustrations? That already I feel guilty I would stoop to such a thing. "I haven't been with anyone since my wife," I say, though my thoughts are more of Chloe than Elizabeth.

"You poor dear." She takes the key from my hands, opening the door herself, clicking on the light. I linger in the hallway, watch as she undoes the back of her dress, lets it fall to the floor. Althea wears no underwear. Naked before me, her small dark nipples hard, her breathing already quickening, she says "Come here, Peter, please," she says.

Nude she looks less like Elizabeth, still pretty but thinner, her breasts smaller, hanging slightly, her belly button protruding. I sigh, give Chloe one last thought and do as Althea requests.

Afterwards, I lie on the bed, my eyes open, while Althea sleeps cuddled against me, her head on my left shoulder, her left hand on my crotch, holding me as if I were hers. My stomach rumbles a little and I shake my head. I won't harm this woman. I'll stay a little longer, then ease away from her and leave. It's bad enough she'll wake in the morning to find me gone, bad enough she'll never hear from me again.

What a pathetic creature I am to use this woman to relieve myself. If Father were here, how disgusted he would be with me. He'd be right to be so. I preach to my son how superior our kind is to humans. "Because we can control our bodies we don't have to be ruled by them the way so many humans are," I say. Then I give in the same way one of them would.

I slip my shoulder out from under Althea's head, gently open her hand and move it from my crotch, then stand and dress. Whether it's from drink or from our sex, the woman hardly budges, continues to sleep. I look at the smile on her face and think, at least I made her happy. But for a creature like me—who can sense how a woman reacts to each touch and stroke and who can control his own body's reactions to her—that's not hard to do.

In fairness, she made me happy too, or at least ensured that I'll be able to sleep through the next few nights. Not that I plan to repeat such a tryst. This time, I promise myself, I won't succumb to any more temptation. I know I have no compact with Chloe yet, but I plan to wait for her acceptance or her rejection.

11

To my surprise, Henri hardly seems to miss our island home. Swimming in the pool becomes one of his favorite pastimes. He pesters me until I have a diving board installed. Granny, who turns out to once have entertained the tourists in Mo Bay with his diving skills, offers to coach my son.

Diving, for a child who knows how to fly, presents no great difficulties and soon Henri is calling me to come out of the house to see him performing swan dives and somersaults and his favorite: the cannonball. Within weeks, he begins to pester me to install a high dive too.

Within a few weeks also, Granny rides to work on a horse, three others and a pony tethered behind him. It becomes a ritual for us all to ride each morning, the Jamaican showing us which trails lead to where.

Some days we ride just to the river; others, we wander as far as Windsor, on the edge of Cockpit territory. At my request, Granny takes us to the caves one day, but Henri, after glancing into the dark maw of its entrance and feeling the strong wind that blows out from the darkness inside, refuses to go.

"I don't blame the boy, mon," Granny says. "They say that cave goes all the way back into Cockpit Country. Cavers are always get lost inside it."

Life settles into routine. Every night after dark, Henri and I change and take to the air and practice his flying. After the boy goes to sleep, I often venture out again. Sometimes hunting over the ocean off Falmouth or inland as far away as Ocho Rios; other times flying into Cockpit Country.

A few weeks after my arrival, two unshaven white men, in rumpled T-shirts and shorts, drive up to the house in a beat-up old Army salvage Jeep. They refuse to deal with Granny, insist on seeing only me, but have difficulty looking in my eyes, as they unload my wood chest and place it at my feet.

Arturo laughs when I tell him about them in our weekly phone conversation. "They're used to smuggling things into our country, not into any others. I couldn't get them to understand — sometimes there are things we don't want to ship openly to Jamaica."

Rita reports regularly to me too. "I think Ian has a problem with me," she says a few weeks after I get to Jamaica. "He's given instructions that only Helen, his secretary, can open his mail. But she's a friend of mine. She tells me Tindall and his friends are going ahead with their purchase of the island. She says he's begun taking a lot of his calls on his cellphone too."

I call Arturo, tell him what Rita has reported. "No problem," he says. From his tone of voice, I can picture him shrugging. "As long as the government won't issue any permits, they can't develop."

"Then why would they complete the purchase of the island?"

"Maybe they had no choice. Maybe they think they have a way around it. But trust me, they don't."

"Just handle it," I say. "No more maybe's"

"Relax, Peter, it's under control," Arturo says. "Just enjoy yourself. Everything will be here when you get back."

As much as Tindall's machinations over Wayward Key irritate me, my focus remains on my life in Jamaica. Except for a few new activities and the daily presence of our household help, Henri and I live much like we did on our island. Perhaps because of that, neither of us suffers from any homesickness.

In early October, a thunderstorm catches me as I fly near Accompang, on the far side of the region. Gusts of wind grab me, toss me around in the air. Rain soaks and chills me. Lightning heats the sky. Rather than endure the abuse of the storm, I take the opportunity of each lightning strike to search the mountainsides for the telltale black opening of a cave.

I search from bolt to bolt, from hill to hill until a flash of lightning shows a large black hole near the top of a mountain. I fly to it, land as thunder rolls across the valley below. The cave is large enough to accommodate me and I back away from its rainy opening, spread my wings and beat them so I can shake the moisture from them, warming my body with the motion.

Someone mindspeaks nearby, *"Mum, the rain's too bad. I'm going to find shelter. I'll be home later."*

I freeze, thinking, Chloe?

Thunder booms again. I move closer to the cave's opening, strain to see the sky through the rain and the dark. A bolt of lightning sears the air, striking the hillside next to mine, illuminating the night for an instant—all the time I need to make out the creature flying so near to me.

I'm sure it's her. She's far smaller than her older brother, but longer than Philip, her underside paler. I want to see her again, compare her to my memory of Elizabeth. I hate the darkness that prevents it.

Another lightning strike. I see nothing. She can't be gone so soon, I think, knowing she may have found a cave of her own, to be protected and drying like me.

"I know where there's a good cave, Mum. I'll let you know when the storm's over."

"Please do, dear," Samantha Blood mindspeaks. *"The rest of us are hungry. We're waiting for you to come back with your kill."*

"As soon as the storm stops."

I'm so intent on the conversation, I wouldn't have noticed Chloe's approach if not for another nearby flash of light. I scurry back into the darkness as she approaches and lands. Thunder fills the night and I take the opportunity of its cover to back up even more, until I feel the cold stone at the rear of the cave.

In the dark, without the benefit of any lightning flashes, all I can make out is her silhouette. She comes into the cave a few more feet from the opening, lays down something large—the body of her prey I suppose—and, like I did, she spreads her wings and beats them to dry.

The next lightning strike catches her in mid-beat. I suck in a breath at the image it leaves with me. She's a little smaller than Elizabeth, her lines a little more delicate, her scales the same light green, her underbody cream colored, her sex not yet swollen the way it will be when she reaches her oestrus.

My body begins to react to the sight of her. I want to rush forward and take her. I take small measured breaths, will my heartbeat to slow.

Chloe continues to beat her wings, continues to stare out at the storm until she dries. She turns then, sniffs the air, stares into the darkness at the back of the cave. I stay motionless, breathing as little as my body will allow, praying no sudden flash of lightning will expose me.

Finally, she turns her attention to her prey, feeding a little, then watching the storm, and feeding a little more again.

The rich aroma of fresh blood wafts back to me. Saliva floods my mouth and I can do no more about it than I can do with my need for sex. I want to join her and feed. Failing that, I want to howl.

Chloe lifts her head. Sniffs the air again as she turns toward me. *"Who's here?"* she mindspeaks. *"Philip, is that you?"*

I hold my breath, close my eyes to slits to eliminate any possibility of their reflecting any light. The wind outside has calmed, the rain diminished to a light patter. Soon Chloe will realize it's safe to leave.

"Something's not right," she says, getting up, walking toward me. *"Is someone here?"*

"Chloe! The storm's over. Come home now. Your father and brothers are hungry," Samantha Blood calls.

Chloe lets out an irritated growl, and says, *"Yes, Mum. Whatever you say, Mum."* She turns around, goes back to her prey, picks it up and heads for the cave's mouth. Stopping, she looks back toward me.

"If anyone is back there, you better pay attention to what I'm about to say. My parents live near here. So do my two brothers. If anyone should harm me or attempt to abduct me, not one of them would rest until that person dies. So go back to wherever you came from. I won't come to term for another six months. If that's what you're here for, come back then."

After she flies away, I rush forward, stare out the cave's mouth at the sky, hoping for a last glimpse of her. But all I see is the night sky and drizzle. A final lightning flash illuminates the valley, revealing only dripping trees. The thunder that follows matches my mood.

Turning, I sniff the air, savor the fresh, sweet leathery scent she's left behind. The smell of her prey remains too and my stomach protests its emptiness.

I can't do anything yet with the need I have for Chloe's touch, but my bloodlust is a far easier thing to satisfy. It's most probably too late to find someone out around Cockpit Country, but I know some fool tourist has to be walking alone somewhere on the beaches around Montego Bay. There always are at least a few of them wandering like that each night.

Sometimes they make very satisfying meals.

12

I'm not sure whether having seen Chloe makes my wait easier or more difficult. I do know I continue to want her. I begin to go into Cockpit Country every night, taking much more care to avoid discovery, avid to see Chloe again, feeling almost like a combination of a peeping Tom and a stalker.

But while, over the months, I see Philip and Derek a number of times, even spy Charles and Samantha Blood once, Chloe manages to evade my scrutiny.

Early in the evening, the third week of April, Rita calls me. "Now I know what's going on," she says.

"About Tindall?"

"Who else? I went out for dinner with Helen last night. She's been a little nervous to talk to me at the office. Tindall's sort of let it be known he doesn't like it when he sees us gabbing together. Well, we ordered some wine and after a glass or two Helen relaxed. It seems that your friend Ian has been very politically active."

"He always is," I say, thinking how his membership in the Democratic Party balances Arturo's support of the Republicans, both parties serving our interests.

"Sure, but not like this. He and his Wayward Key buddies have formed their own political action committee. Guess what congressman they're supporting for governor next year?"

I sigh, shake my head. "Not Muntz," I say.

"Muntz."

"Is he just too stupid to stay bought?"

Rita laughs. "Or too greedy."

I call Arturo the next day, give him Rita's information. "What an asshole," he says. "Don't worry, I'll have a conversation with him, remind him of all the scandals I can have my friends at the *Herald* investigate. When I'm through with him, he'll just be glad to be able to stay in congress. I'm sure he'll be more committed to saving the birds on Wayward Key than he's ever been."

"Good," I say.

"When are you going to let me do something about Tindall?"

"Rita will be through with law school soon. I'd like her to work with Ian for a while before we make any decisions. I should be back by then."

"Can I at least transfer her to his legal department now? That way she can start learning and he'll be put off balance."

Laughing, I say, "He'll crap!"

"He probably will," Arturo says. "But this way I can arrange for a new receptionist before I go on vacation next month. I'll tell him today. He may call you, you know."

"Let him know I'll be waiting to hear from him," I say, but to my surprise Tindall never calls.

May arrives and Henri begins to pester me about taking him with me into Cockpit Country. "I'm almost five," he says. "You said you'd take me after my birthday."

"That's two more weeks from now."

"No fair! You said I can fly better than you did when you were my age and you told me that Grandpa took you hunting with him."

I nod, smile at my son. The boy stands a head taller than he did when we arrived in Jamaica. It seems as if I'm buying him new clothes every week. In truth, he is ready to accompany me. He no longer has any difficulty keeping up with me in the air and has been able to repeat most of my maneuvers without losing control. But if I take him now, what reward can I give him for his birthday? "After your birthday," I say.

"Please?" he says.

He looks so sorrowful that I laugh and say, "Tonight we can fly to the edge of Cockpit Country, past Windsor but no farther, okay?"

Henri can't wait, drags me downstairs a half hour before nightfall. He wanders around the pool, climbs onto the diving board, steps back off as we wait.

I savor the calm of the evening, watch the sky darken, the first stars appear. Barely any clouds obstruct the view. A full moon hangs low in the sky, a silver halo of reflected light around it. "It's a wonderful night to fly," I say, point to the sky. "See the ring around the moon?"

Henri nods, says, "What is it?"

"Humans say it's moisture in the air, reflecting the moon's light. Our kind, the People of the Blood, call it Dwyla's Moon—though my mother always insisted on calling it a Dragon Moon."

"Why?"

"She said it sounded more romantic that way. My father didn't like it, but she always called herself a dragon too. I think it's because she spent so much time with humans when she grew up. Anyway, when I was little my mother used to tell me the story of Dwyla and Kestur whenever a halo appeared around the moon," I say, smiling when Henri comes closer, staring into the sky.

"Tell me," he says. "Please, Papa."

I start it the same way my mother used to. "A long time ago, before there were humans, there was a young maiden called Dwyla, one of our kind, the daughter of a very powerful household. When it came time for her to leave to meet a male of her own, her father, Magnus, who was jealous and selfish, locked her in a cell below his house. Still, there was nothing he could do to stop her scent and soon males of our kind began to come to see if they could make her their bride.

"Magnus fought each one, chasing some away and killing others. But one day a young male came that he couldn't chase away, that he couldn't kill. They fought for days, in the air, on the ground, without either being able to beat the other.

"Finally, the young male, Kestur was his name, suggested that rather than fight any more, they should have a contest. Dwyla would stay with the winner.

"Agreeing, Magnus asked the younger male what competition he had in mind. 'Let your daughter choose it,' Kestur said.

"Magnus brought Dwyla up from her cell and told her about their agreement. She listened and looked at Kestur. As soon as she saw him, she knew she wanted to spend the rest of her life with him.

"She tried to think of a competition that Kestur would be sure of winning. Magnus was known to be powerful so she decided to avoid any contests of strength. He was a renowned hunter so she tried to think of some other feat. But Magnus was also older, heavy around his middle, 'I will stay with whoever flies highest, the fastest,' she said.

"Kestur leapt into the air, Magnus just behind him. Dwyla watched from the ground until both were almost out of her sight. Unwilling not to see who won, she took to the air too and followed them.

"They flew up above the mountains, above the clouds, Kestur always in front, Magnus behind, Dwyla following both. They flew higher as the air grew thin and cold and the earth grew small beneath them. Still Kestur continued, leaving Magnus farther and farther behind him until the older creature knew he had no chance of catching up.

"Magnus turned back, gliding toward earth, passing his daughter along the way. 'He's yours and you're his,' he said.

" 'Forever,' Dwyla said, flying after her mate.

"But Kestur had no idea he had won. He wouldn't risk looking back or stopping. He flew on, away from earth, flying faster and farther than anyone of the Blood ever did, until exhausted, his heart burst and he fell to the surface of the moon.

"Dwyla found him there and circled over him, crying for her lost mate. According to the legend she's flown around the moon ever since. The halo you see are the tears she leaves behind her."

Henri stares at the moon and its halo for a few moments. "That's not true, is it, Papa?"

"Maybe not," I say. "But every Dragon Moon, my mother used to make me wish that I would find a mate who would be as faithful to me as Dwyla was to Kestur."

I allow Henri to change shape first, and follow him into the air. He no longer struggles to flap his wings, no longer loses control on his turns. He knows how to glide now, when to use it to conserve energy. I wish there was someone I could brag to about his progress.

Taking the lead, I fly toward Windsor, diving and turning, spiraling high and diving again. Henri follows, giggling when I dodge in an unanticipated direction and lose him for a moment. {*Not fair!*} he mindspeaks.

{*Life isn't fair,*} I say, studying the land below, spotting a small dog meandering down a path near an empty pasture. {*Tell me what you see.*}

Henri spirals, looks at the ground. {*A dog?*}

{*Make believe it's a human. Bring it to me.*}

{*Do I have to kill it?*} Henri says.

Father would have been furious at his reluctance. It makes me smile. The child has played with dogs his entire life. It's only natural for him to avoid hurting one unnecessarily. {*No, son. Just bring it to me. Then you can put it back.*}

Henri descends in a long wide spiral, gathering speed as he nears the ground, his trajectory flattening as he shoots toward the dog from its rear, his stomach only inches above the dirt path. He beats his wings, rises just an instant before he reaches the dog and grabs it with his rear claws.

The dog yelps as it's jerked into the air. It continues to yowl as Henri carries it skyward.

{*Very good,*} I say. {*Your mother would have been proud of you.*}

{*Did you watch all of it, Papa?*} Henri says, holding the trembling dog close to his body, flying alongside me.

{*Every bit. You're going to be a great hunter. No doubt about it.*}

The dog whimpers and I say, {*Put it back, son. Let's fly the rest of the way now.*}

Henri banks, dives toward earth. I watch him and smile, looking forward to the day I can take him hunting with me, enjoying the serenity of the night, the moonlit beauty of the Jamaican countryside. Spiraling down to meet my son on his way up, I debate whether to let him follow me into Cockpit Country tonight.

The aroma of cinnamon and musk jolts me from my thoughts, envelops me for a moment and disappears as I drop below it. Shocked, disappointed, I roar my displeasure.

{*PAPA! What's wrong?*} Henri mindspeaks.

I know I should answer but I beat my wings and fly skyward, smelling it again for a moment only, passing it before I can level my flight. Spiraling downward slowly, I hit it again. Chloe's scent! I'm sure of it.

It must be the first scent of her first oestrus. Only a few thin wisps of vapor floating on the wind, nothing like the heavy aroma that Elizabeth gave off when I first found her. Still it sends me into rut. I roar into the sky again, my heart pumping so much blood that I can hear the echo of it in my ears.

{*PAPA!*}

It takes all my power to turn my attention to my son. {*It's okay, Henri,*} I say, struggling to control myself before he gets close, dropping below the scent. {*Nothing bad has happened. But we have to fly back home now. I told you one night I would know it's time for me to find Chloe.*}

Henri joins me, flies beside me, his eyes large. {*It's now, Papa?*}

{*I think it may be.*}

I have to force myself not to race back to Bartlet House. I spend an agonizing thirty minutes taking Henri inside, putting him to bed. "If I'm not here when you wake," I say. "Just mindspeak to me. I'll hear you and come home."

Henri hugs me and says, "When I wake up, I hope you're here, Papa."

Even taking the steps two at a time, I'm in the air before I reach the bottom of the stairs to the pool deck. I waste no time spiraling, spare no moments taking in any sights as I race toward Cockpit Country. I do change altitudes as I fly, sniffing the air, seeking that wonderful burst of cinnamon and musk.

It eludes me until after I pass the last lights of Windsor, after I soar over the first egg-shaped hills of Cockpit Country. Again, it's only a hint of cinnamon and musk and again it takes over my body. I revel in it, break the quiet of the night with my roars. I'm done with sneaking through the skies of Cockpit Country like a timid mouse afraid of the cat. I no longer care who knows I'm here. All I care about now is finding Chloe.

The vagueness of the scent maddens me. I find it and it disappears. I follow it for miles and lose it, only to find it again, leading me elsewhere.

I fight to think through the pheromone-induced fog that has overtaken me. If this is Chloe's first night, she has to be either searching for a place to nest or building a bed of branches and leaves in a cave she has already chosen. Remembering the cave near Acoompong that both she and I had taken shelter in, I speed in that direction.

The mixed aroma of cinnamon and musk intensifies the nearer to the cave that I draw. It's still faint enough to make me doubt whether I'll find her there but strong enough to torment me with the promise of a willing mate.

I land at the mouth of the cave to find it empty. But the dank air within is permeated with Chloe's scent. Unable to resist the lure of cinnamon and musk, I venture inward, find a half-constructed bed of leaves and branches and twigs. If I sit and wait, I know she'll eventually appear.

But I'm no more capable of waiting than I am of resisting her scent. I take to the air again, patrol the valley and the others surrounding it. On my third circuit, I finally see her, flying below me, intent on the bundle of branches she carries in her foreclaws.

Chloe has no awareness of my scrutiny until I dive past her and zoom out of her sight.

"Who is that? Philip, it better not be you. Mum told you to stay away."

I circle back, pass her again, this time on her right side before I dive out of sight.

"So soon?" she says. *"My mum said sometimes it takes years to be found. You were the one I thought was in the back of the cave, weren't you?"*

Returning, I fly beside her. *"Yes, I was."*

Chloe's light green scales almost shimmer in the full moon's light. Her scent, finally powerful now that I'm near, envelops me. It's all I can do not to take her now, but I make myself continue beside her and I wait for whatever signal she may give.

She stares at me in silence as we pass through one valley and enter another. Finally, just before we reach the cave, she says, *"Peter?"*

Glad she remembers me well enough to recognize me, I say, *"Yes."*

Chloe bellows as if she were in pain, drops the bundle she's carrying. *"NO!"* she says. *"Get away! Leave me alone! I don't want you!"*

13

Chloe's words hit me like a shotgun blast. For almost five years I've waited for this moment. During that time I'd wondered, over and over, what it would be like. I never once imagined she'd react like this. I contemplate folding my wings and just crashing to earth. But then, I think, what would happen to my son?

Peeling away from Chloe, I climb to look for air clean of her scent. No matter what height I reach, some trace of her remains. Every breath I take keeps me in rut. My heart feels as if it's going to beat its way out of my chest.

Below me, Chloe dives to earth, searches for her lost bundle of branches and twigs. I circle and watch her, the Dragon Moon's light illuminating the terrain below, glistening off her scales—my mind at war with my body.

I know all too well the biological imperatives of my kind. Once one of our females comes to term, she has no more power to refuse an instinct ingrained in a thousand generations of our kind than I do to ignore her scent. Only family members and the underage are immune to such things.

Chloe is in heat. No matter what she says, I know, if I close with her, she can't refuse me. Her body won't let her fight me. Once mated, our kind bond for life. After I have her, after I impregnate her, she'll have no other choice.

Still, I don't want to take her by force. I want her to want me with the same ache and need that I desire her. *"Chloe, look at the moon,"* I mindspeak.

She looks up from the ground, laughs, the sound of it in

my mind harsh, unforgiving, like a short horn burst. *"It's Dwyla's moon. So what? Do you think you're Kestur? Did you imagine me a Dwyla, so faithful to you I'd be willing to sacrifice myself for you, for eternity?"*

I sigh. *"I thought it a good omen."*

"Damn it, Peter, if you were someone else it would be."

"Am I so terrible?"

"You were married to my sister!" She finishes gathering her bundle, takes to the air again. *"I deserve a mate of my own. One who's willing to fight for me."*

Circling wider, to leave her space, I say, *"I came here early to make sure no one else took you—not to avoid a fight. I fought and killed for your sister. I'd do the same for you."*

"You could just leave."

"I thought you liked me. When we were together the last time, it felt to me like we had a special connection."

"I was thirteen! Of course, I liked you. You were so handsome. And Elizabeth said you were strange about human things and humans. I always felt like I was strange too, like I didn't belong with the rest of my family. Elizabeth and Derek teased me constantly about being so different."

"I like that about you," I say. *"My mother was different too. She insisted on sending me to human schools."*

"I know, Elizabeth told me. Mum was sick a lot when I was little and one of our servants, Lila, looked after me. She told me fairy tales and taught me about human things. She taught me to like books. Elizabeth said you liked to read too. And you paid attention to me as if I was another grown-up. I was so envious of Elizabeth, I cried myself to sleep every night you were here. I couldn't understand why you didn't realize you were marrying the wrong sister."

"Which is why I'm here now," I say. *"It was only her scent that lured me here then. I had no choice, you know that. But I did notice you and I did remember how much you and I had in common. I don't think you've changed so

much you can't enjoy those things with me. I know I haven't changed, Chloe."

"Of course, you have! You buried my sister. You're raising her son. That has to have affected you. If it hasn't, I certainly want nothing to do with you." She flies away, toward the cave.

My body torments me. I can't imagine Chloe feels no needs of her own. Whether she does or not, I'm as drawn to her as the moth is to the flame. *"May I follow you, come to the cave and talk with you more?"* I say.

"Just go," she says.

"I can't. I don't want to lose you."

"You never had me, Peter."

"I won't come too close. I just want to talk," I say.

"Do what you want," Chloe says. *"But don't think you can simply take me. No matter how I feel, I will fight you. I doubt my family has heard us, but if I call for help, they will come. Once they know you've been waiting for me, they'll be furious."*

Chloe lands before me, immediately busies herself separating the branches and twigs in her bundle, intertwining them with the others in the partially finished bed. I land, stay by the cave's mouth, watch her as she works.

Her sides heave with each breath she takes. When she bends over to work, her tail raises and exposes her sex, pink and swollen and maddening to see. *"This is as hard for you as it is for me,"* I say. *"Isn't it?"*

She keeps her back to me, doesn't glance in my direction.

"Harder. You've done this before. You've had God knows how many human women too. I've never done any of it. I just came to term today and you show up—my sister's mate!" She stomps one foot, throws down the branches she's weaving. *"I haven't even had time to finish the bed."*

"I don't care about the damned bed."

"I do!"

"Chloe, I've thought about you, waited for you for almost five years. . . ."

"Because I'm so convenient? You already knew where to find me. You had to know around when to be here. You could be pretty sure, if you got here soon enough, you wouldn't have to fight any other suitors. I'm so flattered you chose the easiest possible way to find a mate. Why didn't you just abduct me and hold me in a cell at your house until I came of age?"

I growl at her sarcasm and bitterness. Abduction is as taboo among our people as incest is to humans. Only the lowest of our kind would stoop to such a thing. *"Goddamn it, Chloe! I already told you why I came early. I would no sooner abduct you than I would rape you. I've been on this island since last July, waiting for you. If I wanted, I could have spent that time searching for a mate in Curaçao or Haiti, where I know others of our kind settled, or back in Europe where my father found my mother.*

"I came here and waited because I wanted you. I wanted you because you were different . . . because you read books and liked art and music, because you seemed to think there was more to life than hunting and eating. . . ."

Chloe continues to weave the branches and twigs in her nest, continues to keep her back to me. I'm tempted to grab her and turn her toward me, but I keep my distance. *"How many males of our kind do you think there are that are interested in sharing such interests with you, Chloe?"*

She stops her weaving but still doesn't turn.

"I know what it is to be mated without such fortune," I say. *"Do you want that for you? When I met Elizabeth, she didn't understand any of the things I cared about. The notion of being in love confused her. She thought it something only humans do. I hoped you might understand it better."*

Chloe whirls around, stares at me. *"I understand it, Peter. But I don't know if I ever expected it."* She looks down at the cave floor, says nothing for a few minutes. Finally, she says, *"How did my sister die, Peter? It wasn't childbirth, was it?"*

I shake my head, take a deep breath. The jolt from the sudden intake of cinnamon and musk instantly makes me regret that I did. *"She was killed by a human, Jorge Santos,"* I say. *"My fault. I thought he was a friend and he betrayed me. Humans are such treacherous beings. I never should have trusted one."*

"Poor Elizabeth," she says. *"Poor Peter."*

"At least I have Henri," I say. *"I wish you would meet him. You'd love him."*

"I'm sure."

"But what can I do or say to convince you to consider me?"

Chloe's eyes flick down toward my swollen, rigid cock and then back toward my eyes. *"You could get that thing under control,"* she says.

"Just stop giving off your scent."

She shrugs, smiles. *"I sort of like knowing I have the power to drive you crazy."*

I sigh. *"But now what?"*

"I don't know. Did you mean what you said about love? Do you think it's possible for beings like us?"

How unfair to Chloe and me that biology alone dictates how our kind mates. How much I wish that we could meet and grow to know each other, the way humans often do. *"I know how much I love my son,"* I say. *"I think my mother and father loved each other. Before she died, your sister said she loved me—though I'm not sure she really understood what it meant."*

"I don't think my mother or father ever loved anyone," Chloe says. *"I always hoped I would find someone who could—like in the books."*

"Which is why I came here. Why I waited for you."

Chloe shakes her head. *"This is too sudden. I need to— I want to finish my bed, prepare the cave. I need some time to think. . . ."* She gestures with one claw. *"Why don't you go away for now, come back in two nights? By then the cave will be ready. I promise I'll have my mind made up.*

You just have to promise if I say, 'No,' you'll leave Ja-
maica."

I stare at the woman I want to have as my mate, both of
us breathing hard, our bodies quivering. I know the merest
touch from me would make her self-control collapse. But I
don't want to live a lifetime with a mate who resents my
presence. "I promise," I say, though just the thought of
leaving Jamaica without her tears at my heart.

I find if I fly just inches over the treetops, where the
evening mist is dense and cool, I can avoid smelling
Chloe's scent. By the time I reach Windsor, my body has
surrendered to my control again.

Not so my mind.

My unsatisfied lust combines with Chloe's rejection
and turns to rage. My night of frustration also leaves me
ravenous. I search the countryside for any late-night wan-
derers. Find none.

Farther toward home, near Bunker's Hill, I spot a car's
headlights. Ordinarily, I would ignore such a thing, but
tonight I find the car's lights to be an insolent challenge to
the dark sky.

I turn toward the car, fly over it as it lurches and bumps
along the country road. It's a Porche Boxster, a rich man's
sports car and it's traveling far too fast for the road beneath
it. A white man's at the wheel, another beside him, both
men taking turns drinking from a bottle. Tourists, I assume.

Diving toward the car, I fly across the hood, skimming
the metal, blocking the driver's view only for an instant,
but long enough for him to yank on the wheel, lose control.

The Boxster shoots off the road, mowing down small
bushes, caroming off a low stone fence, racing into a field,
crashing finally into a silk cottonwood tree, the headlights
beaming in different directions. Both men sit motionless
and I land in the dark behind them.

Finally the man on the passenger side gets out of the
car. "Jack. You okay?" he says.

The driver nods, groans. "This is going to cost a fortune," he says. "I sure hope the insurance will cover all of it."

The passenger walks around the front of the car, the headlights shining on him, showing him to be young, muscular, a little beefy. I swallow the saliva that flows in my mouth.

"Damn it, did you see that thing that flew by us? It almost hit us. What the hell do you think it was?"

I roar. I want both men to see me. They turn in my direction and I rush toward them, lashing out at the driver with my right foreclaw, killing him with the one blow. Famished, I let the passenger run off as I rip flesh from the driver—the smell of his blood blossoming around me. I gulp down a chunk of meat, breathe in the rich aroma around me and roar again. Then I take to the air and search for the passenger.

He tries to hide in the tall grass at the end of the field but the quivering movements of the blades around his trembling body, and the acrid sweat his fear produces, betray him. Landing, I flush him from his hiding place—block him with my body each time, in each direction, as he attempts to flee.

Finally he realizes the futility of any escape. To his credit he rushes at me, pummels my scales with his bare hands. I let him wear himself out on my body, then backhand him with one foreclaw, knocking him down. When he works his way to his feet, I twirl, strike him with my tail. He tries to crawl away and I follow him, wait until he stands once more.

The man faces me, his chest heaving, his fists clenched. "What the hell do you want?" he yells. "If you're going to kill me, do it!"

What I want is to rid myself of the fury that fills me. I swivel, strike him with my tail again, the impact throwing him at least ten feet.

He lies facedown, groans. I walk over to him, flip him on his back with my clawed foot. He stares at me and groans again. "Haven't you had enough yet?" he says, barks a short laugh. "Do I have to teach you another lesson?" He turns on his stomach, struggles to rise, pushing up with both arms, weaving in place when he finally gets on his feet.

"So come on now." He motions me toward him with both hands. "Let's get it on."

The anger that has been boiling within me fades. I look at his feeble resistance and feel only shame for tormenting him, rather than finishing him quickly. If I could, I'd let him go. But such a thing is impossible. I slash out, kill him with a simple swipe across his neck before he can realize what I'm doing. The man crumples before me, silent, unmoving.

Slashing him open, I feast on him until my hunger abates. Then I take up his and the other's remains and bring them home so my son can feed too before the sun rises and this terrible long night ends.

14

I lie in bed, my eyes open, aware of every gust of wind, every breeze that comes through my windows, fearful that one of them will carry traces of Chloe's scent. Finally, I get up and go around the house, closing every window, turning on the air-conditioning, even though I have to put it at its lowest setting so it can overpower the cool air outside.

Still sleep eludes me. Staring at the ceiling, I think of Chloe, of her effect on me. If she refuses me, I think, I'll take Henri to Europe. Possibly there I'll find another female. But I doubt I'll find another like her.

Granny and Velda and the other Jamaicans arrive about seven, shortly after daybreak. I listen to them bustling around the house, Velda chiding her cousins about some overlooked dust, Granny telling stories and laughing.

Around ten, someone knocks on my door. "Mr. Dela-Sangre, are you okay, mon?"

No, most definitely not. My life is in upheaval. My heart may be broken in another day. "Just tired, Granny," I say.

"The boy's in bed too. Do you want me to get him up, take him riding or something, mon?"

"You can see if he wants to. Tell him I'll see him later, in the afternoon."

"Sure, mon." The Jamaican's silent for a moment, then says, "Oh, Mr. DelaSangre, the women are complaining. . . ." He chuckles. "Not that they do much otherwise. But they asked me if they can turn off the air-conditioning and open the windows. It is nice outside."

"I want the windows closed and the air on. Tell them if it's too cold, they can go home."

"No, mon. No need to be so harsh. I'll tell them you like it this way for now."

By noon, I've had my fill of sulking and self-pity. I get up, shower and dress. Even with the windows closed, the spring of the diving board and the splashes that follow tell me that Henri is busy practicing his dives.

Going to the window in the upstairs family room, I watch my son execute a wobbly forward flip, Granny applauding his efforts. Smiling for the first time today, I watch him repeat the effort, improving each time. The thought that, no matter what Chloe decides, the boy and I will always have each other, comforts me.

"Life goes on," I say out loud, wishing I believed the words. But a weight still hangs on me. I pick up a book, try to read it, but the words are only black marks on paper for me today. Rifling through the CDs, I try to find some music that will raise my mood, but all of it sounds like noise to my ears. I go through the library of videotapes and DVDs, choose a film and find myself staring at it while I think about Chloe.

It occurs to me I haven't called the office in weeks. I go to the phone, dial Miami. The phone rings three times before it's picked up. "LaMar Associates," a brisk voice answers, feminine but older, deeper than Rita's.

"Where's Rita?" I say.

"She was promoted, sir. May I help you?"

I shake my head. "Sorry, I forgot. This is Mr. Dela-Sangre."

"Oh, sir," she says. "I'm pleased to meet you, sir. I'm Sarah, the new receptionist."

"Welcome aboard, Sarah. Can I have Arturo please?"

"Sorry, sir, he's on vacation. He won't be back for another two weeks." Buzzes from the switchboard intrude on our conversation. "Oh, sir, sorry, sir, may I put you on hold for a moment?"

"Sure," I say, remembering Arturo mentioning his vacation, wondering what else has slipped my mind. I ponder whether I'm in the mood to talk to Tindall, decide to ask for Rita instead.

Sarah returns to the line. "Mr. DelaSangre, sorry for the delay. What can I do for you?"

"Let me have Rita."

"Rita, sir? Not Mr. Tindall?"

Frowning at her question, I say, "Who hired you?"

"Mr. Tindall did, sir. Mr. Gomez was too busy getting ready for his trip."

"Well, contrary to whatever Ian may have told you, I do know what I want when I ask for it. Please connect me to Rita now."

Sarah's voice is barely audible when she says, "Yes, sir. Right now, sir."

"Peter," Rita says as soon as she picks up her phone, her voice brisk and cheerful. "How goes it?"

"It goes," I say in a monotone.

She pauses before she answers and I regret the sadness I let slip into my answer. "Oh, trouble in loveland?"

"When isn't there?"

Rita laughs and I smile at the sound of it. "Tell me what's going on," I say.

She draws in a breath. "Let's see. You know Arturo put me in Mr. Tindall's department. I think you can guess how happy Mr. Tindall is to have me here. You should see the cubbyhole he gave me for an office." She laughs again. "I think it was a utility closet before.

"And I'm graduating Nova Law in another week. I should pass the bar by November."

"There will be another raise for you when you do," I say.

"Thank you, Peter. Anyway, Mr. Gomez is on vacation now. Did you know he's hiking in some Far East country, Bhutan, I think?"

"He mentioned something about it."

"Well, everything's pretty much going on okay here except"—her voice drops to a whisper—"I've seen and overheard some things. I think Mr. Tindall's found a way to get that Wayward Key deal finished."

"Damn it!" I say. "Arturo told me he had it under control. Are you sure?"

"As sure as I can be. I don't have the resources Mr. Gomez and Mr. Tindall do."

"There's no way I'm going to let it happen. I want you to get Arturo on the phone. I don't give a damn if he's on vacation or not. I want him to call me now."

"I can't, Peter. He's in the middle of nowhere. I can't reach him until he finishes his hike."

Sighing, I say, "Then transfer me to Tindall. I'm going to resolve this thing right now."

Rita's voice turns cold. "What about me, Peter? Where's that going to leave me?"

I almost throw the phone at the wall. Why won't any of these humans listen to me today? "You'll be fine," I say, spitting out each word. "It's Tindall that has to worry. Transfer me to him now!"

"So, Peter, are you ever planning to come home?" Tindall says when he answers my call.

"Soon," I say. "But we're going to resolve this now."

"Whoa, Peter, relax. Who stuck a rod up your ass?"

"You did with that goddamned island deal."

"What island deal?" Tindall says.

"Come on, Ian, don't bullshit me. You know I've been blocking you on this."

"Which is why I gave it up after your asshole lackey Muntz sold us out. I'm not stupid, Peter. I'm not going to jeopardize my position with you for a lousy real estate deal. Especially"—he chuckles—"with that she-bitch you put in my department watching everything I do. I know when I'm beat, Peter. You won."

"I hear otherwise," I say.

"She's got you and Arturo really snookered, doesn't she? Check out what I'm telling you, Peter. The deal's done for. My partners are trying to sell the island to the parks department—for a loss. All of us are sorry we ever got involved in this.

"And, Peter, listen to this," Tindall continues. "I don't think that island deal was ever any violation of our relationship. Sure, I knew you'd get snippy if it went through, but if it did, the value of your island would have gone through the roof. You could have sold it and bought any other island you wanted. I would have made you tons of money on this deal, Peter. Isn't that what I'm supposed to do?"

"You're supposed to protect my privacy too."

"Didn't you see all of the plans? Nothing on Wayward Key would have faced your island except for trees, hedges, bushes and a privacy wall. For Christ's sake, Peter, stop thinking I'm stupid!"

I sigh, wish I could trust a word this man says. But he's a Tindall and I know all too well what they're capable of. "Ian, if the deal's dead like you say, then we'll just have a long talk when I get back."

"I look forward to it, Peter."

"But if you've lied to me . . ."

"I haven't."

"Okay," I say. "You know I'm going to have this all checked out. We'll talk again when I know what's really going on. . . ."

"Sure."

"And nothing better happen to Rita in the meantime."

"That bitch? I wouldn't dare." Tindall laughs.

I reach Claudia on her cellphone, tell her of Rita's conversation with me and Tindall. "You know how to get hold of your father's people. I want this all checked out," I say.

"It will take a little time," she says. "I have to go to shore. The man I need to talk to won't discuss anything over the phone."

"Whatever it takes. Just get me the truth."

"Okay."

"And Claudia?"

"Yes?"

"If Tindall's lying to me, I'm going to need you to handle it. Is that a problem for you?"

"Me?" She laughs. "After all that Pops has told me about him, it would be a pure pleasure."

15

Despite Henri's pleas to go outside and practice flying, I spend the evening inside. I don't tell the boy that I don't dare venture into the evening sky. Chloe's scent can only grow stronger as her oestrus continues. I fear the effect it will have on me. I don't want to risk being drawn to her before the deadline she's given me.

To my surprise, sleep takes me as soon as I lie down and, even though dreams and nightmares roil my night, I wake rested, almost cheerful in the morning. Still, I refuse to open the windows, refuse to go outside all day.

Henri stays by my side until I reassure him my odd behavior has nothing to do with anything he's done. After that, he spends the rest of the day tagging along with Granny, helping with chores he always avoided at home.

After dark, I accompany him to his room, sit on his bed. "I saw Chloe the other night," I say.

He stares into my face. "Are you married now?" he says.

I smile, say, "No. If we do decide to get married, you'll be there. But I am going to see her again tonight after you go to sleep. By tomorrow, we'll know whether she's going to come live with us or not."

"You like her, don't you, Papa?"

I nod.

"Then I hope she marries you."

Chloe's scent surrounds me as soon as I walk out the veranda door. The aroma of cinnamon and musk fills my lungs, the scent's chemicals flood my veins. My body begins to change before I even think to, my shoulders widening, bursting through my shirt, my pants splitting, falling off me as my haunches thicken and my tail grows.

I take deep breaths, revel as my skin thickens to scales, as my wings break clear. Spreading them, flexing my claws, working my jaw so my newly lengthened fangs settle into place, I can't imagine why I ever in my life wanted to be such a puny thing as a human. Looking up toward the still full moon, I admire the way the silver disk dominates the sky, bathes the earth with its dull shine, wish it were ringed with a halo again this night.

Springing into the air, I circle once over Bartlet House, smelling the air, following Chloe's scent where it's the strongest. Every nerve I have is energized, every muscle taut. I fly over the dark landscape, the scattered lights, climb high once I pass into Cockpit Country, then dive and skim the treetops and zoom high again, roaring into the moonlit night.

I know that Chloe may refuse me but I can't imagine what would follow. Her scent has me, pulls me toward her, dulls any thoughts of rejection that arise. Flight has never felt so good. Every molecule of air that passes over my skin seems to rub me ever so lightly, tease me further into frenzy. The faster I go, the harder the air presses against me and I strain to speed to the valley, to the cave Chloe has chosen.

Scanning the sky for any sign of her, I growl at its emptiness. I'd met Elizabeth in the air the first time and had hoped I'd meet Chloe that way too. But no matter what altitude I climb to, which valley I fly over, I see no sign of her.

Landing at the cave's mouth, I enter it to find the bed completed, the air flooded with Chloe's scent—with the female nowhere in sight. Weary from my flight, panting from exhaustion and lust, I walk back to the cave's opening, examine the sky as I rest.

Could she be so cruel as to leave me panting in the dark

waiting for her answer? Growling, I shake my head, twitch my tail. Chloe couldn't do that to me. Still, as time passes, my fears grow.

She surprises me by diving from above me, dropping toward the valley floor—a silver streak of movement that rockets across the valley and races back toward the cave. *"Back off, leave me room,"* she mindspeaks moments before she arrives.

Scrambling away from the cave's mouth, I leave enough space for her to shoot past me. She lands only feet from the bed, facing the cave's rear.

Her scent threatens to drown me but I resist its call. *"I was worried you might not come,"* I say.

"Good," she says, her back still to me. *"I wasn't sure I would. I'm still angry with you."*

Her trembling body, her heaving sides, her swollen sex belie her words. But as much as my need for her vibrates within me, I refuse to step forward and risk her rejection again. *"Then you want me to leave,"* I say.

"Would you?"

"It would be the hardest thing I ever had to do. But I would if you told me this was hopeless. Is it?"

"No . . . at least I don't know yet. I want you to be someone else. I want that you never married my sister, that she never died. I'm furious that you've eliminated any chance of any other male challenging you for me. I'm angry that my sister knew you first. I hate that I've been thinking about you almost every minute since we met. I almost came to this cave six times in the past three hours but I still needed to think."

"Chloe, you need to decide."

She turns toward me, lashes her tail from one side to the other as she mindspeaks. *"I don't need to do anything, Peter. You need to somehow make this good for me."*

I look into her emerald-green eyes, admire the sharpness of her snout, her features a little finer than her sister's. A shudder of desire goes through me and I sigh. *"What more can I say?"*

Chloe glares at me. *"I think I could be strong enough to resist you, Peter. I really do."* She breathes deeply. *"You have to give me a reason not to."*

My body aches from need. I'm tired of all this talking. If I'm to be sent away I want it to be soon. *"You want a reason?"* I growl, slam my tail down on the floor of the cave, stand on my hind legs so I tower over her. *"Would you rather I just took you like I was one of the others of the Blood? Do you think you could really stop me? All that holds me back is that I want something more. And that's what I have to offer you."*

"And just what is that?"

"The chance for a real relationship, not the mindless rutting and instinctual coupling of two beasts. I'm worth more than that, Chloe. So are you. We both deserve love."

"Do you really think that's possible? That we can love each other?"

"Yes, I do. That's why I came here. That's why I waited for you." I pause, her scent almost suffocating me, my body so much in need that it's almost in pain. *"Now decide what you want, Chloe. If you want to just be mated like your parents were, tell me and I'll go. If I stay much longer, I can't guarantee what I'll do."*

Chloe shakes her head. *"How can you promise that what we have will be any better than my parents' marriage?"*

"I can't. I can only swear that I'll do my best to make it better. If you do the same, I think we'll be able to do it. Now please, Chloe, either come to me or let me go."

She studies me, says nothing for a few minutes. Finally, Chloe takes a breath, tilts her head a little. *"No, I don't want you to go. But"*—she backs up a few steps—*"you come to me."*

I step toward her, stop just before our bodies touch. Chloe rubs her jowl against mine. I accept her touch, wait for her next move. *"Elizabeth told me you and she made love in the air the first time you met. Did you?"*

"Yes."

She backs away and for a moment I'm afraid again that I've lost her. But she lies on her back on the bed of branches, her sweet cream-colored underbody showing, her swollen sex completely exposed. *"Then I think we should make love here,"* she says.

Standing still, I stare at her, take in her beauty.

"Come on, Peter," she says. *"You're not the only one of us in need here."*

I rush forward, Chloe's scent clouding around me, fogging my mind. There's no need for any further conversation. As frenzied as Chloe and I both are, there's no need for foreplay. I ram myself into her, Chloe shuddering once, yowling as I growl at the warm, tight pleasure of her reception.

She seizes me with her foreclaws, digs her talons into my sides, penetrating my scales, drawing blood as she erupts beneath me, her tail thrashing, her jaws clamped on my throat, the sharp tips of her fangs piercing me. The aroma of my blood blends with the smells of cinnamon and musk, pain mixes with pleasure.

Shocked by her wildness, I bellow, attempt to pull back. I'd expected her to be gentler than her sister, not more forceful. But I can't break her hold. I put my full weight on her, attempt to pin her into submission, but she digs her claws and teeth even more into me as she bucks and heaves against me, her scent growing thicker until I'm powerless to do anything but move in response to her.

Chloe orgasms first, yowling into the night, pulling me even closer to her, her sex spasming, clamping hard around me. I follow only seconds later, my mind devoid of any thoughts, preoccupied only by the sensations that overwhelm me.

Afterwards, neither of us moves. Chloe still holds me with her claws, still clamps her jaws on my throat. A gust of night wind penetrates the cave deep enough to cool us, carry off some of the scents that envelop us. I sigh, breathe the fresh air and then become more aware of the pain of

Chloe's embrace. Groaning, I pull back my head, flexing my shoulders so she'll release me.

This time she relents and I roll to her side, sigh again, rubbing her tail with mine. Chloe half purrs, half growls, her eyes closed, one claw gently tracing the welts and gashes she's inflicted on me. *"I did that?"* She chuckles, presses closer to me. *"Poor you."*

"It's nothing I can't heal," I say.

"I know. I just didn't expect to behave like that. Not that I'm sorry, mind you."

As satiated as I am, I find I'm not sorry either. *"But,"* I say as I will my wounds to close, my skin to heal, *"it might be better if you don't break the surface the next time."*

She nestles against me, gives a little shrug. *"No promises here, Peter. I've never done this before. How can I know how I'll behave the next time? You're just going to have to take your chances."*

We fall asleep, side by side, drowse until our stomachs start to rumble with hunger. Chloe sits up first, leans against me, *"Are you awake, Peter?"*

When I don't answer right away, she slaps my tail with hers. *"Are you going to be like my pa and brothers—always sleeping, expecting a female to hunt for you any time you don't feel like it?"*

The slap barely stings. I open one eye and fake growl, mindspeaking, *"I wasn't expecting to be slapped awake by my bride."*

"Good." Chloe laughs and slaps my tail with hers again, a little harder. *"I don't want you to think I'm dull and predictable."*

"How about just annoying?" I mindspeak, playing along with her teasing, sitting up on one haunch, pinning her tail down with mine before she can slap me again.

"No fair! You're bigger!" Chloe shoves against me, tries to free herself. No matter how she moves, I manage to keep her pinned, both of us laughing as we struggle.

"Okay, you asked for it," she says and gives off a fresh burst of scent.

Cinnamon and musk envelop me. I gasp at my body's immediate reaction and turn toward my bride, releasing her as I do so. But, laughing, she rolls away from me. *"Mum said there are always ways to beat a male."*

Her laugh is deeper than Elizabeth's, full of delight. Even in my state of rut, it makes me smile. *"Now who's being unfair!"* I say and she laughs even more.

I want to approach her, to quiet her laughs with my touch, but I can't help but think about my son at home by himself. The boy's never woken to find me gone. Rising, turning from my bride, I say, *"I need to be home before sunrise. Henri will be worried if I'm not there."*

Chloe stops laughing, says, *"Don't you want to stay in the cave with me?"*

"Of course, I do, but I have to be concerned for Henri too. We can hunt together. After we feed, you can come back to my house, stay there with me, meet your nephew."

I follow Chloe, let her do the hunting as tradition dictates, but insist only that we take no children. *"I don't like hunting them either,"* she says. *"It always makes me feel sad when one of the others bring home young ones. Pa says they taste sweeter, but I don't care."*

We find a shepherd sleeping by his flock on the outskirts of Maroonetown, an older man, gray haired and a little too thin. Chloe lands and kills him before he awakes. We feed alongside each other, Chloe searching for the best parts, pushing them toward me.

After eating, our desire returns and we make love on the ground under the open sky, the shepherd's remains just feet away, his sheep restive and milling near us. This time, Chloe's more subdued, almost gentle at times.

The sun is a thin edge of light between the night sky and the horizon when we finally land alongside the pool deck behind Bartlet House. I shift to my human shape as soon as

I touch ground. "We need to go inside before any of my employees arrive," I say.

Chloe remains in her natural form. "Not bad," she says, examining me.

"You've seen me like this before."

She laughs. *"That was five years ago and only for a little while. I was young then. I didn't know what to look for."*

I frown at her. "Please, Chloe, change so we can go inside. I don't want anyone seeing us like this."

"Turn around then."

"Why? I've seen your human shape before."

"Before I was grown. Turn around, Peter. You'll see me soon enough."

Turning my back on her, I wait for her permission to view her. But, instead, after she changes, she presses her two hands against my back, pushes gently. "Take me inside, Peter, you can see me when we get to your room."

I smile at the sweet sound of her voice. It's deeper than I'd expected—her accent, like her family's, more upper-class British than Jamaican. I toy with the thought of twirling around, viewing her by surprise, but I'm still wary of upsetting her.

She drops her hands down, grabs my buttocks, giggling as we go up the stairs to the veranda.

"Chloe!" I mock complain.

The tile floor is cold under my feet. Chloe's hands grab and touch at my back on the way to my room, both of us laughing, until, afraid we'll wake Henri, I say, "Please shush."

Chloe muffles her giggles, presses her full body against my back once we're in my room, her nipples hard against my back, her pubic hair brushing my buttocks.

Once again I have no choice but to grow hard. "Can I turn now?" I say.

"Just a moment." Chloe backs away from me and I regret the momentary loss of her touch.

"You can turn."

I do and suck in my breath at the sight of her. She's far

darker than Elizabeth, almost a deep milk-chocolate color, but otherwise she could be my dead wife's twin, her body a little fuller, her nose and jaw finer, her lips thick where Elizabeth's had been thin, her hair longer, dark curls spiraling down to her wide shoulders. But her emerald-green eyes sparkle in a way Elizabeth's never did and, unlike my departed wife, her voice turns husky when she invites me to bed.

We lie together over the covers, stroking and caressing each other, kissing for the first time, Chloe's lips soft against mine. Our lovemaking is almost an afterthought to the rest of our activities, our orgasms muted, leading almost immediately to sleep. My new mate surrenders to slumber first, her face close to mine, her lips slightly parted, her breath warm and sweet against my face. I sigh and surrender too, safe, I think, to finally accept that my quest is over, my mate found.

16

The rap of a small hand against my bedroom door wakes me. I stretch, groan at the soreness in my muscles, look toward Chloe and find her sitting up cross-legged in bed watching me. Henri knocks again, says, "Papa?"

"What?" I turn toward the night table, glance at the clock, ten-fifteen in the morning.

"Can I come in?" The knob starts to turn.

Chloe giggles, scoots under the covers.

This is not how I want my son to meet my future wife. "No," I say. "Henri, go downstairs. Find something to do. I'll be down in a half hour or so."

"But I'm bored. Granny says he's too busy to watch me dive."

"So do something else."

The boy clomps his feet as he walks away. "He sounds cute," Chloe says.

"He is cute." I get out of bed, pull the covers off her. "Come on. If you get up now we can shower together. Then, after we get dressed, I'll introduce you to my son."

Chloe stands, looks around the room, furrowing her brow as she does so. Then she puts her hands on her hips, looks at me and laughs.

"What?" I say.

"Okay," she says. "Just what were you expecting me to dress in?"

My mate's small enough that one of my larger knit shirts can act as a short dress, covering her to midthigh.

Still, barefoot, my yellow pique knit shirt cinched at her waist with a red tie, Chloe looks like a little girl dressed in her daddy's shirt—one who's obviously naked under the cotton material. Velda glares at me, as if I've taken advantage of Chloe, when we come down the stairs together.

Chloe holds my arm and toys with her hair with her other hand as she explains. "It's Peter's fault really. If he hadn't pushed me in the pool last night and absolutely ruined my new silk dress, I'd never have to wear such a silly thing. He's going to buy me a completely new outfit today to make up for it. Aren't you, Peter?"

I nod.

Henri just stares at her. Finally he mindspeaks to me, his thoughts masked. {*She looks like the picture of Momma.*}

"You can say it out loud, son."

He looks down, almost mumbles, "You look like my momma did."

Chloe crouches next to him, touches his cheek. "She was my sister, Henri. We always looked alike."

"Are you going to come live with us?"

"If you and your father will have me. Is that okay with you, Henri?"

He nods, turns to me, says, "Can I go swimming now?"

Chloe and I leave Henri in Granny's care, drive to Wakefield, hoping to find enough clothes that fit her, to make her presentable enough to go shopping for better clothes in Montego Bay. She sits as close to me as the Land Rover's bucket seats allow, her hand on my thigh, and stares out the window as she says, "This is my first time outside Cockpit Country. You know how my mum and pa are—they only let Derek venture out."

I nod.

"They already know about us. I told Mum this morning."

It comes as no surprise to me. Henri and I aren't the only ones who can mask their thoughts. "Elizabeth told your mother fairly soon too," I say.

"Well, I think Mum took it a bit differently this time."

I look at Chloe, raise an eyebrow. "Such as?"

"She's in a bit of a snit about it. She thinks it was wrong of you to come back this way—'underhanded,' I think, was the word she used."

Sighing, I say, "Can't she just be happy for us?"

"You have to understand my parents, Peter. Once they get a thought in their minds, it takes a long time to change it. They expected you to protect Elizabeth. They think you took unfair advantage of me."

In-laws. I shake my head. Samantha and Charles Blood had hardly left me with any warm memories from our last meeting. The thought of spending time with them now makes me wish we could leave on the next plane. "Great," I say. "It should make for a wonderful feast."

Chloe laughs. "They'll still have a wedding feast for us. Mum already said she wants you at Morgan's Hole two days from now. They don't hate you, Peter. They're only angry at you. Mum says she can't wait to meet Henri. She'll be even more thrilled when I tell her we're going to have a daughter."

I look at her and my mate smiles, pats her stomach. "You do good work, Peter."

We spend the afternoon clothes shopping in Montego Bay. Chloe buys shorts, blouses, jeans and halter tops, dresses, bras and underwear, shoes and sneakers. "This is the first time I've ever been able to pick and choose what I want," she says, "Usually Mum tells Derek what to bring home." She models each outfit for me, choosing in the end a white sundress and a pair of sandals to wear for the rest of the day.

If anything, a bookstore, Galways Books, thrills her even more than the clothing store. After an hour of browsing, I have to insist she decide on a few books so we can get back to Bartlet House by dark.

*   *   *

After dinner, we take Henri outside and let him fly with us. I lead him and Chloe from our house to Windsor, to Barbecue Bottom and Clarkstown and back. Later, when Henri resists his bedtime, Chloe sits on the bed with him and reads a Dr. Seuss book she bought for him.

Chloe and I fly together after that, hunting again, feeding side by side once more. *"You know I have to go home later tonight, don't you, Peter?"* she says once we're done.

"Why can't you stay with us and go back when we go?"

"Because that's not what tradition allows. We don't want to anger my parents any more. It's just a few days and then we can go to your country. Derek will come to get you the day after tomorrow."

I remember the long trip I made with him the last time and groan. *"Why don't I just drive there myself?"*

"You know you'll never find it. I'm not sure I could. Derek's a bore, I know that. But he's not that bad."

"Then you spend the day in the car with him."

"Not a chance!" Chloe laughs and takes to the air. I chase after her, follow her from valley to valley, my mate always just out of reach. I beat my wings even faster, find myself inches from her tail and, suddenly, she sprays the air with her scent.

A cloud of cinnamon and musk envelops me. *"Not again!"* I mindspeak, breathing in her aroma, surrendering to its effect.

Chloe slows, dipping one wing, turning over in midair so she flies upside down, displaying herself to me. *"Does that make it better?"* she says, slowing even more as I close with her, positioning herself so I can enter her in midair.

"Definitely," I say, joining with her, the night's calm shattered by our roars.

17

Henri and I both wake early and get ready long before Derek arrives. We go outside, wait for Derek on the front steps of Bartlet House, Henri standing, sitting, leaning on me, asking questions until, finally, he sees Granny going to the stables to groom the horses. "Can I, Papa?" he says.

I nod and the boy rushes off.

The stone steps have grown hard and painful to sit on by the time Derek pulls his tan Land Rover into the drive in front of the house. Henri and Granny come out of the stables, to see who's arrived, just as the man gets out.

"Hello, mon," Granny says.

Derek ignores Granny's greeting. He stretches, examines the house, the stables, the cottages, and walks up the front steps to me. He looks like someone on his way to play tennis. The contrast between his pale white skin, blond hair and rosy cheeks and Elizabeth and Chloe's choice of darker hair and skin reassures me that the women's choices were better ones. There's a wasted look to the man and even though he's the larger and more muscular one of us two, I'm sure I'm the more vital-looking one. He shakes my hand, squeezing too hard, and grins one of his empty smiles. "Not too shabby, old man. Not too shabby at all."

"Glad you like it," I say, motioning to my son to join us, introducing Henri.

Derek glances at him, turns back to me. "Let's get going, old man. You know my mum. She'll frown at me for a month if we're late."

At my request, Derek opens the trunk. I put two suit-cases in and place the wooden chest beside them. The man can't keep his eyes off the chest. "Gold, isn't it?"

I nod and he laughs. "You learned your lesson didn't you? At least you know the way to Pa's heart—if the old bugger has one."

Derek continues to talk as we get in the Land Rover. I check my pants pocket, make sure Chloe's gift, the ear-rings to match her necklace, is there before we drive away. "I can't believe you, old man," he says, driving with one hand, gesturing with the other as he talks, Henri, in the backseat, staring out the window ignoring his words, me wishing I could do the same.

"Two brides of our kind in five years. I'm ten years older than you and haven't had one yet. Of course, you had to cheat to get your last one." He laughs. "Not that I blame you, old man. All's fair and all that, what? Don't know why Mum and Pa are so put out. 'Someone had to eventu-ally get Chloe,' I told them. Why not you? After all, at least you're rich."

Derek drones on about the human women he's encoun-tered, his plans to eventually leave his father's house. I nod and occasionally make a monosyllabic answer, but mostly I look out the window and try to memorize key landmarks so should I ever return again, I can do so without the man's company.

We go a different way than I expected, driving through Windsor, past the road to the cave, entering Cockpit Coun-try, crossing the trail that hikers take through it to Troy on the other side. Derek follows a near invisible path through the brush. Having been taken through Cockpit Country be-fore, I'm no longer alarmed by the sheer drops on the edge of our trail, the apparent lack of any real roadway. I realize if I study the ground carefully enough I can make out the faint impressions of tire wheels.

I find myself looking forward to my wedding feast, most especially to the potion of Dragon's Tear wine and crushed Death's Rose petals that Samantha Blood will prepare. Elizabeth and I shared such a potion at our wedding feast and both of us had been stunned to find ourselves sharing every thought, every feeling we had. The potion's effect had mostly gone by the next morning, but it left us with a permanent connection I sorely miss now.

To share such an intimacy with Chloe! I sigh. It had been thrilling to do so with Elizabeth, who'd been so different from me. It could only be better, more intense with Chloe.

We go up and down hillsides, our ears popping in each direction. Derek surprises me by shifting the subject of his conversation from him to me. "Tell me, old man, what it's like living in Miami? How do you manage it? I mean, hunting and all?"

I tell him about life on my island, where I hunt, how I conceal my activities. Derek says, "But what about your wealth? How can you have so much—like all that gold?" He gestures back toward the trunk. "And Pa have so little?"

"Don Henri always saved most of his treasure," I say. "And he learned to invest it too."

"How?" Derek says. He guides the car around deep sinkholes and drives on the edges of circular lakes, steering around some trees, under others as I explain about LaMar Associates, the humans who run it for me, the investments they manage and the miracle of compound growth.

Derek shakes his head. "Pa would never trust any human with any of his wealth. He hates dealing with the creatures. He and Mum barely ever leave left Cockpit Country. I'm the one who has to go to the outside world. Bloody damned pain that. I'm expected to bring back enough money to support us."

"Land Rovers aren't cheap," I say. "You seem to be doing okay."

"Do you know how many fool tourists carry barely anything but credit cards? Sometimes I think it's hardly worth killing them. If it weren't for those street peddlers in Montego Bay selling ganja to the tourists, we wouldn't have hardly anything. Whenever things get tight, I look for one of them, right after an American cruise ship has departed. You can almost always count on finding a big roll of Yankee currency in their pockets.

"But,"—Derek slows the car, steers around yet another tree—"you can only kill just so many of those buggers before you mess things up. Most the time it's tourists—Montego Bay, Negril, Ocho Rios—a little bit of cash, some traveler's checks, jewelry, cameras and watches. I take all of it, except the cash, to Kingston every month, to Virgil Claypool. He turns it into money for us."

Derek looks at me. "I envy you, old man. Your pa set you up proper." He turns his attention back to the wheel. "I bet he left you with a large bit of treasure too. Like that chest of gold you brought? Where do you keep stuff like that, old man? I mean you can't march into a bank and say, 'Store this for me.' Can you?"

I look at Derek, wonder why he would think I'd answer a question like that. "Father made the proper arrangements for everything," I say. "Chloe will be well taken care of."

To my relief, Derek turns silent, concentrates on his driving. Because of the roughness of the terrain, there are times we slow to the speed of a walking man. I doubt we go faster than ten miles an hour anywhere within Cockpit Country.

Henri takes it all in, breaks the quiet periodically by pointing to different birds, asking their names. Green parrots, doctor birds, glossy black grackles and two John Crow vultures circling over a tiny valley are all named and duly noted.

We skirt a deep sinkhole and I recognize it by its steep sides and the jagged stones near its bottom, looking like huge white fangs sticking out of the greenery. I remember it from my previous visit to the Bloods' home. My heart speeds up. I look out the windshield and see, not too far in front of us, the two sheer cliffs that define the pass into Morgan's Hole.

Driving through it, we descend to the flat valley floor. "Home," Derek says and floors the accelerator. We speed across the valley, stopping in its middle by a pile of stones.

Derek honks his horn and in a few minutes a contingent of Jamaican men, dressed in ragged clothes, steel rings around their necks, arrive with two thick wooden planks, stop by a similar pile twelve feet in front of us. Derek looks at me. "You pay your humans. Ours work for free." He guffaws.

The Jamaicans stand the planks on end and carefully lower them directly ahead of each of the Land Rover's front tires.

"There's a fault here," I explain to Henri as we drive across. "Like a big crack in the ground. It runs the whole width of the valley."

My son stares at the ground in front of us. "I don't see it, Papa."

"It's under the ground. If we stepped on it, we'd fall through." I don't tell Henri, the last time I was here I'd tested the danger of the ground by placing one foot on it, bearing down with my weight for only a second. Had I continued, I would have crashed through and fallen, God knows how far.

Speeding past fields, by the tidy wood shacks that serve as slave quarters for the Blood's dozens of forced laborers, we soon come to the stables and the two towering silk cottonwood trees that mark the entrance to Chloe's home. Derek parks next to another Land Rover, a white one, under the trees and we all get out.

Henri tilts his head back, stares at the tops of the silk cottonwoods, over a hundred feet in the air, the massive stone house set into the hillside behind them. "It's bigger than our house, Papa," he says.

I nod, look between the trees at the rest of Derek's family waiting for us on the front porch of the house, all in their human forms. Charles and Samantha Blood stand in the middle of the porch, with Philip to the right of his father. While Chloe's parents have chosen to dress in formal Victorian garb, the teenager wears only a T-shirt and jeans.

Charles and Samantha look as white and aristocratic as ever. Philip however, who, when I last saw him, had chosen to look as pale as his father, now has adopted the dark skin and Jamaican features of his sister. He wears his hair platted close to his skull. I think how irritated Charles Blood has to be with his son's current choice, and have to stifle a grin as I do.

Derek opens the car trunk and Samantha waves a hand toward two blacks dressed in tattered clothes, steel rings around their necks. They rush forward, take Henri's and my luggage. Derek takes the chest himself, walks with it, swaggers really, toward his father. Henri and I follow. "Peter brought this for you—for us, Pa." He hefts the chest and laughs. "From the feel of it, it's a good bit of gold. It should make you happy, Pa."

Charles gives a stiff nod.

"He's so big, Papa," Henri whispers to me.

"That's your grandfather," I say, understanding the boy's reaction. Charles Blood towers over everyone, Derek and me included. I know Derek lives in fear of his displeasure. Elizabeth had told me of the times both she and Chloe had been locked in the cells beneath the house as punishment for their disobedience.

Charles looks at me. "I'm glad to see you believe in following at least some of our people's traditions. Too bad you couldn't follow the others and leave our last daughter alone."

"There's no tradition against what he did!" Philip says.

The elder dragon glowers at his younger son. "There are ways to pursue a mate and there are ways not to." He glares at me. "If it were up to me, sir, you would not be welcome here. But my wife tells me I'm wrong."

"You should learn to listen to your wife," I say.

Charles's glare intensifies.

I return it, refuse to shift my eyes from his. Father-in-law or not, the man deserves to be taught some manners.

Clenching my fists, trying to control the rage that threatens to overtake me, I say, "If I'm unwelcome here, I'll be glad to take Chloe and leave. You don't have to trouble yourself for us. You can keep the gold. It's meaningless to me."

"Chloe will go nowhere until after the feast. That hopefully should be the last time I ever have to endure your presence." He turns, enters the house, Derek following him with the chest.

Samantha Blood smiles at me, but there's no warmth in her grin. "My husband is a stubborn man, as I suspect you are, Peter. He blames you for the death of one daughter and the theft of another. Can you blame him for his anger?"

"I can for his rudeness."

She waves a hand in the air as if to dispel the conversation. "They're only words, Peter. You have my grandson beside you and my granddaughter growing in Chloe's womb. Of course, you're welcome here."

Coming down the stairs, she kisses me on one cheek, bends over and kisses Henri on his forehead. "You look so much like your father," Samantha says. "Too bad he didn't encourage you to look a little like your mother too."

Philip hangs back until she too goes inside, then rushes to Henri and me. He offers his hand, says, "Sorry, mon. Sometimes my parents can be difficult to take." He smiles a wide grin. "Don't think they've never turned their displeasure on me."

The teen kneels, fusses over Henri. "Chloe told me to tell you, she can't wait until the feast's over."

"Me too," I say. "If it's up to me, we'll be on our way out of here tomorrow."

"No fair," Philip says. "That means I'll be stuck here alone with all of them."

"You can come visit us."

He half laughs, half snorts. "Like they'll ever let me."

Inside the house I'm taken again, as I was on my last visit, how far back in time it seems. Torches and candles light the interior. All water for washing and drinking is carried in pitchers to the rooms by black slaves. Windows lack glass and screens and are closed with wooden shutters. I guess my father's house was like this in 1700.

I wonder what Charles Blood did with the gold I sent him for Elizabeth. Surely that was enough to pay for wiring and generators, plumbing and pumps. Not that I really care.

Pacing in my room, anxious for the day to be done, the time for the feast to arrive, I wish Chloe could just leave with me now. If only marriage were possible without involvement with a spouse's family. I hate that my son has to be exposed to these creatures, hope that Chloe can escape the bad part of their genes.

Though Philip too, impresses me as much as his sisters did. So much so that I have no objection to him taking my son and entertaining him for the rest of the day.

Henri returns to my room after dark, babbling about his adventures. Our conversation is interrupted by a knock on the door. I open it to find Samantha Blood.

"I've come to remind you about the antidote," she says. "You do remember you need it, don't you?"

I nod, remembering all too well the warning at Elizabeth's feast. "You told us that the potion of Dragon's Tear wine and Death's Rose we drank altered our body chemistry forever. If either of us ever drank it again without drinking an antidote of alchemist's powder and Angel Wort, we'd die."

"Quickly and painfully," Samantha says. "The antidote is a vile drink. I just wanted to warn you, you'll have to take it after we change to our natural forms. Before you and Chloe share your wedding potion."

"No problem."

"The feast's first bell will ring in about fifteen minutes," she says. "Please come upstairs to the great room when it does."

As soon as she leaves, Henri says, "Papa? Do I have to go to the feast too?"

I turn to him. "Of course, you have to go."

My son's lower lip trembles. "Do I have to drink a potion too?"

Laughing, I shake my head. "The feast is to celebrate my marriage to Chloe."

"What do I have to do?"

"Nothing. You just have to stand next to me. We'll all undress and change into our natural forms."

Henri giggles. "All of us?"

I ignore him. "And then Samantha will mix a potion. She'll say some words and Chloe and I will drink it. Then we'll all feed and Chloe and I will go off by ourselves for a little bit."

"Who'll watch me?"

"Chloe said Philip offered to let you sleep in his room tonight. Is that okay?"

Henri nods.

After what feels far longer than fifteen minutes, a bell gongs, its sound reverberating down the halls. Doors open and close, footsteps sound on the staircase.

I take Henri's hand and lead him out of the room, the hallway lit by wavering candlelight, the dark shadows moving with each flicker. Henri moves closer to me, squeezes my hand.

A second bell rings and we walk up the massive wood staircase, passing the second-floor landing, arriving at the great room on the third floor just as the third gong sounds. Henri and I both blink at the lights of hundreds of candles burning in chandeliers, in wall sconces, in candelabras and candlesticks placed everywhere but the north side of the room. There, a hearth filled with a roaring fire runs almost the whole length of the wall.

Chloe stands in the center of the room. Just as her sister had, she wears a white cotton dress almost translucent in its thinness. It acts as an outline for her dark body accentuating her human curves. I breathe in deep at the sight of her and smile when I see Elizabeth's necklace around her throat—the gold clover leaf and the green emerald in its center, reflecting the lights all around her.

Ignoring Charles and Samantha Blood standing to either side of her, I approach Chloe, dig my hand in my pocket and bring out the earrings I'd bought to match her necklace. My bride smiles when she sees them, mouths the words, "Thank you."

"Chloe, no talking," Samantha says.

I start to put the earrings in Chloe's ears but Derek says, "Don't bother, old man. She's just going to have to take them off again in a second."

Chloe nods agreement and Samantha Blood holds her hand out. I give her the earrings, which she places on the wood floor next to Chloe's bare feet.

"Derek," Samantha says, tilting her head to the corner of the room where a half dozen Jamaicans stand patiently, no fear apparent on their faces. I know all too well the effects of the Dragon's Tear wine they've been forced to drink, how it can numb the mind and body, steal any human's will—or the will of a being like me if he's so foolish to drink such a thing in his human state.

Samantha Blood points to a long table on the other side of the room. A white porcelain bowl and a green ceramic pitcher sit on top of it, next to a pewter mug and a small leather bag. "Philip," she says.

Philip rushes to the table, returns with the bowl and the pitcher, makes a second trip for the mug and the bag. He places all of them on the wood floor in front of Samantha.

Derek ambles over to the Jamaicans, examines them, going from one to the other, feeling their arms and thighs, pinching their skin to check their fat content.

"Bloody well just bring one!" Charles finally growls. Derek grabs a male at random and leads him back to us, the Jamaican's face expressionless, his eyes glazed.

As soon as Derek's in place, Samantha Blood looks at me. *"Peter, do you want Chloe for your mate?"* she mindspeaks.

"Yes," I say.

She picks up the white porcelain bowl and sets it in front of Chloe. Then she takes the green ceramic pitcher and pours a clear liquid into the bowl, until it's half full. *"This is Dragon's Tear wine,"* she says and carries the pitcher back to the table.

When she returns, she picks up the leather bag, undoes its rawhide drawstring and pulls out what looks like a small, dried-out, purple rose. *"Do you know what this is, Peter?"*

"Death's Rose."

"The petals can kill," Samantha says. She crumbles one over the bowl, lets it mix with the Dragon's Tear wine. *"Are you willing to risk death to have Chloe as yours?"*

Looking at Chloe, thinking of the consciousness we'll both soon share, I want to shout out my answer. But I know, to do so would violate custom. *"I am,"* I mindspeak.

Samantha reaches into the bag again. She sprinkles a rust-colored dust over the bowl. *"Alchemist's powder,"* she says. *"To fight the poison."*

It looks lighter colored to me than I remember, but I see little purpose in questioning the woman about it. After all, her daughter will be sipping the potion too.

"It's time," Samantha Blood says. She begins to undo Chloe's dress. Her husband fidgets with my mate's necklace, releasing the catch, removing the chain from Chloe's lovely neck.

Behind me Derek and Peter undress. I help Henri get out of his clothes, rip mine off as quickly as I can. My son looks from person to person, his eyes big, giggling at the women's nudity.

"Quiet!" I say.

Chloe transforms herself first. I watch her as her features sharpen, desiring her more as her skin roughens and turns to scales, her wings unfold behind her. After five years of waiting, I think, she'll finally be with me. I want to roar my excitement, but I know all too well the disapproval such an exhibition would bring from my past and future in-laws.

As soon as Chloe finishes changing, the room fills with the grunts and groans of the rest of us as we shed our human bodies and return to our true and natural shapes. Henri is the last to finish shifting and to my pleasure, all the Bloods wait patiently while he struggles to properly fold his wings.

When he's done, Samantha Blood picks up the pewter mug. She holds it out to me. *"This is a mixture of Angel's Wort and alchemist's powder. It will neutralize the poison in your body and enable you to both drink the wedding potion again and share its effects with your new wife. Without it, you and Chloe would never know the experience or have the connection that you and Elizabeth did."*

Lifting the mug, I smell its contents, almost gag at the aroma, like rotten eggs mixed with acid. I pause, then drain it in only a few swallows, grimacing at its hot, bitter metallic taste.

Chloe's mother smiles at my expression. *"Trust me, the other potion would taste much worse without this antidote,"* she says.

If anything, the taste of Samantha Blood's antidote grows more bitter in my mouth, the hot metal flavor expanding, growing down my throat, heating my stomach.

Samantha looks at me, at Chloe and at her husband. *"Now we have to wait for the antidote to take effect."*

No one speaks. I stare at Chloe, the brightness of her emerald-green eyes and think how close we'll be in a short while. Henri waits and fidgets beside me, twitching his tail, unfolding and folding his wings.

The lights, the heat of the fire, the hot bitter taste that seems to have overtaken every molecule of my body — all conspire to weaken my legs. I sway in place, wonder if the antidote might be too powerful, if the wedding potion will balance its effect.

"Listen to me carefully," Charles Blood finally says. *"In a few minutes, you and Chloe will be offered the opportunity to drink from the bowl before you. What you drink won't kill you, but it will change both of you forever.*

*It will bind you to each other in a way you never imagined.
Peter, knowing you have to do this, do you still want
Chloe?"*

They're the same words he used to marry me to Elizabeth. I stare into his cold, green eyes and mindspeak,
"Yes." I turn, look at Samantha, wait for her to ask Chloe
the same question.

"Chloe," she says. *"Knowing you have to do this, do
you still want Peter?"*

"Yes!" Chloe says.

Samantha points to the white bowl. *"Please drink it at
the same time. Make sure you finish all of it."*

Chloe and I look at each other, staring into each other's
eyes as we drink. When we finish, I wait for her thoughts
to open to me, as Elizabeth's did. Instead, a cloud seems to
settle over my brain.

My bride's eyes glaze and she falls forward.

I catch her just as hot metal sears through my veins.
"WHAT?" I think, her weight dragging me down to the
floor, the pain blocking any further possibility of thought.

"PAPA!" Henri cries. He rushes to me.

Charles Blood bats him out of the way. *"DAMN IT,
DEREK, YOU BLOODY FOOL! TAKE HOLD OF HIM!"*

Derek grabs Henri. My son wails, tries to break free, but
the older dragon holds him in his grip.

Samantha grabs the leather bag, rummages inside it,
produces two glass vials, one filled with a red liquid, the
other with green. She bends over Chloe, pries open her
jaws, and pours the red liquid into her daughter's mouth.
"There," she says. *"In few minutes you'll be fine."*

She turns to me, forces the green vial into my mouth.
The liquid sears its way down my gullet. My arms and legs
turn rigid. Tremors overtake me and I lie shaking on the
wood floor, my body changing form from dragon to
human, once, then twice, then again, leaving me in human
form, twitching and jerking, every cell of my body in pain.

"Bloody stupid charade this," Charles Blood says. *"He*

never would have drunk from the mug without it," Samantha says.

*"I could have just killed him as soon as he arrived.
Saved us all this blather."*

*"You would have had to fight your daughter too. This
way she couldn't resist."*

Charles glares at her, says, *"Bullocks!"*

*"And what about the information we need? Did you
plan to rip it out of his dead body?"*

Samantha's husband ignores her question. He steps over
me, grabs Henri from Derek. *"You damn well better show
us if you can do this thing,"* he says.

"I can," Derek says. His features smooth as he begins
to change to human shape.

Charles shoves Henri toward Philip. *"Take the boy!"*

"I don't want to," Philip says. *"I don't like any of this."*

The older dragon growls. *"Boy, do as I say. I've killed
sons for refusing less."*

Henri tries to rush toward me but Philip holds him,
more hugging than restraining him.

I find if I breathe deeply I can persevere over the pain.
My body fights me, but slowly I turn my eyes to Chloe.

She moves first her arms, then her legs, turning on her
side, forcing herself half up, sitting on one haunch. Chloe
looks at me. *"Oh, Peter!"* She turns to her mother.
"Why?"

Samantha Blood looks past her daughter, grins.

"Bloody good show of that!" Charles Blood says.

I turn my head to see what they're looking at just as
Chloe does too.

"NO!" she mindspeaks, then lets out a long yowl.

If I could, I'd yell too at the perfectly copied blond
human standing before us, completely like me down to his
cleft chin. Only Derek's smug smile mars the replication.

18

"You're not my papa!" Henri says.

Derek laughs, then says in a voice that sounds eerily like mine, "I'm Peter DelaSangre, son of Don Henri DelaSangre. I live on Blood Key, on the edge of Biscayne Bay, between Wayward Key and the Ragged Keys. I get around on the water in my Grady White—whatever the hell that kind of boat is—and I drive either a Mercedes or a Corvette on land."

Samantha Blood claps her foreclaws together. "Go on," she mindspeaks.

"My business, LaMar Associates, is located on the top floor of the Monroe Building, in Coconut Grove. Arturo Gomez and Ian Tindall manage it for me. Arturo's daughter, Claudia, is currently watching my house. Someone by the name of Rita works as my spy at the office." Derek beams. "How's that?"

I groan, realizing now why Derek had been so full of questions about my life. What else did I tell him during our long journey to the valley? But a cloud seems to be filling my mind, blurring my vision. The voices and thoughts around me grow distant and I have to struggle to understand them.

"What are you going to do with Peter?" Chloe says.

"He'll die in a little while," Samantha says. *"Besides the Death's Rose in the wedding potion—and the nightshade I gave you both instead of alchemist's powder—he's drunk a mugful of dogbane, snakeroot and powdered*

*gumbo limbo sap. I've taught you how to mix potions. You
know the strength of all that."*

*"You can't let him die. He's my mate. His child is grow-
ing inside me!"*

"Chloe, you know better," Samantha says. *"Only the
serum of Witch's Tongue I just gave him is keeping him
alive right now. Once it fades, even the antidote I gave you
won't be able to save him."*

Samantha Blood turns from her daughter, motions to
Charles. *"Pick him up. Make him stand beside Derek. I
want to be sure everything matches."*

The big dragon grabs me under my armpits, yanks me
upright, holds me alongside Derek. I try to take control of
my legs but they could just as well be made from rubber.

"There!" Samantha says, pointing at my crotch, then at
Derek's. *"You have it all wrong."*

Derek grabs himself between the legs. "Mum," he says.
"I like my own better than his. Who's to know anyway?"

"Who knows?" she says. *"The way you are, you'll be
using that as soon as you can. You have no way of knowing who he's been with. For this to work, everyone has to
think you're Peter."*

"Are you done?" Charles asks. Samantha nods and he
releases me.

I slump to the floor. Chloe starts to sidle toward me and
both of her parents glare at her, say in unison, *"STOP!"*

Samantha changes into her human form, goes to the
table returns with a pad and pencil. She crouches next to
me, naked, her breasts swaying with each small movement. "I need phone numbers, Peter, names, addresses."

"What about the treasure?" Charles says. *"Ask him
that."*

"You should know that's not the way Witch's Tongue
works. You have to let it build, start with small questions. . . ." Samantha turns her attention back to me. "Tell
me the phone number of your company, Peter."

The question seems to pierce the cloud in my mind. I
answer her. She writes it down and asks another question.

I answer that too, my voice strange to me, too willing. Still I continue to answer every question she asks as she fills a page, then another with her notes. "See?" Samantha says to her mate. "This is the way to do this. This way Derek will know what to do once he reaches Miami."

As the questioning continues, I find I can shade my answers, never lying but, at least, omitting some details. We fill two more pages of notes before Samantha finally asks, "Do you have treasure too, Peter? Gold and silver?"

I tell myself not to answer but hear my voice say, "Yes."

The naked woman grins. "Is it a large fortune?"

"Yes."

"Where is it kept, Peter?"

It's a struggle for me to stop my mouth from revealing the location, but I try to allow myself a partial answer. "In my house."

Samantha frowns, looks up from her pad. "But where?"

"Underneath."

"Tell me more."

"Underneath my house, in a stone room."

"How can Derek find it?" Her voice turns stern. "Where should he look?"

If I could, I would grin at her frustration. "He should look underneath the house."

The woman asks again and I give her the same answer. She rephrases the question and I still repeat the answer. The interrogation continues until pain overtakes me and my words become slurred, then meaningless.

Charles growls. *"What's this bloody nonsense?"*

Samantha says, "The serum's lost its effect. I think we're done."

"Give him more Witch's Tongue."

"It would only give him a quicker, less painful death."

The elder dragon glares at Derek. *"Our fool son managed to miss finding out the most important thing."*

"He has so much else, Pa . . . stocks, bonds, businesses, real estate, all worth millions," Derek says.

Charles whirls, slams his son with his tail, knocking

him down. Then he straddles him and holds an extended talon to his throat. *"I WANT THE GOLD TOO."*

"Mum?" Derek stays down, looks at Samantha. "Please?"

She holds up one hand toward Charles. "Let him speak."

"I found out everything else—just as you asked. I'm sure I can find the treasure. It's probably in a room under his house. By their cells, like ours is."

"If you weren't so useless, if you didn't bring back so little, we wouldn't have to do any of this."

"You could help!" Derek says, sitting up. "There's nothing that stops you from leaving Cockpit Country!"

"Enough!" Samantha Blood says. "There's nothing to be done now but to go on with the plan. If Derek can't find the treasure, so be it."

"You could ask Peter," Chloe says.

Samantha snorts. "He's dying. He already has lost all ability to control any speech."

Chloe forces herself to her feet and faces her mother. *"I know you and your potions. You can save him . . . if you want to."*

Her mother frowns. "If I wanted to . . . maybe. It still might take weeks to bring him back to full consciousness."

"And why would he tell us then?" Charles says.

"You have his son," Chloe says.

Charles laughs. *"I'd give up either of my two for enough gold."*

"But Peter wouldn't," Chloe says. *"He understands what it is to love a child."*

19

{*Papa? Papa? PAPA!*}

I'm lifted, pulled, carried and laid down. A new vile liquid, thick and bitter, is forced into my mouth. I hack and cough, but can't stop it from flowing down my throat, burning my insides. My pain lessens but I begin to shiver. Someone covers my nakedness with a thin blanket.

Still, cold wet air continues to chill me. Not that I care. Asleep or awake, my world's the same. Pain no longer bothers me. Time means nothing. Voices, mindthoughts are just sounds that come and go, like the creak of my cell door's hinges, or the tiny patter of the rats' feet under my cot.

{*Papa, please, he's taking me away! I don't want to go with him! Please, Papa!*}

Darkness comes, settles around me like an ocean of black ink and I sleep.

{*Peter, can you hear me? Oh, I know you can't answer yet but you have to listen to me. You have to make yourself strong. Mum is doing her best to save you. She says her potions alone can't bring you back. Henri needs you. So do I.*}

Gloom replaces dark and doors open and close.

"Here." A liquid is forced into my throat. Cow's blood this time, not medicine and I welcome its nourishment. But the bitter fluid follows, leaves me shivering again.

Dark again, another night with no thoughts, no dreams, no wishes, no hope.

{*Peter, my love. You must grow strong. My mother and*

*father promise me they won't, but I know they'll kill you
when they no longer need you. Derek has already closed
up your house and left with Henri. If he sends back word
from Miami that he's found your treasure room, Mum will
give you poison again. Please, Peter, you must grow strong
soon!*}

Dark turns to gloom, turns to dark and then gloom
again. Each night Chloe mindspeaks to me. Each night I'm
unable to answer. Twice each day, blood is poured down
my throat, followed by more of Samantha's disgusting
potion. But vile as it is, it works. The shivering declines. I
begin to hear more, see more.

On the fifth night, I wake, wait until all's quiet and sit
up. The blood rushes from my head. My ears roar and a
white circle of light blocks my vision. Not willing to risk
fainting, I lie down. When my eyes clear and the roaring in
my ears finally subsides, I sit up again. Flexing my arms
and legs, I'm amazed at my weakness.

{*Chloe?*} I mindspeak, masked.

{*Peter! You can't know how happy I am to hear you!*}

{*Is Henri okay?*}

{*I think so. I'm not sure just when they left Jamaica.
None of us will know anything for certain until Pa goes to
Claypool and Son's in Kingston and finds out what mes-
sages Derek's sent back.*}

Of course, I think. The Bloods have no phones. Certainly no mailman would dare venture into this wilderness.
I could never live like this—so cut off from the world.
But, I realize, for the time being I'm as isolated as they
are. And my son must feel more alone than I do.

Poor Henri, far away with only an indifferent uncle for
company. Rage rises within me. {*Chloe, I am going to kill
all of them—your brother and your parents.*}

{*No. You can't. If Henri hasn't been hurt, you can't kill
any of them. They're still my family.*}

{*And if Henri's been harmed?*} I shudder at the thought.

{*Then I will help you kill each and every one of them,*}
Chloe says.

I force myself to my feet, waver in the darkness. {*Come help me get out of here.*}

{*You need to rest. You need to get stronger first.*}

Feeling my way to the cell door, I say, {*I don't want to wait. Please come.*} I find the door, tug on it. It doesn't budge.

{*I can't,*} Chloe says. {*They've locked me in my room and shuttered my windows. Not even Philip is allowed to visit me. The only time I see anyone beside Mum and Pa is when my servant, Lila, brings me my meals. See, Peter, you have to grow strong so you can escape and come back to rescue me.*}

{*All of it without hurting your family,*} I say.

{*No, dear. I didn't say you can't hurt them. I just said you can't kill them.*}

It takes all my will to feign unconsciousness when Samantha Blood and her servant come in to feed me and administer her potion. But I lie still and allow her to treat me. At first, I doubt whether I have the strength to overpower her anyway. Later, as I feel my muscles growing, I still doubt whether, at full strength, I could best both her and her husband in any struggle.

I begin to pester Chloe about my escape. Each day of waiting must be unbearable for Henri. I can hardly stand it myself. {*No,*} she says. {*Lila's told me of a way you can leave without any chance of my parents' stopping you or finding you. Philip's promised to help. Lila warned it might be very difficult. You must be as strong as you can be before you attempt it.*}

{*Aren't you coming with me?*}

{*I would if it was just me—no matter how dangerous it was. But we have a child to worry about. I won't risk our daughter. You'll just have to remember to come back for me once you get out.*}

I wait, feigning unconsciousness each day, exercising in the dark each night, worrying about my son in Miami and my mate imprisoned above me.

Finally, one night Chloe says, {*It's time. Are you strong enough, Peter?*}

{*Yes.*}

{*Mum told me you're hopeless. I think she may be planning to give you a different potion, a fatal one soon. Lila will come to you later tonight when my parents leave to hunt.*}

{*But if your parents are out hunting, they may spot me once I take to the air.*}

{*That's not the way you're leaving,*} Chloe says.

I stand as soon as I hear the key in the lock on my cell door. Philip swings the door open, gives me a wide grin. A short black, gray-haired and wrinkled Jamaican woman who I guess is Lila, the servant who brought up Chloe, stands beside him, holding a lit candle. I hold up my hands in front of my eyes, wince at the light.

"You sure you want to go that way?" Philip says.

Looking down at my naked human body, I shrug. "Your parents never saw fit to return my clothes."

"They'd just get wet anyway," Lila says and turns. "Follow me."

I look at Philip for an explanation. He holds his hands up, showing me his palms, "Hey, my job was to get hold of the key and let you out. From here on it's up to Lila."

She leads us past the cells to a large empty room at the end of the corridor. Dozens of old, rusty iron shackles hang on the walls. Skeletons and bones litter the floor. The air smells of ancient decay. "This is where the Bloods used to punish their enemies," Lila says.

She picks her way through the bones, walking farther toward the back of the wall. As I follow her, I begin to feel a faint breeze, cold and wet, smelling of bat guano and stale air. "Here," she says, standing in front of a crack in the wall, narrow but possibly just wide enough for a determined man to squeeze himself through.

The candle's flame dances with the breeze. "There's a

river flowing through a cave on the other side of this. Some of us have escaped from here this way," she says.

"Did they make it out?" Philip says.

"I don't know. At least they never came back."

I reach toward the candle. "May I take this?"

"You may, but it won't help very much." Lila hands it to me. "Please lead us out of the room before you leave us in darkness."

Taking them back to the corridor, I say to Chloe's brother, "Are you both going to be okay, once your parents find I've escaped?"

Philip smiles. "They'll rant and rave, but as long as they don't know for sure how it happened, I think they'll leave all of us alone. For sure, neither Lila nor I are going to say anything."

"Thanks," I say to them. "If I can ever help you . . ."

"Hey, we're doing it for Chloe," Philip says. "My parents were wrong to do what they did. This has nothing to do with any tradition. They just want your wealth. Come back, rescue your wife, that's all we want."

20

The ragged masonry scrapes my skin, scratching my back and my chest as I push through the crack in the wall sideways. When I'm finally on the other side of the wall, I hold up the candle and examine my surroundings.

Its feeble light barely penetrates the darkness. A few scattered stalagmites point up, waist high near me; otherwise, the ground looks smooth, wet, slippery. I have a sense of standing inside a huge cavern, but I can see neither the top of the cave nor its other walls. Wrinkling my nose at the dampness in the cold, stale air, I listen, hear only the dripping of water everywhere and the faint rush of flowing water somewhere, off in the dark.

{*Peter. Are you on the way?*} Chloe mindspeaks, masked.

{*Yes.*} I look at the half-melted candle, the darkness crowding around me, and smile. This is a fine mess you've gotten me into, I think. Taking a deep breath, I walk forward, toward the sound of running water.

{*Peter? Is everything all right?*}

My foot slips and I grab onto the tip of a stalagmite with my free hand. {*Everything's fine,*} I say. {*I'm in some sort of enormous cave and I have no idea where I'm going. What could be wrong with that?*}

{*If you think it's too dangerous, come back.*}

I turn, look behind me. Already the crevice is lost in the darkness. {*Not an option,*} I say.

{*We should have thought of another way. I don't want to lose you.*}

The candlelight glints off running water. I rush forward, sigh when I find a rivulet, no more than two feet wide. I decide to walk alongside it, see where it goes.

{*Peter?*}

I sigh again, stop. {*I don't plan to be lost and I don't plan to lose you either. But I need to concentrate now. Tell me what time it is.*}

{*One-fifteen in the morning.*}

{*If I don't call to you by ten, mindspeak me then.*}

{*I will, Peter. Be careful.*}

Sure, I think as I walk forward, I'll try to avoid being lost forever. I'll make every attempt I can to step around any deep holes. I'll be intent on not starving to death.

The bubbling and gurgling of the pool alerts me to its presence before I see it and the wall behind it. About ten feet in diameter, the tiny lagoon accepts the rivulet's flow without rising. I hold the candle high, try to see where the water might be flowing.

I find no sign of it, realize the water has to be flowing out somewhere beneath the pool's surface. Stepping closer, I find skeletons scattered around the water's perimeter. Lila's escapees, I think and shake my head.

Squatting by the pool, I study it, then look at the small nub of wax in my hand. As a youth I used to practice holding my breath underwater. In my human form, I rarely could go longer than six minutes, but in my natural form I never had a problem staying down thirty minutes or more. I put the candle on the cave floor beside me and will my body to change, sighing as my skin and bones shift.

At my full size, I'm almost too big for the pool. I go in headfirst, feeling around the wet, slippery walls until I find the passageway, the rushing water tugging at me to follow it. Once I'm sure the hole is large enough for me, I surface, take a great gulp of air and then another. After my lungs are so full that one more breath is impossible, I dive.

The current takes me and I swim with it as it carries me away from the candle's last few flickers into complete darkness. All I can hope is that the river surfaces somewhere before I run out of air.

Lost in wet darkness, I find only the gradual increase of my need to breathe gives me any sense of how much time has passed. When my lungs finally begin to burn, I sip water to ease my distress. It provides little relief and I sip again. Chloe, I think, I should say good-bye to her while I can.

The passage thins and the water shoots me forward — the walls scraping against my scales, a roaring sound growing somewhere ahead of me. A stone jutting from the wall clips my right shoulder, another cracks into my head and shocked, stunned, I inhale water, my lungs convulsing. I try to expel the fluid from my lungs but have no air left to push it out.

Suddenly, I'm spit out, carried along with a torrent of water falling through dark, open air. Coughing, sputtering, I gasp deep breaths. I try to open my wings but the pressure of the water cascading from above me batters them closed.

I slam into a wet surface and the waterfall drives me under. This time I use every part of my body — my wings, my legs, my tail — to fight the current. Finally, I break the surface of the water and gulp air, filling my lungs once again, swimming forward in the dark until I bump into a muddy bank.

Digging in the mud with my claws, I eventually get enough purchase to climb up and reach dry land. Breathing hard, my body battered and scratched from my underwater journey, I collapse to the ground immediately and surrender to sleep.

{*Peter? Peter?*}
No, I shake my head, try to cling to sleep.
{*Peter, it's after ten. Are you okay?*}
I groan, turn on the sandy ground. {*Mostly,*} I mindspeak. Opening my eyes, I'm surprised to find a faint light illuminating my surroundings.

{*Do you know where you are?*}

My muscles ache. As I stand up, every injured part of me registers its protest. I look around. {*I have no idea. . . . I was in a river last night and I think it carried me a long way. There's a little bit of light here, a very tall waterfall and a huge circular lake. . . .*}

{*Is there an opening?*}

{*I don't know yet.*} I look above the waterfall and my mouth drops open.

{*Peter?*}

{*The cave's gigantic! There's even room for me to fly.*} I stare at the cave's roof hundreds of feet above me, the few thin beams of light coming from narrow crevices surrounded by thousands of hanging bats. {*And every bat in Jamaica must live here. The place reeks of guano.*}

I study everything again. {*But I don't see any crevices large enough to use.*}

{*I wish there were,*} Chloe mindspeaks, her thoughts sad, muted.

For the first time since I entered the cave, I think of my bride's position. What agony it must be for her to sit in her room and wait, unable to do anything. {*Are you all right? Is something happening there?*} I say.

{*Pa and Mum are furious. You had to know they would be. They know we can mask our thoughts to each other— all of us can. They've told me, if you don't return soon or tell me where the treasure is, Henri will suffer the consequences.*}

{*Would they really hurt their daughter's son?*}

{*I don't know. Pa might. It's really up to Mum. Derek will do whatever he's told. Pa said he'll give you a few more days. After that he plans to drive to Kingston, to see what messages Derek has sent. If my brother found your treasure, I'm sure no one will be harmed.*}

I think of the secret passageway, the door hidden in the bushes. {*I doubt your brother will ever find the treasure room.*}

{*Then we need you to find your way out soon.*}

{*If it's possible, I will,*} I say. I wish I were as positive as my words, but I know all too well how much my body needs rest, nourishment and healing.

{*We should have found another way.*}

{*We didn't*}, I say. {*So we'll just have to make this way work.*}

{*What are you going to do?*}

The light within the cave flickers as a few bats leave their perches. I stare at them and scowl. Disgusting foul creatures. But, if I'm to go on, I need nourishment. {*First, I'm going to feed.*}

{*On what, Peter?*}

I look up and scowl again. {*I'll tell you later.*}

Flying to the cave roof, I gorge myself on dozens of bats, gulping them in midair as they swarm and try to escape me, grimacing at my need to feed on the tough, leathery, foul-tasting beasts, wishing there was another way to provide the meat and blood my body demands.

Afterwards, I return to my bed of sand and stone and heal my scrapes and bruises, reinvigorate my muscles. Sleep tries to take me but I resist. Chloe and Henri need me to press on.

I search the cave, working my way around towering stalagmites, scooting under dangling stalactites—like a creature working its way through a giant monster's teeth—until I find a small stream flowing from the end of the lake opposite the waterfall into a dark passageway.

I follow the stream, a weak breeze pushing me forward into the inky black. Stopping just before the darkness engulfs me, I gaze back at the relative comfort of the lighted cavern and a sigh escapes my lips.

Feeling my way forward, I keep my foreclaws in front of me, always following the stream, letting the wind at my back keep me on course. For what feels like hours, or days, I walk through passage after passage, working my way through forests of stalactites and stalagmites as the river widens and strengthens.

{*Peter?*}

I resist the temptation to stop.{*Is it morning already?*}

{*It's already nine, love. Are you doing okay?*}

{*For someone who has no idea where they are, I'm doing fine.*}

{*I hope so,*} she says. {*Pa asks me every morning, when are you going to tell him what he wants? You have to get here before he leaves for Kington.*}

Rushing on as quickly as I dare, I bump against rocks, stumble over projections of stone. One cavern gives way to the other, the river growing, getting louder—the breeze shoving me forward. Chloe lets me know when the day has passed, when midnight arrives.

Not daring to rest, I stumble forward, only stopping when I hear the roar of the river as it falls into a chasm somewhere in front of me. The breeze doesn't follow it and I let it guide me, feeling the way with my feet, smiling when I find a small lip of stone which thankfully skirts the chasm and then widens into a gravelly path.

"Way cool!"

"Fucking A!"

I grin at the sound of the voices, obviously American, almost laugh with delight when I see the faint glow of the cavers' lights.

Changing to my human form, I rush toward the glow, bumping and scraping against rocks, ignoring the scratches and the blood that follows. I find the light comes from a narrow passageway to the right of my path. I squeeze into it, sigh when it widens almost immediately.

The air reeks of marijuana smoke. I follow a curved passage toward its source.

"Come on, man. It's late. You got your pictures. Let's get on to the monument, shoot a few pictures there and get out of here."

"Just a few more."

A camera's flash fills the small chamber with bright light just as I enter from the passageway. I freeze, blink away the dots that flare before my eyes. Two young, white men dressed in muddy clothes, helmets with lights on their heads, stare at me from the other side of the chamber, a dark brown stalagmite—looking like a rabbit sitting on its back legs—between us.

The shorter of the men holds a lit handrolled cigarette in his hand. He draws a deep hit, holds the smoke, then exhales and holds the joint out to me. "Hey, man. Want some?"

I shake my head. That's not what I want.

The other one, the man with the camera, looks to be about my size. He says, "Nude caving? And I thought we were radical."

Smiling, I walk toward him. "I've been lost. It's a long story. Where are we?"

"This is the Brer Rabbit passage," the camera guy says. "You go out to the passageway where you came in, it's a straight shot out to the cave entrance. You got three main chambers, Wharf, Big Yard and Royal Flat, maybe a couple thousand feet altogether and you're out."

"What cave?" I say. My stomach growls, reminds me how long I've gone without nourishment. These two look so young, so full of energy. I wish there were a way I could spare them, know there isn't.

The men look at each other. Again the cameraman answers. "Windsor, man. Just how lost are you?"

I shrug, walk around the stalagmite to them. "Can you guys give me a lift?"

"Yeah, sure." This time the shorter man answers. "Eric's got his dad's Jeep outside. We just need to finish here and then we're going to leave. We want to be long gone before daybreak."

"What are you planning to use for clothes?" the cameraman says. I grab his head, snap his neck. He falls like a rag doll. The shorter man drops his smoking joint, backs up. "What the fuck, man? What gives? We weren't doing you no harm."

"I know," I say, following him, allowing him to back into the wall. "I just need what you have."

I carry both bodies back to the main passageway, drag them back to where the river drops. Stripping them, I change into my natural shape and feed. Fresh meat! I gorge myself, then drop their remains into the river below, kicking the bloodstained dirt after them.

Fighting both the languor that always overtakes me after a large meal and the exhaustion of my journey, I change back to my human form and try on the larger man's clothes. Too snug. Frowning, I flex my shoulders against the fabric, feeling like a sausage in its casing. But I've no desire to waste time and energy shrinking my body to fit the clothes. It's good enough to have clothes and shoes on again and light to show me my way.

I think about going home to Bartlet House for some of my own clothes, but there's no guarantee Derek has left any of it. Besides, as close as the house may be, going there would only take away time I might need to drive to Morgan's Hole and prepare to confront Charles Blood.

Putting on the man's helmet, I rifle both men's pockets until I find the keys to the man's Jeep, their money—only two hundred and twenty-three dollars between both of them—and their credit cards. Then I open the camera and expose the film to my headlamp's light. Dropping it, the camera, the credit cards and the rest of their possessions into the river below, I pocket the money and turn and rush out the passageway. A crudely made path takes me through the three chambers, just as the larger man had mentioned, to Windsor cave's entrance.

Outside, I pause, look up at the early morning sky, the night's dark beginning to be muted by the first brush of dawn's light. A flock of green parrots rustle in the branches of a nearby African tulip tree, breaking the quiet with their cacophony. I breathe in the fresh air, find not a trace of the foul aroma of guano and grin.

The Jeep, its top down, sits not a dozen yards from the

entrance. I walk to it, wipe the wetness of the morning dew off the seat as well as I can and get in. The motor turns over at the first turn of the key. {*Chloe,*} I mindspeak. {*I'm out.*}

I have to call two more times before she replies. {*What?*} she says. {*Peter?*}

{*I'm on the way.*} I put the car in reverse, turn it and drive back to the main road.

{*Where are you?*}

{*Outside Windsor, not far from Cockpit Country. I have a Jeep. I think I can remember the way back to Morgan's Hole.*}

{*And then what? You can't fight both of them. Father's difficult enough by himself.*}

{*If I were going to fight them, I'd just fly to Morgan's Hole. When is your father leaving for Kingston?*}

{*He says tomorrow. I'm amazed he's really going to do it. I had to beg him for months just to get him to tell Derek to teach me how to drive. He only would if I promised to never drive outside the valley. Pa hates cars. I don't think he's been in one since he tried out the Land Rover when Derek brought it home. That was eight years ago.*}

{*And your mother?*}

{*She'll stay here to watch things.*}

{*Can't Philip?*}

{*No. They locked him up too. After you escaped. What are you thinking of, Peter?*}

As much as I'd like to thrash Charles Blood, I worry about his size. {*I'm thinking there has to be another way to handle your father.*} I drive across the path to Troy, turn into Cockpit Country, grin when I find I can make out the faint path Derek had followed.

{*What if you fail?*}

{*If they don't kill me first, I'll tell them everything they need to know about the treasure. There's no need for Henri to suffer. But . . .*} I picture the steep sinkhole near the pass into Morgan's Hole, the large jagged stones pointing up from its bottom. {*I don't think it will come to that.*}

* * *

Even driving slower than Derek had, I reach the pass into Morgan's Hole well before night. I drive past the sink-hole, turn back and drive past it again, looking until I find a place where I can back the Jeep off the road and conceal it in the brush, the greenery making a canopy over the vehicle, hiding and shading it.

I busy myself the rest of the daylight hours, taking leaves and branches, camouflaging the Jeep even more, so there's no chance anyone can spot it from the road.

When night comes, I retreat to the driver's seat. My body aches, my stomach growls, my eyelids threaten to close of their own volition. {*Chloe?*} I call.

{*Yes?*}

{*How will you know when your father leaves?*}

{*I'll hear him.*}

{*Please let me know as soon as you do. I need to rest now.*}

{*I will.*}

{*Chloe, we should be together tomorrow.*}

{*I'd like that very much, Peter.*}

{*I won't let anyone separate us ever again.*}

{*Sleep, Peter. I'll be waiting for you.*}

21

Rain pummels me during the night. Insects try to torment me. Still, no matter what the disturbance, I wake only momentarily, then return to sleep. Only Chloe's call, a few hours after dawn, rouses me completely from my slumber. {*Wake up! Pa's on his way.*}

I jerk upright in my seat, turn the ignition, let the motor idle, warm up. {*He should be here in a few minutes,*} I say.

Chloe's laugh fills my head and I grin. I haven't heard such a happy sound from her since before our feast. {*You've never seen Pa drive,*} she says. {*It will be longer than you think.*}

Fifteen minutes pass, then a half hour before I hear the low grumble of the Land Rover's engine. I stand, lean over the windshield and push some branches out of the way, to give me a better view. Then I sit and put the Jeep in gear, wait for Charles Blood to come into sight.

The Land Rover finally creeps into view, Charles Blood squeezing the wheel with both hands, like an old man, as he peers through the windshield, through the side windows, from left to right, staring at the path.

I wait until the car is directly in front of me and then jam the gas pedal to the floor. The Jeep leaps forward, crunches into the Land Rover's driver's side door. The door buckles, window glass crumbling and falling as, *bang,* the driver's airbag inflates. To my dismay the impact knocks the Land Rover only a foot to the side.

Stunned by the crash, pinned momentarily to his seat by

the airbag, Charles turns, stares at me. *"YOU!"* he mind-speaks. *"YOU'RE DEAD!"*

My foot remains mashed down on the pedal. All four tires spin and dig for purchase. The Land Rover skitters a few more inches to the side. I grit my teeth, hold the wheel, my foot pressed down.

Dust and exhaust surround the Jeep. The other car skitters sideways a couple of inches more, then a foot.

Charles realizes my intent. "Damn you!" he shouts. He jams his gas pedal to the floor a moment too late. The car attempts to shoot forward just as two of its tires slip over the edge of the sinkhole. The Land Rover's tires spin, touch only air.

I take my foot off the pedal, shift to neutral, hit the brake and watch the Land Rover slip, almost in slow motion, into the sinkhole. It catches on some vegetation or a ledge, its motion frozen for a moment, the two driver's side wheels up in the air, the car's underbody exposed to me.

"Enough," Charles Blood mindspeaks. *"You've bloody well beaten me. Help me out of this thing."*

"And then?" I say.

Charles's arms reach out of his window. His head emerges. I watch as he begins to force himself out the window. *"And then I'll rip you to bloody shreds!"*

I throw my car into gear, jam down the gas pedal again. The Jeep jumps forward, crashes into the Land Rover's underbelly.

I slam on the brakes as the Land Rover falls over, somersaulting down the side of the sinkhole, Charles Blood still inside.

Getting out of the Jeep, I rush to the side of the sinkhole, watch the car hit and turn as it descends, striking trees, caroming into boulders, until it finally reaches the large white rocks jutting skyward at the depression's bottom and crashes top down, impaling itself on the largest of the rocks, the car's wheels continuing to spin, engaging only air.

I'd hoped there would be a huge ball of flame, like in the movies. But I shrug—this way the vile creature will just be injured, not killed, as Chloe wishes.

As if to confirm my suspicions, Charles mindspeaks, *"Samantha! I need you. I'm pinned inside this bloody car."*

"What? What happened?"

"Damn it, woman! I'll tell you the story later. Right now everything in my body is broken. I need you to help me. I'm right outside the pass, in the sinkhole."

"How did that happen?"

"That damned Peter. Come quick!"

Samantha Blood, in her natural form, flies over me as I drive into the valley. She sees me and circles back. *"If you stop to fight me, your husband may die,"* I mindspeak. *"Go help him. I've no need to kill you."*

"If you and our daughter aren't gone before we return, you will be attacked," she says.

I think of Charles's many injuries. How weak he'll be. How much need he'll have for food, rest and sustenance. *"If you do fight us now, you'll both die. Do you want to force your daughter to participate in your deaths?"*

She flies off without answering.

{*Peter! Are you almost here?*} Chloe mindspeaks.

{*Almost. Are you ready?*}

{*Ready? I can't wait to get out of this damned room. I've had all my clothes and things laid out on my bed since Pa left this morning. Just get my door open, let me find a few bags to pack it all up in and we can be gone.*}

As soon as I drive up to the front of the house, I jam on the brakes and jump out. Grabbing a tire iron from the back of the Jeep, I rush to the steps, take them two at a time and hurry to her room.

I find her door held closed by an iron bar secured with an ancient iron padlock, fastened to a rusted hasp. I shake my head—that any parent would imprison their daughter like this—and swing the tire iron at the lock. Sparks fly.

The clang of metal striking metal reverberates through the house. But the lock holds.

{*Peter, you could go for the key, you know. I've a fairly good idea where Mum keeps it.*}

{*This is quicker,*} I say, drawing in a breath, raising the tire iron over my head. I swing again and once again. The lock holds.

I can hear Chloe's laugh through the door. {*Silly,*} she mindspeaks. {*It might be quicker if you go down the corridor to my parents' room and look in the top drawer of—*}

"I don't need to do that!" I shout, swinging the tire iron again, as hard as my body allows, the shock of the impact numbing my hands, the hasp tearing free of the wood, the padlock shattering into pieces and falling to the floor. Throwing the bar away from the door, I open it.

My bride greets me in her human form, sitting on the edge of her bed, her hands clasped together, tight to her chest in an adoring pose. "My hero," Chloe says, her voice mock serious.

I frown at her obvious teasing. "The door's open isn't it?" I say.

Chloe nods. "And a key might have made a whole lot less fuss," she says, grinning. She gets up and comes to me, wrapping her arms around me. "It looks like you might get to be a little bit too stubborn sometimes. But"—she kisses me—"this time I think it was cute."

I hold her, return her kiss, revel at the softness of her lips, the press of her body against mine. I'm tempted to hug her as long as she permits, but I know too well that Charles and Samantha Blood will return soon.

Breaking free, I say, "We have to go."

Chloe nods, but doesn't move away. She stares into my eyes, smiles.

I shake my head. "We need to get away from here," I say.

Still she stares. "I'm glad you're here."

"Me too." I look at her clothes laid out on her bed. "Where can we find suitcases?"

"You don't get it. I think I'm really falling in love with you. I never was sure I could feel like this."

I sigh. "Chloe, I'm glad. I love you too, but we have to go. What about Philip?"

"This is his home. He doesn't want to leave."

I shrug. "Then we need to go."

Chloe nods, motions for me to follow her and leads me to her mother's room. I stand by, tapping my foot while she rummages in a closet and finally comes out with two leather suitcases. She hands them to me, gives me an impish smile, says, "I need to find a couple of other things," and goes back into the closet.

She emerges a few minutes later with a small wicker box and an ancient book, its leather binding cracked and peeling.

"What's all this?" I say.

"Oh, all of Mum's herbs and roots and leaves, all the ingredients . . . and her recipes, everything we need to make potions, especially wedding potions." She giggles. "Mum may be mad now, but she'll be furious when she finds all this gone." Chloe smiles wide enough to show all her teeth. "But you didn't think I'd go away with you without knowing how we could finally wed each other properly. Did you?"

"Mum, we're on our way," Chloe mindspeaks to Samantha Blood as we speed through the valley in the Jeep.

"Good riddance to both of you."

Chloe winces at the cold tone of her mother's thoughts. *"It's not fair of you to be like this. I'm your daughter. That should matter to you. I've done you no wrong."*

"You've chosen against us."

"What do you expect? He's my mate, the father of my daughter."

"He betrayed your sister. He'll betray you too."

"He will not!"

"He almost killed your father. Come see him, Chloe. It

will take hours for me to maneuver your father out of this wreck. Look at your pa's bloody mangled body, pinned inside the car by rocks and twisted metal and tell me I should accept Peter as part of our blood."

"Pa would have killed him, if he could have."

"I wish he had."

"Mum, I wish you would accept us. You have two grandchildren you'll never see."

Samantha's harsh laugh fills our minds. *"Who said you'll ever get Henri back? My husband isn't the only Blood who can best Peter in a fair fight. Look at Derek and look at Peter and tell me which one is more powerful."*

"Mum, please!"

"Leave! Just remember my husband will heal. Once he does, you'll have more than Derek to worry about."

Chloe shakes her head, bites her lip. She shuts herself off, accepts no further thoughts from her mother, though the woman keeps calling out, scolding her the whole time it takes us to exit the valley and skirt around the steep sinkhole in front of the pass.

My bride stares through the windshield as we drive. Her legs drawn close to her, her bare feet on her car seat, Chloe says nothing, and hugs her knees.

I resist the desire to stop the car and take her in my arms. Likewise, I avoid trying to talk her out of her mood. Her mother has injured her and nothing I can say or do will heal that wound.

Reaching for her, I rub her cheek with the back of my hand. She leans into my touch and I smile. It's enough for me now to have her by my side. We have years for talking.

The terrain passes and I barely take notice of it. Samantha Blood's warning impresses me as a sincere threat. What to do now that my mate sits safe and secure at my side occupies my thoughts. I weigh our options, try to decide the best way to travel back to Miami — without papers or enough money to buy our way.

Chloe finally turns to me, as we drive out of Cockpit

Country, onto the road to Windsor. "We have to go to Kingston," she says.

I look at her, cock an eyebrow, say, "Now?"

"Claypool and Sons is in Kingston. Virgil Claypool will be holding all of Derek's messages for Pa. Don't you think we need to see what they say?"

"Sure." I look at the sun, how low it sits in the sky. "It's going to be dark soon. What good will it do for us to get there after the office closes?"

Chloe shrugs.

"Kingston can wait until tomorrow," I say. "We can stop at Bartlet House for the night."

"And do what?" My bride grins at me, puts her hand on my shoulder.

I smile at her touch. "Whatever we want, Chloe," I say. "Whatever we want."

22

By the time we reach Bartlet House, the day has turned dim. Shadows stretch over us as we make our way up the driveway. To my relief the yellow Land Rover, while now covered by a canvas tarpaulin, still remains parked by the front door where I left it. I hope that the small magnetic box holding the car's spare key remains in place where Granny said he secreted it—inside the front driver's side tire well.

I'm well aware that we're driving in a Jeep that belongs to two missing men. "We can get rid of this car after dark," I tell Chloe, then point to my car. "We can use that one tomorrow."

She nods, gets out of the Jeep at the same time as I do. Silence greets us.

No household staff comes out to welcome us. No watchdogs show themselves. No horses bray or whinny in their stalls. Chloe follows me to the stable. "This must be what a ghost town feels like," I say, throwing open the door, finding each stall empty, the dirt floor raked clean of any sign of hay.

Chloe puts her hand on my shoulder. "I told you Derek closed up the house," she says.

I nod. "It's still spooky," I say. I go back to the car, pull off the tarpaulin and feel for the small box in the tire well. Once I find it, I pull it out, open it and show Chloe the spare key.

She smiles, says, "Too bad you didn't hide the house key in there too."

Too bad indeed. I test the front door, find it locked. We walk around the house, find every window closed, every door locked too. At the veranda door, Chloe says, "We don't have to stay here. We could stay at one of the hotels on the coast."

I think of all the nights I just spent sleeping in the cell beneath Chloe's house—the miserable and meager rest I had, both in the cave and in the Jeep. Shaking my head, hard, I say, "No," and slam my shoulder into the veranda door. The door shudders, but doesn't give way.

"I want to sleep in my own damned bed tonight!" I say as I smash into the door again, the frame splintering but still holding.

Chloe stares at me, a bemused smile on her face. "It might have been easier to drive to a hotel," she says.

Glaring at her, I thud into the door again, splinters flying as the frame gives way. Pushing the door open, I give Chloe a triumphant smile and motion for her to enter.

Inside, the only light comes from around the edges of the drawn curtains and closed shades. Sheets cover all the furniture. The air is warm and stale, as if the house has been closed for weeks. Chloe wrinkles her nose at the musty smell, watches as I flick a wall switch.

Lights go on. "At least we still have power," I say, going to the thermostat, turning it until the air-conditioning kicks on. Just the drone of the compressor and dull whir of the fan operating makes the house feel less dead.

"And not much else," Chloe calls from the great room.

I join her. Except for two CDs and one videotape, the entertainment center's bare, all electronics gone. In the kitchen we find the pantry and the freezer devoid of food, all the smaller appliances missing too.

Chloe picks up a phone, holds the handset so I can hear the dial tone. "They haven't turned off the phone yet," she says.

"Great!" I take the telephone from her and dial Lamar Associates in Miami. A recording comes on, Sarah's voice, explaining the office has closed for the day and detailing the company's business hours. I disconnect and dial Arturo's cellphone number. It rings at least a dozen times before a mechanical voice asks me to leave a message. I hang up.

Chloe puts her hand on the phone when I start to dial Claudia Gomez's number and says, "Peter. They're all going to think Derek is you. You have to know that. What are you going to accomplish by calling any of them now?"

Hanging up the phone, I sigh. "I just want to know that Henri's okay."

"We'll find out at Claypool's tomorrow," Chloe says. She hugs me. "I'm sure Derek hasn't harmed Henri. He has no reason to."

My bedroom is as stripped as the rest of the house, my clothes all gone, the mattress bare. Chloe goes to the linen closet and returns empty-handed. "They've taken everything," she says. "We'll have to use the sheets on the furniture to make the bed."

I shrug.

"Of course." Chloe approaches me, puts her arms around my neck, smiles at me, her lips only inches from mine. "We could use it just as it is." She kisses me once, softly, then backs up, saying, "You know what we never got to do on our wedding night?" as she pulls off her top—revealing her bare chocolate breasts, her dark soft nipples just starting to grow taut.

Shaking my head, I breathe deep at the sight of her. Chloe and I have spent so little time together. Nothing would be nicer than to lie down with her, forget my responsibilities for a while. But I know there are things we have to do. "We have to get rid of the Jeep yet," I say.

"We will." Chloe grins a bad girl grin at me, undulates her hips as she shimmies out of her jeans. "We just should do this first."

"We need to find food."

Chloe makes a fake pout. "I'm not hungry." She pulls

down her powder blue bikini panties and kicks them out of the way. "I want something else."

Watching me as I stare at her, she flops back on the bed, naked, lying on her back, her legs spread, every part of her in view. "It's your turn now," she says.

I stand at the foot of the bed and fight to control my body. But my loins stir anyway. I can't turn away. I can't keep my eyes off her. "We need to leave early in the morning," I say. "We should rest."

Chloe moves down in bed, reaches with her foot, pushes it against my crotch. "There's plenty of time for that later," she says, rubbing me with her foot, smiling at my hardness.

After lovemaking, after we've disposed of the Jeep, after we've hunted and fed together, after we've made love again in our natural forms, after we've returned home, Chloe and I gather up sheets and make the bed as best we can.

Because Elizabeth preferred sleeping in her natural form and I preferred my human shape, we often slept separately. Chloe delights me by joining me in bed, snuggling close, her head on my arm, her bare back pressed against my front, her smooth skin warm against mine. "I hope you don't mind," she says. "I'm used to sleeping in my human form."

Her body heat wakes me in the middle of the night and I attempt to pull away—to cool myself. But Chloe moans in her sleep and pins my arm with her head. I grin and cast off the sheets instead and Chloe pushes against me. Embracing her, I put my lips on the back of her neck and, feeling the rise and fall of her breathing, loving being so close to her, I drift off again.

The touch of hands on my body, holding me, stroking, teasing and then the touch of lips on my flesh, rouse me from deep slumber. I lie half awake, my eyes closed, and let the hands move me where they will—let the lips, the mouth, bring me to a sore, but willing tumescence.

When Chloe rolls me onto my back, straddles me and slides me inside her, I smile at the warm, wet pleasure of her and reach up with both hands to fondle her breasts. But they're fuller than I remember, more pendulous. I crack my eyes open—just enough to see that the first rays of daybreak have already penetrated the bedroom. Then I open my eyes farther and see the pale skin and the blond hair of the woman above me.

I gasp and pull my hands away.

The blonde guffaws and collapses against me laughing as I slip away from her. The woman says between whoops of laughter, "Peter, it's me! It's me, Chloe!"

But the yellow hair that cascades on me is soft and silky with none of the wiry body of Chloe's hair. The skin is creamy white, without any hint of ever having been exposed to the sun. Chloe sits back up, still straddling me, cups her breasts in both hands and laughs again. "I thought I should change before we left for Kingston," she says, swiveling from side to side, exposing her breasts, fluffing her blond hair, modeling her new appearance for me. "Don't you think Virgil Claypool would find it odd that Charles and Samantha Blood have a black daughter?"

I know she's right but still she looks too much like a cross between a Barbie doll and a younger edition of her mother for me to be comfortable with her new look. Touching her breasts again, I say, "Did you think Mr. Claypool would be put off with your own breast size too?"

Chloe puts her hands on top of mine and giggles. "I just thought these went better with the blond hair."

"You are going to change back after we leave Claypool's, aren't you?" I say.

"That depends on you," Chloe says, moving her body against mine, touching me until I grow hard again. "Show me how much you want me to be back to my old self."

We stop in Falmouth long enough to shop on Market Street for fresh clothes for me and a new outfit to show off

Chloe's new, more ample body—a green silk dress, she decides, with a plunging neckline.

After the bumpy, slow country roads of the interior, the A1, the modern highway that runs along the coast, is a pure delight. It's still early enough in the day for the road to be relatively uncongested and we speed along past Runaway Bay and Ocho Rios without incident. But once the highway curves inland at Port Maria, traffic thickens with cars packed with passengers and trucks full of produce and other cargo, all heading for Kingston.

Drivers jockey for position, shouting, cursing at each other, beeping their horns. At an intersection where I seem to be the only driver unwilling to creep through a red light, Chloe loses patience. "Let me drive," she says. I shrug and change places with her.

"Our women are the true warriors among us," my father used to say, chuckling. *"None of us would dare be as reckless as they."* Chloe is no exception. She accelerates into traffic and weaves around a Toyota compact, swerving just in time to barely miss an oncoming pickup truck.

She turns, flashes a wide smile. "I love this!" she says. I nod, make sure my seat belt is properly fastened.

Just before Annoto Bay, Chloe turns onto the A3, driving through the center of the country, climbing the foothills of the Blue Mountains. "Look," I say to Chloe and point at the beauty around us, but she stares forward, her jaw set, intent on the road and the competing drivers.

We reach Kingston well before noon, descend from the mountains with the whole city laid out beneath us. "We're going to New Kingston," Chloe says. "Derek talks about it all the time. Claypool's offices are at the top of the Garvey Building at the intersection of Halfway Tree and Hope Road. Derek says it's the tallest building around and the only all white one."

I point to a white rectangular building, inelegant in its simplicity, surrounded by smaller but much better designed office buildings. "That must be it," I say.

Chloe nods and maneuvers the Land Rover through

traffic that suddenly is as intense as in any other large city. It takes us thirty minutes before we finally find a parking spot in a lot across the street from the Garvey Building. Once Chloe turns off the ignition, she looks at me. "Please let me do the talking when we get up there," she says.

Claypool and Sons offices may be on the top floor of a major office building, but they possess neither the size nor the elegance of LaMar Associates. We enter through a poorly finished wood door, marked only with the suite number, 1512, and a small brass plaque proclaiming: CLAY-POOL AND SONS, EXT. 1715.

The receptionist, an elderly Jamaican woman, thin, very light skinned, her face and hands textured with wrinkles, sits at a mica desk in the middle of the room, four folding wooden chairs lined up against the wall facing her. All the walls are dull white, marred and bare, obviously in need of a new coat of paint. The woman looks up at us as we enter. "Yes?" she says. "May I help you?"

"We'd like to see Virgil Claypool," Chloe says.

"Do you have an appointment?"

Chloe makes a show of examining the empty room, the empty chairs. "My name is Chloe Blood. I'm Charles and Samantha Blood's daughter," she says, her tone suddenly aristocratic, tinged with a hint of disdain. "I think Mr. Claypool will want to see me if he isn't too busy."

"One minute," the Jamaican woman says. She motions for us to sit.

"We'd rather stand," Chloe says, shaking her head.

The receptionist nods, goes through an inner door to another office.

I look around the office while we wait. "Why does your family use these people?" I whisper. "It looks like they can barely afford their rent."

Chloe shrugs. "Pa's always used them. His father used them before that. They've always done whatever we needed."

Virgil Claypool comes through the door, followed by

his receptionist. He's even lighter complexioned than she, his face sporting the nonspecific features of generations of intermarriage and the tautness of a recent facelift.

His well-tailored black silk suit, his gold Rolex watch and his three jeweled rings—one diamond, one emerald, one ruby—all contradict the first impression of impoverishment his front office made on me.

"Chloe," he says, grinning a wide, white-toothed smile. "Your family's women don't ordinarily grace us with your presence. Most often I have to make do with your brother and we both know he has nowhere near the beauty that you do." He extends a manicured hand to her. "Please come into my office."

As we follow him into the office, I mindspeak to Chloe, *"How old is he?"*

"Derek says he's at least sixty-five and"—she looks back and grins at me—*"he's the son in Claypool and Sons."*

Virgil's office is as elegant as the front office is bare. The desk is a rich mahogany, the seats leather, the oak-paneled walls covered with pictures of a younger Virgil Claypool playing cricket and sailing on his yacht with his light-skinned family. Other pictures show him posed with various Jamaican politicians—Seaga, Manley and others. A large frame holds an obviously prized photo of Virgil and Bob Marley, both men grinning as if they had just shared a joke. The window behind Virgil's desk offers a panorama of downtown Kingston—all the way down to the harbor.

Virgil grins as I examine everything and then says, "And you are?"

Before I can answer, Chloe says, "This is my fiancé, John Ames. He's visiting from the U.S."

Claypool cocks an eyebrow, motions for us to be seated, sits himself after Chloe does. "Derek didn't mention you were engaged."

"John?" I mindspeak. *"You couldn't come up with a more original name?"*

"Live with it," Chloe says.

She motions with one hand, as if to wave Virgil's question away, says to the man, "He wouldn't know. Johnny just asked me, a few days after Derek left."

The Jamaican nods, leans back in his chair. "And how can I help you today?"

"Pa asked us to come by and pick up any news you've received from Derek. He's anxious to hear how everything's going in Miami."

"I've been anxious to hear from your father. I was worried I'd have to hire a helicopter soon and fly out to see him. You know how much Charles hates to be visited. And there's always a problem of what to do with the pilot when we return." Virgil chuckles then pauses, looks at me. "Will your pa be comfortable with us discussing all this in front of him?"

"Look at his eyes, Virgil," Chloe says. "Johnny's family too. My second cousin. There's nothing he can't hear."

"Of course. Please excuse the suspicions of an old man. Caution, I fear, sometimes gets the better of me." Virgil opens a side drawer on his desk, rifles through some papers. "Here," he says, pushing three sheets of paper across the desk. "I'm afraid these are all the faxes I've received so far."

Chloe scans them, then says, "I assume you've talked to my brother too."

"Yes." The man nods his head, smiles. "Not very often, but enough. Fortunately, his people are much better communicators. We're all very excited."

"About?" Chloe says.

Virgil Claypool's eyes narrow. "The merger, of course."

"Of course," Chloe says, "When will it all finally be done?"

"Ian Tindall, from LaMar Associates, is due here in two weeks. Actually, I was beginning to worry I wouldn't hear from your father in time. Please tell him we need his presence here two weeks from next Monday. By then all the papers will be drawn and ready for his signature."

"I'm sure he'll be pleased," Chloe says.

It takes all of my self-control to sit still and show no emotion. *"What the hell is going on?"* I mindspeak to Chloe.

"You know as much as I do," Chloe says.

"What about Henri?"

"Oh," Chloe says to the Jamaican, "did Derek mention my nephew Henri? He has him in his care."

Virgil nods and chuckles. "I think the boy's been a bit of a trial for him. But Derek said to tell your father that they've reached an accommodation. The boy now knows better than to defy him."

"Good," Chloe says. "I'm fond of him but I'm afraid he's been very spoiled."

"Not anymore. Derek was quite specific about the boy learning to behave."

"But Henri's well?" I say.

The Jamaican frowns at my interruption. "From what Derek has told me, except for possibly a sore rear end, the young man is perfectly fine."

I want to reach across the desk and grab Virgil Claypool, beat him until he tells me everything he knows about Derek's trip to Miami. Then I want to beat him again for being so blasé about the treatment Henri must be receiving.

Chloe surprises me by standing up. "I appreciate your time, Virgil." She rolls up the faxes. "With your permission, I'll bring these to Pa."

The Jamaican nods.

"We need to leave now to make it home by dark," Chloe says.

"We're leaving?"

My bride ignores me. "I'm sure Pa will be just as excited as you are about the news."

Virgil Claypool grins. "I know how much Charles has been worried about money. Without the gold he sent me five years ago, I doubt we'd have been able to keep the government away from Morgan's Hole. Tell him, once the merger's done, we'll have more than enough assets to protect his home for as long as any of us can imagine."

As soon as we leave the building, I say, "Why the hell did we leave? We could have forced him to tell us everything. . . ."

Chloe whirls around, faces me, "And then what? Kill him and his receptionist?"

"Why not? How could anyone trace their deaths to us? No one knows us here. Hell, we'll probably be gone from this island long before the police even start investigating. And killing Virgil would certainly stop any possibility of a merger."

"And it would serve as a warning to Derek that something has gone wrong here. This way there's a decent chance no one in Miami will know we're coming. Besides," she says, frowning, her eyes turning moist, "my family needs Claypool and Sons."

"My son needs me."

"Damn it!" Chloe stamps one foot. "I'm going to do everything I can to bring us all together. I've chosen you, Peter. I'll love you. If necessary, I'll die for you. But I have no wish to destroy my parents and my brothers. No matter how they've wronged you—they're still my family. Didn't you hear what Claypool said?"

"About the money?"

"That's why they turned on you. They needed your money to survive."

"If they had asked, I would have helped them. I have more than enough."

Chloe shakes her head. "Charles Blood never asks for anything. The only thing he knows is to take what he needs."

"Well, he can't have my son or my wealth."

"No, of course not. But, Peter"—my bride stares into my eyes and I want to take her in my arms and kiss the hurt away from her face—"they gave birth to me. They raised me. Please don't do anything to make me sorry I married you."

"Once this is over," I say, "if this gets over, we'll see what we can do."

23

At the car, Chloe hands me Derek's faxes and gets in on the driver's side. "I could drive if you want," I say.

She shakes her head, motions for me to sit on the passenger's side. Having seen how intense Jamaican traffic can get, I'm just as glad to let her cope with it. Chloe's temperament seems far better suited for it than mine.

We drive out of Kingston, neither of us speaking. Chloe, lost in her thoughts and concentrating on maneuvering the Land Rover through traffic, seems not to notice me studying her, admiring her.

She surprised me today. My fault really. I've thought of her for years as the bright, precocious thirteen-year-old I met when I wed Elizabeth. I'd always assumed she'd retain her enthusiasm for human things, her delight in gathering new experiences, but I never considered how she would be grown up, never wondered about the other aspects of her personality.

I hadn't expected her to take charge at Claypool's. I've seen now some of what lies beneath her sweet exterior and I find myself as attracted to her strength as I am to the rest of her.

Chloe finally glances toward me, catches me staring. "What?" she says.

"Just thinking that I love you."

"Good, you should."

Traffic thins a bit as we climb up into the mountains. The land becomes more rural, dotted with small farms. We pass the occasional dilapidated store and dozens of wan-

dering goats and chickens. I turn to my bride and say,
"What do you make of what Claypool said?"

"Read the faxes first," Chloe says, returns her attention
to the road and whatever thoughts she might have.

I unroll the papers, smooth them on my lap and arrange
them in chronological order. All are typed on LaMar sta-
tionary, the first fax dated June 12th, the last July 20th. I
think back, exhale a large breath. When Chloe and I met it
was still May. I can't believe so much time has passed
since then.

> *6/12*
> *Pa—*
>
> *All is well. I'm typing and faxing this myself—prying
> eyes and all, you understand.*
>
> *We arrived here without incident and I hired a cab to
> take the boy and me to LaMar Associates. There my recep-
> tion was warm, particularly from one of Ian Tindall's asso-
> ciates, Rita Santiago (Peter's spy, I think) and Arturo
> Gomez, the company's president.*
>
> *Tindall, the fellow who comanages with Gomez, barely
> gave me the time of day.*
>
> *Since I was anxious to get to the house, I didn't dither
> around the office very much learning about the business.
> Gomez called his daughter to come get us and she picked us
> up in DelaSangre's boat. She gave me an odd look when I re-
> fused her offer to let me take the wheel. But I'm glad I didn't
> take it.*
>
> *I spent the whole time out watching her and trying to re-
> member everything she did. Coming into the channel by the
> island looked especially difficult, but I'm proud to say I
> memorized all the twists and turns it requires.*
>
> *Gomez's daughter gave me an even odder look when I
> didn't help her tie the boat off at the dock, but I watched her
> do it and memorized that too.*
>
> *Otherwise, all went well on the island. The house is
> smaller than ours but, Pa, they have everything! Plumbing,
> power generators, water pumps, lights, air-conditioning,
> TV. Once we have enough money, we should do the same at
> Morgan's Hole.*

I searched every room from the top to the bottom of the house and found no trace of the merchandise you asked me to find. But I have to tell you, from the look of LaMar Associates, we hit the bloody jackpot anyway.

I told Gomez to arrange for a meeting in a week to review everything.

I'll fax you again after that.

Derek

6/24
Pa—

Things are mostly smashing. We had our meeting the other day and there's more money here than any of us imagined. I told them about your idea to move control to Claypool and Sons in Jamaica. Gomez and his daughter were hostile to the move, but I think they'll do whatever I say. Especially because Rita pointed out the tax advantages of moving the corporation offshore.

Tindall seemed impressed with the savings. He said it might work.

The boy is a bloody pain. I had him with me at the meeting. He kept quiet for most of the time but towards the end, he went over and whispered to Rita. She whispered what he said to me—Don't listen to him. He's not my papa—so I slapped the boy in the face and sent him out of the room. Gomez and his daughter gave me odd looks again.

I've also had a bloody hard time with DelaSangre's boat, the Grady White. I don't know why people like dashing around on the water in those blasted things.

Anyway, I thought I'd already observed and memorized enough to look like an old salt to anyone. For Christ's sake, I even practiced tying off the bloody boat's lines. But the channel going to the island is deucedly hard. I'm afraid to say the wind was up the other morning and somehow when I was going out the channel to leave the island, I was careless and let a wave knock me off course a tad. Just like that I hit a rock and gouged a huge gash in the hull and the damned thing sank!

I could tell Gomez's daughter thought it strange when she came out to rescue us. Still, she didn't say anything, but just took me to shore and arranged for a rental boat.

They say it will be about a month until the Grady White's hull is repaired and new motors are installed but, honestly, I could care less. The rental's fine with me. Of course, I'm taking much more care with the bloody channel now.

Pa, I've searched the whole island now and the house again and I still haven't found that room you want to know about.

But in a few weeks it won't matter. Ian Tindall and Rita are now in direct communication with Claypool. They tell me everything's going along well.

I can't wait to hear what you say when you see how huge their assets are.

Derek

7/20
Pa—

Rita told me today that everything's finished. All that remains is for her and Tindall to prepare the final paperwork and deliver it to Claypool's. Ian is supposed to call Virgil soon to set up the final meeting.

I'm afraid you'll have to attend that one. Ian will go over to represent LaMar and me, but I think it best I stay here and watch our interests.

Gomez and his daughter have impressed me as very unreliable, possibly dangerous. They constantly ask me about the boy's welfare and seem shocked that I no longer bring Henri to the mainland. But I can't trust him to be quiet or to behave. The whelp even bit me the other day! You should have heard how he wailed when I beat him for that. So now I simply lock him up whenever I leave the island or need some peace and quiet.

Gomez's daughter even had the effrontery to come out to the island by herself and ask to see the boy. I sent her packing. I have it in my mind to dismiss her tomorrow.

Her father is quite another matter. I've received some advice at the office—on how to handle getting rid of him—but from what I gather, the man has the capability to strike back. I'm not quite sure the timing's right yet to take him on.

In the meantime I must say, I'm having a smashing time. The hunting is easy—mostly I go out on the water and search for stray boats far out to sea. And Rita's arranged a permanent suite for me at the Grove House Hotel, quite swank you know, quite elegant, only a short walk from the office. I stay there at least two or three nights a week. I'd stay more if it weren't for the boy.

I'm afraid I'm becoming too spoiled for Morgan's Hole. Once all this is over, I'd think I'd like to stay here in Miami, run this end of things—that is if you agree and if I can send Henri back to live with you and Mum.

I've found some good company here and until I find a mate of my own, I think this can be as good as it can get.

I have searched again, everywhere I can think of for the other things you want me to find. If they're anywhere on the island, they're hidden too well for me.

Please arrange to call me from Claypool's once the deal is done. I'd love to hear how you feel about it.

Derek

Shaking my head, I fold the faxes, fold them again as if neatly reducing their size will somehow make the problem go away. How could I leave Henri so undefended? How abandoned he must feel. I fold the papers again. How I look forward to confronting Derek. The papers have become compact and stiff, and still, I fold them again.

"I have to call Miami," I say.

"We'll be in Ocho Rios in an hour. We can find a phone then," Chloe says.

"I can't stand what your brother says he's done to Henri. The boy's just five years old!"

"He never did understand children. All of us have felt his wrath at one time or another," Chloe says. "At least he hasn't done any permanent harm to Henri."

"It's still not acceptable."

"Of course not. I expect you'll show him so."

I will indeed, I think; then the effrontery of the rest of it overwhelms me. "Can you believe they're trying to steal everything?"

Chloe nods. "I believe it. But we're going to find a way to stop them."

"Damned right we are. First thing, we have to get to Miami, soon."

"With what?" Chloe says. "We have no papers, no ID. How much money do you have left?"

I pull out the cash wadded in my pocket, count it. "Forty-three dollars, twenty-five cents."

My bride laughs. "That will fill the gas tank again and pay for some prepaid phone cards, but then what?"

"All you have to do is get me to Montego Bay and I'll take you home in luxury." I grin at the confusion evident on my bride's face but only say, "Trust me."

Maxim's General Store on the outskirts of Ocho Rios offers everything we need. Chloe fills the car's fuel tank at their pumps while I go inside the brightly painted store and buy phone cards. Afterwards, it takes me a few minutes to find the pay phones, but I'm glad to see they're located in the back of the store, in a quiet, deserted alcove near the storeroom.

Inserting my card, I dial LaMar Associates. Sarah picks up on the third ring, offers the standard greeting. I make my voice higher, a little harsh. "Arturo Gomez please."

"Sorry, sir, he isn't in. Can I get anyone else for you?"

"When is he due back?" I say.

"I can't say, sir."

"Is Claudia available?"

"Ms. Gomez no longer works here," Sarah says, her voice turning brittle. "Perhaps if you could tell me your name and the purpose of your call, I can find someone else to help you."

"I'll just call back later for Arturo."

"Sir, he won't be here. He's out for an indefinite period. Either Mr. Tindall or Ms. Santiago can explain—if you'd like to speak to one of them."

"Put me through to Rita."

"Who may I say is calling?"

I try to think up a name, blurt out the one Chloe made up. "John Ames."

Rita doesn't pick up for almost five minutes. When she does answer, her voice is brisk and impersonal. "Yes," she says, "What's this about?"

Using my own voice, I say, "Rita . . ."

Her tone goes soft. "Peter dear," she breathes into the phone. "I wasn't expecting to hear from you until later. . . ."

Unprepared for the intimate tone of her voice, I slam the phone into the receiver. Rita had never been that familiar with me. She could only have thought she was speaking with the other Peter.

I dial Arturo's cellphone again and once more get no answer. Then I dial Claudia's.

"Hey," she says.

"Claudia, it's me, Peter."

"So?" Her voice turns guarded, sounds careful to me.

"I'm concerned about your dad."

"Me too," she says. "Though I didn't think you'd care."

"Of course, I do."

She says nothing.

"Claudia listen," I say. "I need your help."

Claudia spits her words out. "You forget. I don't work for you anymore. Ask your flunkies, Rita or Tindall, to help you. I have more important concerns." She disconnects her phone.

I slam the receiver down. No Gomez has ever spoken to me like that. I doubt any Gomez has ever used such a tone with any DelaSangre. None would ever dare. I'm tempted to think of Claudia—of all of them—as traitors. But as much as I would have liked them to see through Derek's façade, I know in reality, to them, Derek is me.

Taking a deep breath, I try to calm my anger away. Of course, Rita would welcome his advances—just as much

as she would have mine. Why wouldn't Arturo and Ian follow his orders—no matter how illogical—without much
resistance? If I told Gomez to fire his daughter, the man
would, no matter how much it pained him. Why should I
expect him to disobey Derek's?

I pick up the phone, put it down again, take another
deep breath before I dial Claudia's number once more.

Claudia answers on the first ring this time. "Leave me
alone," she says before I can blurt out one word.

"Claudia, wait. Don't hang up. Let me explain. It's not
the way you think it is!" I say.

"What am I confused about?" she says. "You fired me.
My father was almost killed."

"Arturo? What do you mean? What happened?"

Claudia laughs into the phone. "You're pathetic. You're
one of the ones that found him."

I shake my head. I wish I were there, face-to-face with
her, so she could read my expressions. "Claudia, you have
to listen to me. . . ."

"I don't have to do anything."

"This is going to sound strange. The Peter you're talking about isn't me. I'm still in Jamaica."

"Bullshit! I just saw you out on the bay in your crummy
rental boat, less than an hour ago."

"That wasn't me," I say, trying to think of a way to convince her, looking around me for anything I might be able
to use. To my relief, the pay phone still has its number
printed on it, faint but readable, even showing the Jamaican area code, 876. "I can prove it! Call me back, here
in Jamaica." I read off the number to her.

"How do I know this isn't something you and Ian
arranged?" Claudia says.

"Why would I bother? If I am the Peter you think I am,
what reason would I have for pursuing you? You're already out and it appears so's Arturo. Take the number.
Check the area code out with an operator if you need to.
Just call me back."

For the first time Claudia's voice sounds closer to the

way I'm used to hearing it. "Give me the number again, Peter. I'll check it out and call you back in a few minutes."

Minutes pass.

I sit. I stand. I drum my fingers on the top of the pay phone. Chloe walks to the back, smiles, says, "There you are," and comes over and hugs me.

It's the first time she's been in physical contact with me since we left for Kingston and I realize I've missed her touch. Elizabeth had rarely touched me except during sex, but Chloe, to my delight, seems much more physical, always resting a hand on me or standing close enough to brush against me. I smile, hug her back, tell her all I've learned.

The phone remains silent.

"I need her to believe me," I say to my bride. "She's the only one I think might be willing to help us. I can't be sure of any of the others. And poor Arturo—I need to know what happened to him, how badly he's hurt."

"If she doesn't call back, so be it," Chloe says. "Why is this woman so important to you? We don't need any humans to help us defeat my brother."

I smile, rub her arm lightly. "Of course," I say. "But my father taught me, 'Only fools take action without first gathering all the information they can.' No one knows Miami like the Gomez family does. If Claudia decides to help, believe me, we'll be grateful for her assistance."

More minutes pass. "Let's leave," Chloe says. "You can try her again in Montego Bay."

I shake my head.

My bride frowns. "I don't see what makes her so special that you let her make you wait so long. I'll wait in the car," she says and stomps off.

Time drags by. I sit and stare at the phone. When it finally rings, the harsh sound of it startles me so much that I don't pick up until the second ring.

"You're at a pay phone in Maxim's General Store in Ocho Rios, right?" Claudia says.

"Yes," I say, smiling that Claudia has already taken the

opportunity to trace the number. Arturo would have done the same.

"Two men, employees of one of Pop's smuggler friends are on the way there. What are you driving?"

"A yellow Land Rover."

"Yellow?" She laughs. "Could you be any more conspicuous?"

"Claudia, tell me what's going on."

"I've faxed a photo of you to these people. If they find you look like the picture, they'll give you a cellphone, an untraceable one like we use in Miami. Then we'll talk. And, Peter?"

"Yes," I say.

"If you aren't who you say you are, you better leave now."

The blare of reggae precedes a huge black SUV as it pulls into Maxim's parking lot. Leaning against the trunk of the Land Rover, Chloe close beside me, I watch it slowly cruise toward us. "Your special friend's been reading too many spy novels," my bride sniffs.

"She's not special and she's just being careful," I say.

The car pulls up to us and the dark tinted front passenger window rolls down revealing a large, well-muscled dark Jamaican, talking into a cellphone, the phone looking like a child's toy in his huge hand. "Ya, mon," he says into the phone. He motions for the driver, another oversized Jamaican, equally black, to turn down the music.

The first man holds up a piece of paper studies it, then looks at me. "Ya, mon, he matches the fax you sent us." He listens for a moment, stares at my eyes and nods his head. "Ya, his eyes are very green, like you said."

He holds out the phone to me. "For you, brother. The lady, she wants to talk with you."

I take the cellphone and walk away from the SUV. The car sits, its motor idling, the two men watching me, waiting, I assume, for instructions. "Claudia?" I say.

"Peter, I don't know what's going on but I think I'm relieved to hear that you're you. What can I do?"

"First tell me about Henri."

"He looked okay the few times I saw him. A little subdued, but he looked healthy. I can't really report anything recent. Peter, the other one, stopped bringing him to shore a while ago."

"And Arturo?"

Claudia sighs. "Two nights ago Pop left work at his usual time. According to Ian, he and Peter—the other Peter—and Rita stayed to work late on this merger they're doing. You can't believe how Pop hated the whole idea. He kept trying to talk all of them out of doing it. But Peter and Ian insisted.

"Anyway," she says. "When the others left, they found Pop by the side of his car, all bloody, bruised and unconscious. At first they thought he was dead, but Ian finally felt a pulse. The police think it was a mugging—his money and jewelry were all gone—but I'm not sure. You know how tough Pop is."

"What does he say happened?"

"He's still unconscious. I contacted some of his people; they're putting the word out on the street, trying to find out who did it and why. My bet is we'll find it's someone connected to Tindall."

"Because?"

"Pop thought if he and Ian went to Peter and presented a united front, they'd be able to change his mind about the merger. Ian refused to risk it. The two of them had some pretty brutal screaming matches. Pop told me they both threatened each other."

I nod, even though Claudia can't see me. "I can see how they would," I say.

"Who is this other Peter?" she says. "How can he look and sound just like you?"

"Claudia, you know there are things about my family that we never discuss."

"Yes," she says. "Pop was real clear with me on that."

"Let's just say he's a relative—a not very friendly one."

"Whatever you say."

"What's more important is our getting to Miami and resolving this whole situation."

"Our?"

"I'm married now. My wife, Chloe, is with me."

"What can I do?"

I know there's no time for false papers to be made. Without them any commercial air travel is out. "Can your friend smuggle us into the Miami?"

"His next shipment leaves in two weeks."

"I don't want to wait that long. Find out for me what cruise ships are in Montego Bay and what their itinerary is."

"Sure," Claudia says. "I'll have to call you back on that."

"Fine," I say. "Do you think your friends here can help with a few things?"

I hand the cellphone to the Jamaican in the SUV. He listens, nods a few times, saying, "Ya. Ya," then disconnects and hands the cellphone back to me. He opens the glove compartment, gives me a charger for the phone and a manila envelope.

"A thousand dollar in twenties, mon." He flashes me a wide smile. "Your lady friend on the phone must like you very much. She said you have some things for us."

Opening the trunk, I say to Chloe, "We'll never get your herbs and potions through customs." I take the wicker chest and our suitcases and hand them to the Jamaican. "This way everything will be in Miami in a few weeks."

After the SUV drives off, Chloe folds her arms, gives me a hard stare. "'Your lady friend must like you very much,'" she says, mimicking the Jamaican's accent and tone.

"She works for me," I say,

Chloe shrugs, obviously not pleased with my answer.

*   *   *

The cellphone rings just a few minutes after we leave Ocho Rios. As soon as I answer, Claudia says, "You may want to stay where you are. The *Carribean Queen* is in port at Ocho Rios right now. It's due to leave at six. Their schedule calls for a stopover in Cayman, a sea day and arrival at the port of Miami the next morning."

I check my watch. Three P.M. With luck we have plenty of time to find our way aboard the ship. "Can you arrange for some of your people to watch my island and some others to watch the office — so we know what's happening with the other Peter?"

"Sure."

"And can you get Arturo's SeaRay and meet us in Key West the day after tomorrow?" I say.

"Why Key West?"

"I don't want to contend with customs in Miami," I say. "Key West is the first place we can get off."

Claudia says, "But the ship doesn't stop there."

I sigh. If all goes as I plan, arriving in Miami could prove inconvenient. For beings like Chloe and me, leaving a ship at sea is a simple matter. But I've no desire to explain any of it to Claudia. It's none of her business just how I intend to get on the ship or how I plan to leave it. "Didn't your father tell you there would be questions that go unanswered? I just need you to meet us."

"Sure. Whatever you say. It's a push but, yeah, I can do it," Claudia says. "Then what?"

"Then we have some people to visit."

Chloe shakes her head when I tell her to turn the car around. "Why? Did your special friend tell you to?"

I glare at her. A little jealousy may be cute and endearing, but enough is enough. "Why would you be jealous of any human women, let alone this one?"

My bride shrugs. "I don't like that you're making plans with her and not discussing them with me. And don't tell

me you never took any of them to bed. Derek brags about
the hundreds he's had."

"I'm not Derek," I say. "Since Elizabeth, there's only
been one—and I regret that. Most certainly it was not
Claudia. We need to go back to Ocho Rios because there's
a cruise ship there that I want us to catch."

"How?" Chloe says. "We have no papers."

I tell her.

24

The *Carribean Queen* sits at the end of a long, narrow concrete pier jutting into Ocho Rios bay. Painted a brilliant white, with six tiered levels above its waterline, it looks more like a floating wedding cake than a majestic ship of the sea.

Dozens of tourists stroll along the pier: some going back to the ship; others heading for some last-minute shopping on land. A number of them wear loose-fitting T-shirts decorated with a large blue trident, the same insignia that decorates the ship's three smokestacks.

"That's what's taking us home," I say.

We cruise past the harbor as I study the sidewalks for likely couples. But most seem to be paired with other couples or using guides.

The crowds of tourists thin out as we pass a clock tower in the center of town. I grin when we approach a farmer's market after that and see a couple—both the man and the woman wearing blue trident decorated T-shirts and carrying shopping bags in both hands—arguing with a cab-driver. They look to be in their mid-thirties—the woman attractive in a sort of suburban, overdressed, country club way; the man smaller than me, balding, but trim.

The taxi drives away, the man and woman frowning as they begin their long walk toward the pier. I motion for Chloe to drive up to them. Putting down the window as we approach, I call out, "Would you like a ride?"

The couple stops, the man peering into the Land Rover. "You American?" he says.

I nod. "Miami," I say.

"No kidding? We're—Marcia and me—we're from Boca. Barry and Marcia Liebman . . ."

"And believe me, we wish we were back there, right now," the woman says. "I can't believe these people. Would you believe that cabdriver wanted to charge us extra to turn the air-conditioning on? Uh, don't think we're too spoiled. . . ." She looks into the car, smiles at Chloe. "But neither of us think that perspiration makes for a better vacation experience. You understand that, don't you, honey? After all, if Barry and I wanted to sweat, we could just as well stayed home and turned our air-conditioning off."

"We have to make a stop first, but if you don't mind that, we'll be glad to take you to your ship," I say.

"Great," Barry says. He and his wife rush into the car's backseat.

"Thank God! Air-conditioning!" Marcia says, arranging the bags on the floor before them as Chloe drives forward, heading out of town. "I told Barry if he wanted sun we could have stayed home and gone to the beach club. At least there, the floor doesn't move. They say they have stabilizers on the ship but, honestly, I don't think they ever use them. The boat was rocking so much last night I was positively green."

"Marcia," Barry says. "You wanted to come."

"Only because of the food—which I haven't had any appetite to eat—and because he got us a free stateroom," she says. "Barry does the cruise line's books."

Barry grins. "It's one of the perks of being a CPA."

"Next time"—Marcia looks at her husband—"tell them to give you a bigger check instead."

Chloe puts her right hand on my thigh, mindspeaks to me. *"How long are we going to have these people in our car?"* I smile.

We drive out of town, Marcia and Barry talking nonstop, neither even asking what our names are.

"I'm telling you, as soon as we left Miami, I got seasick. We haven't been out of our room the whole time. I don't even know where our dinner table is," Marcia says.

"It's okay, Marcia. You're better now," Barry says.

"There's a road over there," Chloe mindspeaks. I look up ahead, at a dirt road to the right, just past a run-down shack, three half-naked children playing in its overgrown front yard.

I nod, say, *"Take it."*

"Look at that," Marcia says. "How can these people live like that?"

A handmade sign says, WHITE RIVER, with an arrow pointing to the road. "We're almost there," Chloe says out loud, turning onto the dirt road, the Land Rover sending up a cloud of brown dust behind it.

Marcia and Barry complain about the road's condition, the jungle desolation we drive through. Neither Chloe nor I speak until we come to a small clearing by the river's bank. My bride pulls into the clearing, turns off the ignition. "We're here," she says and gets out of the car.

Marcia and Barry look around. "Where?" Barry says.

I open my door, get out. "It will be cooler for you if you get out while you wait," I say.

The man and woman both get out slowly. "This is the middle of nowhere," Marcia says.

Chloe gives her a sympathetic smile and walks over to her. "True," my bride says, changing the shape of one finger, slitting Marcia's throat with a quick slash, grabbing the woman by her hair, holding her so no blood stains her clothes.

"No!" Barry shouts. Before he can move, I grab him by the neck and hold him in place as I strangle the life from him. After he goes limp, I lay him on the ground and undress him. Chloe does the same with Marcia.

Once their clothes are off, folded and placed in a neat pile on the car's hood, Chloe and I take our clothes off. "Me first," she giggles, and studying the dead woman lying before us, she shifts shape until I see her becoming Marcia, her hips widening, her legs thickening, her hair growing longer, turning dark. Likewise, I change until not even Barry's best friend could tell I wasn't him.

Chloe stares at me, says, "Well, you look like him."

I examine her. "You did fine too."

My bride shakes her head. "Look at her face. I'm sorry," she says. "I have no idea how anyone can put on so much makeup. I don't know how to do it."

"You're fine," I say.

"They were such disagreeable people."

"True," I mindspeak as I remember how long it's been since I've eaten. I shift into my natural form. *"But I bet they make a most agreeable meal."*

We leave the Land Rover in a parking lot a few blocks from the pier and walk to the *Carribean Queen,* carrying the bags of souvenirs that Barry and Marcia had bought. I offer to carry all the bags but Chloe refuses, even though she clearly has a problem remaining upright in Marcia's high heels while carrying two shopping bags and Marcia's oversized sequined, leather handbag.

After she twists her heel the third time in almost as many steps, she says, "Why do their women do this to themselves?"

I shrug, don't even attempt an answer.

Our suite looks as large as most homes' main bedrooms. Chloe flops down on the queen-sized bed as soon as we get in the room, pulls off her shoes. She points to the closet. "She better have some sneakers or flat shoes in there or I'm going barefoot the rest of the time."

I grin, say, "Whatever. We don't even have to leave the room until we get near Key West." I point to the wide pair of sliding glass doors leading to a private outdoor balcony overlooking the water. "We can watch the ocean from here."

"Uh-uh," Chloe says, shaking her head. "I'm not going to let you off that easy. Don't they have shows on board these ships?"

"And gambling . . ." I say.

"And dancing and movies?"

I nod my head.

We don't get back to our room until after three in the morning—after losing four hundred dollars at blackjack, after seeing a truncated version of *A Chorus Line* performed on an impossibly small stage, after watching a comedian tell jokes that made most of the audience groan and mostly confused my bride and after dancing for hours in the ship's club.

"I loved all of it!" Chloe says, pulling off her clothes, dancing her way across the room, naked. "Didn't you?"

"Not all of it," I say. "I could have come back sooner."

"I think you're taking your impersonation of Barry Liebman a little too seriously," she says, coming to me, rubbing my bald spot, kissing me, undoing my clothes for me. "Don't be an old fuddy-duddy accountant. Wouldn't you like to balance my register?"

I look at the dark-haired woman in front of me, attractive but not my Chloe. "I'd rather make love to my real wife," I say.

Chloe smiles, changes before me. "You too, Peter," she says.

It takes me only a moment to shed Barry's image. "Wait for me on the bed," I say, going to the sliding doors, pushing them open.

The room fills with the fresh, salt smell of the open ocean. I breathe it in. "This is what it smells like on my island," I say, returning to my bride, admiring her brown body, her chocolate breasts.

"I like it," she says and we make love surrounded by the salt air, the ship gently rising and falling as it makes its way through the waves.

Afterwards, we lie on our backs, naked on top of the sheets, letting the ocean breeze cool our bodies. Chloe nestles against me, her head on my shoulder, her hand on my thigh. I sigh, glad to just be lying beside her, happy that for the next day, we have nothing we must do. So much has happened since Chloe and I met, that all I want right now is to take this time for us to pay attention to each other.

This evening on the ship was the first time we were able to relax and to play together. Chloe's enthusiasm to try to do everything available almost wore me out, but it also delighted me. "This can be sort of like a mini-honeymoon for us," I say.

"That sounds nice," Chloe says. "Of course, you know, technically, we're not married yet."

"No?" I frown. "Screw the technicalities, I think we are."

"Don't worry, I think we're already bound to each other for life too." She pats her stomach. "Your daughter thinks so too. It's just that, according to our tradition, you're not officially wed until you've shared the potion."

"Is this your family's tradition or our people's?"

"Didn't your mother teach you anything about your heritage?"

I shake my head. "My mother was raised by humans. All that she knew about our people's traditions, she learned from Father. I don't think he taught her very much. He certainly didn't teach me any of it."

"Not even which castryll you're from?"

"I don't even know what that is," I say.

Chloe turns on her side, looks at my face. "It's sort of like a clan or a tribe. Mum taught me we're all descended from one of the four castrylls—the Zal, the Thryll, the Pelk and the Undrae. According to Pa, we're of the Undrae castryll but with Zal blood."

"Which means what?"

"In the old days, it sometimes meant war. Do you know any of our history?"

"Only that our kind once ruled the world. Father said we only lost control after the humans outbred us. He said we couldn't cope with their numbers."

"You can thank the Undrae for that. They're the ones who bred them into what they became."

"And how's that?" I smile at my bride. "Did they raise and breed humans like cattle?"

She nods. "After the great explosion—the same one, I think, that killed the dinosaurs. And only after they won the war."

"Okay, I don't know any of this."

Chloe says, "Before the explosion there were no humans. Our kind, the People of the Blood, were free to hunt and feed as we wanted. We developed into four almost separate species. The Zal were the largest and most ferocious of our kind, the fire breathers. They hunted the big beasts, the tyrannosauruses and brontosauruses. The Thryll were the smallest. They spent most of their lives in the air, living in treetops, hunting whatever flew near them. The Pelk took to the sea, living in the oceans, hunting fish and whales. The Undrae chose to live on the ground and cultivate herds of beasts so they had no need to constantly hunt."

"They sound like the smartest ones," I say.

"Maybe too smart." Chloe kisses my chest. "Something happened, a great explosion. The human scientists are saying now that it was caused by an asteroid. Whatever it was, it turned the sky dark, killed all the vegetation. Almost all the beasts died. There wasn't enough to eat to take care of all the castrylls. Rather than starve, the four clans turned on each other."

My bride sits up, holds up one hand showing three fingers. "The war lasted three hundred years. The Thryll were the first to go, most of them dying, the remaining few changing, merging with the Undrae. The few Pelk who survived either merged with the Undrae too or retreated to the sea and cut themselves off from the rest. Ma says some of them still exist. She told me they're the ones who used to pose as mermaids to draw ships to their death.

"Toward the end, only the Zal and the Undrae were left. There were fewer of the Zal but they were huge, powerful beings. As much as the Undrae tried, they couldn't kill any of them without receiving massive casualties, and while the Undrae could change shape, they were incapable of growing that big."

"So how did they win?" I say.

"One of the Undrae women, of course," Chloe says, grinning. "A potion maker named Lystra. She found a combination of herbs that enabled the Undrae to grow as large and as powerful as the Zal." My bride shakes her head. "Only once the potion was taken, the Undrae warriors had just twelve hours to take an antidote. Otherwise, they were doomed to continue to grow until their hearts burst.

"By the end of the war only a pitiful few of either castrylls were left, but there were more Undrae than Zal. The remaining big beasts finally agreed to join with the Undrae. Mum says all of the People of the Blood can trace their roots back to to those mergers."

I shrug. "Not me," I say.

Chloe gives me a grin, puts her hand between my legs, stroking me until I respond. "From the size of it," she says, "I'd say you have to have some Zal blood in you too."

I want to sleep in late but Chloe seems determined to take in every experience the ship has to offer. Venturing forth as Marcia and Barry Liebman again, forgoing any shore trips to Cayman, we start with yoga on the top deck, followed by an aerobics class in the gym and massages after that. Later in the day, after an interlude in our cabin and a few hours in the pool, we return to the casino, taking advantage of the light late-afternoon crowd to try each game, losing equally as well at blackjack and roulette as at craps and the slot machines.

Through all of it, Chloe can't seem to keep her hands off me, touching me absentmindedly, stroking my arm, holding my hand. Since I do the same to her, everyone takes us for newlyweds, teasing us and fussing over us.

We spend our evening much as we did the evening before, though this time we win in the casino, taking away the grand sum of thirty-three dollars after two hours of play. And this time, once we return to our room, we undress and shift into our natural forms, flying away from the ship as it cruises in the open sea, hunting together.

A Russian-made Cuban patrol boat, searching the dark waters off the island's coast—looking for rafters, I presume—catches my attention. I explain their mission to Chloe, say, *"Shall we?"*

Chloe strikes first, swooping down on the bridge, slashing out at the captain and his mate while I descend on the gun crew on the bow. It takes only moments until all is quiet.

My bride insists on examining the bodies, choosing the most palatable ones for our meal. She carries them to the rear deck, waits for me to take the first bite, then feeds beside me. Afterwards we make love on the deck in our natural forms, growling and roaring as we couple, filling the night air with our sounds.

Before dawn, just before we leave, I go below and open all the seacocks. We take to the air as the ship begins to settle, circling above until it and its dead crew sink from sight. *"Let the Cuban authorities try to figure out what happened,"* I say as we veer away and fly back to our ship.

Once we return to our bed, Chloe insists on making love once more in our human forms. I give a mock groan and comply, thinking how relieved my aching body will be once we arrive in Key West and our mini-honeymoon ends.

We sleep in late the next morning, but then spend the rest of the day in much the same way as we had the day before. But because we are at sea, we also have the opportunity to shoot skeet off the stern of the ship and to drive golf balls into the sea. After a few missed tries, Chloe proves to be amazingly adept at both pursuits.

In the evening, my bride sees a notice that a movie will be shown in one of the ship's auditoriums. "Can we?" she asks. "I've never seen one."

I sit with Chloe, my arm around her, her hand on my

leg, content to feel her warmth next to me as we both watch the movie. My bride enjoys every moment, gasping and laughing and crying along with most of the rest of the audience. I find I enjoy her reactions and enthusiasm more than I enjoy watching the screen. I've already seen my share of Hollywood movies. I know the handsome leading man will end up with the pretty leading woman—after some mutual misunderstanding and some manufactured crisis or chase. Besides, I'm aware the ship will soon be passing near Key West and my mind's on what we must do.

We take to the air shortly after midnight, when the ship is closest to Key West. I'm tempted to fly all the way to Caya DelaSangre, but I have no way of knowing where Derek is or where he's put my son.

Chloe follows me as I head for the glow of Key West's lights, a small bag held in one of her foreclaws. I carry a similar bag, filled with a change of clothes, money and the cellular phone Claudia arranged for us.

"What are we going to do when we get there?" Chloe mindspeaks.

"We'll find a place to rest until morning. Then we'll meet up with Claudia."

"We only have the Liebmans' clothes. I don't want to stay in that woman's shape any longer than I have to."

I sigh. *"In the morning, you'll just have to shift into Marcia's shape one more time. We'll go shopping before we meet Claudia."*

"Good," Chloe says. *"I wouldn't want her to think I'm that woman."*

25

The lack of motion wakes me. I sit up, momentarily confused, until I remember we're no longer on a ship. Careful not to disturb Chloe, I get out of bed, look out the sliding glass doors, past the shutters I removed the night before, to the ocean behind the house. A few boats are cruising offshore, even though the sun sits barely a few degrees above the horizon.

I sigh, wish Chloe and I could have more time to play. But all the problems waiting for us in Miami flood my mind. Even though the distance may still be too much, I try mindspeaking to my son, masking my thoughts. {*Henri! Henri! It's me, Papa!*}

No answer. I try again and get the same result. I sigh once more, go the the nightstand, pick up the cellular phone Claudia's Jamaicans gave me and dial.

Claudia doesn't answer until the fifth ring. "Yup," she says.

"We're here." I say. "Where are you?" I whisper in the cellphone so as not to disturb Chloe. I don't see any reason to explain that we broke into someone's shuttered beach house and slept in their master bedroom.

"Land's End Marina, slip four," she says.

"Everything go okay?"

"Yeah, I had to burn up almost a whole gas tank to do it, but I got in last night."

"Any word on the other Peter?"

"You've got to be kidding. Your call just woke me up." She pauses. "It's only eight-thirty. No, I haven't talked to any of our operatives yet. I didn't know when I'd hear from you today."

Chloe makes a contented sound, almost a purr and I turn, look at her, her eyes still closed, stretching under the covers, moving like a cat just waking up. So much for being quiet, I think. "We still need to get up here and get dressed," I say in my regular voice.

"We need new clothes too," Chloe says.

"And we need to go shopping for some clothes," I say into the phone.

"Do you want me to get a cab and come for you?" Claudia says.

"No. We can get one ourselves. We'll be a while yet. Why don't you call Miami, see what's happening?"

"Sure," she says. "Have fun shopping."

Chloe gets up, shifts one last time into Marcia Liebman's form. Frowning I do the same, adopting the build, the balding head of her husband. We both dress as quickly as we can, leaving the house from its rear.

My bride takes the beach and surrounding hotels in stride. We go inland to the first road and walk on the sidewalk ten blocks south to Duvall Street. Once there, we head up the street, searching for a store that sells more than trinkets or T-shirts. She says, "It doesn't look much different than Ocho Rios."

Looking at the bars and restaurants, the souvenir and T-shirt joints, I nod agreement. "Pretty much one tacky tourist trap looks like another," I say. I tell her about my unsuccessful attempts to reach Henri.

"Poor you." She puts her hand on my shoulder. "It's too far yet. He's too young to be able to hear from such a distance."

"Poor Henri," I say.

She nods, says, "That too."

On a corner, a few blocks before we reach the end of the street, we come upon what looks like a small department store, its windows filled with fine clothes and gifts. I read the sign out loud, "Fastbuck Freddies."

"Now this," Chloe says as we enter, "is what I expected America to be like."

I call a sales clerk over to show me some khaki shorts while Chloe takes some clothes into a changing room. After she emerges, newly dressed in shorts, sneakers and tank top, changed from Marcia Liebman into the brown beauty I love, I carry my new clothes into a different changing room and gladly shed Barry Liebman's appearance and clothing.

We buy enough other clothing to last a few weeks. The sales clerk seems confused to have lost track of the Liebmans, but thrilled to make such a large sale so early in the day. She follows us out of the store, gushes, "Please come back soon," as we leave.

I can see slip four and Arturo Gomez's SeaRay from Land's End Marina's parking lot, the boat's sleek white hull gleaming in the morning sun. "That boat can cruise at over twenty-five miles an hour," I say to Chloe as we get out of the taxi and I pay the fare. "We'll be in Miami before dark."

"And then what?" Chloe says.

We walk toward the dock. "That depends on your brother and my son," I say. "The first thing I'm concerned about is Henri. If we can find him and get him somewhere safe, then we can deal with Derek."

"Are you sure we can deal with him? He's larger than you, you know."

"Not large enough to defeat the both of us. My hope is he'll realize that before anything starts."

"That's a good hope to have," Chloe says. "But I have to tell you it doesn't sound anything like the way my brother would behave. Derek's not quite that smart."

"Then we'll have to teach him, won't we?" I say.

Claudia comes up from the cabin as soon as we step on board the SeaRay. "Peter!" she says, rushing forward, wrapping her arms around me. Chloe stands back, watches, no expression on her face.

I disengage, motion to my mate to come forward. "This is Chloe, my wife," I say.

"She's adorable!" Claudia extends her hand to Chloe. "Young of course, but Pop told me you like them that way." Looking at my bride, she says, "Welcome to Key West." Then she glances from Chloe to me and back. "Congratulations!"

My bride shakes her hand. "Thank you," she says, a hint of sarcasm in her voice. She eyes Claudia. "You're adorable too."

Claudia either doesn't notice or chooses to ignore Chloe's tone. She takes our packages. "I've been straightening up the cabin, putting my stuff in the Vee berth in the bow. You guys are the newlyweds, so you can have the stateroom in the middle. I'll put your gear there. But"— she laughs—"we do have to share the head."

"How soon can we get underway?" I say.

"Maybe thirty minutes." Claudia shrugs. "All we have to do is settle up at the marina office, take on some fuel and cast off."

I take the wheel, guide us out of Key West Harbor, Chloe standing next to me, watching the boats as we pass them. When we go by a cruise ship docked at Mallory Pier, the massive ship towering above us, my bride presses against me, whispers, "I love the time we spent together on the *Carribean Queen*."

Kissing her on her cheek, I say, "Me too." As soon as we pass the cruise ship, I jam the throttles forward, the SeaRay's twin Mercuries growling as they accelerate, our wake rising and spreading behind us.

Claudia joins us, grinning. "Couldn't wait, huh? It's good we're going today. They say a storm may be coming tomorrow. The sea's not too bad yet," she says. "We should be able to run full speed all the way home."

"Good." I guide us out the channel, turn the boat so we

can go around Key West on the ocean side. "What did your people report?"

"Wait a second." Claudia goes below deck, returns with a small pad. "Peter left the island yesterday at about eleven. He spent most of the day at the office, returned to the island before dark and left about nine in the evening, carrying a large bundle. My man says, after Peter docked at Monty's, he carried the bundle to a truck in the parking lot and put it in the truck's back. After the truck drove away, Peter walked over to Grove House and spent the night."

"What was in the bundle?" I say.

The girl shrugs.

"Didn't any of your people follow the truck?"

"No. I had someone watching the island and a few others by the office, like you asked. They did what I told them. They followed Peter. None of them thought to follow the truck."

"Damn it!" I shake my head. "What else?"

"After ten this morning, a little after you called me, he left the hotel in your black Mercedes." She grins. "A redhead, Rita Santiago they think, was driving. And yes, Peter, my people followed them. They drove to Miami International."

"Who'd they meet?"

"No one yet," Claudia says. "My people tell me they're waiting by the Air Jamaica concourse. They're supposed to call me as soon as they see who Peter meets. That is, of course, if we're in cellphone range."

"I'm thinking of running up on the Atlantic side. We can get back in range the quickest by coming in at Caesar's Creek, off of Homestead, and running up the bay from there. Can you set the GPS for that?"

"Sure," Claudia says.

"The bundle could have been Henri, you know," Chloe says.

I know all too well. "He wouldn't have killed him, would he have?"

"There would be no reason for that," Chloe says. "Yet."

It weighs on me. That and the mystery person or persons that Derek's waiting for at the airport. I ignore the beauty of the day and the calm ocean around us. Even though we're already going at full speed, I tap the throttles forward to see if the boat can go any faster. All I want is for the day to pass, for me to be close enough to reach Henri.

"Could your father be healed already?" I say.

Chloe pauses, thinks, before she says, "It's been over forty-eight hours since you pushed him into the sinkhole. Don't you think you could heal in that much time?"

I nod. "But without a phone or a car, what could he do?"

"That depends on Virgil Claypool," Chloe says. "Maybe you were right. Maybe we should have killed him."

26

Henri finally answers me, five hours after we leave Key West, just as we're passing Key Largo, nearing Carrysfort Reef. {*Papa?*} he says. {*Where are you?*}

{*Coming home soon, baby. Soon. Tell me where you are.*}

{*I don't know. It's dark, Papa. I don't like it.*}

{*Is it on the island?*}

{*Maybe. But I'm not so sure, Papa. Sometimes Derek just locks me in my room. Other times, he wraps me up in a blanket and carries me someplace else. He never lets me see where he takes me.*}

I hold back my anger. It will serve no purpose right now. {*Are you hungry?*}

{*No. They always leave me meat and water.*}

{*They?*}

{*A lot of times, Derek has someone with him. I don't know who. He doesn't let me see. They never talk around me. Only Derek does. I don't like him.*}

{*I don't either.*}

{*Papa, he says he had to take me away from you because I was bad. I promise, I'll behave, Papa.*}

{*I never wanted you to go away from me!*} I say, wishing I could have Derek in my hands right now. {*You never were bad.*}

{*Sometimes I did bad things.*}

{*Sometimes you behaved like a normal child. And no matter what, I always loved you and I always wanted you.*}

{*I want to come home now, Papa.*}

I let out a breath, breathe in deep. {*I'll come get you as soon as I can, Henri. As soon as we can find you. You have to pay attention to everything around you. You have to let me know what sounds you hear. What you smell. Can you do that?*}

{*I think so,*} he says. I can picture him nodding as he says it, his eyes big.

{*I love you, son.*}

{*I love you too, Papa.*}

At my request, Claudia relieves me at the boat's wheel. I take Chloe aside and tell her about my conversation with Henri. A flush of anger overtakes her face, just as it had mine, when I repeat what Derek said to my son.

"What an ass!" she says. "If there was any doubt I ever had about harming him, it's long gone now."

She hugs me. "We'll find him, Peter. Don't worry. Derek's too stupid to hide him well."

If it weren't for the alarm going off on the GPS, I'd never have realized we were near Caesar's Creek. From the ocean all I can make out is a continuous line of green, tree-covered land hugging the ocean. Of course, I know from long experience, as soon as we draw closer, the channel will show itself, first as a break between the trees, then widening as we near until we see the full size of it—a green expanse of water, hundreds of yards wide, separating two tree-covered islands.

As soon as we pass the first channel marker, Claudia motions for me to take the wheel. Once I do so, she rushes below, returns with her cellphone, punching in a number. She listens, frowns and punches in the number again. This time she grins, gives a thumbs up. She jots notes on her pad as she listens, asks questions and listens again.

After she disconnects, she joins Chloe and me at the helm. "Got a description of the man they met at the airport," she says.

"And?" Chloe asks.

"An old guy." Claudia looks at the pad. "He arrived at 11:45 on flight 763 from Kingston, traveling by himself, carrying an overnight bag, no other luggage. My man describes him as tall, around mid-sixties, light-skinned but probably black, wearing a really expensive black silk suit."

"Virgil Claypool," Chloe says. "We were just in his office the other day. I don't think he'll be too much of a problem for us."

I nod agreement, say, "What else?"

"They drove back to Grove House and checked him in, then they went to the office. They left there, together, a little while ago. Right now all of them, Peter, Ian, Rita and Claypool have just arrived for an early dinner at Detardo's."

"It's a steak restaurant," I say to Chloe. "I used to go there a lot."

Squinting at the sun, now low enough in the sky to make looking due west painful, I take the final turn of the channel, past Adam's Key, a small island with a half dozen assorted wood homes on it, into Biscayne Bay and tell Claudia to dial her man again. "Tell him to call you when they leave the restaurant. Even if the other Peter decides to come back to Caya DelaSangre after dinner, I think we have plenty of time to visit the island before he does."

I jam the throttles forward, smile at the surge of power that follows. As we speed up the bay, Chloe points to three towering, red-topped smokestacks showing from across the bay, and to a large hill, almost a mountain she sees to the north of it. "What are those?" she says.

Both man-made structures serve as useful landmarks from the water but they've always struck me as a jarring reminder of what mankind sometimes does to sully the beauty of nature. "The smokestacks are from a nuclear power plant, Turkey Point," I say. "They call the hill, Mt. Trashmore. It's a city dump."

Chloe frowns. "They don't belong here."

I nod, say, "But look at everything else."

We have the bay to ourselves, the waters so calm that

our wake seems to spread out forever behind us. To our left, the sun has begun to sink out of sight, its last rays glinting on the rippled water, the sky and clouds streaked with reddish colors, the mainland darkening. To our right, a string of tranquil, tree-covered, barrier islands—Elliott, Sands and Boca Chita keys—all appear to grow greener in the waning light. Only our motors break the calm of the dying day, their drone filling the quiet air around us. Chloe presses close beside me. "It is beautiful," she says.

The sun has set by the time we reach Caya DelaSangre. To our west, the city lights of Miami and Coral Gables glow in the sky. The lights of Key Biscayne and Miami Beach illuminate the dark to our north. No lights show from my island, only the dark gloom of land contrasted with the black liquid of the sea.

I grin. "Think I still know the way in?" I say.

"For sure, better than the other Peter," Claudia says. "He actually managed to miss the channel and sink your boat. I didn't know whether to laugh or cry when I saw what he did to it."

"Something else he'll pay for," I mutter and turn into the island's channel, barely slowing, taking turns from memory, easing on the throttle just yards before we enter the small harbor.

Only a few barking dogs greet us from the dock. "Where are the rest?" I say.

Claudia shrugs. "They were all here before the other Peter came."

{*Do you think Derek would have eaten them?*} I mind-speak to Chloe.

{*He's lazy enough.*} My bride frowns. {*My parents always had to remind him to leave our servants alone. He never understood why we hunted when we had so much fresh meat readily available.*}

As soon as we dock and tie up, I turn to Claudia and say, "Stay with the boat. Sound your horn if your man calls to say they're leaving." Jumping off the SeaRay, I run toward the gate, Chloe following close behind me.

{*Henri!*} I mindspeak. {*Henri!*} I throw the generator switch on, so we'll have lights, take the steps to the veranda two at a time, rush to my room, open the doors. {*Henri!*}

{*Papa?*}

{*I'm on the island, in our house.*} I shout, "Hello!" {*Can you hear me?*}

{*No, Papa.*}

I flick on the lights, dart through the room, barely noticing the mess Derek has left—the crumpled sheets, the piles of dirty clothes—and go through the doors into the interior of the house. I shout again. Chloe calls from behind me. {*Can you hear anything?*}

{*No, I can't.*}

Going around the second-floor landing, I open Henri's doors, then all the others, one at a time, turning on each light, finding nothing. Chloe follows, turning off each light, closing every door as soon as I leave the room. "In case we have to go quickly," she says.

Running upstairs to the great room, I shout again. {*Anything?*} I say.

{*I'm sorry, Papa.*}

{*There's nothing for you to be sorry for.*}

Chloe helps me throw open each cabinet, search all the cupboards—all to no avail. She closes up behind me again as I run down the spiral staircase to the bottom floor. "Henri, can't you hear me?" I shout. No one answers.

I go from cell to cell, from storeroom to storeroom without finding any sign of my son. I shout again and Chloe shouts in tandem with me. {*Henri?*} I mindspeak.

{*Papa, I didn't hear anything except a bell. I tried, Papa.*}

{*What kind of bell?*}

{*I don't know. Sometimes it rings a lot, loud. Then it stops. Then after a little while, it rings a lot again and then stops for a long time.*}

{*Good, Henri, that's the type of thing you have to notice and tell me about so we can find you.*}

{*Yes, Papa.*}

{*We'll come for you soon.*}

{*Please, Papa.*}

I look at Chloe. "He isn't on the island."

"I didn't think so," she says. "He would have heard us." She walks along with me, her arm in mine, as we climb the stairs, leave the house through my room. I tell her about the ringing sound Henri's noticed. "It's a start," she says.

Chloe stops on the veranda and I stop with her, standing still while she stares at the house, over the dark island, out to the sea already dotted with boats' lights. "It's beautiful here," she says. "Peaceful. I know why you love it."

I nod.

She presses against me and I hold her, both of us looking out to sea, the bright light of Fowey Rocks lighthouse flicking on, then off, repeating every ten seconds, a little more than a mile offshore.

"I like it here," she says.

The SeaRay's horn sounds and we turn and walk down the veranda's steps, holding hands.

As soon as we're under way, Claudia says, "It looks like Peter and Claypool plan to be spending the night at Grove House."

"Can you get us a slip at Dinner Key or Monty's?" I say to Claudia. "I want to be close enough to LaMar that we can get there as soon as we know everyone's together."

"Let me try," the girl says. She gives me the wheel while she phones.

"Okay," Chloe says to me, leaning against me. "I have to admit—she is helpful. I guess I'm going to have to learn to like her."

"Or tolerate her," I say, grinning.

{*Would you mind if I spoke to Henri?*} she mindspeaks. {*He must feel so alone. He's just a little boy. It can't hurt if he has more than one person to pay attention to him.*}

{*Do you know how to contact him masked?*}

{*No, but you can show me.*}

{*I guess so,*} I say, thinking about how to do it. {*It's really just like thinking on other frequencies, the way you tune a radio. We can try later, after we're docked, when we can concentrate.*}

"Hey, you guys. I got us a great slip," Claudia says.

We turn and stare at her.

"We're at pier sixteen, right behind city hall. The mayor's window overlooks us."

I shrug. "Hopefully we won't see him," I say.

Claudia insists on staying with us. "I want to go with you tomorrow," she says. "This way you won't have to wait for me. I'll sleep in the Vee berth. Don't worry, I'll be very quiet so I don't bother you two newlyweds."

Chloe and I go to the stateroom, fold out the bed, close the thin wood, folding doors. We hear no sounds from Claudia, but still, it's hard not to be aware that another person is sleeping just a few yards away. We find ourselves whispering.

Chloe giggles. "Is this what a sleepover is like?"

But in bed, she turns serious. "I want to be able to mind-speak with Henri."

"Sure," I say, concentrating on how I mask my thoughts with Chloe, trying to decipher the differences when I mask to Henri. {*I can feel it,*} I mindspeak to Chloe. {*But I don't know how to say it.*}

{*Think it to me,*} she says.

"First let me make sure it's okay with Henri," I say.

I mindspeak to my son, {*Chloe wants to be able to speak with you, masked, like we do. Is that okay with you?*}

{*I think so, Papa. She's nice.*}

{*I think so too. But if I teach her how to reach you, she'll be able to hear us anytime we mindspeak. Is that okay with you?*}

{*Is it okay with you, Papa?*}

{*Sure.*}

{*It's okay then. Oh, Papa,*} Henri says, {*I heard the bells again, just a little before now. I heard a horn too, before the bells.*}

{*What type of horn?*}

{*A loud one. And a rumbly sound too.*}

Deciphering a five-year-old's descriptions can be a challenge. I smile. {*What's a rumbly sound?*}

{*I don't know. It's loud and shaky, sort of growly.*}

{*Like an animal?*}

{*Papa!*} Henri giggles. {*Like a big machine!*}

Shaking my head, I try to figure out what he's talking about, but I have no idea. {*Mindspeak me the next time you hear any of it,*} I say.

{*Yes, Papa.*}

"Henri says it's okay for me to teach you. He likes you," I say.

Chloe smiles.

{*This is the way you and I communicate masked,*} I mindspeak, pressing my forehead against Chloe's.

{*Yes?*}

I nudge my thoughts a little toward the way I reach Henri. {*Can you follow this?*}

Chloe frowns. {*It's a little fuzzy. Say more.*}

{*Check, check, testing, check, check . . .*} I repeat, suppressing a smile as I realize I sound like a roadie. I watch my bride's face, the furrows on her forehead as she tries to follow me.

Finally, she smiles. {*Okay, it's clear.*}

Once again I nudge my thoughts, and once again Chloe works to follow. We repeat the procedure, over and over, coming tiny steps closer each time.

Hours pass and I wonder if we'll finish in time to get any sleep. But the next time I ask, {*Can you follow this?*} Henri and Chloe both say, {*Yes!*}

I stretch out on the bed, smile as my new bride and my son chatter away. After Henri's assured Chloe that he's well and that he's been well fed, she asks if he'd like her to tell him a story.

{*Please,*} he says.

Chloe says it's a tale her mum used to tell her, about a dragon warrior and his battle for his own kingdom. I listen to her, just as Henri does, her words turning into a murmur as I close my eyes, not sure whether it's me or my son who drifts off to sleep first.

27

I wake to find Chloe pressed against me, her breath hot on my neck, her arm across my chest, one of her legs thrown across mine. Opening my eyes, I stare at the cabin's ceiling, listen to the rhythm of my bride's breaths, try to match mine with hers. I'm tempted to fall back to sleep but, I know, there's much to do today.

A large boat nearby starts up its motors and the SeaRay vibrates in sympathy with their watery growls. In the bow of the boat, Claudia coughs, her curtain rustles, and I hear the pad of her bare feet as she makes her way to the head. I jostle Chloe gently, kiss her on her forehead, her closed eyelids, her sleepy lips. "It's time to get up," I say.

She shakes her head and burrows against me. I kiss her more and she says, her eyes still closed, "Okay, okay, I get it." Chloe stretches beside me. "What time is it?" she says.

Claudia's voice comes to us, through the stateroom's thin wood doors. "It's almost eight."

Chloe and I look at each other and laugh. "So much for privacy!" I yell out.

A thirty-foot-long boat can feel very crowded when three people all try to get ready at the same time, especially when the boat has one small head. Still, within forty-five minutes, all of us manage to gather at the galley table, fully dressed, Chloe and I wearing linen street clothes we bought at Fastbuck Freddies, even Claudia forgoing her usual boat clothes for business casual attire.

To my delight, Chloe has chosen to wear the necklace I

sent her and the matching earrings I gave her on the night of the feast. Claudia examines the four-leaf-clover charm with its inset emerald and the emeralds on each earring. "Wow. They match her eyes," she says.

But when I find a package of frozen hamburgers in the boat's freezer and defrost and warm them in the microwave, the Latin girl looks up from her cup of black coffee and her toasted and buttered bagel, and curls her lip at the plateful of meat. "Are you two really going to have those for breakfast? Do you realize how much cholesterol and fat there is in just one of them?"

"Yes," Chloe says. She makes a show of cutting a large bloody piece, pops it in her mouth and chews it as if it's the most delicious thing she's ever eaten. Then she turns her attention back to the small portable TV on the table and watches the local news.

The TV has been on ever since Chloe discovered its existence, shortly after she emerged from the stateroom. "You two have been watching this stuff all your lives," she says. "I've never seen any of this before."

"Look, they've posted a hurricane warning," Claudia says.

I glance at the screen, listen to the weatherman say the main storm could hit before morning tomorrow, maybe sooner. Scattered thunderstorms will probably start hitting soon. He then gives wind speeds and the storm's probable track. I shrug. "It's just a category one hurricane, a two at worst."

Claudia shakes her head. "It'll still kick up some major winds and waves. We're going to have to tie this boat up pretty damned good."

"Depends on how everything goes." The TV switches from a map of the Carribean, showing a graphic of Hurricane Eileen, to a local shot, a newswoman speaking from the side of the road. "If we can take it out there," I say. "The best place for the SeaRay is in my harbor. A boat could ride out any storm there."

Claudia says something, but the newswoman on TV

catches my attention. "And Jack," the woman says into the camera, "boat owners have begun to take their boats to safety. Hundreds of them are bringing traffic to a standstill as they try to bring their boats up the Miami River." An air horn sounds and the camera pulls back to show cars stopping, traffic backing up as a drawbridge drops its gates— a loud, harsh bell ringing continuously. "Not that anyone in rush hour traffic is very happy about what they're doing."

The reporter continues to talk about boat safety as the gates finish lowering into place and the ringing finally stops. Chloe, who's never seen a drawbridge, stares at the TV as the bridge goes up. "Did you hear that ringing?" I say to her.

"You think?"

I nod, mindspeak my son. {*Henri, did you hear anything?*}

{*No, Papa.*}

Chloe looks at me. "Are there other bridges?" she says.

"Could be, but do you have any idea how many drawbridges there are in South Florida?"

"What are you guys talking about?" Claudia says.

The bridge begins to go down. On the screen the picture returns to the weather map.

"Drawbridges," Chloe says.

{*Papa?*} Henri mindspeaks to me. {*I hear a horn now.*}

"Yes!" I slap the table, grinning.

Claudia starts, stares at me.

{*That's wonderful, Henri,*} Chloe says.

"Which bridge was that on TV?" I say to Claudia.

She looks at me, her forehead furrowed. "Why?"

"Which one?" I growl.

Claudia says, "Didn't you see the Hyatt on the other side? That was the Biscayne Boulevard bridge, over the Miami River."

I nod. "How far upriver is the next bridge?"

"South Miami Avenue? Just a few blocks."

"Do we own any property near there?"

"I don't know. Why?" Claudia says.

{*The bell just started.*}

Chloe answers Henri, tells him to describe the sounds he hears.

I say to Claudia, "We think Henri might be near there."

The girl's eyes widen. She reaches for her cellphone.

Henri says, {*There's the rumbly sound again.*}

"The drawbridge gears!" I say out loud. "He has to be close to the bridge to hear them."

"How do you know what he hears?" Claudia says.

I frown at her question. "Just check to see what we own near there. Check if Ian owns any property around there too."

Claudia nods. She punches a number into the phone while she walks toward her berth, away from the noise of the TV.

Chloe and I mindspeak to Henri while Claudia makes one call then another, then two more. Once the bell stops sounding, and the machinery sounds stop, Chloe asks Henri to tell us about the room he's in. {*It's dark in here,*} he says. {*I can't see anything. I don't like it.*}

{*I know. I wouldn't either. Henri, can you put your hands out and feel your way around?*} Chloe says.

{*Guess so.*}

{*Then I want you to walk forward until you feel a wall.*}

Silence, then he says, {*There's some boxes.*}

{*Walk around them.*}

A few moments pass and Henri says, {*Okay, I feel a metal door.*}

{*Can you count?*}

{*Of course! I'm over five. My papa taught me that.*}

{*Then, Henri, I want you to turn around and walk from the door to the other side of the room. Take regular steps and count out each one to me.*}

Listening to him count out each step, picturing him doing so, alone, in the dark, makes me grit my teeth. I hate my powerlessness to spare him this ordeal. Fortunately, it takes him only six paces. Chloe has him repeat the procedure from one side of the room to the other, with much the same result. "It's not a very large room, maybe twelve-feet square," my bride says.

I frown, shake my head. "Which leaves us not knowing much more than we did before."

"We know he's somewhere by the river's South Miami Avenue bridge."

"Which is smack in the middle of downtown Miami. There are hundreds of buildings and warehouses around there, dozens of cargo ships."

My bride puts one of her fingers on my lips, as much to calm me as to silence me. "And we know more now," she says, "than we did before."

"It would be a lot easier if I were still at the office," Claudia says when she rejoins us at the table. "If I could get to the phone numbers in Pop's desk, I could get answers quicker. My people say it will be at least until this afternoon before they can tell me everything, for sure."

She and my bride watch the TV as the hour turns and the news is replaced by a morning talk show. I've no patience for the hostess's inane chatter with her guests, her promise that before the end of the hour all her guests will receive complete makeovers. I can't believe that Chloe and Claudia seem content to watch it, discussing each person's appearance.

Rather than sit in the cabin and watch the TV and them while we wait for the call telling us that Derek and the rest have arrived at LaMar Associates, I go above deck, stand in the cockpit, admire the day.

The sky shows little sign of the pending storm. Only a few gray clouds float overhead; otherwise, all is clear, the sun hot enough to make me reconsider staying above deck. Still, the wind has turned brisk and seems to be building between strong gusts, and while there's a clarity to the sky, there's also a hint of ions in the air that I know predicts a coming storm. Let the weathermen say what they will, I've been through enough hurricanes to realize when one can't be very far away.

Not that Hurricane Eileen concerns me very much at the moment. I pace the deck, try to think of a good way to search out my son, should Claudia's inquiries bear no results. The best thought that I have is that we can take hand-held air horns and sound them as we go from block to block around the South Miami Avenue bridge, asking Henri how close the sounds seem.

I shake my head. There has to be a better way.

Claudia's cellphone rings below. I rush into the cabin.

The Latin girl has already finished her call. She and Chloe look up at me from the table, Claudia's cellphone and a massive, stainless-steel semiautomatic pistol on the table in front of them.

Claudia picks up the pistol. "Pop gave it to me for my last birthday. It's a Desert Eagle, fifty caliber, magnum. It kicks like hell when I fire it." She grins. "My hand aches for hours after I take it to the range, but the damn thing can bring down an elephant."

I stare at the impossibly thick barrel on the pistol, made to look thicker by its shortness. No more than six inches, I calculate. "It looks like it could bring down a herd of elephants," I say.

Claudia nods. She pulls back on the pistol's slide mechanism, racks a round, the motion making a harsh, loud click. She snaps the safety lever, checks it and puts the pistol into a red leather handbag. "One of my people called," she says. "Peter, Claypool, Rita and Tindall are all at the office now."

28

The Monroe building sits on a corner only a few blocks north of Dinner Key Marina. The three of us walk the whole way, no one saying a word, more clouds darkening the sky as we walk. When we stop in front of the tall building, Chloe says, "This is it?"

I nod, point to the windows on the top floor, all overlooking the bay. "LaMar's offices are up there. Let me do the talking this time."

Both guards look up from behind the security desk in the lobby as we enter, their mouths open, each man gawking. The older guard, the balding one says, "Mr. DelaSangre, you were—"

"I snuck out when you weren't looking," I interrupt, grinning. I certainly can understand their confusion. The other Peter, Derek, couldn't have crossed this lobby more than thirty minutes before us.

"But she"—he points to Claudia—"Ms. Gomez isn't allowed upstairs anymore. Mr. Tindall ordered it."

"She's allowed now," I say. "Mr. Tindall will understand." I walk to the private elevator, Chloe at my side, Claudia at hers, and realize, I have no key.

Claudia notices me pause, fumbles in her purse, the large red leather bag hanging from her left shoulder. After a moment, she fishes out a key. "They took mine," she says. "This is Pop's."

*   *   *

When we get out of the elevator, in front of the receptionist's desk in LaMar Associate's offices, Sarah reacts much the way the guards had below. "Sir," she says, looking toward the closed door to the conference room. "I thought . . ."

"Never mind," I say, walking past her, shepherding Chloe and Claudia toward the meeting room. "I assume they're all in there."

Sarah stands. She's younger than I would have guessed, heavier, her jowls frozen by the frown on her face. "But, sir, Claudia's been barred from the office. The meeting's closed."

"Sarah, they're my offices aren't they?"

She nods.

"That's my meeting isn't it?"

"Yes, sir."

"Then sit down and do your job." I open the door to the conference room and we enter.

Seated at the far end of the glossy, mahogany conference table, Derek looks up first. "Well, well," he says. Rita, sitting to his right, and Tindall to his left, both turn their heads toward us and stare.

Leaning in a corner at the far end of the room, his eyes shielded by dark, thick sunglasses, Virgil Claypool gives us a mocking grin. "If it isn't Mr. Ames. And this is your new fiancée, isn't it?" he says.

I flash the older man a cold smile. "Actually," I say, "it's Peter DelaSangre and his wife, Chloe."

Only Ian Tindall's face registers any shock. I'm not surprised that Derek remains so calm. If Virgil is here, Derek has to know of our visit to the Jamaican's Kingston office. But Rita Santiago's lack of expression concerns me.

"Rita," I say, nodding to her. "Ian." I nod in his direction, study him, the papers spread on the table. "Going over the merger documents?" I say.

Tindall gathers up the papers, stacks them, and straightens them as he speaks. "It seems there are some things I don't know about." He looks from Derek to me and then to Rita. "Did you know about this?"

The redhead gives him a dead stare, says nothing.

"We were readying these papers for *that* Peter DelaSangre to sign." Ian tilts his head toward Derek. "I guess you have an objection?"

I nod. "He isn't Peter DelaSangre. His name is Derek Blood. He's an imposter."

Ian looks from me to Derek and back. "And how would we resolve this?"

"Rita," I say. "Ask Derek where you and I bought the earrings Chloe's wearing."

The redhead looks at my wife, then glares at me. "I don't need to." She turns to Ian, puts her hand on Derek's. "This is Peter. He told me a fake might show up with a Jamaican woman. I've spent almost every night with Peter since he came back from Jamaica, Ian. I'd know if he weren't for real."

"Yeah, sure," Ian says, a pink flush blossoming on his usually pale face. Hands shaking slightly, he gathers up the papers, drops some as he jams them in his briefcase. "The fact he promoted you to equal status with me wouldn't affect your judgment, would it, Rita?" The thin man picks up the papers he dropped, throws them in the briefcase, slams it closed, gets up, walks past us to the door and turns.

"I have no idea what the hell is going on, but I'm not about to make a fatal mistake here," he says. "Whichever of you is the real Peter, I want you to listen to me closely. There is no reason for you to take any action against me. All I've done is to follow the orders which a man, who I thought was Peter DelaSangre, has given me. I had nothing to do with deciding to fire Claudia. I had no involvement in the attack on Arturo and no knowledge of who did it, either before or after the fact."

Tindall opens the door. "Whatever is going on here is none of my business. None!" He looks at me, then at Derek. "What I'm going to do now is leave and go home. I'm going to take a few days off while you all work this out. By the time I come back, I hope the two of you will have decided just which one of you is the real Peter. I'll be delighted to follow that Peter's instructions, whichever one of you it turns out to be. Unlike this one here"—he nods toward Rita—"I'm unwilling to risk my life gambling on one side or the other. I wish you both the best."

I grin as the door closes. "He couldn't have covered his ass any better," I say.

"Now what?" Derek says.

"Now I want my son back. Now you should leave," I mindspeak.

The other Peter laughs out loud. *"Why should I, old man? I like it here."* He glances toward Rita. *"She's wonderfully helpful and damnededly good in bed too. So bloody good, I've managed not to feed on her so far."*

Chloe says, *"If it comes to a fight, Derek, you have to know I'll be with Peter. You can't defeat us both."*

Both Rita and Claudia look confused. They have no idea we're communicating. To them, they're just watching people changing expressions, laughing, frowning, smiling inexplicably. Virgil Claypool shows no expression whatsoever, his eyes hidden from sight by his sunglasses.

"So you're going to kill me, both of you together?" Derek says, grinning.

"Not if we can avoid it," I say. *"I just want my son back—soon. And I want you to go back to Jamaica."*

"Sorry, old man." Derek shrugs. *"Can't do. You know, if I come home empty-handed, Pa will kill me."*

"We'd be willing to help you out," I say. *"I wouldn't mind arranging to send some money to Claypool's for all of you every year."*

"Why bother with that when we can have it all?" Derek's smile widens.

The anger that I've kept within me, heats my face, makes my jaws clench. I want to slash out, slice Derek's smile away. *"Then you'll leave us no choice. We will have to kill you."*

"Don't be so bloody sure you can. If you want, we can end this right now."

The mindthought isn't Derek's. I look at Virgil Claypool. He smiles as he removes his sunglasses. Chloe gasps, says, "Pa!" and I find myself staring into Charles Blood's cold, hard, emerald-green eyes.

29

"What the hell is going on here?" Claudia Gomez says, reaching into her purse. She pulls out the Desert Eagle and snaps off the safety, her words and the click of the safety lever breaking the silence in the room.

"Relax, Claudia," I say. "Nothing bad's happening—yet."

"Should I put the gun away?"

I shake my head. "Point it at him." I nod my head toward Virgil Claypool. "If I tell you to shoot, kill him."

The Latin girl nods. "But I wish some of you would say something. It's real creepy, all of you making faces at each other, nobody talking. It's like being with a bunch of deaf people—without the signing."

"Just go with it, Claudia. It's never going to be explained."

"Whatever you say, Peter."

I look at Charles. *"That's a Desert Eagle semiautomatic. It fires fifty-caliber magnums—more than enough power to penetrate your skin, even if you were in your natural form. There are nine rounds in the magazine. If she empties the gun at you and Derek, most probably neither of you will survive,"* I mindspeak.

"Then, without us to release him or bring him food, your son will starve to death," Charles says. *"Don't you think I know you've had to be in contact with him? If you could have found him, you would already have rescued him."* He flashes a cold smile. *"He could be starving*

within yards of you and you still wouldn't be able to find him."

"Pa! That's Elizabeth's child," Chloe says.

The Jamaican shrugs. *"And you're my bloody daughter. Tell me you care what happens to me and Derek. Your poor ma. You took all her herbs and potions. You stole her book! How do you expect her to get on without it?"*

"I intended to send it back after I copied it. And why should I feel bad after what you did to Peter?"

"So we have a standoff," Charles Blood says. *"There still is the matter of the treasure."* He glances at Derek. *"My useless son assures me it's nowhere to be found."*

A flush rises on Derek's face and Charles laughs. *"We could trade Henri for that. We could give you and Chloe a chest of gold too and let you go on your own way. You could choose to live somewhere else. That way no one need be hurt."*

"How can we know we can trust you?" I say.

{*No, Peter!*} Chloe mindspeaks to me, her thoughts masked. {*He'll kill you after he gets the treasure.*}

{*I know that,*} I say. {*But we need time to find Henri.*}

Charles Blood says, *"And how do we know we can trust you to stay away? In the end, all any of us can do is trust and be ready to respond if that trust proves unwarranted."*

Rain splatters on the conference room's window. I look out. The sky which, was so clear such a short time ago, is now turning into a solid gray quilt of angry clouds. The wind gusts outside, rattling the windows, and I wonder if this could be the first outer band of the storm. I stare past the boats—bobbing and dancing, tugging at their lines in the marina—to the murky, whitecapped waters beyond.

"The treasure's on the island," I say. *"But there's a hurricane coming soon. I can show you where it is once the storm's passed."*

"Show me now," Charles Blood says.

I shake my head. *"Not until I know my son's safe. You can arrange to have someone bring him to a neutral place. I'll send Claudia there. We can use our cellphones. Your people can release him to her at the same time as I show you the treasure."*

Charles nods. *"Let's do it now."*

Smiling, I say, *"Derek, look out the window. Your pa wants you to take him to the island now."*

Derek gets up, walks to the window, stares out at the churning water, the pitching boats, and blanches. *"Pa,"* he says. *"The boat would have a bloody hard time of it. There's no harm in waiting for a day or two."*

"It's just a damned storm!" Charles says. *"I've flown in worse."*

"So have we all, Pa. Why go out in it if there's no need? We can go back to the hotel and ride out the storm there."

"What's going to stop them from searching for the child or attacking us?"

"No problem, Pa." Derek grins. He walks over to Rita, kisses her on top of her red hair. "Rita dear, I need you to do me a favor. Will you?"

"Of course, Peter," she says.

"I need you to go visit Henri now."

She nods.

"Bring your cellphone, of course, and your gun."

Rita smiles. "I always do."

"It's a smaller gun than that." Derek points to Claudia's Desert Eagle. "But"—he shrugs—"Henri's just a small boy." He looks in Rita's eyes. "I'm going to call you every six hours, starting at noon. If you don't get my noon call, shoot him. If I don't call at six, shoot him. Until I phone and tell you everything's okay—anytime I miss calling you every six hours, anytime, shoot him. But if I call and tell you to bring him to Claudia, I want you to do that as quickly as you can."

"Okay," Rita says. She checks her watch. "I should go now, so I can be in place for your first call."

Derek looks at me. "Okay?"

I nod.

She gets up and leaves the room. "See, Pa," he says, smirking, clearly pleased with himself. "Now there's nothing they can do to us, nothing they can try without risking the boy's death."

At Derek's insistence we sit in the conference room and wait. After a half hour, he takes out his cellphone, dials a number. "Are you there?" he asks. He nods, says, "Good," and disconnects.

"No one interfered with her," he says to Charles.

"Then, if no one objects, we have to go secure our boat," I say. "Once the hurricane has passed, we can meet and discuss how to exchange the treasure for my son."

Charles Blood nods. Derek forgets his role as Peter, says out loud, "Jolly good."

As soon as we get in the elevator and the doors close, I turn to Claudia. "Tell me someone followed her."

The Latin girl shakes her head. "Someone followed Tindall and someone will follow those two upstairs, but I never assigned anyone to Rita. I never thought she'd go anywhere important without Tindall or the other Peter. I knew she was a no-good bitch. I just didn't think she was an important no-good bitch."

"You knew?"

Claudia nods. "Shit, I should have known better. So much has been going on, I forgot to tell you. Remember when you asked me to check out her story about Tindall keeping on with that development?"

I nod.

"Tindall was telling the truth. The whole thing was dead. Rita was playing you and Pops."

"I guess I'll have to apologize to Ian the next time I see him." I shake my head at the thought of it. "It looks for once that a Tindall has been falsely accused."

"It appears a Santiago is our problem now," Chloe says.

Claudia nods. "And we don't know very much about her at all."

"But," my bride says, "didn't she have to fill out paperwork when she applied for work at LaMar? Wouldn't that help?"

"Some," Claudia says. "I need to talk to Lisa Stanwell, my pop's secretary. She's the only one at the office I know I can count on. But with Pop out, she only comes in after lunch." Claudia takes out her phone and begins to dial.

"So who are you calling now?" Chloe says.

"I told my people to check on LaMar and Tindall property near South Miami Avenue and the river. I think I should have them check for Santiago property too."

"Of course," I say.

I welcome the rain that soaks us on our walk back to the SeaRay. I welcome the wind that assaults us, the cold chill that penetrates to my bones. If my son must suffer, why shouldn't we?

Chloe and Claudia walk in silence beside me, their heads bowed against the wind, their clothes soaked and plastered to their bodies. I'm sure, like me, their thoughts center on how to save Henri. I'm sure, like me, they've found no solution.

Even in the marina, the water has come alive. The boat heaves and bucks in its slip like a wild horse newly restrained, and we have to time our jumps onto the SeaRay to avoid injury. Once aboard, Claudia throws open the hatch and we scramble below.

We have to brace ourselves to stay upright against the boat's sudden movements but, still, the warmth and quiet of the cabin are a relief after the wind and rain outside. Rather than going forward to the privacy of her berth, Claudia strips off her own wet clothes as soon as we enter the cabin, dialing her phone, barking orders, asking questions as she grabs a towel and dries her tanned, naked body.

The girl seems too busy to care about our presence. Still, I look away from her nudity. Chloe, however, stares at Claudia's body. I prepare for another jealous comment, or at least a catty one. But instead, my bride shrugs, strips off her wet clothes, and begins drying herself too. When I make no motion to do the same, she looks at me. "What's the matter? Would you rather stand there dripping?"

The three of us use up every dry towel on the boat, but within minutes we're all dressed in sweatshirts and jeans, Claudia already opening a few vents before the cabin becomes too oppressively warm.

"Tindall owns nothing near South Miami Avenue," the Latin girl says. "Neither does LaMar Associates. I left a message on Lisa Stanwell's voice mail. I'm waiting for her call back and for a report from my people on any property Rita Santiago, or someone close to her, may own. I also told one of my men, Umberto, to go get Dad's Hummer out of the garage and bring it to the marina. This way, as soon as we hear something, we can get going, no matter what the weather."

Chloe looks at me, her eyebrows raised.

"It's the civilian model of an army vehicle," I say. "It costs a fortune. I thought Arturo was nuts when he bought something so ugly. It's wide and squat, like a smashed Land Rover on steroids but it can handle almost any terrain or any weather. If we need to go anywhere today, we'll be glad to have it."

Waiting irritates me. I want to be out doing something, anything. Chloe and Claudia handle the time better than me. They turn on the TV and watch the endless hurricane reports. Rather than stay below and sit with them until Claudia's people call, I throw on foul-weather gear and go above deck, busying myself securing extra lines, making sure the SeaRay won't be destroyed by Hurricane Eileen.

I become so involved in my task, I don't notice at first when the hatch opens and Claudia's hand waves for me to come inside. Finally, she sticks her head out and shouts. I scurry below.

"While you've been playing outside, I've been on the phone," Claudia says as she tries to dry her newly wet hair

with a damp towel. "Rita Santiago owns no property anywhere."

"Damn!" I say.

"But," my bride interrupts us, "an Homar Santiago
owns a home on Southwest Tenth Street and Fifth Avenue.
Claudia checked. He's Rita's uncle."

"It's too far." I shake my head. "That has to be six or
seven blocks away from the river. Henri couldn't hear anything from there."

"It's close enough so Homar can walk to work," Chloe
says, grinning like she knows something I haven't figured
out yet.

I look toward Claudia. She has the same smirk too. I
glare at both of them, begin to regret that I've left my bride
and the Latin girl alone together long enough for them to
bond. "So what?" I say.

My bride turns to Claudia, says, "Tell him."

"It was Chloe's idea to look at Rita's employment ap-
plication for LaMar Associates. Lisa Stanwell pulled it out
and read it to me over the phone. Homar Santiago was one
of Rita's personal references. She listed his occupation as
'bridge tender.' "

Now I grin. "You've both been busy, haven't you?"

"Yup," Claudia says. "I checked. Homar's been working the evening shift at the South Miami Avenue bridge for
the last five years."

"But that still doesn't tell us exactly where Henri is," I
say.

The Latin girl nods. "Maybe not. But I think we're getting close. One of my people lives near downtown. I asked
him to take a drive around the bridge, on both sides of the
river. He just called back a few minutes ago. There isn't
much around it—on any side—just empty dirt lots and
some docks. But, he said, a road runs under the south side
of the bridge. When he took it, he found a small parking lot
built directly under the bridge, on the river side of the
road—you know right into the bridge's foundation, under

the concrete spans. He said, the lot was empty except for a black Ford pickup and a new green Acura—"

"And," Chloe interrupts, "Claudia says Rita Santiago bought a new Acura just like that a few weeks ago."

30

Umberto looks large enough to carry the Hummer on his back if he wanted to. He drives, Claudia in the front passenger seat and Chloe and I in the Hummer's two rear bucket seats. As wide as the vehicle is, as far apart as the chairs are spaced, I'm tempted to shout my words, even though the sounds of the gusting wind and driving rain outside are muted by the vehicle's rugged construction.

We drive north on Bayshore, one of the few cars braving the storm. The full strength of Hurricane Eileen isn't forecast to arrive until early the next morning, but the squalls now hitting, one after another, pack enough wind and rain to keep most people in their homes.

Although it's only four-thirty in the afternoon, the day has turned as gray as dusk. I peer out the rain-streaked windows at the gloom, the shuttered stores and homes, the palms bending before the winds, the downed branches already cluttering the road. A strong gust hits the Hummer, barely nudges it and Umberto turns, flashes a toothy smile and says, "Man, you got to love this car."

From the Grove, downtown Miami's only a short drive away. With no traffic to impede us on Bayshore Drive or Brickell Road, we reach the South Miami Avenue bridge within twenty minutes. Umberto barely slows, turns a hard right onto a sidestreet just before the bridge and almost immediately takes a sharp left onto a road that curves underneath the bridge's structure.

"Stop!" Claudia says.

The Hummer slams to a halt, just a few inches of its

hood exposed to the opening to the undercover parking lot, the rest of the car's body shielded by a concrete wall. It sits for a moment, its motor idling, its windshield wipers snapping from side to side, squeaking against the glass, until Claudia reaches for the ignition key, turns it off.

The car goes silent. "Shit! You think you could find a way to be more obvious?" she says. Umberto's face blushes pink. He looks away. The wind, gusting from behind us, shoots rain and spray under the bridge, spattering the Hummer's rear window.

"Now what?" Claudia says.

I hold up my index finger. "Give me a second," I say, and mindspeak to my son. {*Henri?*}

{*Papa! She's here. She just came in and turned on the lights.*}

{*Rita?*}

He doesn't say anything.

{*Henri, you have to tell me what's happening. I think we're near you.*}

Chloe, who can hear every word my son and I share, opens her door and motions for the rest of us to get out too. We all do—Claudia carrying her Desert Eagle, Umberto holding an almost as lethal-looking black semiautomatic pistol.

{*It's Rita, Papa. She says I have to stay quiet. She has a gun. She says she doesn't want to, but if she has to, she'll hurt me.*}

Umberto rushes forward at a wave of Claudia's hand, points his gun into the garage, swivels his body from side to side as he examines the interior. When he's sure of no threat, he waves us forward. We all enter the garage at the same time, Umberto and Claudia's pistols at the ready.

{*Do as she says, son.*}

{*I'm scared, Papa.*}

{*I know. We're coming. Just do as she says for now.*}

Inside the garage, the only noise comes from the wind at the entrance; otherwise, all is still, calm, quiet. We wander the interior, staring at an asphalt floor laid out with twenty parking spots, looking up at a concrete ceiling held up by concrete spans and pillars and concrete walls. The light fades at the back of the lot, and in that darkened area we find an U-shaped anteroom packed with road signs, safety cones, barricades and other traffic control equipment stacked to the ceiling.

On the left side of the three-sided room, a narrow, clear path leads to a single bathroom door. Umberto tries it. "Locked," he mouths.

"The bridge tender probably has the key," Claudia whispers to me. "I can send Umberto up to the bridge house to get it."

I nod.

The Latin girl whispers instructions to Umberto and he rushes off.

{*Papa, she's holding me near the door.*}

{*Don't fight her, Henri.*}

{*She's mean. I don't like her anymore.*}

{*I don't either, Henri. We'll be there soon.*}

{*Please, Papa.*}

Umberto returns, his clothes drenched, his hair plastered to his skull, a small key ring, with two keys on it, in his left hand. "Sure hope no one needs this bridge to go up," he whispers, grinning. "Somehow the bridge tender ended up falling into the river—after he gave me the keys."

Claudia takes the key ring. I hold up my hand, signaling "Wait."

{*Henri, where is Rita pointing the gun?*}

{*Right now it's in her hand, pointed at the ground, Papa.*}

{*Is she holding you tightly?*}

{*Not very.*}

{*Good. We may be coming in—in a few moments. As soon as the door opens, I want you to push away from her. Run to the other side of the room.*}

{*Okay, Papa.*}

I nod to Claudia. She tries one key in the door's lock. It

doesn't budge. She tries the next and flashes a smile when the knob turns.

She and Umberto rush in first. Chloe and I follow. We find only an empty bathroom. "What the hell!" Claudia says, checking the two stalls, examining the plain white-tile walls. We all look at each other.

Chloe points to the keys in Claudia's hand. "The second key has to be to another door, doesn't it?"

We leave the bathroom, go back into the garage, search for any sign of another door. We find nothing. "Pa warned we could be yards away from Henri without finding him," Chloe says.

I nod, wander back to the storage area. On the right side of it, folded barricade signs are stacked from floor to ceiling. But when I get close, I can see that the stacks start about twelve inches from the wall—enough room for someone to make their way to the back sideways. I motion for Claudia to hand me the keys and begin to sidle my way back. The others follow.

Halfway into the alcove, the closest stack of barricade signs stops and the passageway widens. I stop, look around, spot the steel door at the rear of the area, located on the right wall. I dash toward the door, Chloe behind me, Claudia following, Umberto just emerging from the narrow passageway.

The large man snags the leg of one of the barricades as he rushes toward us and the stack teeters, then falls with a loud, metallic crash.

{*Papa, is that you?*}

{*Yes.*} I glare at Umberto.

{*Rita's right next to the door with her gun. She has her hand over my mouth—hard—so I can't make any noise.*}

{*Henri. Where is she pointing the gun now?*}

{*Toward the door, Papa.*}

{*Away from you?*}

{*Yes.*}

{*When I say so, I want you to change as quick as you can. Can you do that?*}

{*In front of a human, Papa?*}

{*It's okay this time. You have to bite her hand as soon as you start to change.*}

{*Bad?*}

{*As bad as you can.*}

After telling Claudia and Umberto that Chloe and I will be going in alone, I insert the key and try it just enough to see that it will release the doorknob. I take a deep breath. If Henri is shot, I doubt I'll ever forgive myself. I nod to Chloe.

She strokes my cheek and nods.

{*NOW! CHANGE, HENRI!*} I mindspeak. {*BITE HER!*}

Rita's scream pierces through the door. She howls again as I throw the door open and dart inside, Chloe right behind me. I shove the yowling redhead out of my way, ignore her bloody fist, the pistol at her feet and rush toward my son.

Henri, now in his natural form, stands nearby, blood on his mouth and chest. {*Are you okay?*} I say.

He nods, spits out three of Rita's fingers.

"Damn you!" Rita screams. She tries to reach for her gun with her good hand, but Chloe grabs her and throws her down to the floor.

{*Change back!*} I say and Henri reverts to his human form, his clothes ripped and tattered by his shapechange, his face and clothes still splattered with Rita's blood.

"Papa!" he shouts and grabs me as if he'll never let me go.

I hug him too, pick him up, kiss his face, his cheeks.

"You can come in now!" I shout to Claudia and Umberto. They enter, their eyes wide at the spattered blood, the moaning redhead seated on the floor, clutching a bloody, near-fingerless hand with her good hand while Chloe tightens a makeshift tourniquet around her wrist.

"Wow," Claudia says. "I guess you guys didn't need us."

* * *

Henri clings to me, refuses to get off my lap as we drive back to Coconut Grove, the storm's strength growing, rain pelting our car, winds howling. I hold Rita Santiago's cellphone in my right hand, stare at it and frown. Soon it will be six and Derek will call.

I hate that it all isn't over, that I must be apart from my son again, but I'm all too aware that finding and rescuing him was the easier of our tasks. "We still have to deal with your father and Derek," I say to Chloe.

She nods. "I know," she says. "I was thinking the same thing. But how?"

Not sure myself, I shrug. "We can offer to buy them off again. Now that we have Henri and she"—I motion to the redhead huddled in the back of the Hummer, nursing her injured hand—"is no longer available to help them, they may be willing to go away—for a price."

"I doubt it."

"Me too," I say.

Rita's cellphone rings a few blocks before we reach the Dinner Key Marina. I let it ring a few more times, then answer. "Hi, Derek," I say.

Silence.

"Derek, it is you, isn't it?"

"Bloody hell! Where's Rita?" he barks.

"We have her," I say.

"And the boy?"

"He's fine. He's sitting on my lap right now."

Derek doesn't answer. He muffles the receiver with his hand, but still I can make out enough of his conversation to know he's telling his father what's transpired.

Rather than take over the phone, Charles Blood mind-speaks, *"DAMN YOU, BOY, I THOUGHT WE HAD AN AGREEMENT!"*

"You were never going to keep your word, Pa. We both know that," Chloe says.

"I regret your mother and I ever had you."

My bride's eyes water over. *"Me too,"* she says.

"Listen," I say, and I make the offer Chloe and I had

discussed—to send Charles and his family an annual allowance if he and Derek go back to Jamaica.

Derek says, *"It's not a bad idea, Pa. We can't count on Ian Tindall, and without Rita's help, it's going to be sticky making the merger work. . . ."*

"No!" Charles says. *"Quiet, you fool. Don't you have any pride? You could learn from Peter. He knows better than to give up. Besides, he knows Tindall will go with whoever wins. Don't you, Peter?"*

"Yes."

"So, Peter, are you and my ungrateful daughter prepared to face us?"

"We will be," I say.

"Bloody good. Spoken like one of us. Where can we expect to find you? You're not going into hiding are you?"

"No," I say. *"We'll be waiting for you at the house my father, Don Henri DelaSangre, built on the island that bears his name."*

31

At the dock, Claudia offers to let us keep her Desert Eagle, but I shake my head. "I just need to borrow your boat. I'd rather you keep the gun, in case any of those others come after Henri."

"They'll never be able to find us," the Latin girl says.

"Good," I say. "Still, this way my son has some extra protection. Besides, I have guns of my own on my island. If I decide to use them."

"Okay," Claudia says as we leave the car. "Don't worry about Henri. We'll keep him in hiding with us as long as it takes."

I pause by the car door, leaning against the wind, rain stinging my face as I look at Chloe. How could I live if any harm came to her or to my daughter growing within her? "You could go with Claudia too, you know," I say.

Chloe pushes the car door closed. "Don't be silly," she says. She stands by my side, the wind buffeting both of us as we watch the Hummer drive away, even its brake lights obscured by the rain long before it should have been out of sight.

We bow our heads against the wind, tighten our foul-weather gear as we make our way to the boat. Still, rain manages to find its way through all the protection we wear and trickle onto our clothes, soaking us before we reach the SeaRay.

Even inside the marina, the water never ceases jumping. Waves crash into pilings. In every slip, boats pitch and yaw, tugging, jerking on their lines. The SeaRay is no exception and we wait for a lull in the wind, when the boat's movements are a little less violent, before we leap on board.

Chloe jumps alongside me, slips as soon as her feet hit the deck. I catch her, pull her upright and rush to the helm. My bride follows. "Don't you want to go below and change?" she shouts against the storm.

I shake my head. "It wouldn't help—too much wind." For the same reason, I don't bother putting up the dodger. The wind would probably tear it away before we had it in place. I hit the switch to lower the boat's drives into position, then put the key in the ignition, turn it and nod when both motors cough to life.

"Good thing we're backed into the slip," I say, going to the stern, casting off lines. "I'd hate to back out in this weather."

Giving Chloe a knife, I tell her to cut the bowlines when I signal. "We have more lines on board," I say. "There's too much strain on those to risk undoing them."

As soon as I motion, Chloe cuts both lines and I gun the motors, trying to get enough forward momentum to overcome the resistance of the wind and the waves. My bride rushes back off the bow and joins me, watching me turn the helm, sharp, as I jam down the throttles.

Just before we make it all the way out of the slip, the boat shudders as we crunch into a piling. I motion for Chloe to look over the side while I continue taking the boat out of the marina. "The side is cracked just below the deck," she says.

"Too high to threaten us," I say, give Chloe a thumbs-up and steer the boat toward the channel.

Once outside the marina, into the open bay, we feel the full strength of the storm. Rain blinds us. Winds push us off course. Waves toss us as they wish.

As much as I would rather be in my Grady White, the SeaRay surprises me with its ability to plow through the churning water. Between the darkening day and the thick rain and salt spray, we have no visibility. I steer by compass and instinct, reacting to waves as they rise up before us, speeding and slowing as the conditions dictate.

"At least we know that Derek wouldn't dare bring his boat out in this," I say.

Chloe hugs my arm, looks at me with her brown, rain-dampened face. "True," she says. "But what guarantee do we have that they'll come by boat?"

Near Caya DelaSangre, the wind lessens, blocked by the island's mass. Still, the bay leaps all around us; so much so that I give up all hope of following the channel. I can only pray the storm surge is high enough to let us pass safely over the rocks.

We hit bottom at least a half dozen times, each crunch and scrape loud enough to convince me that we'll sink any moment. But the boat continues to amaze me with its resilience, finally delivering us into the island's small, relatively calm harbor.

"My father built four arms rooms when he constructed our house," I say as I pull up to the dock and tie the boat off. "He stocked them with pistols, rifles, large guns and cannons—with lead and shot and powder. Some of the guns are large enough to stop your father and your brother."

Helping Chloe off the boat onto the dock, I take her hand and pull her toward the house. "They're called rail guns. Elizabeth was almost killed by one. We can open one of the arms rooms and load two or three for each of us. Then let Derek and your father come attack us."

My bride stops walking, tugs back on my hand. "What?" I say, look at her face.

But she looks past me. I turn, follow her gaze, see the two large dragons waiting in the rain, at the top of the veranda's steps. Chloe says, "I don't think that plan's going to work anymore."

"Change!" I say, ripping off my clothes. Chloe nods, does the same with hers.

"We've been waiting for you." Charles Blood laughs. *"It's a pity the weather's so bloody awful. It would be so much more fun if the sky were clear. Wouldn't you agree?"*

"No. This way, in this weather, we can do what we need to do without any humans noticing us," I mindspeak, willing my body to change, regretting that Chloe and I have nothing to feed upon.

"So you've no intention of running?"

I flex my shoulders as my wings form behind me. I curl and uncurl my taloned fists. *"Why would I? This is my home, my wife. Why would I let you take that from me?"*

"Well said." Charles Blood begins to walk down the steps, Derek just behind him. *"Chloe, I may have underestimated your man."*

My bride, now fully in her dragon form, says, *"You did, Pa."*

The large dragon pauses on the staircase's middle step. *"Jolly good. Then we'll have a proper row today, won't we?"*

{*Fly, Peter!*} Chloe mindspeaks me, masked, and takes to the air. I follow her just as Charles and Derek both launch themselves toward us.

"WAIT!" Charles mindspeaks. *"I thought you wanted to fight."*

"Follow me," I say. *"You'll find me soon enough."* But I don't feel half as brave as my words. Both Charles and Derek are larger, heavier and more powerful than me. Only Chloe and I, working together, have any chance of victory and that's only if we can find a way to separate Charles and Derek and engage them one at a time.

{*Higher,*} I mindspeak to my bride. {*We have to get far above them.*} But the rain blinds us, the wind tumbles us across the sky as we try to climb.

{*At least, they have to fight the weather too,*} Chloe says, beating her wings, straining skyward.

The storm surges around us, dark clouds racing by, lightning crackling across the sky, thunder shaking the sea beneath us. One flash reveals a scaled creature flying at least five thousand feet below us. {*Derek!*} Chloe says.

We both fold our wings and fall toward him, our speed increasing as we dive, our talons ready to rip through him. He roars as we appear, as if out of nowhere, and bellows when Chloe rips through his right wing and I tear through his left.

"*Pa!*" he mindspeaks as he falls toward the sea. "*They surprised me and tore my wings. I can't fly!*"

"*You didn't even fight them?*" Charles says. "*You useless child.*"

Derek sends up a white plume of water as he hits the angry sea. "*Pa! Help me!*"

"*You bloody well know how to swim. Save yourself. Rejoin me when you're healed.*"

Chloe and I beat our way skyward again.

"*Peter, Chloe, good show that,*" Charles Blood calls. "*I must warn you. You won't find me so easy.*"

Neither of us answer. We save our energy, concentrate on gaining altitude, ignore the constant driving rain, fight each gust of wind as if it were as much an opponent as Chloe's father. My muscles ache. My lungs struggle to take in enough air to renew my tired blood. I know if we don't win soon, exhaustion will defeat us before Charles can.

The air is too rough, the day too dark, the rain too thick for us to soar and examine the sky beneath us. We fly as high as we can, until the air grows too thin, then spiral down, looking for Chloe's father.

He strikes at three thousand feet, diving from above us, slashing open my back, from my shoulders to my midsection, as he passes. He catches Chloe too, ripping through her right wing, tearing a gash on the side of her throat, striking an artery, her blood spraying into the sky around us.

My bride roars from the pain, tumbles in the air as she falls. "*Peter! I'm sorry!*" she calls.

I howl into the stormy night, circle once, looking for Charles, and, unable to locate him, I dive after my bride.

He swoops up from the dark sky beneath me, rushing toward me, his talons extended. I know my best course would be to turn away, evade him, but my injured bride lies in the sea beneath him. I fold my wings even more so I dive faster, shoot like a bullet toward the large dragon.

We collide in midair, both roaring, his claws tearing into me, his teeth ripping large chunks of my flesh. I tear into him too — not as deep, not as damaging as him, but enough to injure the older creature. He howls and breaks free before we hit the water.

"Not bad, Peter," he says as he flies away. *"I didn't think you could hold up so well."*

I don't answer. As much as I injured Charles, he wounded me doubly. If the fight had continued, I know which dragon would have won. I wonder why he chose to break away without finishing it.

"Save your wife now," Charles Blood says. *"She's shown her bravery. There's no reason either she or my granddaughter should die. We've plenty of time for you and me to end this, after they're safe."*

I hit the sea and writhe in agony as the salt water finds each cut, each tear, each scratch. *"Chloe!"* I mindspeak. *"Answer me!"*

"Peter, I'm floating somewhere near you. I think. I mended my artery. I'm so tired I can't heal anything else."

"Wait," I say. Other than stopping my bleeding, I heal nothing else. Chloe needs me to conserve whatever energy is left. Gathering my strength, I surge out of the water, take to the sky and skim low over the waves, fighting the storm as I search for my bride.

"Chloe!" I mindspeak. *"Can you see me?"*

"The waves are too high. I can't see anything!"

I circle and circle, my muscles protesting, my breath coming in ragged gasps, my wounds searing with pain. *"Chloe!"* I have lost one bride. I will not lose another and a daughter too. *"Chloe!"*

"Peter? I think I see you — or something in the sky above me."

Looking down, I see a dark object floating in the white froth of a broken wave. I dive toward it, scoop my bride from the water. She goes limp as soon as I have her in my grasp, the burden of her dead weight almost taking me from the sky. But I fight upward, away from the sea and let the winds rush me toward my island.

Landing alongside the dock, next to the steps to the veranda, I lower my near-comatose bride to the ground. I scan the sky above, find no sign of either Derek or Charles and rush up the steps. I nod my head when I find the veranda empty. But I know there's no guarantee either of them won't choose to avail themselves of the house's shelter at any time.

Going back to my bride, I pick her up and carry her into the bushes, to the secret entrance leading to the treasure room. The wind fights with me as I pull open the passageway's oak door but within moments, Chloe and I are inside, the storm's fury blocked and silenced by the thick oak door.

32

With barely any strength left, I struggle to half carry, half drag Chloe up the passageway to the small chamber that houses the door to the treasure room. Leaving her on the floor, I feel on the wall for the light switch and flick it on.

I gasp. My poor Chloe! Cold to the touch, she lies with her eyes closed, breathing in rapid, shallow gasps. White bone shows at the bottom of the long, red gash on her neck. Her scales have turned dull green, her torn wing lies unfolded and laid out at her side.

It takes all my willpower to resist lying down beside her, resting in the quiet safety of the chamber, but I know both of us need food if we're to rest and heal. I nuzzle Chloe with my snout, say, "I'll be back as soon as I can."

She shows no sign of hearing me. I force myself to leave her, enter the dark passageway that leads to the cells above. In my natural form, the passageway and steps leading up to the cells are almost too snug. I shrink myself a little to speed my way up the steps and, at the top, I push up on the bottom of the floor above me until it begins to rise and pivots out of the way. As soon as it does, I rush to the storeroom which holds the freezer and study the dozens of frozen sides of beef hanging dangling from hooks.

The meat will be cold and hard but so what? As long as it nourishes Chloe and me it will have served its purpose. One side, I think, will feed us for now, but I have no certainty how long it will be before Charles and Derek decide to search the house.

I take down three frozen sides of beef. Since there isn't

enough room in the passageway for me to carry more than
one side of beef at a time, I leave two of them on the floor.
Picking up the other, I tear off a chunk of frozen meat and
chew on it as I carry it back to my bride.

I find her lying as I left her, her eyes still closed. Well
aware that Charles and Derek might rush into the house at
any moment I hurry back up the steps, make two more trips
to bring down the rest of the meat.

At first, Chloe can take only small pieces, which I rip
from the beef carcass and force between her lips. Swallowing my own saliva, I ignore my hunger, forgo eating
any more myself until my injured bride feeds enough to
start healing.

I wait while she chews each bite, then feed her another,
lying on her, hoping my body will warm hers. *"Chloe. You
have to eat. You have to heal."*

"I want to sleep."

"Not yet," I say. *"You have to eat more."*

She shakes her head, but takes the meat from my claw.
"More," I say.

"I'm tired."

"So am I. You still have to eat."

I start giving her larger pieces which she chews and
swallows. *"It's cold,"* she says. *"Can't you warm it?"*

"No." I nuzzle her, feed her another chunk. I mask my
thoughts. {*We can't risk going upstairs. We might run into
your father or your brother.*}

Chloe's eyes open. {*Where are they?*}

I shrug.

{*Where are we?*}

Still masked, I say, {*We're in a secret passageway
under my house. Derek never found it. He and your father
have no way of knowing where we are. We're safe as long
as we stay here.*}

{*My father,*} she says. {*Peter, he could have killed both
of us. Why didn't he?*}

{*I'm not sure. I think he's enjoying all of this. Maybe he*

*doesn't want it over so soon. He definitely made it clear—
he wanted me to save you.*} I feed Chloe another chunk of
meat.

Wincing, she shifts her body, pushes me off her and sits
up on one haunch. {*Pa wanted you to save me?*}

I nod. {*He said you'd shown your bravery, there was no
need for your or our daughter's death.*}

{*I guess Pa isn't quite the monster we thought he was.*}
Chloe looks at me. {*Still, look what he's done to you. My
poor Peter,*} she says, stroking my jowl with a foreclaw.
{*All you wanted was a wife and a family.*} She examines
my wounds, shakes her head at each rip, each bite. {*Look
what loving me has brought you.*}

{*Look what it's brought you,*} I say, tearing off another
bit of meat, offering it to her.

She pushes it back. {*You need to eat. You need to heal
too.*}

{*You take that one. I'll eat another.*} Chloe accepts the
piece I offered while I tear off another chunk of cold meat
and bite into it.

We both go silent while we feed and concentrate on
healing our bodies. I think over what Chloe said as I gulp
and chew large chunks of meat, shifting my body back to
its full size as soon as I've regained enough energy to do
so. No matter what the outcome of our conflict with
Charles and Derek, I have no regrets that I chose to pursue
her or that she chose to have me.

{*Are you sorry now that I came for you?*} I say.

Chloe stops feeding, looks at me. {*Not for a moment,*}
she says. {*I'm only sorry my family treated you the way
that they did.*}

"Peter!" Charles Blood's thoughts interrupt us. "Where
are you, boy? Haven't you had enough time?"

"No," I say. "Chloe and I are still healing."

"Forget Chloe. You two injured my fool son so badly
he's still off healing himself. It's just you and me, boy.
There's no reason to involve my daughter. You and I can
settle things."

"Pa. Why can't you just leave both of us alone? Peter already offered to help you," Chloe says.

"I've never backed off from a fight in my life. Besides, your Peter has been giving me a good what for. I'm curious to see how well he can stand up."

"But you might kill him."

"I may very well. It is my intention, you know. But don't forget, he may kill me."

"Pa, I'll have to help him."

"I'll understand if you do. He's your mate after all. Your ma would do the same for me. But I hope you don't. You've always been too willful, Chloe. That doesn't mean you and your child should die.

"And you, Peter," Charles continues. *"Please convince my daughter to stay out of this. It's time now for us to end this. Show yourself, boy. Don't make me come searching for you."*

"I'm not your damned boy!" I say. *"Search whenever and wherever you wish. My father taught me long ago that only a fool fights at his enemy's convenience. I'll show myself when and where I please."*

Charles says nothing.

I tear off another morsel of meat, push it toward my bride and say, {*I think your pa was right. I should fight him alone.*}

{*I'm not going to let you face him without my help. I can't sit in safety and watch you go to your death,*} Chloe says.

{*Look at yourself. You've lost too much blood. By the time you're healed, Derek will be too. I should fight your father before he has help.*}

{*You were talking about getting guns from the arms room. I'm well enough to pull a trigger.*}

I shake my head, bite off more meat, force my body to mend as quickly as it can. {*Face facts,*} I say. {*Your father has to be waiting for me somewhere nearby. The arms rooms' doors are outside, on the veranda. I don't know if I can reach one without him seeing me. If I do reach one, I don't know if I'll be able to get any rail guns loaded and ready before he attacks. And even if the guns are loaded I don't know if they'll stay dry enough to fire in this storm.*}

{*So you think I should stay here and wait while you may go to your death? Don't you realize what your dying would do to me?*}

{*Of course.*} I sigh. {*But now that we know your father doesn't want to kill you, it would be foolish for you to risk your own death. We have to think of our daughter—and of Henri. At least if you survive, they'll have a mother.*}

Chloe says nothing. We feed in silence, only stopping once we're gorged. Lassitude overtakes us and we lie for too long, half dozing, side by side.

A loud crash comes from the floor above and I sit upright, wondering what might have been shattered, what could have broken to make noise penetrate the stone walls around us.

"Peter, I'm tired of this!" Another crash breaks the calm quiet around us. *"Show yourself soon or I'll destroy everything in your house."*

"What's the matter, Pa? Can't find us?" Chloe mindspeaks.

I wince at the crash that answers her. {*Good, why don't you taunt your father more. Let's see if he can break everything I own,*} I say.

My bride's eyes twinkle. {*Okay,*} she says, then mindspeaks, *"Please, Pa, don't do anything to the dining table. Peter and I love it."*

Charles doesn't answer, but a few minutes later something large slams into the floor above us. I wince at the thought of the massive oak table dropping three stories to the stone floor of the bottom landing.

Chloe stifles a giggle. {*Sometimes he's so predictable,*} she says.

{*I can see why he may have thought you were difficult,*} I say.

My bride nods.

{*You know I'm going to have to go soon.*}

Chloe lays her tail over mine, strokes me with it. {*Not yet.*}

I lie back down, nuzzle the back of her neck. {*If I could, I'd stay here with you for days,*} I say. {*But if I go soon, while your father's still inside, I may be able to get in position to surprise him.*}

"*PETER, YOUR BOAT WILL BE NEXT!*" Charles says.

A laugh erupts from Chloe. "*IT'S NOT EVEN OURS!*" she mindspeaks, then giggles.

Something else breaks overhead and I can't resist laughing too. Then we both go silent, ignoring the noises, paying no attention to Charles's angry outbursts, stroking each other, not as a preliminary to sex, but as an acknowledgment of the pleasure we take from each other's presence.

Chloe stretches, looks around the chamber and lazily motions to the steel door nearest to us. {*Is that the door to the treasure room?*} she mindspeaks.

{*Yes.*}

She points to the other steel door, across the chamber from us. {*Then what's that door lead to?*}

Bolting to a sitting position, I stare at the ancient steel door, the aged, rusted locks and the equally rusty chains that protect it. {*I've never been inside,*} I say, remembering my father's words. {*Father said I should only open that door if there's no other hope. I think this qualifies.*}

Standing, I walk to the door, examine the locks and chains and reach up and run my right foreclaw over the stones to the right of the door.

Chloe sits up and stares at me. {*What are you doing?*}

Stopping at the third stone, I tug on it. It moves and I pull on it, work it out and put it on the floor. {*Father told me there's a chest inside. With some sort of weapon. I'm getting the key.*} I reach into the cavity, feel a small wood panel, slide it out of the way and find a thick, rusty key. Taking it out, I show it to Chloe. {*See.*}

She gets up, hobbles toward me as I attempt to put the key in one of the ancient padlocks. At first, it doesn't fit. I hit the lock with my claw and rust falls away. I strike it again, knock off more rust and then try the key again. It slides in and, after a little initial resistance, it turns.

Undoing that lock, I use it to bludgeon the others, knocking off rust, loosening their mechanisms. They too click open and I pull the chains off the door, swing it open.

The room is empty except for a small wood chest left on the stone floor, near the back of the room. I go in and carry it out.

{*That's going to have to be a mighty small weapon,*} Chloe says.

I lay the chest on the ground, stare at it. {*It barely weighs anything,*} I say.

Chloe opens the chest, takes out its entire contents—two small wood boxes. One has a painting of a large fire-breathing dragon on it, an X etched beneath it. The other has a painting of a smaller dragon.

My bride opens the first box. It holds twelve glass vials, seven empty, five filled with a green fluid. {*Oh, my,*} Chloe says. She opens the second box, once again finds twelve vials, four empty this time, eight filled with an amber liquid. {*Oh, my,*} she says again. {*Do you think this could be what I'm thinking?*}

She closes the boxes and I study the two dragons on their covers. Chloe puts her finger on the larger, fire-breathing dragon. {*I think that's the image of a Zal warrior.*} She moves her finger to the image on the other box. {*And that's an Undrae.*}

{*Father said this came from an ancient war, before the time of humans,*} I say. {*You think this is the potion you told me about? The one the Undrae used to fight the Zal?*}

Chloe nods.

I open both boxes, take out a full glass vial from both. {*No wonder Father said this was dangerous,*} I say.

{*Remember, if you take it, you only have twelve hours. If you don't drink the antidote by then*}—Chloe points to the amber liquid—{*you'll die.*}

33

Chloe's color still hasn't returned. Every movement she makes causes her to wince. It will take hours more before she can mend all the damage to her body, before she regains most of her strength. I don't want to leave her, not yet, not ever.

Another crunch of something breaking above resonates through the house and I look at Chloe. {*I need to get ready for him outside,*} I say.

My bride nods.

{*Do you have any idea how much potion I should drink?*} I say. {*How long it will take to act?*}

{*No,*} Chloe says. {*All I know is that Undrae warriors took it to grow as large as the Zal.*}

{*How large was that? Twice as big? Three times?*}

She shrugs. {*No one ever said. Look at the pictures on the boxes.*}

I hold them up and compare them. The picture of the Zal warrior is no more than half as large as the Undrae. But was size dictated by the amount of potion taken? Could too much potion prove fatal?

In the absence of any answers, I can only act from my own guesses. I thin my body, shrink my size so I can haul two sides of beef at the same time through the passageway to the outside door. {*To grow that much must require a tremendous amount of energy,*} I say to Chloe. {*I'm going to put this meat outside, so it will be there for me after I drink the potion.*}

{*Why don't you take the potion first?*} she says.

I shake my head. {*We don't know how quickly it acts. If its effect is immediate, I'll grow too large for the passage-way.*}

Leaving the two vials with Chloe, I carry the meat to the door. The winds outside have intensified and I have to push my shoulder against the oak door, use all my strength to force it open. Wind lashes at me as soon as I go outside. Rain slams against me. I calculate it must be near midnight now, the storm building toward its full strength.

The wind tries to tear the sides of beef from my grasp but I manage to hold on to them. I carry them to the dock, lay them down near the foot of the veranda stairs, where the storm's fury is partially blocked. Then I return inside for the vials and to say good-bye to my wife.

{*Stay here with me,*} she says.

I shake my head. {*You know better than that.*}

{*We could go away together. Forget about my father and Derek.*}

{*I'd no more run than your father would. If I did, I wouldn't be the man you married.*}

{*But we haven't had any time.*}

{*We've had enough to make me sure I love you,*} I say.

{*And I you. Wait at least until I'm strong enough to help.*}

{*No,*} I say, stroking her face with my foreclaw. {*Don't forget. I have the potion now. If anyone will have an ad-vantage, it will be me.*}

{*If it works. It must be older than the millennium.*}

I laugh. {*A fine thought to send your husband as he leaves for battle. It will work and I will be back.*}

Chloe presses the side of her face against mine and we stay that way for a few moments before I break away, take the vials and head for the door—and for the storm that waits for me outside it.

34

Wind pummels me, rain blinds me as soon as I emerge from the house's protection. I shift my body back to its normal full size and feel my way through the bushes, turning to where I left the meat, not twelve paces away. A lightning bolt cuts its way through the sky overhead, illuminating the night for an instant. The flash shows the image of the large dragon nearby, hunched over a side of beef, feeding.

Dark returns almost instantly, but too late to prevent my discovery. *"Peter. How good of you. I came out to begin destroying your boat and I found you set out this food for me. How kind of you to make yourself so available too,"* Charles says.

"Are you finished destroying everything in my house already?" I say, holding both vials in one hand, trying desperately to remember which one is which. In the dark, in the rain, it's impossible to tell green from amber. *"I'd hoped you'd be busy a little longer so I could eat before we began."*

Charles Blood laughs, tears a huge chunk of meat with his teeth. *"Come join me, boy. Feed as you wish."*

"And you, of course, will back away, leave me enough room to be able to dodge your attack."

"Possibly yes, possibly no." Charles laughs again. *"You'll have to decide if the food is worth the risk."*

"I thought you believed in being sporting," I say, transferring one vial into my left foreclaw. Deciding to chance it, I hold it up to my face.

Charles says, *"But not on being foolish."*

Another flash of lightning lights the island and I see Charles has changed his position to a crouch, like a cat ready to pounce. Thunder rolls over us and a second flash makes the amber fluid in the vial in my left hand momentarily glow yellow. I gasp, throw it toward the bushes and leap into the air.

"Peter, leaving so soon. Is it something I said?"

The wind catches me, throws me up, drops and tumbles me. I try to gain altitude, fumbling with the cork stopper sealing the vial of green potion, as I beat my wings, straining to fight the wind, but finding myself flying sideways.

"Isn't this a grand night?" Charles says, passing me in the dark, slashing out, missing any vital part of me, engaging only the tip of my tail, ripping it.

I bellow, as much from the surprise as from the pain. Enough, I think. I put the vial to my mouth and bite down, ignoring the pain of the broken glass as it cuts into my lips and tongue, swallowing every bit of the potion.

It tastes rancid, spoiled, like fish oil left out in the noonday sun. My stomach revolts and I struggle to keep it down, gulping air, swallowing rainwater to dull the taste.

Nothing happens. My tail still throbs. The storm still batters me. The wind still pushes me where it wishes. Even worse, I know Charles Blood is somewhere in the night, close, waiting for another opportunity to strike.

I work at gaining altitude, search the sky at every burst of lightning. See nothing.

The air around me crackles with static electricity and I prepare for yet another lightning bolt. It shoots through the air so near to me that I can feel its heat. Its brief light reveals the beast hurtling toward me from above.

Folding one wing, I tumble out of his path. I fold my other wing after he passes and plummet after him, falling a thousand feet in seconds, catching him, ripping through his back with my rear claws. Roaring, I finally spread my wings and shoot away from him.

He bellows, soars off in the other direction into the dark.

Once again, I beat skyward.

"Well done, boy. I'm impressed. Nobody has ever been able to stand up to me. Not that you won't lose eventually, mind you. But it seems we'll both have fun tonight."

"You think this is fun?" I say.

"Bloody good fun. I haven't had such a good row since I fought to win Samantha."

Another lightning bolt illuminates the world, but I see nothing. Charles hits me from the side, folds his wings over mine and sinks his teeth into the back of my neck as we fall. Howling, I thrash and twist to break his grip. His claws dig into my side and I twist even more, ignoring the pain as talons rip through my flesh, finally grabbing his side with one of my foreclaws, slashing through it.

We hit the water, Charles on top of me, and the momentum of our fall carries us deep below its surface. The older dragon kicks free, swims away.

Pain rages through me. Unable to move at first, I can only drift upward as quickly as my buoyancy takes me. I slowly force my muscles back into action, barely paddling until my lungs begin to burn, taking stronger and stronger strokes after that.

Breaking through at the crest of a wave, I gasp a breath, then another. My heart pounds so much that I fear heart failure. I breathe in again, tread water as one wave after another lifts and drops and tosses me.

I doubt whether I can survive another attack. The pains from my wounds sicken me and leave me weak. My heart hurts. My lungs beg for more air. My muscles ache. My stomach churns and rumbles and begins to burn. How can I hope to face Charles again?

My head throbs with each beat of my heart. As many gasps as I take, my lungs still beg for more air. I've never felt this way, no matter how injured. I consider mind-speaking to Chloe, saying my last good-byes.

My entire stomach and chest feel as if I've swallowed

hot coal. I open my mouth and a small flame shoots out. I gasp, swallow a gulp of salt water to diminish the heat. It doesn't help. But my pains begin to diminish, replaced by the familiar pangs brought on by growth.

I flex my wings in the water and smile at their new strength. I stretch my shoulders and growl in pleasure at their increasing bulk. The potion! I think. Finally, it's begun to work. I burst out of the water, take to the sky and roar out a challenge.

"Peter? Is that you?" Charles Blood says. *"Are you ready for more already?"*

I'm amazed at the strength I feel coursing through me, the size I've grown to, the fact I'm still growing. My blood pounds in my veins and arteries, my lungs pump great quantities of air. Heat continues to grow within me. *"More than ready,"* I say.

This time Charles chooses to attack from below. I see him coming, do nothing to avoid him. Just before he hits me, he says, *"My God! You're as large as a Zal!"*

Blocking his attack with a rear claw, I tear his face with it. *"Yes, I am,"* I say.

Charles sinks his teeth into my leg, slashes at my underbelly with his foreclaws. I shake him off, like a Great Dane pushing away the nuisance of a Cocker Spaniel's attack.

"Give it up, Charles," I say. *"This is no longer a fair contest."*

He drops away from me. *"I've never given up in my life. I don't know how you did this, but nothing, bloody nothing is over. DEREK!"* he mindspeaks. *"I NEED YOU!"*

"Yes, Pa! I'll be there in a few minutes."

"I thought you said it was just us two."

"And I thought you were an Undrae," Charles says, flying away from me.

If I wanted, I know I could catch him before his son can join him. But I let him go. Roaring, I beat my wings, fly higher, faster. The storm rages around me. Gusts of wind try to stop me and I roar again. I am too strong to be deterred by a mere hurricane, too powerful to worry about the combined attack of any two ordinary beings, even if they are People of the Blood.

Let Charles and Derek worry about me. I roar again, continue to climb. My heart shudders with each mighty beat. My muscles continue to swell. I climb, piercing angry cloud after angry cloud, flying upward until I finally emerge into clear, dark sky, sprinkled with stars and overseen by a silver splinter of the moon. Breathing cold thin air, I coast over the black blanket of storm clouds below me.

My size amazes me. I must be more than twice my natural size by now and, although my growth seems to have stopped, my heart continues to beat faster, harder. My wounds no longer bother me, but hunger overtakes me and with it, exhaustion. I think of the sides of beef lying by the dock on my island and my saliva almost drowns me. Folding my wings, I sigh and drop into the storm again.

I descend so rapidly that when I finally open my wings, I shoot past my island. Banking, I circle back, land on the dock near the meat. Thankfully, it's still there, one carcass untouched, the other only partially consumed by Charles.

Rushing forward, I tear a chunk from the untouched side of beef and swallow it almost whole. I bite another piece, then another, desperate to fill the void inside me. It takes half a side of beef before my hunger begins to subside. Even then, I continue to gorge, my heart still thumping too quickly, aching as it shoots blood to my tired muscles.

I bite into the frozen carcass again, rip another chunk of meat and chew it—more slowly this time as I begin to concentrate on mending the wounds Charles inflicted on me.

Something, someone? slams into me, landing on my back hard enough to force the air from my lungs and send the meat shooting from my mouth. Another beast crashes into my head and neck, dazing me. Teeth bite into me, claws rip through my scales. *"In the old days, Zal warriors were sometimes defeated by the Undrae,"* Charles Blood says. *"All it took was teamwork and surprise."*

Roaring, I twist under them, flailing my tail, raking the air with my claws. A clawed foot appears before my face and I bite into it. Derek howls and loosens his grip on my neck. I push up against their combined weight and force myself erect. Standing on my hindquarters as they rip and bite me, I knock Derek away, then Charles.

Bleeding in more than a dozen places, aching in a hundred more, I leap into the air, the other two creatures in close pursuit. Flying low, I skim over the island, race above the crashing waves, beating my wings as fast and hard as I can, finally climbing skyward in order to gain enough room to whirl and attack.

"What's the matter, boy? Must you run? Have we been too rough with you?" Charles Blood says. *"Turn and face us. It's just a matter of time before we catch you and finish this."*

Each beat of my heart sends jolts of pain into my shoulders and foreclaws. My lungs already hurt again. My burning stomach feels as if it will burst. I open my mouth to relieve the pressure and a blast of flame erupts from it, turning the raindrops before me into steam.

I shake my head as I continue to build distance between me and the two dragons. Why hadn't I thought of that and used it before? The picture on the box had shown a fire-breathing dragon. The Zal could do such things. It only makes sense that I can too.

If not for my pains and aches, I'd roar out in celebration. But hunger returns again and exhaustion and I begin to understand Father's and Chloe's warnings about the potion. As large and powerful as I've become, my body can't seem to cope with such rapid growth. Worse, I can't do anything to stop my heart from growing. Only the antidote can do that and it's in the bushes by the dock on my island.

Suddenly my conflict with Charles and Derek becomes

less worrisome to me than my body's capacity to fail me. *"Charles,"* I say. *"You're right. It's time to end it."* I whirl in midair and race back to confront both him and his son.

Lightning crackles through the sky, bolt after bolt of it. Thunder shakes the night—the wind gusting, shooting bullets of rain as I race through the storm. I see Derek and Charles in the brief flashes of light well before they're aware of me. They're both too intent on scanning from side to side, searching the sky above and below them, trying to anticipate a sneak attack, to notice my frontal approach.

I zoom straight at them on a collision course, almost laugh when they finally see me, both flaring their wings and attempting to peel off, one to each side. But I'm already too close. I open my mouth and release a burst of flame. The blaze engulfs them, sears their skin, evaporates the rain near them, surrounds them with steam.

Both creatures yowl and contort their bodies, but somehow they continue to fly. I bellow fire at them again and they fall from the sky like moths who've come to close to the flame.

Spiraling down after them, I mindspeak, *"Charles, Derek, can you swim?"*

Neither answers.

I skim over the roiled sea. *"Charles? Derek?"*

Nothing again.

Circling over wave after wave, I search for them. *"Damn it,"* I say. *"I promised Chloe I wouldn't kill you."*

I find Derek first, floating, his scales no longer green but bright red, like a lobster fresh from a boiling pot of water. As I descend to rescue him, I see Charles, just as red, only a few yards away.

Landing by Derek, I grab him by a scalded foreclaw—to pull him with me toward Charles. He moans as soon as I touch him, mindspeaks, *"Leave me be. I hurt too much. Let me go."*

"The hell I will." I tug him through the water, grab Charles too.

He lets out a yowl. *"Boy, you beat us. Let us die in peace."*

"Can't do that. I made a promise."

"We're baked through our scales. Neither of us have the energy to mend ourselves. We've no food, barely the strength to stay afloat. Can you lift either of us into the air and fly us back to your island?"

In truth, I've barely the energy to take myself back to the island. My breath comes in rapid gasps. My heart has begun to break rhythm at alarming intervals. I shake my head.

"Then leave us, boy. We knew the risk we were taking."

I shake my head again. *"I can't fly with you, but I think I can swim with you."*

"You're daft. We're more than a mile from your island."

"I know," I say as we come to the top of a wave. I look around, searching for the light that I think should be near. A glint of its flash shows through the rain and the light repeats itself ten seconds later. I begin to swim toward it, tugging each creature along with me. *"But we're not too far from the Fowey Rocks Lighthouse."*

For every ten yards of progress I make, the pounding waves push me back six. I swim on my back, ignoring the rain, the whipping wind, stroking the water with my wings, sculling with my tail, holding Derek with one claw, Charles with another. Neither of them able to do much more than moan.

I mindspeak, masked, to Chloe as I swim, {*It's over.*}

{*Peter, are you all right?*}

{*I'm here.*}

{*And my father and brother, are they dead?*}

{*They seem to wish they were.*}

{*Are you on the way back?*} she says.

{*Not yet.*}

{*What's wrong. What aren't you telling me?*}

A wave crashes over us and I fight through its foam. {*Neither Charles nor Derek can fly. I'm towing them to the lighthouse. After they're safe from the storm, I'll try to fly home.*}

{*Try, Peter? What's wrong? How badly are you injured?*}

{*It's not any injury. It's the potion. I've outgrown my ability to maintain my body. I can feel my strength draining away.*}

{*Take the antidote!*}

{*I don't have it. It's on the island—in the bushes by the dock.*}

{*Then forget my father and Derek. Fly home now, while you can.*}

Even though Chloe can't see me, I shake my head. {*Neither of them have the energy to change to their human forms. Can you imagine if one or two dragons washed up on a beach, what a fuss there would be? Besides, I promised I wouldn't kill them. There's no need for their deaths now.*}

{*There's no need for yours either,*} Chloe says. {*I'm coming. I'll meet you at the lighthouse.*}

{*Can you, without hurting yourself? There's still a storm out here you know.*}

{*I've healed well enough to fly a little ways. I'm my father's daughter, damn it! I'm not about to be intimidated by a storm and I'm not about to lose a husband to his own stupid stubbornness.*}

By the time I reach Fowey Rocks, the storm has started to abate. Still, the waves push and pull at us, threaten to beat our bodies against the wrought-iron legs of the unmanned lighthouse's skeletal structure.

It takes most of my remaining strength but, by timing my shove to the surge of the waves, I manage to heave first Charles and then Derek onto a metal platform, a walkway that circles the lighthouse's frame just above the tips of the highest waves.

But when I try to climb up with them, my body betrays me. All I can manage is to hold on to a girder and let the waves pound me.

I forget about Charles and Derek safe above me, concentrate instead on breathing, on trying to slow my racing heart. I measure time by each wave that strikes and fails to dislodge me, by each gust of wind that rips at me to no avail. When Chloe finally says, *"Peter?"* I try to answer, but have no energy left to do so.

A cold glass tube is pressed against my lips and my bride says, *"Drink. Drink all of it."* I let some fluid flow into my mouth and it's as if I'm swallowing liquid ice. The cold fluid tastes of apples and citrus—and something bitter, with a hint of ammonia. It quenches the burning within me, but makes me shiver. I stop drinking. *"All of it,"* Chloe says.

"Pushy woman," I say, emptying the rest of the vial.

"Wait until all this is over," she says, helping me up to the platform. *"You haven't seen anything yet."*

35

Ever since Chloe and I rescued Charles and Derek in the final dark hours of the storm, we've barely had a moment alone. Sometimes I regret having ferried the two injured creatures back to our island on Arturo's SeaRay, their natural forms shielded from view by the rain and the night's last moments of gloom. Certainly, I wish there had been somewhere else for them to stay while they healed.

I never thought my house could feel so crowded, especially during the first few days. Charles and Derek seemed to never stop moaning—both creatures sprawled on their beds of hay in their natural forms, demanding food and care. Henri seemed to need endless attention too, rarely leaving my side unless Chloe lured him away. And Claudia seemed always to be visiting, bringing out supplies, updating me on her father's rapid recovery, laughing and whispering with Chloe, helping us straighten out the house after its months of neglect and Charles's rampage of destruction, but always staying far too long.

With no more need to fight for our survival, I yearn for time that Chloe and I can spend alone, learning more about each other. But not even our bed belongs to us.

Every night Henri comes to sleep with us. "The poor boy needs to be with us now," Chloe says when he first asks. "He needs time too—to get over being taken away from you and to get used to me. Don't worry, it won't be forever."

As much as I hug and kiss my son, as much as I reassure him that everything bad is over, he rarely ventures off by himself. Once Derek heals enough to leave his room, the boy clings to me even more, hugging my leg whenever he's present. Not that I blame him.

Derek barely talks to any of us, only mumbling, "Sorry about all that, old man," as a preface to asking me about Rita.

He storms off when I shrug and say, "They took her away. That's all I know." Fortunately, he stays mostly in his room after that.

"Don't mind him," Charles Blood says. "The boy never did handle disappointment well. He made the mistake of thinking all this was already his." The elder creature laughs. "As if I would have trusted him to run such a large company."

I find myself enjoying Charles Blood's company. Once he heals enough to sit up and talk, he surprises me, saying, "You needn't worry about me, boy. You won. I'll never bother you again. It's over for me as long as it's over for you."

Something in his gruff manner reminds me of my father. Like Don Henri, he loves to play chess. He challenges me to a game the first time he sees the chessboard set up in the great room.

"My father liked to play chess too," I tell him.

"Most of our kind do," Charles says. "Strategy is strategy, no matter what kind of creature you are." He plays me every night, often winning, regaling me with stories his father had told him about sailing with my father.

Charles accompanies Chloe, Henri and me each morning too when we visit Elizabeth's grave and tend to her garden. The first time he does so, I tell him the true story of how Elizabeth died at the hands of a human who betrayed me. "You know I blamed you for her death," he says, putting his hand on my shoulder. "I don't anymore, son. You did everything you could."

It takes all my self-control not to hug him. Not that the elder creature can't still be irritating. Sometimes he reverts to his old, unpleasant self. "Bullocks!" he shouts when told he must assume his human form whenever he wishes to go outside or whenever Claudia visits the house. "I'm not some bloody human who delights in chewing on dead cows!" he rails when Chloe and I serve him steak instead of fresh prey.

Still, grumble as he might, he accepts what we give him and does as we ask. He also never turns his gruffness on my son. The boy soon makes a habit of visiting with his grandfather at least a few times each day, sitting with his mouth open, his eyes wide as Charles tells him tales of the old days when our kind, the People of the Blood, flew openly wherever they wanted.

Claudia calls early on the morning of the eighth day after we took in Charles and Derek Blood. "Good news. Your Grady White is finally ready. I'll bring it out later this morning," she says. "After I pick up Pops. The hospital's releasing him today. I told him to take it easy, but he insists on my bringing him along."

I tell Chloe about the call, then say, "If I tell Arturo to arrange things, we can have your father and brother gone in a few days. It's time for them to go, Chloe, especially your brother. They've healed well enough to travel. It's time for us to be alone."

My bride smiles. "I'd like that, Peter."

"It's time for Claudia to stay away for a few days too," I say.

Chloe nods. "I'll tell her."

I take her in my arms, hug her, feel her warmth against me and whisper in her ear. "And it's time for Henri to start sleeping in his own damned bed again."

I don't know whether I'm happier to see my Grady White or the wan Latin sitting beside his daughter by the wheel. "Pop tried to take the wheel," Claudia shouts as soon as the boat pulls up to the dock. "I told him you'd be pissed if he screwed your boat up."

Arturo flashes a full-toothed smile. "I told her it would only be fair after all you put my SeaRay through."

Jumping on board, I accept Claudia's kiss on my cheek. Then I turn my full attention to her father, helping Arturo stand, clasping his hand in mine.

"Claudia's told me everything's that's gone on," he says.

Looking at the man, I wince at the bruises still apparent on his face, the bandage wrapped around his head.

"Don't worry. The doctors say I'll be fine. I will too— as soon as the bastards that did this to me are taken care of. My people think they found them. So it shouldn't be long."

Chloe lets out a happy squeal and we both turn and look at the dock just as Claudia hands my bride the wicker box we sent from Jamaica. My bride hugs Claudia, holds up the box. "Look!" she says.

I nod and the two woman walk off, talking and laughing.

"They're awfully tight," Arturo says.

"Like schoolgirl chums," I say, wondering what they're discussing now. "Claudia was great. Without her, we'd have had a hell of a time."

The Latin nods. "I told you she was good." He turns the subject to business, asks me what else I may want done. I tell him.

It takes only a few days for Arturo to arrange documents and airplane tickets for Charles and Derek Blood. "Ian will fly over with them. That way everyone can sign the necessary papers at Claypool and Sons," he says.

I explain it to Charles the day after that, before I take him and Derek to shore. "I've had my people make arrangements," I say.

"Oh?" Charles arcs an eyebrow.

"We're buying out Virgil Claypool's interest in Claypool and Sons. Don't worry, we'll let him stay on as long as he likes. But his main job now will be to protect your interests. We'll be sending over enough funds to support you and let you invest, plus enough to pay the politicians each year to keep the Jamaican government away from Morgan's Hole."

"Not necessary, but still it's bloody decent of you."

I shrug. "Or sensible self-protection. We're going to keep Bartlet House. Chloe wants to be able to come visit and I'd like to do so without worry."

"I gave you my bloody word," Charles says.

Putting my hand on his shoulder, I smile at him. "No offense intended. You gave your word but Samantha and Philip didn't. Neither did Derek and we both know how furious he is. This way, no one will have any need to be anything but pleasant. Besides, Chloe and I wanted to help. If you ever want to modernize, we'll help you with that too. It would be nice if you had a satellite phone so Chloe can call when she wants."

Chloe insists on saying good-bye at the dock. "Henri and I have things to do," she says, grinning.

"What?" I say.

"Things. You go ahead take Pa and Derek to the airport. We'll show you when you get back."

"You're being pushy again."

Chloe smiles. "So? I warned you I would be." She kisses me and, frowning, wondering what she has planned, I do as she says.

Once Charles, Derek and Ian walk up the concourse to Jamaica Air, I rush from the terminal to my car and speed back to Coconut Grove.

The day couldn't be more perfect for boating. White powder-puff clouds sit, hardly moving, in a clear, light blue sky. The breeze barely ruffles the surface of the bay. I can't wait to take my Grady White from the dock and race across the calm water to my island, where only Chloe and my son now wait for me.

But as I near Caya DelaSangre, a new, shiny, dark blue speedboat emerges from the island's channel. I slow down and study the boat. Now what? I think, as it speeds up, throwing a rooster tail of white water behind it, turning and shooting toward me.

I gun my motors too, prepare to veer out of its way, should it not turn. But as it closes, the boat changes direction, so it will pass to my right side. I laugh when I realize that Claudia's behind the wheel, wonder when she bought this boat, what new clothes or books or music she brought Chloe today.

She waves as she passes. I wave back, dropping my hand when I see Henri seated beside her, waving too.

"What are you doing there?" I mindspeak.

"I'm going to sleep over at Claudy's. It's going to be fun!"

"Who said you could?"

"Mommy did. It was her idea."

"Okay." I say, waving until they're well past, smiling at what Henri said, remembering our conversation just a few days ago.

"Would it be okay if I called Chloe 'Mommy?'" he said.

"Sure."

"Would my real mommy be mad if I did?"

I hugged him. "No, she would think it's just fine."

But tears had welled up in Chloe's eyes the first time he called her that.

"Hey, Mommy," I mindspeak to my bride now. *"How come you're sending my kid away?"*

"It's our kid and don't you forget that. How far away are you?" she says.

"In the channel. Almost home."

"Good. Come up to the great room after you dock."

"Why?"

"Never you mind."

The last few watchdogs come to the dock to greet me. I shake my head at their pitiful number. It will take years to breed the pack back to full strength. Cowed by their experiences with Derek, they barely growl or bark at my approach. After I tie off the Grady White, I brush past them, take the veranda steps two at a time and rush up to the third floor of the house.

I stop at the doorway, my mouth open. Even though the day is warm and the sun has yet to set, a fire rages in the hearth on the far wall and candles blaze everywhere—on tables, on countertops, on shelves, even on top of the television and the DVD player.

Chloe stands waiting for me in the center of the room—barefoot, wearing a sheer white, cotton dress, obviously naked underneath it. "I've been waiting for you to come back," she says. "Are you planning to keep me waiting even more?"

Shaking my head, taking a deep breath, I walk toward my bride. I can't keep my eyes off her, can't stop from growing hard, the way her brown body shows itself beneath the dress—her hipbones and nipples jutting against the thin fabric, looking as if they might break through. I stop a foot from her, facing her.

She glances down, grins a wicked grin. "Mr. Dela-Sangre," she says. "Control yourself."

"It's been too long."

She breathes out her words. "And don't I know it too."

"Is this what I think it's about?" I say.

Chloe nods. "It's time we were properly married."

"I agree." I look around the room, see the white bowl and green ceramic pitcher on the table, the pewter mug and small leather bag beside it. "I'm just surprised you got it all ready so soon."

"It wasn't easy," Chloe says, walking toward the table. "Would you bring her over while I get the rest?" She points to the shadows in the farthest corner of the room.

My mouth falls open again. Rita Santiago, naked, her eyes glazed over and staring at nothingness, her damaged hand still bandaged, stands calmly, waiting.

"Couldn't we have had someone else?" I say. "Anyone else? Someone I never knew?"

"Why not her, Peter?" Chloe frowns. "She's just another human. One who, if I can remind you, was perfectly willing to kill your son."

I nod. "I know," I say, not wanting to argue with my bride, feeling a little foolish, knowing that Father would have scolded me about my queasiness. "I just know her too well. I expected that Claudia would have disposed of her. . . ."

"So you don't care if she dies. You just don't want to kill your pet yourself."

"She's not my pet."

"Peter, you know I haven't had any time to hunt. We needed fresh prey for our feast," Chloe says, picking up the bowl and pitcher. She carries them to the center of the room, sets them down and then walks over to Rita and takes the redhead by her good hand. "I had Claudia bring her out this morning after you left. This one put up quite a fuss until we forced some Dragon Tear's wine into her."

Rita follows without any resistance as Chloe guides her to the center of the room, near the bowl and pitcher. "Anyway, she's the best choice. Remember, Rita betrayed you and put your family in danger. Peter, you know she won't suffer barely at all, certainly not as much as she deserves to."

Before I can reply, Chloe shapeshifts her index finger into a clawed talon and slashes it across Rita's neck, killing her almost instantly. Then she lays the body down near us. "There," Chloe says, shifting her finger back to human shape. "You didn't have to do anything."

"But," I say, "I would have . . ."

"It's okay," Chloe says, smiling at me. "There are more important things for both of us to do." She returns to the table, brings back the mug and the leather bag.

Picking up the pitcher, my bride pours Dragon's Tear wine into the bowl. "Death's Rose," she says, taking a petal from the leather bag, crumbling it into the liquid, following it with a few sprinkles of alchemist's powder.

"You look like you know what you're doing," I say.

"I should. I'm my mother's daughter." She motions to the mug. "I mixed your antidote too. You worried?"

I shake my head.

Chloe turns around. "Help me," she says, taking out her emerald earrings.

Caressing her shoulders first, I kiss her neck and then undo the gold-and-emerald, clover-leaf necklace that I first gave to her sister. I take both it and the earrings and put them on the table. Chloe begins to undress as soon as I return. Watching her, I do the same.

"It's time," Chloe says and my eyes never leave hers as we both change, stretching and shifting into our natural forms.

My bride picks up the mug, offers it to me. *"This should neutralize the wedding potion for you,"* she mindspeaks. *"I hope I did it right."*

"You are your mother's daughter," I say. *"Of course, you did."* I drain the mug without looking in it or smelling its contents, prepared for it to be vile. But this time the fluid only tastes slightly metallic, only warms my throat as I drink.

"We have to wait," Chloe says.

"We have all the time we want," I say, standing, looking at my dragon female, the candlelight all around us. I'm content to wait as long as it takes.

"Peter," she finally says, *"do you remember that this will change you and bind you to me forever?"*

"Yes," I say.

"Knowing this, do you still want me?" Chloe says.

"More than ever." I stare into her emerald-green eyes. *"Knowing this, do you still want <u>me</u>?"*

"Forever," she says.

We drink the clear, slightly bitter liquid at the same time, our jowls touching. Neither of us stops until the bowl is empty. I look up, thinking how lucky I am to have her. Chloe gasps, thinks, *"I'm lucky too,"* both of us hearing each other's thoughts, seeing each other through the other's eyes.

"Is this how it was for you before?" she says.

I nod, feel my bride's heartbeat quicken. *"Soon,"* I say/think. *"After we feast."*

"When we make love, will we both be able to feel what each other feels?"

"Sure." I nuzzle her and feel the warmth that grows within her. Chloe gasps as she feels my body respond and grow hard again. *"I guess we could skip the feast part for now,"* I say.

"Oh, no," Chloe says. *"I'm supposed to feed you now and I will."* She turns to the body beside us and rips off a piece of flesh for me.

I take it from her and feel her stomach rumble as I chew. We feed together then, gorging ourselves, neither of us talking, neither of us thinking. As soon as we're satiated, I push everything out of our way, take her right there on the floor, Chloe and I moving with a unison we've never experienced before, both of us growling, roaring, climaxing at the same time.

Afterwards, we lie together, stroking each other with our tails. *"Don't think this is terrible,"* Chloe says and immediately knows I couldn't. *"But as sad as I am that my sister's dead, I love that we ended up together."*

I get up, open the windows so the late afternoon air can course through the room. It cools me and Chloe sighs. I lie down beside her and begin to stroke her again, aware of every part of her body, every breath, every fleeting thought she has, every heartbeat.

Chloe sighs. *"I hate to think this will go away by tomorrow."*

"But we'll still be here and we'll still be together," I say, wondering what the future will bring, what surprises will come our way.

"Can't you feel it?" Chloe says.

"What?" I say, then realize what she means.

"Shush. Listen."

The heart beats so faintly that it's barely noticeable. I

concentrate, touch it with my mind, feel the warmth around it, its simple awareness of being here.

"Our daughter," Chloe says. *"I hope Henri likes her."* She presses close to me.

"He will," I say, my eyes closed, my mind intent on listening to the rapid beat of the child's tiny heart.

"I'd like to name her Elizabeth," she says.

"Of course," I say, enjoying Chloe's warmth. In a little while, I know, we'll make love again. But for now I'm content to lie beside her almost dozing, trying to picture what my little girl will look like, imagining life in my house with a wife and two children.

Outside, the restless ocean continues its endless rush and tug on the beach. Seagulls caw as they fight over some morsel of food. The wind rustles the trees—a cool gust coursing through the window, enveloping us with the salty smell of sea air, its chill reminding us that night will soon arrive and after it, yet another day.

About the Author

Alan F. Troop's poems, essays, short stories, and articles have appeared in Miami's *Tropic* magazine, Fort Lauderdale's *Sunshine* magazine, and a number of national publications. A lifelong resident of South Florida, Troop lives near Fort Lauderdale with his wife, Susan, and manages a hardware-wholesale business in Miami. He often spends his leisure time sailing his catamaran around the islands off the coast of South Miami. You can visit him on the Web at www.DragonNovels.com.

See what's coming in May...

Roc   (0451)

THE DRAGON DELASANGRE

Alan F. Troop

Here, at last, are the confessions of one Peter
DelaSangre, who tells of his life on an island
off the coast of Miami...of his lonely balancing
act between the worlds of humans and dragons...and of the overwhelming need that gives
his life purpose:
To find a woman of his own kind...

0-451-45871-0

"The most original fantasy I've read in
years...Terrific."   —Tanya Huff

To order call: 1-800-788-6262

S341